Read what bloggers are  saying about

Sofia
Khan
is NOT
Obliged

"**Never in my life has a character touched me as much as Sofia Khan did.** She is funny and ridiculous and she has the biggest heart anyone can have . . . It's refreshingly original with characters that feel so real, you'd expect them to walk into your room at any second. Don't just take it from me, go on and read it."

Books and Other Distractions

"**The most delightful surprise of this summer** was *Sofia Khan is Not Obliged* . . . a cheeky, intelligent, fallible heroine who . . . I could identify with more easily than most of the other protagonists in the genre . . . it's the only thing I've read this year that kept me up past midnight."

The Captive Reader

"A brilliant first novel . . . In some ways **I enjoyed this book even more than *Bridget Jones*** as Sofia felt like a stronger character"

The Book World of Anne

"I loved it . . . whilst religion and racism are portrayed unflinchingly, it's also a great piece of entertainment . . . **If more people read books like this, I think the world would be a better place**."

Social Bookshelves

"The book is actually HILARIOUS and I mean hilarious . . . **a funny, honest portrayal of one woman's journey through some of the hardest and happiest times**, featuring a great band of diverse characters full of life and lessons."

Crooked Bookshelves

"**This book captured my heart in the way that very few romance books do.** Sofia was just such a great character. She was strong and well written, with a voice that felt more like she was just chatting to you than that you were reading a book."

The Whispering of the Pages

"It's funny, it's heart-breaking, it's heart-warming . . . **Malik shows us what's unique about life as a hijab-wearing Muslim.** She also shows us how much of Sofia's life is no different to any other young woman's life in a western city."

The Writes of Women

"**This fast-paced, engaging novel will entertain and educate you.** If you're looking for a book to cheer you up on these drab and drizzly autumn evenings then this is the book for you."

Writer's Little Helper

"Ayisha Malik's debut is funny, current and **a really exciting addition to the face of women's fiction.** She's not afraid to take on cultural stereotypes and clichés, often to genuinely humorous effect . . . Malik's characters are relatable and larger than life, and in Sofia she has a universal heroine."

Chicklit Club

"How can this novel go wrong? . . . It's intelligent, very funny, sharp, heart-breaking, witty, superbly plotted, realistic, and a feminist love story without gush . . . **This is a superb novel about modern Britain and modern living.** Go buy a copy immediately."

Katemacdonald.net

"**I need to implore you to read this book.** It's just darling . . . You fall in love with Sofia as she navigates her own love life, the problems of her family and friends, and trying to write a Muslim dating book that she feels is true to herself"

Amy Elizabeth

"What a fantastic and fun read this was. **I was hooked from page one and fell in love with the characters** . . . it's funny, fast-paced and gives the reader an insight into the day-to-day life of a single Muslim woman living in the UK."

Wee Shubba's World

Ayisha Malik is a British Muslim, lifelong Londoner and lover of books. She read English Literature at Kingston University and went on to complete an MA in Creative Writing. She has spent various spells teaching and being a publicist at Random House. Now she splits her time between writing and working as managing editor at Cornerstones Literary Consultancy.

Sofia Khan is NOT Obliged

AYISHA MALIK

twenty7

First published in Great Britain in 2015 by Twenty7 Books

This paperback edition published in 2016 by

Twenty7 Books
80-81 Wimpole St, London W1G 9RE
www.twenty7books.co.uk

A CIP catalogue record for this book is
available from the British Library.

Paperback ISBN: 978-1-78577-003-6
Ebook ISBN: 978-1-78577-004-3

1 3 5 7 9 10 8 6 4 2

Typeset by IDSUK (Data Connection) Ltd

Printed and bound by Clays Ltd, St Ives Plc

Twenty7 Books is an imprint of Bonnier Publishing Fiction,
a Bonnier Publishing company
www.bonnierpublishingfiction.co.uk
www.bonnierpublishing.co.uk

For my mum and dad.

Obviously.

SEPTEMBER 2011

I Was Told There'd Be Light

Thursday 1 September

'Fight the Good Fight' by Yes, I'm Muslim, Please Get Over It

On www.sofiasblog.co.uk

You'd have thought that a break-up just before Ramadan would have inspired some kind of empathy from extended family members.

'O-ho,' one auntie might've said, 'I'm sorry that your potential husband wanted you to live with his family and a hole-in-the-wall.'

Perhaps even a show of shock – a gasp, a hand to the chest or to the mouth … 'Hain? A *hole-in-the wall*? What is this?'

Nope. An entire month and all my aunties (even the occasional uncle) felt compassion was redundant. For spiritual sustenance, they used their obsession with marriage instead. There was no sympathy at the mention of my no longer marrying the lawyer, and no shock when I explained why the hole-in-the-wall was an impediment to marital bliss. At every iftari party to break fast, all I did was wait seventeen hours to have a decent samosa, and instead I had nothing but the question of marriage shoved down my throat.

'Maria is getting married, Sofia. Now it is your turn, nah?'

I tried! I did! But what *normal* human being would ask another human being to live with a cohort of mother, father, brother and sister-in-law with two children, complete with a sister and brother-in-law and three children next door, and a hole-in-the-wall joining the two houses? (Just writing that sentence about so many people confused me; imagine living with them.) I had to pretend it was the chilli sauce that made my eyes water.

Every time someone mentions the 'M' word, they become monochrome to me – like the first half of *The Wizard of Oz* – and at least Dorothy was looking for something more interesting. Home. If little old Dot was Muslim (and not that much older, to be honest), that wizard would be an eligible husband, they'd get married and she'd spend her days popping out babies and choosing suitable flooring. (Not that I have anything against babies or flooring – both are reasonable pastimes if you're into that kind of thing.) On the plus side, she'd not have to worry about things like pouring water into authors' champagne, or being thirty and waking up to her parents clattering around the house.

But it seems that this is life. The yellow brick road is paved with babies and just too many questions about the 'M' word ...

7 a.m. The truth is, if your (ex) boyfriend has a habit of shaking his leg and all you want to do is chop off the limb in question, you're probably not *that* in love with him – despite any affection that might bubble to the surface. (Incidentally, if you don't have any kind of physical relationship with someone, can they really be your boyfriend? Shouldn't there be a word for someone between a friend and a potential husband?) And then of course there's the hole-in-the-wall. After a month of fasting and praying, and praying and fasting, I decided to write a list, because as Anaïs Nin said, 'We write to taste life twice.' I'm not sure she knew what she was talking about: we write to get rid of the taste certain morsels of life leave us with. But I don't think I should be accused of never giving things a chance and writing is very useful for reference's sake. Now where the hell is it. Ah, here we are:

Post-Ramadan/Hole-In-The-Wall resolutions:

- Give up smoking. Especially when Hannah says, 'Some Islamic scholars say it's haram. "Haram" is just "harm" without an extra "a".' Sigh. Knowledge is so inconvenient sometimes. (I do think it's rather good of me not to judge her potential polygamous marriage given her raised eyebrows whenever I decide to get a fag out.)

- I'll maintain my philosophical take on the entire Imran and hole-in-the-wall situ. There are people who like walls, and there are people who like holes-in-the-wall, and that is that.

- I'll also unglue the phone from my hand. One should be selective with their obsessions and mine should be my job rather than social media and checking if Imran has emailed/Facebooked/texted/whatsapped/tweeted/instagrammed/pinterested etc.

- Which leads me to the importance of being a brilliant publicist. I won't PR my way into a comfortable afterlife, but surely serving literature is like serving education, and education is the pinnacle of Islamic philosophy. Not sure how my current campaign for Shain Murphy's *Facts About Hippos* book fits in, but then life is mysterious sometimes. Also I can prove that wearing a hijab does not make me a social pariah. I will *not* get sacked for being a practising Muslim. Getting sacked for being a shit book publicist, however, may be unavoidable.

- I won't eat the entire contents of fridge to make up for severe Ramadan calorie cutback where my body went into shock and believed itself to be in a state of famine. (What I've lost in weight, I've gained in spirituality. I think.)

- Since I'm on the path to enlightenment I'll also avoid any (unintentional, of course) *ho*jabi tendencies. I.e. stay away from jersey, Lycra, tight-knit material that leave little to the imagination, and expose what can only be described as the *wrong* type of lady-lumps. This, I think, is rather a win-win for myself and society. (My community spirit begins.)

- More importantly – sod relationships. It's either that or sod what I want, and I'd really rather do the former. So what if Imran and I wanted different things? That's the way life rolls; downhill, some might say. Emotional dependency is bad for personal growth. (And a little too good for physical growth. Obviously.) As a woman of the twenty-first century, I should be enlightened enough to not obsess over my single status. I'm going to do more meaningful things. Voluntary work? Help London's homeless? Bake cakes for people? (Learn to bake?) The list is endless.

I checked my phone to see if Imran had texted a belated Happy Eid. He had not. Maria burst into my room in her bathrobe and threw a bunch of swatches on my bed. It's now four months until her wedding to Tahir. Her dress is going to be maroon, so everything has to be a shade of maroon. I wouldn't be surprised if she took down my curtains and used them for the stage's backdrop. I want to say: keep the curtains, dear; you'll need them for covering that hole you'll probably end up living with. She went through my wardrobe, leaving puddled footsteps on the flooring as I picked up one of the swatches.

'This is one of the many reasons I've turned my back on marriage,' I said.

'Yeah, right.'

She doesn't understand the spiritual transformation of the past month. Images of hazelnut Dairy Milk only occasionally punctuated the formation of my new Zen-like personality. If life were meant to be spent in a constant attempt to be *with* someone, I'd have been born in Lahore in, well, the 90s.

'I can't find my black pointies,' she said, stretching so far into my wardrobe she was in danger of getting lost in there. She emerged with said black heels and inspected them. 'Thanks for scuffing them.'

I got out of bed and rummaged around for a black marker.

'Don't worry,' I said, lifting the marker in the air, trying to take the shoes. Maars snatched them back.

It was my face, I think. Perhaps I looked hurt, or just pathetic, because Maars then looked at me the way she and my parents have been making a habit of and said, 'Oh, it's fine. Gives them a vintage look. Here, have them.'

She tried to hand the shoes to me.

'I don't want them,' I replied.

A person only accepts sympathy in the form of presents if they need it. And I don't need it.

'Are you OK?' she asked.

I bunched my hair up in a clip and straightened out my bed sheets.

'I'm *fine*,' I said, for perhaps the thousandth time. Just to prove how fine, I turned to her and did a jig on the spot followed by jazz hands.

Maria looked at me, adjusting the towel on her head. 'Freak.'

'Look at these walls,' I said, caressing the smooth Egyptian Cotton paint. I rested my cheek against the wall and gave it a kiss. 'Every morning I wake up and look at the fullness of them and think ... Ah, *this* is how God intended walls to be.'

Maars sat on the bed. 'Living with a hole-in-the-wall was taking it a bit far.'

Exactly. That's not living with the in-laws, that's living in an institution. But she *has* decided to live with the in-laws (without a hole-in-the-wall, which apparently makes all the difference) and anyway, Dad came thumping up the stairs and appeared at the door.

'I'm leaving your mother.' He rested both hands on his poorly back and puffed out his chest.

'We know, Dad. Any decade now ...' I said.

Mum appeared from behind Dad and made him jump. It's really rather impressive that such ampleness can move around so noiselessly.

'Hai!' Dad exclaimed. 'You gave me a heart attack.'

'No such luck.' She shoved a tray in front of him. 'Take your dogskin.'

Dad threw the Digoxin into his mouth, gulping it down with a glass of water. I hope Mum doesn't go around saying she gives her husband dogskin. People already think Muslims are weird enough. Mum set the tray on my bed and handed Maria and me a plate of toast.

'Look how kamzor you've become,' she said to me.

Kamzor? I might be in danger of looking many things, but frail is not one of them. Three faces collectively leaned in and peered at me. I knocked on the wall.

'But isn't it better to have complete walls than a fat face?' I asked. (Rhetorically, obviously.)

'See her fussiness,' said Mum, looking at Dad.

Dad came and placed my hand on the wall. 'Now tell me,' he said, walking to the other side. 'How big was this hole?'

That's the thing – I didn't know. Did it have a door? Did the door have a lock? Or were the two houses separated by those long strings of beads where you can hear and see from one living room what's going on in the next; people swishing in and out at will. Did this mean the family had voyeuristic tendencies?

'But what if they have one *big*, big house?' said Mum. She looked at Maars who was nibbling her toast. 'At least we should have seen before Soffoo said no.'

'What? said Maria. 'She said no. End of.'

'*Thank you.*' Love Maars.

It's so weird how our parents are constantly nagging us to get married when they're ready to leg it out of their own marriage at any given opportunity. Is that what they think life is: a combination of resilience and resignation? No, thank you. They didn't have choices – which is depressing – but surely they should be pleased that we've managed to inherit some. Though I suspect this much choice is not what they intended.

'Kismet,' I said, widening my eyes. 'Can't fight destiny, Mum.'

'Le, *kismet* told you, say "no".'

'Kismet, right now, tells me I need the toilet.'

With which I walked past the family congregation and locked myself in the bathroom.

7.05 a.m. Wish I could have a fag. I could lean out of the window, but surely the fumes will penetrate the gap between the door and floor? Also, I'd have to go back into my room, lift the mattress for my secret stash and bring it back into the bathroom without being caught by either parent. (Which will make me feel as if I'm sixteen rather than thirty. Not particularly good for my sense of self.) Perhaps I should just jump out of the window and that will be the end of it.

Except I'm being a saint-like offspring to my immigrant parents.

8.15 a.m. What is the point of being a saint-like daughter to immigrant parents when my decisions are met with derision?

Mum took one look at my scarf and then outside at what promises to be a scorching day.

'Hai hai, you want to die from heat?'

Dad was armed with his tool-belt in an attempt to fix the kitchen light. I pat him on the back.

'Yes, Mum. One day I'll sweat to death in my hijab.'

Mum fixed a roller in her hair as she told me about her friend Nargis's daughter, who put on a hijab and had some gang follow her after work, calling her a Paki and telling her to go back home. Her daughter was so scared she took the hijab off the next day.

'She should've said I *am* going home ... Around the corner!'

'Exactly,' said Maria, taking two maroon swatches and checking them against the light.

'O-ho! Bastard,' Dad exclaimed. Not sure if he was talking about the kitchen light or the gang.

'Your hair's your one beauty – all covered up,' said Mum, looking at my head.

I suppose since Mum created me, and I created the hijab situation, covering my hair must feel like a personal affront to her. It's not *you*, Mum, it's me. Honestly, it's bad enough having Imran prefer spending a lifetime in a weird extended family living situation, but to have to explain what you do or don't put on your head is really the limit.

'Acha, maybe put on some more makeup.' Mum looked at my apparently frail features. 'Or you'll look like one of those *Gontonomo* Bay wives.'

Dad looked over his shoulder and pointed the screwdriver at Mum. 'Mehnaz ...'

'But at least they have husbands,' she added, and was so impressed with this joke she began laughing out loud, hitting Dad on the back. He turned around and grabbed her by the shoulder, waving the screwdriver in the air.

'Girls, your mama has loose screws in her brain. I will fix it.'

'Haw, look at the time. Soffoo, you'll be late.' With which Mum handed me a banana and pushed me out of the kitchen, moaning about my state of being wrapped up in too much material and her state of being wrapped up in anxiety.

Angry-looking, tattooed next-door neighbour witnessed Mum trying to loosen my scarf to at least show that I have a reasonably long neck. He looks exactly like the type of person to tell me to go back home – even though he knows where I live. But no one ever said racists were sensible.

11

9.10 a.m. Oh my *actual* God. What just happened? I stepped onto the escalators at Tooting Broadway station thinking about my last exchange with Imran.

'But girls move in with the in-laws all the time,' he said. 'It's normal.'

Normal? Whose normal? I suppose another reason to not marry someone is differing ideas on concept of normality.

'Why can't you make a compromise?' he asked, looking at me with that impenetrable stare he has – as if nothing could move him. Nothing *has* moved him – certainly not out of his family home. I wasn't sure whether to cry or throw my coffee in his face. It was just so absurd. But then one person's absurdity is another person's obsession. *You make the compromise. No,* you *make the compromise. No,* you *do it . . .* How about no one does it and we all live uncompromised ever after?

'Remember one of the first times we went out?' he said. 'You were pissed off because no one offered an old man a seat on the train and you forced someone to get up for him?' He finally cracked a smile. 'Everything you say, everything you do, there's fire in your belly. *And* you wear a hijab.' He glanced at me. 'You should never change.'

That made something constrict in my chest. I don't care for *I love you*s – they're for people who don't know any better. *You should never change* is the culmination of all your flaws made necessary: the imperfect sum of an imperfect past, which turned out to be a good thing for someone.

'Do you really think you'll find someone who adores you as much as I do?'

Thanks. I hadn't realised I was a puppy. Sigh. Logically speaking, it's not as if it's the end of the world, but it's the end of something. I'm not fond of endings.

I was brought back to the present as people flooded out of the train. Before the doors closed I made a run for it, accidentally bumping into a man who was walking towards me. *Accidentally.* I heard him mumble something, but the doors were beeping and I was too busy pushing through the rush of people to really hear. As I stepped into the (non-air-conditioned) crammed carriage, the word finally penetrated my commute-fogged brain. I turned around, mouth open in delayed realisation. *Terrorist? Me?* What the *actual* fuck! I tiptoed and angled my head to catch sight of the perpetrator of this most unexpected opinion. The tube doors were still open. I saw him turn around to disentangle his jacket that had got caught in someone's briefcase. Someone else got stuck between the doors.

Please stand clear of the closing doors.

No one heard him. Everyone just carried on reading their papers, listening to their iPods as if someone hadn't just pulled normality from under my feet and smacked my head against some bizarre reality. In my daze, I got my book out from my bag. *Forget him*, I rationalised to myself, *you should be used to racist abuse, Sofia. Such flimsy words make no difference to me.* It was a decent rationale, but didn't quite do the job of putting my world back into balance. I stared at the ground and looked at my shoes: my lovely, teal, snakeskin, peep-toes (which, by the way, are offset perfectly by my coral scarf). I was like, hang on – I don't look like a terrorist.

Ladies and gentlemen are reminded to keep clear of the closing doors as it can cause disruption to services. Thank you.

I looked up, and just as the doors were about to close, a very clear bout of logic possessed me.

'Oi,' I shouted. 'Terrorists don't wear vintage shoes, you ignorant wanker!'

I kind of hoped my usefully loud voice would carry. Of *all* the things in the world I could be, that was the brush he decided to tar me with. But what was the point in my outburst? The doors had already closed between us and he was long gone. You know who wasn't gone? Me. Surrounded by a tube full of people who were now casting me sideward glances and inching away tentatively. How is anyone meant to explain reasonably to a train full of people that they are *not* a terrorist? I mean, I work in publishing for goodness sake! So I did the next best thing and in poised fashion focused on my book (or pretended to focus, as how was such a thing possible?). Unfortunately I didn't take into account that I was reading *The Reluctant Fundamentalist*.

I need a fag.

9.35 a.m. *Terrorist!* T-E-R-R-O-R-I-S-T. The word keeps knocking around in my head, denting and scratching the surface of my, quite frankly, already fragile brain. It's giving me a headache. My innards declared a state of emergency. I sat on the step in the empty smoking area at the back of the building. Managed to bum a cigarette from Colleen in reception.

'All right?'

Charlie from the post room, who seems to live in a perpetual state of annoyance, came out with a trolley, his gold bracelet glinting in the sun, as a van pulled in.

'Do you have a light?' I asked.

He reached into his pocket and threw it towards me.

'Haven't seen you here for a while.'

'I was fasting.' I inhaled the smoke and looked at the lovely thin white stick: the embodiment of nicotine and guilt.

14

'Oh yeah, you're Muslim.' I do wonder why Charlie thinks I walk around with this neon-sign-of-a-cloth on my head. Actually, I suspect he doesn't think about it at all. I fiddled about with my phone, and had an urge to text Imran to say: *Can you believe it? Can you* actually *believe I was called a terrorist?*

Oh, bollocks. Late for meeting!

10.35 a.m. I walked into the conference room for our catch-up meeting and finger-sniffing Brammers had popped out to get her notes.

'Nice scarf, Sweetu,' said Katie.

Which was nice of Katie to say, because Mr Racist clearly didn't think so.

'Is it from Zara?' she asked.

'Huh?'

'Are you OK?'

So I told her what happened. As soon as I uttered the words, Katie bellowed, 'Everyone, listen! Guys! Sofe was just called a *terrorist* on the Northern line!'

Fleur's head shot up. 'What?' Then there was a general outcry of, 'How ghastly!' 'No!' 'What an awful thing to say.'

Katie put a plate of biscuits in front of me as Fleur brought me a cup of coffee. I looked around the table at my fellow publicists' concerned white faces and told them about terrorists not wearing vintage shoes. Everyone exploded with exclamations of, 'No. You didn't!'

I bloody well did, and they bloody well don't. It was like that time Katie and I were at Paddington waiting for a train to Bath for an author event.

'Do you remember that mad brown man?' I asked Katie.

She nodded. 'Don't worry. You're not going to hell for being friends with a white person.'

'He made my chips go cold,' I mumbled. And my blood, to be quite honest. A person really does get it from everyone sometimes. Every time I think, *Hurrah!* No one cares about my scarf, some miserable random person calls me a terrorist (or Paki, ninja, bomber – you get the idea). I took out my notepad and pen as Katie patted me on the shoulder.

'I should just wear a niqab if I'm going to get called a terrorist. At least I wouldn't have to worry about wearing lipstick,' I added.

A few of the girls laughed. I don't know why. It wasn't a joke. Brammers came in wiping what appeared to be some dried-up vomit on her Armani suit jacket – the juxtaposed lifestyle of publicity director and mother of three.

'Alex threw up on me *just* as I was leaving home,' she explained. 'Right, everyone. Before we start our catch-up, anyone have ideas for me to take to the editorial meeting? Make them good.'

Every month, Brammers uses catch-up meeting to try and get us to come up with ideas, which she can then take to editorial and bask in the triumph of being *more* than just publicity. Every month she fails. I was supposed to have thought of ideas on the way to work and I would have done if *someone* didn't think I spent my time Googling chemical formulas. I began doodling a house in my notebook, while looking at my phone, briefly wishing Imran would call, the way he used to, just because he wanted to hear the sound of my voice. No one was more aware of Imran's affectionate stream of consciousness than me and my phone provider. One of the issues about the whole 'being alone' stance is not having anyone to share the world's problems with. A person's been scooped out of your life and so you speak into a pit of noth-ingness. Or you don't speak at all, depending on your tendency towards soliloquy. I'd say my tendency ranges between average to excessive.

Fleur went through her list of points, including potentially writing a book called *The Virgin Cyclist*, which would've been funny – I imagined myself on the book's cover – under normal circumstances.

'Sofia? Sofia?'

Brammers looked at my blank face, which nicely complemented my blank brain. I experienced a tie-dye of emotions in the shape of holes-in-the-wall, professionalism and racists as I glanced at my drawing.

'I don't suppose anyone would like to read about my string of God-awful dates?'

I'm still undecided as to whether saying something is better than saying nothing at all. I tried to give my most winning smile, which, I think people would agree, was quite a deal given the state of affairs.

'Yes, well, intriguing as that might be, we've published three dating books in the past year,' replied Brammers.

She was about to move on when I said, 'Bet no one else's boy-friend ever asked them to live with their parents and a hole-in-the-wall.'

I was too busy figuring out how one draws a hole-in-the-wall to notice everyone looking at me.

'Your boyfriend asked you to live with his parents and a hole-in-the-wall?' asked Brammers.

'Yes.'

Emma pushed back her fringe. 'Your boyfriend wanted you to move in with him and his parents, and a what?'

Trust me to get a career in quite possibly the most white-centric, middle-class industry there is. I explained to the confused faces about the conjoined house, living with the in-laws, and, of course, the hole that holds the entire story together. After I'd explained about common Asian practice, not only did I feel like a black sheep, but I would've quite liked to be a sheep. Sheep are not judged.

'But *why?*' asked Emma.

God, Emma asks a lot of questions. I find this to be a problem. Not the questions, per se, just the assumption that I have answers. I'm not an anthropologist.

'Can't be arsed to hire a removal van?' I suggested. 'Problems cutting the cord? Filial sense of obligation to immigrant parents?'

'And do men move in with their wives' parents?' Brammers asked. She was taking notes, I saw with some alarm.

'No. It's always the woman,' I said, agitation rising in me.

'Gosh,' said Emma. 'It's so difficult for you, isn't it? Did you read the *Metro* yesterday? About the Asian girl in Birmingham?'

Fleur put her highlighter down. 'Awful. Just because she wanted to go to university.'

Don't know what that had to do with me and the hole-in-the-wall (HITW?).

'Well, there was no gun to my head,' I said.

Brammers looked intrigued. 'Could there have been?'

'No, no,' I said, waving my hand. 'I just mean, a person can say no. I said no.'

OK, we all know the HITW is a whack situ, but there was no need for everyone to look so uncomfortable: as if Asians were *all* a bunch of lunatics. There are crazier things that happen. Then Hannah sprang to mind.

'It's not like he asked me to be a co-wife.'

'A co-wife?' Brammers had her pen at the ready again. I mean, a HITW was one thing, polygamy was another. So I explained my friend's whole being a second wife scenario.

'But that's not even legal!' Fleur exclaimed, going red in the face.

Err, hello! Neither is murder, but that doesn't stop people.

'Is your friend mad?' asked Emma.

Brammers scratched her head. 'This is fascinating, Sofia. Just the kind of thing *The Times* would love.' Which isn't particularly helpful as Hannah hates *The Times*.

'Yeah,' I said, laughing, 'Someone should write a book about it.' I carried on doodling, but there was a pause.

'Sofia,' said Brammers, shaking her head and smiling. 'This is an amazing idea.'

'What?'

'A book about Muslim dating.'

'Oh, no. No,' I said, picking up a chocolate digestive. 'I'll gag on my biscuit.'

'It'd give a fascinating insight into modern Muslim dating and marriage.'

I sighed. Who'd have thought my parents and the publishing industry would share such similar interests?

'What other situations are there, dating-wise?' she asked.

I shrugged. I'd been through a hole-in-the-wall or two, and Hannah wanted to marry a married man, but conjoined houses and co-wives do not a book make.

Katie then said, 'Remember that guy you once met? The beardie?'

'The one who called me a disco hijabi?' And, by the way, suggested my clothes weren't that bad – they just needed to be painted black. Gloomy bastard.

'This is good, Sofia; this is *very* good.' I could see the vein in Brammers's forehead protruding. 'We could think of all types of things – forced marriages, honour killings.'

Oh my God. You read about that kind of stuff in the papers but no one I ever knew was forced to marry someone. The only reason my dad *might* brandish a knife would be to make sure a man doesn't step out of line. Mum would probably offer him a lifetime of chicken biryani.

'Illicit sex stories ...' Brammers added.

'Sex?' I asked. 'What's that?'

Apparently this wasn't funny because only Katie let out a stifled laugh, whilst the others weren't sure whether to laugh or be shocked. Indeed, my friends, indeed.

Brammers nodded passionately. 'The sexual politics of double standards ...'

I straightened up in my seat. OK, if you were to do a survey then I'm guessing there would be far more Muslim women that are virgins than men, but talk about limited observation – as if this double standard is just a Muslim phenomenon.

'It's all a bit dark, isn't it?' I said. 'I couldn't *really* say I have much experience with the whole forced marriage, honour killing thing.'

I impersonated the *Psycho* knife-killing scene to properly demonstrate my point.

'So a *funny* Muslim dating book?' Brammer's vein was practically doing a jig.

'Yes, exactly. Something *light*.'

As everyone filed out of the meeting, I asked Katie if people at work secretly thought I looked like a terrorist, but were too middle class to say so. 'Don't be so utterly ridiculous,' she said.

'Should I do a poll?' We sat down. 'Might look a bit desperate. But better to look desperate than like a terrorist.'

'People are just curious. Fleur once asked me about your scarf and the whole Muslim thing. At the Heyworth launch. You were Rammer-ing and couldn't find a place to pray.'

I looked over at Fleur who was inducting the new work experience guy.

'Bad praying space, good canapés. Thanks for saving those for me, by the way,' I said.

'Standard. To be honest I think she just admires your dedication. She found it very interesting when I told her no one in your family wears a scarf.'

'That's like saying, *I find it very interesting, given no one in your family is gay.*'

'You don't have to tell me.' Katie began plaiting her blonde hair.

I considered it. 'Some people like shopping, some people like therapy, I happen to like praying.'

'The other day I went to church with my granny and lit a candle, and I don't even know what I believe. Religion has a bad name.'

'Hmmm. Maybe I need to swap campaigning for books about hippos and start a PR campaign for Muslims,' I said.

'You'll never please everyone. Anyway,' Katie added, her hair shining in the stark office light, 'Most of us know that terrorism is all relative.'

I bought Katie (and myself) some chocolate to celebrate my non-terrorist-looking accomplishment. I'm also going to start celebrating the small things in life – they are, after all, the things that matter.

3 p.m. I had five missed calls from Fozia. I think it says something about the dedication of our friendship that we're able to make time for these calls in the middle of our respective professional endeavours (often crises). Apparently Kamran's in 'talks' with his parents about their relationship. The Geneva Conference of marriage. His parents aren't happy about him wanting to marry someone who's *dye*-vorced (as our parents would say). I tried to explain to her it was a typical case of the ball-less men, but no one ever listens to me. There are far too many holes (in walls, of course), and not enough balls, if you ask me.

4.30 p.m. What length of time is appropriate to text an ex and see how they are? Especially when your parting words to them were, 'I don't need to be adored.' Which in and of itself is a fair point, but having had a month of reflection, perhaps even valid points need to be delivered with sensitivity.

To Imran: Hello. Hope Ramadan went well and you had a good Eid. Just wanted to see how you were. Take care, and remember: never tie your shoelaces in revolving doors. Sofia. X

See. I can be caring too.

7 p.m. Bloody hell. Tattooed neighbour was out front, leaning under the bonnet of his car. Katie's long-term advice has always been to kill things with kindness. I wasn't going to bother, but just as I walked past him he stood up, resting his hands on his hips and frowning at his handiwork. Given what happened today, I thought

I might be doing my community a favour by being friendly and gracious in the face of prejudice.

'Car trouble?' I asked.

'The oil's gone,' he replied without looking my way.

'Hmmm, yes. Oil is important.'

I mean, what else is a person to say?

He looked at me. 'What?'

'Keeps things smooth. Running smooth-*ly*.'

Unlike this conversation. What was I saying? He slammed the bonnet shut, his look loosely translating into, *What the hell are you talking about?* Which was fair enough. A person should know when to quit while they're behind so I smiled my best fake smile and left him to it.

10.30 p.m. I prayed and checked my phone to see if Imran had replied. Perhaps he's changed his number? Dad was smoking in the garden while listening to old melancholy Indian songs. I hung my head outside my bedroom window in an attempt to inhale as much second-hand nicotine as possible. Got a bit bored, so decided to go and sit with him. For company and not just close proximity to nicotine.

I looked at his cigarette – the only relief for living on the edge of anxiety. (But not as good as praying. Obviously.)

'You know smoking kills?' I said. Yes, I know – hypocrisy. But what I mean is smoking ten-a-day kills, not smoking once when you're feeling especially stressed, or have just been called a terrorist.

'Soffoo, you will learn that a person should be allowed some vices.'

I propped my feet up on the chair.

'I don't know how I feel about gender discrimination with these vices.' Because I mean, it's all right for a man to light up and puff away, imagine if I decided to join in?

Horror!

Scandal!

Bullshit.

The politics of double standards. Dad patted down his flyaway grey hair. He seemed to contemplate something, giving me a sideward glance. For a minute I wondered if he knew about my ocaasional smoking ... but in that eventuality I'd kindly point to his packet of cigarettes and hypocrisy. It's good to have pre-prepared comebacks.

'I can't argue,' he said, nodding. 'Acha, shh. This is a beautiful song. Wah!'

He sat back and closed his eyes. Mum walked into the garden and looked around at the flowerbeds.

'When will you put on my solo lights?'

Had an image of Dad wearing a blanket of solar lights. Dad opened an eye and closed it again.

'Who wants tea?' shouted Maria from the kitchen.

Everyone. Obviously.

We sat around quietly (shockingly enough), drinking tea, the music still playing in the background. It won't be long until Maria leaves and it'll be just me, Mum and Dad. There are talks of converting the attic after the wedding's over ... (Will I be the Mad Woman in the Attic?)

'Oh, I know this song,' said Maria.

I think parents reserve a certain look for their first-borns, whatever's happening in the world. Perhaps having children is an attempt to try and glue that world back together. There's optimism – although I doubt a person who has babies gives it that much thought. Mum and Dad both watched Maria – the departing daughter – sad and proud. Parents can be so *Bollywood* sometimes. She's only getting married, though it'll be a bore not being able to throw my dirty socks at her. Don't think my parents would ever look at me with that kind of pride. But then her life's as orderly as Mum's Tupperware cupboard; she finished her studies, got a job, found a boy (though granted she had to sit through about fifty different ones, with their parents, in our living room. Ungh – never doing that, thanks). But at last she found one and now she'll marry him. One petite foot in front of the other: clean, consecutive, steps. I prefer hopscotch. Just so happens there's more chance of a stumble and fall.

Dad turned up the volume on the iPod and he and Mum thought it perfectly acceptable to start singing along. Maria and I exchanged looks and quietly laughed. At least they find harmony through their mutual love of old Bollywood music. I looked over the fence and the neighbour had the door open. Was that him leaning against the wall? I turned the volume down, explaining to Dad that not everyone on our street is a fan of Bollywood. He looked at me in mock horror. We really should stop giving people an excuse to dislike us anymore than they probably already do.

But, honestly, but if you don't like it, you really shouldn't leave your door open.

11.40 p.m. The other problem with my being alone stance is being celibate and believing in no sex before marriage. Surely never having a shag, ever, will have an adverse effect on my health.

11.45 p.m. Hmmm, I've just Googled 'lack of sex in life' and it seems there's no such thing. There is 'Marriage sex problems', 'Bring your sex life back to life' (ha!), 'Lack of sexual intimacy', etc. but nothing about not having *any* at all. Clearly no one's deemed the possibility of having no sex and its adverse effects important enough to put up online. Perhaps I should instead search 'celibacy'.

11.47 p.m. 'The effects of celibacy on obsession and arthritis ...' Hmmm.

2.15 a.m. I can't sleep. I keep thinking about arthritis. Is being celibate really making me obsessive??

Friday 2 September

'Blah, Blah, Black Sheep' by Yes, I'm Muslim, Please Get Over It.
On www.sofiasblog.co.uk

I've never liked talk of 'otherness'. What a breeding ground for division and, quite frankly, stupidity. But, unfortunately, just because you don't like a thing doesn't mean you won't

feel it. Whether this feeling karate-chops you – as it probably will at some stage in your Muslim or non-Muslim life
(I don't pretend to have ownership over 'otherness') – or
whether it slowly takes the oxygen from the bubble you
realise you lived in, it's the after-effects that are the most
interesting. If things are thrown off balance, you shouldn't
worry about it too much, God'll chuck down something on
the other side of the scale to even things out, though it may
very well be a shaky start.

9.40 a.m. I've strolled in with pastry and coffee in hand, but
the only person here is Fleur. She was in a frenzy because she
couldn't find the stapler to staple the Events Schedule together.
I handed her some paper clips, before checking my phone for
any message from Imran. *Again.* Positives about being alone
include being able to focus on other people's problems, which
is very selfless, and far more in keeping with being a good Muslim. Except that getting married is apparently completing half
your faith. Does this mean I'm less successful in Islam as well
as society?

9.55 a.m. Balls! Fleur just asked me why I'm not in the editorial
meeting. Why are these now starting at nine-thirty?? Changing
face of publishing – there's crack of dawn prayer, and now there's
practically crack of dawn meeting. But how is anyone to take my
professionalism seriously if I miss them?

'Can I still blame it on Ramadan?' I asked Fleur.

'Wouldn't that be lying?'

I like Fleur. Her obsession with highlighting things is very
entertaining, but when she looks at you in that earnest way she

makes you question yourself. I think it's hard not to like the people that make you question things. Unless you don't like answers.

Well, so long as everyone's away, no harm in checking my Facebook.

9.58 a.m. Ooh. Who's this hot guy that's just poked me?

10.05 a.m. Oopsies. Was just going through photos of hot guy standing on mountains and at weddings, and didn't see Brammers come up behind me. God knows how long she was looming over me.

'Can I see you in my office in ten minutes?'

Now I'm going to have to persuade her that I really am a professional publicist, not professional cyber-stalker.

Katie came over to my desk and handed me a smoothie.

'Happy non-fasting! It's a bit healthier than the biscuits yesterday.'

She perched on my desk, hugging her notebook.

'Don't worry, I missed most of the meeting too. Forgot my wallet on the train and then my shoe fell on the track,' she said.

There should be a book written about Katie. Just then John Trumpet, the publishing director, walked past us and into Brammers' office, closing the door behind him.

'What's going on in there?' I asked.

'Oh, Trumpet's all "Ghastly situation we're in, ahem. Something needs to jolly well be done. What we need is a book with real *punch*."' Katie thrust her fist in the air. 'They might be laying people off.'

Oh my God, is this why Brammers wants to see me in the office? Despite my brilliant idea yesterday? Though firing me would mean they wouldn't be able to tick the ethnicity box for the division. Hurrah for equal opportunities! Shame if someone better than me had to lose their job, though, would feel guilty.

Katie was just about to say something when Brammers poked her head out of the door and asked me to come through.

10.45 a.m. Erm, what just happened? I walked into the office and Trumps was still there. I thought this was them saying sod ticking equal opportunities box, let's get rid of the scarfie who spends her time looking at strange men's pics on FB.

'So, Sofia, you know your idea in yesterday's meeting was great. Contemporary, fresh, good fun,' said Brammers.

'Thanks. You know, glad to help.'

Trumps sniffed and seemed distracted by the pigeons outside the window. 'Terribly filthy things,' he said.

Brammers cleared her throat, 'Yes, well, John and the team *loved* the idea.'

Even Brammers couldn't hide the excitement in her voice. I suspect because she delivered the idea to them. Trumps, who was still distracted, looked at me as if he'd only just noticed me. 'Brilliant idea! Excellent! Muslim dating? Well, I had no idea you were allowed to date.' He heaved towards me and looked at me sympathetically. 'Are your parents disappointed?'

In life? Me? My inability to find a husband? Their own loveless marriage?

'Erm, well ...'

'It's all very *western*, isn't it? Must be hard for them. Out with the old, in with the new.'

Felt I should've played along and said, *Yes, they cry about the loss of their culture and roots and curse the day they immigrated to England.*

'I, er, don't know.'

Trumps looked a bit dissatisfied. Then something important seemed to occur to him. 'Now, you're not going to get *stoned* to death for this, are you?'

Brammers cleared her throat and then laughed. 'Of course she's not going to get *stoned to death*, John. Really.'

Wait, what? 'Why would *I* get stoned to death?'

I'm sure fundos have better things to do than give out fatwas on hijabis who come up with dating book ideas. And then Brammers really did drop the bomb.

'Because we want *you* to write the book.'

At first I thought she was joking, because, *hello*, I'd be better as a farmhand than a writer (although they *probably* wouldn't take to a scarfie in the country). I've never tried to write a book in my life. I *read* books, obviously, but when I laughed Brammers just looked at me. Even Trumps was no longer distracted by the three pigeons – one of which, by the way, had propped itself on top of the other. Imagine; even *pigeons* are shagging.

'Oh, but don't you think it might be better if someone who *knows* how to write, writes the book?' Silence. 'I could always help them with stories and things.'

I looked at them, hopefully. What were they thinking??

Brammers looked like she needed to take a laxative. She then turned her computer screen around and lo and behold, what was facing me but my very own blog?

'Katie told us about this …'

Katie is going to die.

'Over five thousand followers … We've had a meeting with the team,' she continued, looking at Trumps. 'John and I agree that it would be somewhat *authentic* coming from you. From a market-ing angle.'

'Yes, that scarf thing.'

Brammers opened up her hands towards me. 'You're energetic, Sofe. Always telling funny stories; everyone in the editorial meeting thinks you'd be great. And this blog shows you *can* write.'

It's always nice to be appreciated. Also, felt like reporting *that* to people with a 'No one wants a scarfie in the workplace' attitude. This is London, thank you.

Trumps scratched the flesh of his belly that peeped through the strained buttons of his shirt. 'It's a bloody brilliant idea.'

'Sales and Marketing think so too,' added Brammers. 'No mean feat.'

Has Trumps's looming retirement turned him from ingenious to insane? But what was I meant to say to the divisional publicity director and publishing director? No, loves, find another scarfie to do that for you?

'We know it's a somewhat unusual request, Sofia. But your idea is great, and your stories, well, who can tell them better than you?' said Brammers.

Obligation came with its vice-like grip. There were people who thought *I* was the one to make it work. People who didn't think I was a terrorist. *Look!* We Muslims can be fun too! It just didn't feel wholly comfortable.

'The thing is, I've never written *stories*, you know.'

'Small, minor detail, Sofia. If it's awful, well, that's what editing is for.'

Yes, I'd like to be known for writing that *one* awful book that had to be edited to within an inch of its life.

'Of course we've discussed an advance.'

I looked at both of them. Nothing makes the ears perk up more than the mention of an advance. Especially since the salary jump from press officer to publicity manager wasn't exactly nigh. Probably rightly so. Shame.

'We'd like the first draft in July, we're thinking, aren't we, John?'

'Yes. Good month. And October for final delivery. Fifteen thousand. Lucinda will be your editor, but Dorothy here, well, she's interested in being hands-on with the editorial process so she'll also be working on the book.'

My heart began to race, which was rather uncharacteristic of it. Obligation's grip turned out to have padding in the shape of *fifteen* thousand pounds. I could quit work for a year and go travelling. Or add it to my savings and try to buy my own place – if I'm not getting married I can't live with my parents for ever. All kinds of other possibilities came popping out from the seams of professional opportunity.

'And such a huge commitment from you wouldn't go unnoticed.' Brammers smiled, her V-shaped vein threatening an appearance. Trumpet's bushy eyebrows were raised expectantly, and then I suppose you could say the trumpet had sounded ...

2 p.m. Katie was so excited she insisted on going for lunch to celebrate after I'd prayed.

'You do know this doesn't just happen? This is a real opportunity, Sofe. You should be ecstatic.'

One emotion at a time, please.

'What you need to do is go online dating.' Katie took a bite of her quiche. 'Don't give me that face, you know what I mean. If

I hadn't been with Tom since the beginning of time, it's exactly what I'd be doing. Inspiration.'

'Uh-uh. There has to be a simpler way. Let's look into ghost-writers.'

'*You* need to be open to new experiences. I'm learning to do the same. Going to India taught me this.'

'Yes, going online is the same as travelling around India. Anyway, what if people find out?' I said, lowering my voice. 'And plus, I'm sworn off men.'

'You need *stories*.'

I put a chip in my mouth.

'And you won't get them listening to your mum going on about lamps. Also, it's a good distraction from, you know, *stuff*.' I assume she was talking about Imran, who still hadn't messaged me back. 'What about that website? I've seen those ads and one of my Indian friends signed up for it. She said it was good. Sh ... sha-something?'

'Shaadi.com?'

'Yes! Shaadi! What does it mean?'

'Wedding.'

'Well then – that's just what the publishing house ordered.'

Man, I could do with a fag. Hmmm, maybe I can bum one off the workie.

2.15 p.m. Love our workie. I put the cigarette safely in my bag as I called Hannah.

'This is fantastic news!' She'd just come out of the doctor's surgery and got my message. My new career path apparently made her day better. I'm a philanthropist! Although I did use her polygamous life as an anecdote for the office. Honestly, what was I thinking? Thankfully Hannah's response was, 'Finally. Someone who actually gets to benefit from my ridiculous relationship.'

Love Hannah. Perhaps this is like karma for intentions. I was thinking of ways to help people and it turns out people's relationships are going to help me. Maybe being asked to write this book is not such a bad thing. Perhaps this is God's way of saying, here, you might not have a man, but have a book instead. I was, after all, looking for something meaningful, and this is like volunteering my literary services to help people have a better understanding of the Muslim world: a bit of light relief in the face of chronic darkness.

From Suj: You're a fucking genius! We're going to be famous!

From Sofia: When are you back from Miami?

From Suj: Who bloody knows! I have another spot on my chin. Men in Mee-ami are HOT! Always knew you'd be famous. Love you and your big brain! Xxxxxxx

The cons of having a best friend who's a model includes having to wait until she's home to have a proper conversation. I won't yet break it to Suj that Muslim dating books do not make a person famous.

10.55 p.m. The girls and I had a post-Ramadan commencement of our monthly meet in Spice Village in Toots (sans Suj), which turned into a celebratory dinner. I'm going to be a writer! (With fifteen thousand pounds!) Fozia came after work drinks with her banking lot and said it'll show people that we Muslims aren't boring bastards. Double hurrah! And I can also use Fozia's stories.

'I've been out with most of the Muslim men in London ... And look who I've ended up with.' She slumped her head on the table. 'Good for you, though,' she mumbled before looking up with distressed Bambi eyes. 'Can I have your job? God I hate mine.'

'All you need is a plan, Foz,' said Hannah. She got out her phone and started making a list. I patted Fozia on the head as I began to see that actually the picture here was bigger than I'd thought.

'I'm beyond a plan.'

'No one,' said Hannah, 'is beyond a plan. No weeping over the mixed grill, please. '

That's obviously because Hannah (whose activism against the objectification of women includes forgoing makeup. I'm against this too – obviously – but inflicting social trauma because you can't be arsed to put on mascara is a little selfish. We're not all blessed with natural beauty) can't live without a plan.

'Is it weird that Imran hasn't texted me back?' I said.

'Do you think he's got married?' asked Hannah.

Why does everyone act as if there's a marriage marathon going on? 'It's only been five weeks.'

Foz sat up and sighed. 'Maybe he went to Pakistan and found himself a wife.'

I stared at her as the awful possibility dawned on me. But then I remembered who we were talking about.

'No,' I said. 'Not Imran. He's too ... what's the word?'

'Idealistic?' Hannah offered.

'Exactly.' I remembered how much that used to annoy me about him. Until it stopped annoying me and then just made me laugh. 'Maybe life played the irony card and he fell down a hole?'

Hannah cleared her throat. 'Girls, I've decided – I'm giving Zulfi an ultimatum ... It took him *two* years to tell his wife about us. He needs to either set the wedding date or I'm gone.'

Foz gulped down some mango lassi. 'My friend who's a second wife never had any of this, Han.'

Hannah's makeupless face went a shade of red.

'She's really happy,' added Fozia. Honestly, Foz reads a situation as well as she can read Chinese. It looked like Hannah might throw her chicken tikka across the restaurant and storm out.

'I've given up fags,' I interjected. 'I'm against any kind of dependency – nicotine included.' (This morning's fag doesn't count. Nor does the one in purse.)

Hannah stabbed at her plate (possibly visualising Foz?). We needed Suj to diffuse the situation but she was on a beach in Miami, modelling, and we were in Spice Village, eating a mixed grill.

'I *am* happy,' said Hannah.

I tried not to look at Fozia.

'Good,' I said. 'Excellent. That's the goal, isn't it?'

Hannah looked at me. 'You hate it when people say they're happy.'

'Yes, but look at me. I have an ex-boyfriend who's either married some boatie or fallen down a hole. Listen, you do what you have to do, and leave the rest up to God. That's what we do. Action followed by a substantial leap of faith.'

I wanted to add that perhaps the action should be a little more thought out, but you don't blame the person who lit a fire while they're still in the middle of a burning building. To think: there are all these people in polygamous marriages, and one of my best friend's about to join in. A person could get used to the practicalities of it; seeing your husband half the week (less time spent shaving), being home alone (brilliant – you get quality couple time together *and* alone time), not quite having legal rights as a wife since you'd only be married by Islamic law (hmmm) ... It's the emotional part-ownership that's surely the biggest drag. That and also sex sharing. Except it's not PC to judge – we are all autonomous beings, blah blah blah.

When I got home and told the family about the book, they were almost rapturous. (I suspect Mum more so because of the advance.) Dad took my hand, kissed it and looked at Maria and Mum.

'See? You *make* your luck.'

I didn't go into detail about the *nature* of the book. Then Maria asked Dad to take some decorations out of the attic so wedding shenanigans trumped literary endeavours, which was useful in this instance.

The more I think about it, the more I realise some good can come of these bad stories. And why can't I write? One can do anything one puts one's mind to – it's all a matter of perspective. I've cut down smoking by *at least* half. I'm a marginally intelligent, selectively confident, assertive woman who isn't defined by what's *on* her head, but by what's *inside* it. I could become a role model for Muslim youth: wise, sage-like and revered in the community. This week will be the beginning of a long line of incredibly productive weeks. Now must call Hannah to make sure she's not in a stupor of depression, and keep my anti-polygamy feelings to myself in the manner of a truly non-judgemental person.

Oh dear, fag broke in purse.

11.20 p.m.

From Katie: Shaadi, Sweetu. It's the literary way forward. Xxx

When God sends signs, who can ignore them? Perspective. Positivity. Sage-like.

Saturday 10 September

10.10 a.m. Shaadi.com? More like Shady.com. Yesterday I was mentally constructing an online profile while Tahir's parents were over to discuss wedding plans. It hardly seems fair that I have to make all this wedding effort only for Maria to have a lifetime of getting laid. When they left and I finally managed to go online, I realised this was no normal site. According to Shady, being fair or wheatish (in skin tone, one presumes) affects my marriage prospects. As does the number of married siblings I have, and my blood group. Who's ever described themselves as *wheatish*? When I voiced this concern to Mum, she just handed me a tube of Fair & Lovely. 'I've told your chachu to bring more when he comes from Pakistan for the wedding.' My dad's brother must love all this task setting. She looked at my face. 'You need it more than me.'

Don't marry a white person but do try to look like one. Sigh. But I must remember inheritance of choice, etc.

There were a number of *interests* (the cyber equivalent of a lingering look?) from members of the non-Muslim kind and

I wondered whether they could actually see I wear a hijab. Which was inclusive enough, but really, marrying a non-Muslim would be the most nonsensical thing for a hijabi to do. A) You're meant to keep it in the religious family, which I'm very happy with because B) if ever I were to get married I'd rather like to grow in faith with the person who I've committed to *for ever*. While I'm not quite a 'let's live in each other's pocket' type of girl, sharing the fundamentals is rather basic. And anyone who says *love* is all that matters hasn't quite grown up. This is long-term planning ... and I mean *afterlife* kind of long term.

I also received a picture match. How do they decide a *picture match*? Do they look at your photo and start filtering in accordance to what type of man you should marry, based on looks? In which case apparently I should marry a man whose goatee makes him look like he has testicles in lieu of a chin. Not that I've seen what testicles look like, but one gets the idea.

Hey! Salaamssss! Am Pakistani man lukin Pakistani girl good and desent. She be good girl I be good husband happy we be Insh'Allah Allah blesing always.

I called Foz, and thanked God I'm not actually looking for a husband on this thing.

'Sofe,' she replied in her ever calm manner. 'If you want to find guys for research then you need to be proactive. Search for the type of man you'd like to go on a date with and send him an interest.'

Note for book: Cyber-dating rules are different to real-world rules ...

'Han hasn't responded to any of my messages. Is she pissed off?' Foz asked.

'No, but next time try to keep the salt away from her emotional wounds.'

'What's wrong with being honest? I like blunt advice.'

'Dump Kam,' I said.

'Right. Point taken.'

I flicked through some profile pages and ignored the under six-footers. Obviously.

'OK, I'm going to call her again,' she said. 'You'd have thought after fifteen years of friendship she'd know what I mean.'

'You'd have thought after fifteen years you'd know what not to say.'

I clicked on a hottie's profile. Non-Muslim. Shame.

'Another good point. OK. Remember, Sofe, be proactive, not ho-active.'

'Thanks, Foz.'

I've expressed interest in four men who all seem relatively normal, don't have a problem with spelling or grammar, and aren't overly fond of emoticons.

11 a.m. I've already received one response from Shady:

A hijab???? Seriously??!! You're living in the West!!!

Who is this prejudiced person who suffers from punctuation hysteria, one might ask? A BBC correspondent. Had to double-check he was actually brown. In true Zen manner I wished him luck with his identity crisis.

Maybe this is the scrutiny sage-like people suffer.

3 p.m. Were the great writers in history also interrupted mid-writerly flow to visit people's houses and give out celebratory ladoos? My pen will have to wait because everyone needs yellow sugar balls the size of a fist to clog their already ghee-filled arteries.

Maria suspended wedding planning and tried to be helpful by giving me a writing timetable for the next month.

'See, today you have between twelve and two-thirty to get started. We take a break, give out some invites and ladoos, come home, have dinner and you can carry on between ...'

To be honest, I stopped listening. I looked at the colour-coded paper.

'The writing process is a creative one, Maars. You can't just box it up and label it.'

It's not her fault she doesn't get it.

'I don't want you wasting time,' she said. 'I can't wait to tell people I have an author for a sister.' Yikes, Maria saying it out loud like that made it feel rather real. She looked at the timetable. 'You have to be *disciplined*.'

I'm beginning to realise the strain of people not understanding artistic development.

3.15 p.m. Hmph, Dad's managed to get out of parental duties by complaining about high blood pressure. Though God forbid he give up smoking. Mmmm, smoke ...

7.45 p.m. 'Are you all right?' Maria asked, stacking wedding invites (that weren't going to be hand-delivered) on the coffee table.

'Yeah,' I said, glancing at my reflection in the living-room mirror. Eugh. 'Do I look like shit?'

'No, you idiot. I mean are you all right with the whole Imran thing?'

'Oh. Yeah. Fine. Although the next time an auntie or uncle asks when I'm getting married, I'm going to say I've taken a vow of chastity.'

Nothing makes our people more uncomfortable than the mention of sex (or lack thereof).

She inspected my face. 'Not exactly what I'd planned. Me getting married and you dealing with a break-up.'

Poor Maria was being elder sisterly, but I hadn't even paid attention to that particular irony.

'Well, thankfully break-ups aren't fatal,' I said, taking an invite and throwing it at her. 'And stop pretending to worry about things other than your wedding.'

'Shut up. It's just if you were any more miserable, we'd have to disown you.'

Hmph. And there's me thinking I was putting on a relatively good show.

'Don't worry. Anyway, I've got a book to write.'

'And that's a lot more interesting than men.'

Which I knew was a lie, but I let it slide. 'It would just be far easier deciding to live life as a single person if everyone would let me.'

'People are always going to ask when you're getting married,' said Maria. 'That's what makes people *actually* get married.'

I think there should be a 'Marriage' jar. Anyone who mentions it has to put in a pound. The proceeds can go towards funding research into arthritis and obsession.

7.50 p.m. OK, must sit down and write. *Write, write, write.*

7.55 p.m. Why are there no biscuits in the house? How can this be?? It's probably a good thing though, as I'll end up eating an entire packet and then spend the next three days wasting prayer time on asking for a stomach bug.

7.58 p.m. I can't live like this. Surely it's bad for my mental state to deprive myself of things in life. It's like in Islam where everything should be in moderation, and not having biscuits at all is the opposite of moderation if you think about it.

8.45 p.m. Honestly. You can't even go to Sainsbury's and get a packet of Lemon Puffs without being given advice. I had my headphones in and was speaking to Fozia.

'I'm going to give Kam an ultimatum. Hannah's on to something.'

'I'm not a fan of those,' I replied, remembering being on the receiving end of Imran's ultimatum. 'I prefer a more organic approach to love and life.

'You know what the problem is?' I continued. 'There are the men who'll marry a hijabi – but then expect her to move in with a hole-in-the-wall, or think she's going to be this weird paragon of traditional values.' I sighed. 'And then there are the men who are all, *"You're living in the west – what's with the hijab?"* Honestly, I can't help it if I like God. Life would feel so much harder without God, you know?'

The person next to me glanced at me and moved swiftly away.

'Well, I'm no hijabi and look at me.'

'Excuse me? Excuse me, hi . . .'

I turned around and looked up to see a brown (wheatish?) man standing in front of me.

'You dropped your, er …' He looked at the packet. 'Lemon Puffs?'

He scanned my basket that was stocked with cakes and muffins (because what if there was an emergency like today, except it was in the middle of the night – where would I get my biscuits from? And with my spirituality at stake too).

'Oh. Thanks.'

He leaned forward a little and stared at me as if I had something on my face. I leaned back.

'Sorry. Have we met before?' he asked.

I looked at his unfortunate pink shirt, green scarf ensemble. 'Don't think so.'

'It's not a line,' he said. 'I swear.'

'OK.' I didn't think it was a line – if I thought it was a line I'd probably have laughed in his face, they never fail to amuse me – but there was no need for him to look so horrified at the prospect. I waited for him to give back my biscuits.

'So, are they good – your Lemon Puffs? I need some good cookies.'

'What's going on?' asked Fozia on the phone.

'You're American?' I asked.

'No,' she replied.

'Not you, Foz – hang on, I'll call you back.'

'What gave it away?' he said in his distinct American accent.

'Your lack of knowledge of Lemon Puffs, obviously. And the fact that *cookies* in England are these things.' I picked up a packet of Marylands to demonstrate. 'These,' I said, taking the Lemon Puffs from him and putting them back in my basket, 'are what we call *biscuits*.'

'Oh, I see. Biscuits.' He gave me a weird look again. 'You're sure I don't know you?'

'No. I have a vague face. People I don't know think they recognise me all the time, and people I know never do.'

He picked up another packet of Lemon Puffs, looked at me and put them back. 'I don't think I trust your opinion.'

'OK.' Weirdo.

I was about to call Foz back when he said, 'You know the problem with Muslim dating?'

'Sorry?'

'I couldn't help but overhear,' he said, gesturing towards my headphones.

Err, actually, I believe you'll find you can help by not eavesdropping.

'What would that be?'

'So many restrictions,' he said, eyes hovering over my scarf. 'Don't get me wrong, I get if you're conservative, but everyone's too ready to jump from coffee to marriage.'

OK thanks, strange person, for your opinion, but who said *I'm* conservative. Talk about judging a person by their scarf.

'And why do you assume that everyone who wears a hijab is conservative?'

'Oh? Is there something you're not telling people?'

He raised his eyebrows suggestively. That's not what I bloody meant! I'm not some dodgy hijabi, rocking up in a scarf everywhere but secretly conducting illicit liaisons.

'I mean *generally*.'

'Hey, I don't mean to sound obnoxious.'

'Do you live in London?' I asked.

'Just moved.'

'Then don't worry. You'll learn that eavesdropping isn't in keeping with British culture.'

Moron.

'Is being rude in keeping with British culture?'

Hm. I cleared my throat.

'Being rude's not the same as giving an education,' I replied.

'Oh, you're an *educator*?'

'More a fountain of knowledge, actually.'

'So when I visit my aunt today and she asks what I found in the confectionary aisle, I'll put the bag of shopping down and tell her, "biscuits and wisdom".' He paused. 'From an unexpected source.'

That, despite my better inclination and his ironic tone (which I'll forgive in this instance), did make me smile.

'Isn't life a wonder?' I said.

'Well, life and Lemon Puffs,' he replied.

'Exactly. Remember,' I added, pointing to the Lemon Puffs, 'biscuits.' I picked up the Marylands. 'Cookies.'

'All I'm saying is if you're going to eavesdrop then at least have the courtesy to pretend you didn't hear,' I said to Fozia when I called her back.

'Teaches you to stop being so loud.'

'You know I can never tell. *"Everyone's so ready to jump from coffee to marriage."*'

'Was he good-looking?'

'He needed a haircut. Looked a bit like a jumped-up tosser with a scarf flung over his shoulder. But you know, whatever.'

Silence. Fozia can speak volumes with her silence. She can argue a point and win the argument just with how carefully

46

she positions these silences. I've always been an admirer of this (being of the non-silent type – clearly). I glanced around to see if jumped-up tosser might be in one of the queues, so I could smile to show that I can be friendly. But he was lost amidst the throng of weekend shoppers.

Sunday 11 September

10 a.m. Maria was organising tea lights in boxes according to colour. Dad sighed and drank his tea as he watched bearded faces splashed across the TV screen – ten years since 9/11. I remember that day so clearly. This is how we were – glued in front of the TV, anxious, depressed. A shift had taken place, and for a while we'd been displaced.

That evening Dad had suggested we go to the mosque, which didn't happen very often. The imam gave a sermon about our duties as Muslims and told us to pray for the people who had lost their loved ones in New York. You hear all these stories about mosques being breeding grounds for radicals, so, I have to be honest, I was relieved this imam hadn't lost the plot.

'It is a test from Allah; for all of us.' He paused and sighed. It took a few moments before he carried on. 'One of the greatest things a person can face on earth is the test of separation. Separation, in any form, *is* loss, but remember: the greatest separation is that of hope. Ignore people who blame us for the actions of a few, because a person who has faith is never separated from hope. Do good deeds, Brothers and Sisters. For everyone. Start with your neighbour – even they have rights over you – because when life is over, your good deeds will be all you take.'

Two weeks later, I wore the hijab. Good deeds are kind of limited to giving up my seat on the Tube. And as for the neighbour! What if he's a (miserable) racist? Hmm?

Mum shouted from the kitchen, 'Did you bring the potatoes?'

Dad smacked his hand against his head without looking away from the TV.

'You remember your cigarettes but not food for dinner. Very good.'

'Panchods, look at it.' Dad's swearing always peaks at bad news. He leaned forward, stretching out his hand as if he were holding something between his fingertips. 'People don't care about *life* any more. We either shout at each other, or shoot at each other.'

'I'll get Tahir to bring potatoes on his way here.' Maria put the box of tea lights to one side and picked up the phone.

I thought about The Racist. 'As if shouting ever made a difference.' Not that shooting does. Obviously.

'Shakeel!' Mum exclaimed. 'The toaster has broken!' Dad stood up and looked down at me and Maars. 'Look at what your baba's become, girls. There is a technique to shouting.' He winked as he added, 'Learn from your mama.'

Since I'm not really in the mood to learn from Mum, I might as well learn from the Qur'an.

12 p.m. Here's a thought (the Qur'an's always been very good at helping me produce those): perhaps *everyone* should feel guilty on behalf of whatever stupid killing spree someone's decided to go on, even if they're not responsible. Guilt equals productivity.

6.10 p.m. Oh, God. I got ready to see the girls and came downstairs. The news was *still* on. Mum was telling potato-bearing Tahir he should've got a maroon tie in the summer sales. Maria was telling him that she won't speak to him at their wedding if the tie doesn't match her bridal suit. Dad turned up the volume as Mum said, 'When you've both finished lunch you can put on solo lights before it gets dark.'

All I did was ask that the TV be switched off.

'It's bad enough being called a terrorist, do we have to watch news about it all day too?' I said. As if the news was going help keep hope alive.

Slight mistake mentioning The Racist to the family.

'I told you, don't wear that hijab,' said Mum.

'O-ho, Mehnaz, calm down. She is a grown girl.' Dad said this with more conviction than I suspect he felt.

'Who was this guy? Where was it?'

'Calm down, Maars. He never *did* anything. He wouldn't have the guts.' Maria flashed a look at Tahir, who leaned back in the sofa.

'I'll tell you what I'll do with his guts, calling my little sister a terrorist.'

Unlike myself, Maria isn't all words and will pack a punch harder than Tahir can imagine. Maybe he'll become personally acquainted with it when they're married.

'You're always coming home late. Have you seen outside, how bad the world is? Shakeel,' Mum said, looking at my dad, 'tell her how bad the world is.'

'It's not good, you know,' piped up Tahir. 'I think you should stay home today.'

Unbelievable. I sat down and looked around the room. 'What's next? Should I stop going to work? Stay in the house all day, maybe? Tie the apron strings and resign myself to life within four walls?'

'Soffoo, you know I don't like sarcasm,' said Dad.

The doorbell rang and it was Auntie Reena with her six-year-old granddaughter, Asma.

'Remember Nargis's daughter?' she said, joining in the discussion *du jour*.

How can we forget Nargis's daughter? Our very own cautionary tale of belief gone wrong.

'See what you've done? You always let her do what she likes,' said Mum, looking at Dad. She turned to Auntie Reena. 'If I had left him years ago there wouldn't be this problem.'

According to Mum, the world is falling apart because she and Dad stayed together. Maria and I looked at each other – Tahir glanced uncomfortably at our parents. I really wish they wouldn't publicise their lost dreams of divorce. I tried to catch Tahir's eye, give him an *isn't it funny when these two start this nonsense?* look. He, unfortunately, was too busy spectating.

'Haan,' responded Dad. 'Then I also wouldn't have a heart problem.' He leaned towards Tahir. 'Your auntie is meant to help with my blood pressure.'

'Le, *pressure*,' scoffed Mum. She opened the box of solar lights, handing them over to Dad, who inspected each one before putting them on the floor. Maria looked as relieved as I felt. One never can tell whether our parents' arguments are going to turn into a full-scale recounting of all that was wrong with their marriage. Those late-night prayers of mine when they used to shout at each other have come in handy, I believe. Maria and I are constantly impressed at the convenience of time too – it's sapped both parties of their energy to hurl accusations.

'I'm *thirty*,' I said, getting back to the issue before time decided to go into reverse.

'Sofe, that doesn't mean you don't listen to your parents.' Tahir had got comfortable again and began chomping on some crisps.

Asma started swishing around in her dress and flashing her knickers, while dancing in the middle of the room.

'Stop doing that.' Auntie Reena grabbed her and Asma started crying – all the while I had my heels on, ready to meet the girls.

The doorbell rang (again!). I went to answer it as I heard Tahir say, 'Well, just sometimes, Maar, Sofe can be a bit, you know, la-di-dah.'

La-di-dah? I opened the door. Uh-oh, tattooed neighbour. The last thing we needed was for him to see that he lives next to a zoo. He stood there as I heard Mum say, 'O-ho and now it's getting late and you haven't put on my solo lights.'

I looked at him, expectantly. He stood there as if *I'd* disturbed *him*.

'Hi?' I said.

'Chalo, let's not get hot-headed or we won't get dessert,' said Dad.

'I think you have my package.'

'Excuse me?'

Before he could answer, something smashed and I heard Mum exclaim, 'Oh my vase!'

Back in the living room shards of glass were scattered over the flooring. Auntie Reena was comforting Asma, Mum was already sweeping the floor, and Maria was telling Tahir he should be careful about what he says. Dad looked behind me and frowned, then ushered the neighbour into the room with a wave of his hand.

The neighbour looked around, towering over the brown jungle he'd stepped into.

Maria nodded towards the door and mouthed, 'Go.' What will I do when she no longer lives here? But I wasn't about to be a prisoner in my own home. Like a prisoner of war. Except the war is outside, and not a real war; rather, more like guerrilla warfare where no one's sure whose side anybody's on.

'Right. Bye, everyone,' I shouted. Before anyone could respond, I legged it and as I shut the door behind me I heard Mum ask tattooed neighbour, 'Do you know how to put on solo lights?'

Tuesday 20 September

6.45 a.m. 'Soffee toffeeeeee!'

Honestly. The only person who can get away with such a chirpy call at six in the morning is Suj.

'Suj fudge, you're back.'

'Who's the lucky bastard dating you and when the hell is he putting a ring on your finger?'

She's been asking me this question for the better part of ten years. I sat up in my bed and rubbed my eyes.

'Any day now.'

'I'm knackered. Five weeks doing photo shoots has done my head in.'

'I always knew you belonged on the red carpet,' I said.

'*We* belong on the red carpet.'

I didn't bother going into the fact that I didn't look like a model, whereas Suj certainly did.

'Has Foz quit her job yet?' she asked.

'No.'

'Has Zulfi set the date?'

'No.'

'Has Imran decided to move out of the hole-in-the-wall?'

'No,' I replied. 'Forget that. He can't even reply to a message. Poor you, coming back to Neverland. Actually, come to think of it, poor *us*.'

'What the fuck is wrong with him?' she asked.

Oh, God. I just spent a whole month praying away the question *What is wrong with* me *that he didn't want to move out*, but I swear if people keep asking about it I'm going to have to become a hermit.

'Anyway, forget him,' said Suj. 'Let's see if that Zulfi shapes up.'

'Isn't it slightly, you know, *risky*?' I asked.

She paused. 'I dunno, Sofe. When you see them together you're like, yeah, this is all right. But then it's like, he already *has* a family.'

Oh dear.

'Thank God you're home,' I said. I told her about all these ultimatums flying out of our friends' mouths.

'Damn right. You know you don't get things unless you demand them. Speaking of, I've met the fittest bloke, but he's *black*. Right, just got off the plane and wanted to call my Soffee toffee before I spend the next three days sleeping off my hangover. Love you.'

7 a.m. Ooh dear – jeans feel a bit snug. But it's better to be a little bit fat and embroiled in a struggle to become a size eight than actually being a size eight – where would you go from there? It's not the destination that counts, it's the *journey*.

7.05 a.m. Wish the journey didn't involve having a muffin top.

10 a.m. Actually, journey into work did include a muffin, which won't help the muffin top but does help my general happiness.

I had forty-six new messages on Shady. I scanned down the list, squinting to get a better look at the photo next to each message and stopped short. Surely it couldn't be … I clicked on the profile and who was it other than the jumped-up tosser from Sainsbury's! According to his profile, he's very serious about settling down. I think he should first learn about cookies and biscuits to be honest. Bloody online dating. Now he really will recognise me. Weird, cyber-stalking, OCD-inducing tools show you who's checked your profile.

3.20 p.m.

> **From An American in London:** Hello. Just so you know, I told you I recognised you from somewhere.
>   PS The Lemon Puffs were interesting.

I looked at his message. A response wasn't really warranted, but if he wants to make a point then I have those too.

3.25 p.m.

> **From Hello, Publicity:** OK, fine. I told you so about the Lemon Puffs. I'm happy to impart knowledge.

3.30 p.m.

> **From An American in London:** Just to clarify, I didn't say thank you. I was just appreciating Lemon Puffs.

3.34 p.m.

> **From Hello, Publicity:** I say potato, you say patata.

3.36 p.m.

> **From An American in London:** Bit soon to call the whole thing off.

6.45 p.m. I've spent the majority of the afternoon not pitching books to news and mags editors, but firing emails back and forth with the American (New Yorker), aka Naim. Since signing in and out of Shady will probably alert the IT police, I gave him my Gmail address. I do wonder what type of man has the time to respond almost instantly to emails. Is he bored? Does he not have a job? Is emailing women online his job? To which I couldn't say much, considering emailing men is forming a part of mine.

8 p.m.

> **To: Sharif, Naim**
> **From: Khan, Sofia**
> **Subject: Hi**
>
> So, what brings you to our little island?

8.15 p.m.

To: Khan, Sofia
From: Sharif, Naim
Subject RE: Hi

I want to say Lemon Puffs, but actually most of my dad's side of the family live in Slough so that's where I am for now. I was just visiting my aunt when I bumped into you. My mom passed away a year ago so Dad wanted to be with his brothers and sisters. I guess I wanted a change and joined him, helping out with the family's business. I'm still figuring out what your city has to offer that New York doesn't.

And what brings you to Shaadi?

Death is an odd kind of thing; both imminent and surreal. I remember Suj's mum dying when we were in college.

'You think the world's going to stop,' she said. 'And it doesn't. It just fucking carries on.'

I saw the world through Suj's blurred vision and wished I could make it stop for her. Even for a moment. It all seemed to be a dream. An absurd, abstract dream.

'Is she in a better place now, Sofe? You believe that stuff, don't you?'

I told her I did. It makes me shudder to think about people who don't.

I re-read Naim's email and realised that one shouldn't form opinions based on articles of clothing. I, of all people, should know this ...

From: Khan, Sofia
To: Sharif, Naim
Subject RE: Hi

I'm really sorry to hear that.

I think you'll find London has plenty to offer that NY doesn't. You just have to look in the right places.

I'm actually on here as a bit of a project. I'm (trying) to write a Muslim dating book so this serves well as research.

Sofia.

8.25 p.m. Dad came into my room and sat down, clasping his hands together.

'Soffoo.'

'Baba.'

He looked at the boxes containing wedding stuff in the corner of the room.

'The wedding is in four months.' Before he could continue, his mobile rang. 'Haan!' he barked down the phone. He grunted a reply before swearing at the person on the other end of the line and putting the phone down.

'Your mama tells me I can't smoke.' He poked his head out of the door. 'And then she is the reason I smoke.' *Word, Dad. Word.* 'So, as my daughter, you have to hide my cigarettes in case she catches me.'

Ha! Five years ago, the idea of hiding anything from Mum would've had my dad in a rampage. Amazing how heart problems can solve anger problems.

'How much will you pay me?' I asked.

He narrowed his eyes and leaned back.

'My daughter is blackmailing me?'

'Yep. And you might as well make it worth my while. Your wife has the eyes of a hawk and the hearing of a bat.'

'Haan. Bat.' He sat, thinking about this for a while. 'By end of the wedding I'll give you fifty pounds.'

'You want me to hide your cigarettes for the next four months and all you're giving me is fifty lousy pounds?'

He flared his nostrils.

'Baba, listen.' I got up and put both my hands on his shoulders. 'Let's call it a hundred quid a month, you'll get your (rationed) cigarettes and I'll lie for you. And you know a daughter should never lie to her parents.'

'Fittaymoo.'

I shook my head – honestly, my own father cursing me.

'If you'd just given me and Maria pocket money when we were kids instead of saying how western that was, we wouldn't have had to learn how to hustle.' I took my hands off his shoulders as he got up. 'I think an advance is important. To foster trust.'

I put my hand out as he reached into his pocket and got his wallet out, handing me two crisp fifty-pound notes. He squeezed my nose between his fingers, squinting at me, and said, 'I'll be keeping count of my cigarettes.'

Damn.

Wednesday 28 September

What's Love Got To Do With It?' by Yes I'm Muslim, Please Get Over It

On www.sofiasblog.co.uk
(NB: Recycle material for dating book. Because it's good for the environment of my brain.)

When our immigrant parents crossed an ocean, for evermore, they also crossed certain boundaries of understanding, which, of course, they didn't quite understand. My sister came home from a date once. Mum asked what happened.

'Nothing,' she replied. 'Just didn't really click.'

Mum nodded, a confused expression forming as she went back to grinding the ginger. I went on a date a few months later and Mum asked how it had gone.

'Nice guy.'

Mum's face went from disgruntled housewife to hopeful mother.

'But no click,' I added.

The same confused expression was etched a little deeper as Mum went back to chopping up the parsley.

A friend of mine came over one day and was describing a man her parents had set her up with. 'What was wrong with him?' asked Mum.

'He was a bit quiet. We didn't click.'

Confusion had morphed into incomprehension. Thoughts of ginger, parsley, garlic, were all abandoned. Mum leaned forward, bringing out her hands as if she were about to make a sacrificial offering.

'What is this ... click?'

And there it was, that very ocean in our living room.

9.10 a.m. I signed into my Gmail account, trying to figure out how to pitch to *Stylist* for Shain Murphy (how, how, how do hippos fit into contemporary, city women's lives?) and noticed I hadn't received a reply from Naim. Was it wrong to have mentioned the dating book? Should I go undercover?

10.05 a.m.

From Hannah: Brace yourself ... I'm getting married! Next month!

10.40 a.m. I can't believe it! Zzzz Zulfi has pulled his finger out and set a date. Does this mean that people can change and surprise you? Or did he just break under the weight of ultimatum – which is a charming story.

I asked whether she's sure. I mean *really* sure – because humans are pretty great at self-delusion. She said she loved him, which didn't really answer my question. But apparently if you argue with that logic (if that's what you want to call it) then you're a cynic, God forbid. That, and of course Hannah's thirty-one – funny how age is always inserted into the equation of love. I can sit here and argue about the implications of polygamy until I'm no longer brown in the face, but no one's allowed to contest matters of the heart. Unless the heart wants religion – in which case there is no shortage of people to tell you that you're a nut.

12 p.m. Still no email from the American.

4.55 p.m. No email, and I want a muffin.

9.45 p.m. 'I thought you wanted a simple wedding?'

Suj, Foz and I looked at the pile of magazines Hannah slammed on the table as she ordered a virgin mojito.

'I'll have a skinny cappuccino, thanks, babe,' said Suj, handing the drinks menu back to the waitress.

'Sorry, we only have semi-skimmed.'

'Oh. All right, I'll have a vodka then.'

Hannah and I cleared our throats.

'Bollocks, I forgot I'm with a bunch of Muslims. Black coffee then.' Poor Suj.

'Yes. Simplicity is key. But there's no need to be ghetto about it,' said Hannah.

Note for book: When people say they want a small wedding, they almost always lie.

I told them about the brief emailing episode with the American.

'Small world. Great story for the grandkids.' Hannah picked up a magazine from the pile.

Weddings also give people tunnel vision; at the end of which there is always some form of extravagant party – for everyone. She's obviously forgotten that I'm a conscientious celibate now, as opposed to one by default.

'He's gone AWOL because I mentioned the book.'

'Why are you being honest?' said Foz. 'So soon?'

Sigh.

'I like that she doesn't care what people think,' said Hannah, flicking through the magazine. 'It's refreshing.'

'This is your fault, you know.' Foz jabbed her finger in Suj's direction. 'You need to stop letting her take everything so lightly.'

'All right, love. Why don't you use that finger to call Kam and tell him he's a tosser?' Suj put her hand on my knee and squeezed it. 'And Sofe can do whatever she wants.'

'Forget Kam,' I said. 'Call post-divorce Riaz. He was a good egg.'

'Now, what do you think of this flower arrangement?' Hannah slid the magazine towards us.

Note for book: Weddings also cause selective hearing.

'No carnations,' said Foz, colouring a little, presumably at the mention of Riaz.

Suj didn't think the arrangement was big enough. I personally didn't think anything, but felt it my duty to be involved so started Googling more options.

'How about just a single orchid?' I said.

The girls shook their head in unison.

Suj then took out her phone, presumably to also Google flowers, but got distracted and showed us photos of Charles instead.

'Is that an eight-pack?' Foz exclaimed. She grabbed the phone and zoomed in. 'Jeez.'

I glanced at the screen and nodded.

'Forget your American unless he looks like that,' said Foz.

'If anything happens with the American,' I said, 'I'd eat my own hand.'

'Well, make sure it's your left one if you're going to write this book,' said Hannah.

'Speaking of which, I think I need to be professional and do things like interview you guys. Since you're getting married and apparently have the most *Times*-worthy relationship, I'll start with you, Han.'

Earnest writer that I've become, I put my Dictaphone on the table. Hannah sat up and cleared her throat.

Me: *Soooo, do you think this'll work?*

(Silence.)

Hannah: *Well, yes. I do.*

Me: *Hmm.*

Hannah: *Don't you think it'll work?*

Me: *Me? I er, yeah, no, why not.*

(Gulping of drink.)

Me: *Future's a murky place. I mean, we're not psychic. Also, people that give definitive answers are arrogant know-it-alls.*

(Silence.)

(More silence.)

(One of the girls coughs.)

Me: *You know those people who say, 'Go with the flow?' They're idiots. Question everything and, more often than not, you'll stumble across an answer.*

Foz: *Sofe, you should probably question things less.*

Me: *You wait your interview turn.*

Hannah: *I need another drink. Hi, can I have another virgin mojito, please?*

Waitress: *Virgin?*

Me and Hannah: *Yes, virgin.*

Me: *What was it your dad said again when you told your parents about Zulfi?*

(Suj laughs out loud.)

Suj: *He's so fucking funny.*

Hannah: *(In Arabic accent) 'You are almost thirty-one, never married, I show you man and you say no … Maybe you are lesbian.' Mum walked in and said 'Habibti, life is not like this, what do you call that programme you girls watch?* Sex and the City.'

She's right. You can't reject a man because he wears Y-Fronts instead of boxers. Another won't just come along and sweep you off your feet.

Me: *Yeah, namely because by the time you find out he wears Y-Fronts you'd be married to him anyway.*

Hannah: *I thought, excellent. Telling him I'm becoming a second wife will pale in comparison to me being gay. (Sound of glasses being set on table.) I think he'd have preferred it if I was a lesbian.*

(Pause.)

Me: *How do you feel about, you know, husband-sharing?*

(Pause.)

Hannah: *It's not ideal, is it? But then what's ideal? (Pause.) Have you interviewed anyone else yet?*

Me: *No.*

Hannah: *Let's put Foz under the microscope. Or Suj.*

Suj: *I'm not Muslim.*

Me: *Muslim, brown – all begins to leak into the same thing.*

Hannah. *Hardly. You know, actually I should finish this drink and then go. Early start tomorrow.*

Me: *Oh, are we done?*

Hannah: *Yeah. We're done.*

Friday 30 September

8.30 a.m. ARRRRRRGHHH! Mortification! Why, why, why is technology both friend, by introducing me to Muslim dating case studies, and foe, by stripping me of dignity in the same technical breath? I woke up to message failure emails. Wasn't sure what that meant until I got an email from Shain:

> **From: Murphy, Shain**
> **To: Khan, Sofia**
> **Subject: (no subject)**
>
> Sofia, wow – what an offer. Is this part of the service when publishing with you guys? Haha. Or a personal entrepreneurial endeavour?! Anyone who has the balls to sell Viagra to their author is the kind of publicist I want! ;)
> PS Did I get the *Guardian* slot you pitched?
> Shain xxxxx

My stupid email's been hacked and is now sending out Viagra promos to everyone in my contacts' list, including authors. If Brammers finds out, it'll be death by administrative tasks. HITW Imran's also in my contacts' list. For a moment I thought: maybe this will induce him to drop me a line. And then I realised he'll just be glad he didn't marry a Viagra-selling hijabi.

10.30 a.m. Brammers is in a meeting. Granted I was a little late for morning prayers, but I dragged myself out of bed eventually. Surely that should help protect me against possible disciplinary.

Anyone would think I've given the new workie the task of sending out aid to Africa when explaining how to do a mail-out. I passed him a list of contacts as I was checking my Shady account, and he just stood there. I looked up from the screen.

'Benjamin ...'

'Benji.'

'Right, Benji, you print these out onto the sticky labels I gave you and put them on the jiffy bags, in which you'll add a copy of the book with a press release.'

Of course, as I was explaining this, he was staring at Fleur's legs. People and their distractions. Honestly.

12.45 p.m.

From: Sharif, Naim
To: Khan, Sofia
Subject: Thanks for the kind offer ...

Good afternoon, I'm just wondering if there's a reason you sent me a link to purchase Viagra/Cialis? Just so you know, I don't have a problem that might require those. Unless, of course, you're trying to suggest something ...

Please, Earth, open up right now and swallow me, and my laptop, whole.

1 p.m.

From: Khan, Sofia
To: Sharif, Naim
Subject Re: Thanks for the kind offer ...

I'm conducting a survey. Congratulations on being one of the chosen participants.

1.09 p.m.

From: Sharif, Naim
To: Khan, Sofia
Subject Re: Thanks for the kind offer ...

Participants? Plural? Next time I think you should keep your men separate. Creating a competitive environment might not work to your advantage. What are you going to do if they all show up, pumped-up on Viagra?

1.25 p.m.

From: Khan, Sofia
To: Sharif, Naim
Subject Re: Thanks for the kind offer ...

Excellent story piece, don't you think?

3.11 p.m.

From: Sharif, Naim
To: Khan, Sofia
Subject Re: Thanks for the kind offer ...

Maybe I need to hear more about this book. Quick question, does the one who buys the most Viagra win or lose? Interesting ...

3.47 p.m.

> **From: Khan, Sofia**
> **To: Sharif, Naim**
> **Subject Re: Thanks for the kind offer ...**

> For the person who buys the most, surely it's a win-win situation. The future's bright.

4.05 p.m.

> **From: Sharif, Naim**
> **To: Khan, Sofia**
> **Subject Re: Thanks for the kind offer ...**

> Apparently for you the future's looking limp. How many orders does it take to get a phone call? 07700 900 988. I'd like to hear more about this book.

Note for book: The way to get a man's number is to send him a link for sexual enhancement drugs.

4.25 p.m. Arrghhh! I've just seen the list I gave to Benji! He's sent out sixty copies of *Facts About Hippos* to all the financial editors on our list. Bollocks! I called Charlie in the post room. He said I'd missed the delivery truck by two minutes. Maybe this is God's way of telling me to be nicer to work experience people.

5.05 p.m. Oh dear. Brammers has just asked me to come into the office.

5.20 p.m. 'Anything you want to tell me, Sofia?'

Brammers scratched her head. *Sniff sniff.* I had a flash of wanting to blame work faux pas on the workie, and then felt guilty for having such a thought. I prefer not to think about what a person's instinct says about them.

'About the hippo campaign?'

She looked at me blankly. 'What? No. Shain seems to be happy, though, well done,' she said, distracted.

Thanks to God! Maybe she hasn't found out, and there's no reason I can't order some more books and send them out to the right editors ASAP.

'Sofia …' Brammers tapped the desk with her pen. 'The book?'

'Oh, going really well.'

'Really?'

I swear her pupils dilated as her eyes bore into mine.

'Great,' she said. 'I'll have a look at the first chapter draft before we show Lucinda. Here's the contract. Have a read …'

I held the mini booklet in my hands.

'You know, it's important that this is delivered on *time*.' She looked pointedly at me.

Honestly. Anyone would think I'm not responsible or focused enough to meet a deadline.

10.24 p.m.

To Naim: Just so you know, this is a private number. Any orders relating to Viagra/Cialis should be made online. Obviously. Sofia.

10.32 p.m.

From Naim: Are you really writing a book or is that just a cover story for your real job, selling Viagra?

10.41 p.m.

To Naim: Of course I'm writing a book. Hijabis don't lie. I'm very professional.

10.42 p.m.

From Naim: Professional what? That's what I'm asking. Although, nothing like a bit of mystery to keep things interesting.

I've discovered that it's very liberating being immune to flirtatious banter. Once one is sage-like and focused on the task at hand, they are also impenetrable; emotionally speaking.

OCTOBER 2011

Out of the Frying Pan

Muslim Dating Book

~~When Muslim dating, forget sex. Don't think about it except momentarily when you're sitting opposite someone and ask yourself, can I imagine having sex with this person? Because that's all you'll be able to do – imagine it.~~

Ugh. No. I forgot I'm against the sexualisation of society. Goes to show that marriage isn't the only thing ingrained in us.

Muslim dating shouldn't be confused with Asian dating. Plenty of clichéd stories exist of girl likes boy, boy likes girl – except girl has to marry her cousin from Pakistan or India or wherever – girl's parents take her abroad for forced arranged marriage, so on and so forth. I mean authentic Muslim dating, where often chaperones are present, where first dates consist of discussions about living arrangements, how many times you pray in the day, conversation about the socio-political effects of 9/11 and skinny jeans. There is one purpose, and that is marriage. You are diving, head-first, into the fire.

Saturday 1 October

9.10 a.m. Oh, Lord, incessant phone bleeping woke me up. I'd been sent seventeen pictures of what is basically the same shoe in a different shade of gold.

9.12 a.m. Maria came in and sat on my bed.

'Did you like the one with two straps at the front, or the slightly thicker single strap? The thing with the single strap is the heel's a little shorter but ...'

She flicked through *Asian Bride*. I sat up and looked at the pics with her, pretending to sound passionate about diamantés.

Once we'd gone through the five thousand shoes, she put the magazine to one side.

'How's the book going? Actually, you can tell me all about progress on our way to Green Street. Mum doesn't understand about the golden shoes and just keeps handing me tubes of Fair & Lovely.'

8.20 p.m. Well, thanks to God that's done! We came home and Mum was looking impressed with my purchase until I draped the scarf over my head. I didn't have to – but who can resist?

Oh, Naim's calling ...

Wednesday 5 October

9.30 a.m. I came in to work early to write but a fuzzy wall stood between creativity and me. Katie came bounding in to work early too. She ran here. *Five miles.*

'Training, Sweetu. I'm doing a half marathon.' Her hair was still wet from her shower.

'Are you mad?'

'It's important to have goals,' she said, collapsing in her chair and switching on her computer. 'Don't you find that life is otherwise just, *stagnant.*'

'You do know that when you run, *you're* the one moving, not life?'

Katie looked at her screen. 'Ugh. Thirty-nine emails.'

'Let me buy you a cake. Or a disgusting spinach and kale smoothie.'

We both went to the canteen while Katie told me about her running routine. I was exhausted just listening to her. By the time we'd come back up, Fleur was also at her desk, and Benji was hovering around her.

'How's the book?' Katie asked as she stared at the muffin in my hand.

I watched Benji tell Fleur a joke as I told Katie about the American and my research being underway.

'He needs to just ask her out,' I said, surveying the situation from the side of my computer. 'I want to say, "Benjikins, time is of the essence."'

'Exactly,' she replied.

Honestly, Katie is such a nudger: clearing her throat here, a meaningful raise of the eyebrows there. I ignored her and continued to observe Benji fannying around with Fleur's notepad when I felt Katie's eyes still on me.

'What?'

'This American. Nice, is he?'

I told her that I ended up spending three hours on the phone to him last night.

'What on earth did you talk about?'

'Erm, Billy Bob Thornton, garlic sauce and that ad with the cow running down the beach.'

'This is hopeful!'

Which is a lot better than Hannah asking whether we had phone sex. Ungh. If you're not having sex before marriage then don't have any kind of sex at *all*. Honestly.

'Pink shirt and scarf – that's all I have to say.' Was it worth reminding Katie that I'm also no longer looking for a relationship (now, I just write about them)?

Note for book (and life?): Compartmentalising is a useful and essential tool in order to maintain focus.

To which she didn't reply. Five seconds later I received an email:

From: Byrne, Katie
To: Khan, Sofia
Subject: ...

WHATEVER.

Just as I looked over the computer and laughed, my phone beeped.

From Naim: So I was thinking we should discuss your Viagra-selling strategy over some coffee and Lemon Puffs. Saturday work for you?

'Who is it?' Katie's also nosy as hell.

'Speak of the devil.'

She jumped out of her seat, took the phone from me and read the message.

'He's asking you out.'

'No, he doesn't really know anyone in London. I'm his port of call. Literally.'

Katie had my phone clasped in two hands. 'You're very flirty.'

'I am not and stop reading all my messages,' I said, snatching it back. 'I'm going to see him as part of my professional endeavour.'

'Oh, God,' she said, wrapping her cardigan around her and walking back to her desk.

'I am,' I replied.

'Fine. And I'm going to record a conversation between you and George in Facilities and replay it in our catch-up meeting. Then we'll see whether or not you flirt.'

Hmph. Friendliness is now mistaken with flirtation. The world's moral compass is askew.

To Naim: Lemon Puffs on a Saturday sounds fine to me.

Saturday 8 October

2.30 p.m.

From Katie: Good luck, Sweetu! And remember – open mind and positive thinking! Xx

Pfft. If that worked, we'd all have positive-thought our way into world peace, surely. Mum came into my room while I was trying to write and started showing me her sale shopping, including clothes for mine and Maria's (unborn) kids, more solar lights, ruby earrings (forty per cent off!), nose trimmer for Dad – 'Just because you're getting old and blind doesn't mean everyone is also blind' – and a dress for me, which will be nice for when I visit my in-laws, apparently.

'And which in-laws would they be, Mum?'

Since we were talking clothes, I abandoned my laptop and decided to go through my wardrobe to look for a dress to wear tonight. I pulled out an animal-print number and tried it on.

'Do I look like a camel-humped Dubaian in this, Mum?' The last thing a person should do is look like they have a huge head, as well as bum. This growing obsession with ever-expanding hijabs is very disturbing.

'Hain? It looks nice,' she replied, smiling at my attire in an all-too-approving way.

'I'll take that as a yes.'

'O-ho, you will get married *one* day.'

'Mum, I told you I'm not getting married.'

I got out of the disastrous Dubaian ensemble and tried on my orange dress. Mum looked at the clothes I'd flung on the floor as I tried on a pair of jeans.

'Are you meeting a boy?'

My leg froze mid-air.

'Huh?'

She repeated the question in Urdu.

'What? No.'

Those sin points for lying seem to be stacking up. But it was either that or a floodgate of questions from her, and I was already drowning in clothes.

'Why aren't you marrying him? What happened? Didn't he like you? Why didn't you like him? You're too fussy. It's the hijab – I told you to wear it after you got married. Look at Ambreen, she was clever, she didn't wear a hijab.'

Sometimes it feels like my decision to wear a scarf is a perpetual punishment. It's bad enough to get raised eyebrows from the outside world, but Mum seems to think that she'll huff and she'll puff, and that one day she'll blow my scarf off.

'Shame, Soffoo,' she replied. 'People get married three, four times and you can't even meet a boy.'

'Yes, Mum, thanks. Now can I pray and then get some work done, please?'

I ushered her out of the room and just before she crossed the threshold, she said, 'Pray for a husband or go and find somewhere to live.'

I'm not sure what's worse; being grey-haired and wrinkled, sitting with my parents and watching TV, or being grey-haired and wrinkled, sitting *alone* and watching TV.

10.20 p.m. Nerves are an odd kind of thing. At first I thought I might have heartburn, and then I thought, *Hmm, no, I've had this feeling before.* It's just been such a long time I didn't quite recognise it.

Naim suggested meeting in Leicester Square. I waited outside Burger King, which is depressing at the best of times but then he is a foreigner so I decided to be accepting and forgiving.

'You're late,' I said as he approached.

He was taller than I remembered and seemed to have forgotten to shave, which was a little distracting. Who doesn't like a bit of stubble or a beard, eh? Thank God he wasn't wearing that stupid scarf. We stood for a few seconds and I was caught in that dilemma of whether I should shake his hand. A hijabi shouldn't really hug a man, but then shaking hands is like we're about to have a business meeting. I put my hands firmly in my jacket pockets.

'But wasn't I worth it?' He smiled, rather too widely. What was it about this smile? He had, after all, reasonable teeth. I have doubts about a person who smiles too widely or readily. It suggests something like smugness.

We walked towards Patisserie Valerie and sat down. He fiddled around with his phone as I ordered a cappuccino.

'So what's your family business then?' I asked.

He tucked a strand of hair behind his ear. 'My dad's always been hung up on the idea of a restaurant. Like *that's* not been done before. Anyway, we've just leased a place. It's work, right? Can't complain.'

Nothing like a bit of passion. The waitress brought over our coffees and his apple tart. Granted, she was rather beautiful, but he could've been a little subtler when he checked her out. Honestly. He turned his plate around.

'Here, try some,' he said.

I got my spoon to take a bite when he picked out a raisin and put it to the side. 'Isn't it weird how these are dried grapes?'

What an idiot! And the sentiment of what I thought was written all over my face. I sat back, empty spoon in hand.

'Raisins aren't dried grapes.' You *moron*, I wanted to add.

He looked, momentarily, embarrassed. 'What?'

'How are raisins dried grapes?'

'Yeah, yeah, they are – what else are they?'

'I don't know, but not *dried* grapes.'

Then he got his phone out and started Googling it and, of course, found to my profound horror that they are *indeed* dried grapes.

'Where did you think they came from? Raisin trees?' He was laughing so hard the table was shaking.

'All right, calm down,' I said with whatever dignity I could muster. WTF? How have I gone through life in such ignorance??

'It was the look on your face. This, like, conviction, that I'd said the stupidest thing ever.'

'And yet *you* had to Google it.'

By this time the waitress had come back to our table. He looked up at her, his eyes resting momentarily on her rather voluptuous frame.

'Thank you for bringing this dessert. It has, quite literally, made my day.'

Hmph. She looked a little confused.

'Excuse him, he's easily entertained. And a public hazard,' I said.

'I hope you don't go around telling authors that raisins grow on raisin trees.'

This doesn't bode well for my writing career. Surely this is the kind of thing a writer (and normal human) should know?

'They're not included in your dating book, are they?' he asked.

'I think it's best to stay away from shrivelled up things.'

Like my ovaries, for example.

'So, what are you going to say about our people's dating rituals?'

'Not sure. A bit of research should get the wheels in my head turning.'

'Are you just using me?'

'Are you telling me you're useful?'

He laughed. 'Well, I've already told you that raisins are dried grapes. Let's take this further. Did you know that prunes are dried plums?'

'Fascinating.'

His phone beeped and he checked the message before turning it upside down.

'So you don't actually want to get married?'

'No.' Right now I'm in the process of getting over the fact that I DIDN'T KNOW WHAT RAISINS WERE.

'Well, that explains it then.'

'What?'

He took a bite of the dessert.

'Why you're still single.'

Now, I'm as big a fan of irony as the next person, but only when I can detect it. Was that a compliment? I don't know why the hell it made me blush. On one hand it serves very well as a natural rouge, on the other hand it can also be a bloody nuisance.

'Hey, you wanna go get dinner?' he asked.

I hesitated and looked at my phone. Maybe during dinner I could redeem myself and pretend I did actually have a functioning brain. Just as I was about to say yes, he looked at his phone again.

'Actually, better not,' he said. 'My friend keeps messaging. I've kinda bailed on her a lot.'

And there was me thinking I'm the only one he really knew here.

'Oh. Fine. Good,' I replied. 'Lots of wedding stuff to deal with anyway.' Although, I did think an extended evening might've been quite fun. 'Listen, there's no obligation or anything ... but if you're in the mood for answering questions and me generally being nosey about your perspective on matters about faith and commitment, I'd be more than happy to listen.'

He wiped his mouth with the napkin. 'Sure. I reckon it could be interesting.'

Ooh, Hannah calling.

11.23 p.m. 'So?' she asked. 'How was the date?'

'Perfectly amicable.'

'Any potential?'

'For help with the book? Yes, plenty.'

'That's not what I meant.'

'Did you know that raisins were dried grapes?'

'Yes, of course.'

Maybe I need to read less fiction and more newspapers. I received a FB notification on my phone and checked it.

'What is it?' asked Hannah.

'Oh, nothing. Just got a friend request from Naim.'

'That's one of the good things about dating an older man,' she said. 'You don't have to analyse your relationship status through the medium of social media.' She paused. 'Zulfi still writes letters.'

'Bloody hell. That's a bit long. Although, I suppose there's longevity in letters.'

11.55 a.m. Keep thinking about raisins. Can't sleep. Also keep thinking about endings.

Note for book: Endings are never absolute.

The idea of getting married is so ingrained in us that even when one decides to be alone, all a person has to do is say 'keep an open mind' and the notion leaks out of some unknown fold. I don't have time for leaks, especially when there are still the odd dust particles of the HITW. I looked at Naim's friend request and wondered about extracted moments of my life being available to him.

As I went through some of Imran's old messages on my phone I moved my finger over the screen and the 'delete' button appeared. I read each message one last time before I brushed each particle of dust under the carpet, with every tap of the button. Then I accepted Naim's friend request.

12.05 a.m.

From Naim: We are now fraands?
To Naim: We are, indeed, fraands.

Note for book: You can't employ cleaners for emotional matters, but now you can de-clutter with the tap of a button. Who has time for the ritual of letter-burning, anyway?

83

Sunday 9 October

11 p.m. Genius new idea to be used, as a back-up, should book and life-plan fail: sing Bollywood songs in English and get the other person to guess it! Perhaps idea needs to be tweaked. But have just spent two hours on phone to Naim and we both agree that this is how we could make our mark in the world.

Tuesday 11 October

10.45 a.m.

From Naim: I think we should set up our own Bollywood Winter Wonder band.

10.50 a.m.

To Naim: Will it help with non-music related matters?

10.52 a.m.

From Naim: Sofia – you manage to sing your way into my evenings; now apply the same talent to singing your way out of non-music matters too.

10.55 a.m.

> **To Naim:** If we're going to have a Winter Wonder band, we should go public and charge.

10.56 a.m.

> **From Naim:** Of course. Who wouldn't pay to listen to our genius? But given I'm clearly the brains in this set-up, leave the logistics to me.

11.03 a.m.

> **To Naim:** But then what do I bring to the set-up?

11.04 a.m.

> **From Naim:** The looks, of course.

Hain?

12 p.m.

> **From Hannah:** All I want to hear you say is that you think this is a fine idea and that getting married to a married man is not ridiculous.

Called Hannah on her lunch break. She was shopping in Selfridges for wedding shoes for her cold feet.

'What if she turns out to be this psychopath who decides to kill me for marrying her husband? What if his kids hate me now they know I'm not just a friend but his soon-to-be-*wife*? What if they begin plotting an elaborate revenge attack?'

All questions to have asked oneself a little more than just three weeks before a wedding, surely?

'She's not going to kill you, his kids will love you, and I don't think a person has time to plan revenge attacks when they have children. Most mothers barely have time to brush their hair.'

'Trust me. She has time to brush her hair. They have a nanny.' She paused as I tried to think of something positive to say. 'What if I don't end up like Fozia's friend who goes out to Pizza Express with her co-wife?' she added. 'Not that I *want* to.'

I've always hated words of comfort. I don't know if you should trust a person who says 'It's going to be OK' unless they're going to personally try and fix it. The best thing in such circumstances is to do damage control, because surely whatever spectacular mess you might get yourself into, there's always a way out. Unless you're stuck in a mine or something.

'Divorce is a handy option.'

'That's your solution?' replied Hannah.

'No. But I'm just saying that it's a possibility.'

'You girls don't think I should do it, do you?'

I paused. Well, who in their right mind would say 'Yes! Fabulous idea!'

'Only you can know what's right for you,' I replied. This might mean I can't be trusted.

Note for book: If entering polygamous relationship, get CRB check on the first wife. Just in case.

9 p.m. Naim called around half five saying he was in the area and asked whether I could grab a coffee.

'Sorry, can't,' I said. I looked over at Katie and mouthed that it was the American. 'I'm having dinner with Katie.'

'Oh come on. *I'll* buy you dinner ...'

Katie watched me and raised her eyebrows.

'Listen, she knows you have a book to write. I'm your inspiration. It doesn't come along every day.'

'You're so full of shit.'

I lowered the phone and informed Katie of happenings.

'Oh, God, Sweetu,' she whispered. 'Just go. We'll have dinner next week.'

If I were Katie, I'd want to smack me right now. 'Are you sure?' I asked.

'Yes,' she said, sighing. 'Just tell him he owes me.'

We met at Tate Modern and I told him I'd be poor company because I couldn't go back to sleep after morning prayer.

'You never miss a prayer, do you?' he said.

'Nope. Once a bunch of people walked into the conference room while I had my forehead on the ground.'

'With your ass in the air? They lucked out, huh?'

I smacked his arm. Honestly.

'What did you do?' he asked.

'Well, I had to choose between God and a bunch of sales execs. I carried on praying, of course.'

He laughed as I guided him towards the Black History Month exhibition.

'You know, I did the whole drinking, girls scene and then there was a time when I really got into going to the mosque. But I dunno, shit happened and it just kind of stopped.'

I wasn't quite sure what to say to that. We were both looking at a selection of framed pictures, drawings and posters.

'You know, the thing about garlic sauce is that it makes everything taste better,' I said.

'Mixed with chilli sauce.'

'Obviously. But not too much.'

'You want it spicy, though,' he said.

'Oh yes. Everything in life should be.'

'Apart from raisins.'

'Very funny.'

He laughed again.

I leaned in to look at a poster, which said: 'Made for Kisses – The Lighter, Smoother Skin Men Adore'. He leaned in too.

'That's some bullshit, huh?' he said.

I was about to reply when his phone rang. He looked at the name and excused himself as he took the call. The exhibition really was very interesting but my eyes kept wandering towards Naim, who seemed to be engaged in a rather entertaining conversation. I got my phone out to message Katie that I was sorry when I realised Naim was behind me.

'Hey. Sorry about that.'

A big group of people entered the room.

'I'm so sorry,' he said, 'but can we take a raincheck on dinner?'

One of the girls in the group stepped away to take a photo. She flicked back a cascade of brown hair, distracting Naim before he looked back at me.

'Oh.' I realised that I might've been looking forward to an extended evening more than I thought.

'Dad needs me to sort out a work emergency. Is that OK?'

It's not as if you can ignore an emergency, but this rationality didn't quite quell the disappointment. Also, that was a very animated way of speaking to one's dad.

'Maybe you can still have dinner with your friend, Caitlin.'

'Katie.'

'Right, sorry. Katie.'

Ugh. I hope he's not the type of person who thinks that it's acceptable to cancel on someone and then un-cancel just because it's convenient.

'No. I should do some writing.'

'You should write another blog.'

I didn't even know he'd read them. Hair cascader walked past us, but I don't think he noticed.

'Blogs are on hold until I've written the book.'

'I'll make it up to you. Do you mind?'

Constant questioning about whether something is OK is very annoying.

'Don't worry about it,' I said. 'Human interaction beyond a two-hour window bores me anyway. Plus,' I said, tapping on my phone, 'I've received a non-idiotic email on Shady. It's my duty to investigate.'

I showed him the profile on my phone, which, luckily, happened to be rather witty.

'He's good-looking, isn't he?'

'Why are you asking me? Make sure you tell him about the two-hour window,' he mumbled.

Note for book (and life): Test a person's capacity for annoyance.

I put my phone in my bag and we walked towards the escalators in silence.

'Hey,' he said when we got to the top. He stepped towards me. 'You should brush up on your research skills. Ask me a question.'

'Good point. OK. Worst date?'

'Oh, God, girl who wouldn't leave me alone, calling me Poopy Poo in all her messages.'

I laughed.

'Yours?' he asked.

'When I said raisins aren't dried grapes.'

ARGH! Why, why, *why*, did I say that?

'Not that it was a date. Obviously. You know what I mean.'

He smiled and we both stepped onto the escalator. 'One of my top three moments in London. My friends in America are going to love that story,' he said.

'Tell me more about this Poopy Poo. Is it a nickname you're fond of?'

'I could write a Bollywood song about raisins.'

'Knowing Bollywood, it'd be a hit.'

And, right there, in the middle of the Tate, Naim opened up his arms and decided to sing a song about raisins.

Who'd have thought that writing a book could be such good fun?

Sunday 16 October

2.20 p.m. Dad came in earlier and I attempted to steer him away from taking a cigarette, but I felt sorry for him so gave in. I haven't heard from Naim the entire weekend, though he said he'd call. How long does it take to sort out an emergency? At least it's given me time to email Tate guy (Jawad) on Shady, while downstairs, Mum, Dad and Maria discuss Chachu and maroon drapes. Sigh.

6.30 p.m. It's not as if people do as they promise. Like when HITW Imran said we could live wherever I wanted and then, three months later, he decided he couldn't leave the parental womb. It's just as well I've decided to be alone, I suppose, given that the idea of spending the rest of one's life with me makes a man cling to his parents for dear life.

If HITW Imran marries someone and moves out I will be very annoyed.

6.52 p.m. Or maybe Imran realised that I have a big bum and used living with his family as an excuse to spare my feelings. A farce because of my arse!

Ooh, girls are here.

9 p.m. Foz was already warming a plate of food in the microwave and Suj was eating an apple when I came downstairs.

'Where's Han?' I asked.

'Shopping with Zulfi,' replied Suj.

'A wedding present,' Foz added. 'And she gets to choose.'

'I suppose she has important things to do given the wedding's less than a week away.'

I relayed my conclusion about the real reason Imran didn't marry me. Bits of apple came flying out of Suj's mouth.

'You were only ready to book a ticket to California with me the day he wanted to tell his parents.'

Hmm, I'd forgotten about that specific panic attack, but I think that's a natural reaction in the context of deciding to make long-term commitments.

'What's wrong with wanting an extended holiday?' I asked.

Foz took her plate of saag aloo and rice out and leaned against the counter. 'Oh, my God, Auntie. This is *so* delicious.' With which she forgot all about us and went to sit with Mum and Maria.

'How's Charles?' I asked Suj.

'He's *black*, that's what he is.' She threw the apple core in the bin. 'Can you imagine what my family would say: her mum died and then she fucked off with a black guy.'

'People are shits.'

'I'm seeing Charles tonight, but after that, Toffee … if my dad ever found out he'd have a heart attack.'

I wanted to say that's outrageous, but somewhere in the gaps of my high morality there was a morsel of understanding. I can't imagine what my parents would say if I brought home someone of the non-brown variety. 'Just so you know, confessions about black boyfriends doesn't give heart attacks.'

She laughed. 'It does! Don't you watch Zee TV?'

'No, and neither should you because that's what happens.' I nodded towards Mum and Co. who'd moved on, naturally, to discussing maroon drapes.

'If the old dear was here, she'd probably have a heart attack too,' said Suj.

I took Suj's arm.

'From where she is she wouldn't care if he were Flamingo Pink. It's all the same in the end. Plus,' I added, surveying the swatches on the coffee table, 'she's undoubtedly looking down and shaking her head at our collective stupid preoccupations.'

Foz came in for second helpings. 'Have you spoken to the American?'

'No,' I replied. 'He said he'd call.'

'Don't be fooled by these men, Toffee. Mind games.'

To be honest, I don't know where that comment from. What have Naim's phone calls got to do with mind games? We're just friends. Dad walked past and went into the garden.

'Actually, he's really more into singing games,' I replied.

'Is he five?' asked Suj. Poor Naim. 'Why hasn't he called you?'

'We're just friends.' But it is annoying – when someone says they'll do something and then they don't. 'Imran always called when he said he would,' I added. 'Although, I prefer failure to call over failure to move out.'

I looked into the garden but couldn't see Dad. As I craned my neck I saw him hiding in a corner, having a cigarette! You'd think he'd be more discreet about it. He saw me and put his finger to his mouth. Granted he looked rather at peace, but I don't really want to be the reason he carries on smoking. Mum, who always seems to know what's going on, marched into the garden and began telling him off. Maria came into the kitchen as all four of us watched the battle of the wills. 'He really needs to stop this nonsense,' said Maars.

'This is only pleasure I have left,' exclaimed Dad.

'Where did you get this?' she demanded.

I ducked, as if that was going to help.

'Panchod, I can't do what I want in my own home.'

At which he carried on smoking, while Mum decided to stand firm and watch until he finished, presumably to minimise any joy.

'Sofe,' Foz added, 'Men are never the ones to make the sacrifices.'

Seems all the goats in the world are female.

9.40 p.m. Well, I've not heard from Naim but I have heard from Jawad. Jawad would like to have coffee on Wednesday. As it happens, I am available.

Note for book: DON'T BE A GOAT!

Wednesday 19 October

10.20 a.m.

From Naim: Hello, dear raisin. How about we have a coffee tonight?

Oh, hello. Five days later!

10.30 a.m.

To Naim: Sorry, can't tonight. Tomorrow?

10.31 a.m.

From Naim: Keep a guy waiting. OK, sure. Tomorrow.

9.40 p.m. Basically, perceived reality is pants. Take, for example, Jawad, who looked like a decent enough kind of guy in his profile picture. I'm not being superficial but he *actually* looked like sewer rat guy from *Teenage Ninja Mutant Turtles*. Every time I looked at him, I expected him to perform ninjitsu in the middle of Costa.

Points from evening that might be useful in book:

1. He received a call from his dad about some plans to do with getting pizza. (Parental dependency?).
2. He mentioned my age several times. 'How come you're not married?' 'Do you see yourself having children sooner rather than later?' (Thanks, God, by the way, for the actual ticking of the clock that we could hear in the coffee shop.)
3. His profile said he was tall, but he was no taller than 5 feet 8 inches. Suggests self-delusion or entirely different perspective on concept of tall.

Ah, Naim calling …

10.25 p.m.

From Jawad: Hi. So, good to meet you. Let's take this forward. When do you want to meet again?

11.45 p.m. Just got off phone to Naim. Oh, my Lord. Is it me, or is that message total presumptuous twattishness?

11.55 p.m. I forwarded to girls. They all agree. Twattish.

'Haha. Defo a twat!' shouted Maria from her room. To which Mum asked, 'What is twat?' and Dad intervened with 'Language!'

Mum, Maria and I, from our respective rooms, told him to stop being such a pot.

Whatever the twat factor, having to text back 'thanks, but no thanks' is definitely on my list of top ten most hated things. So I spent some fifteen minutes devising a text message, sending it to the girls and Maria for approval, editing and finally sent it:

> **To Jawad:** It was lovely to meet you, but I don't think we're compatible. Take care and it'd be good to stay friends.

Which it wouldn't. Obviously. But a person has to try to be nice about these things.

Thursday 20 October

8 a.m.

> **From Naim:** Tonight I'm bringing a book that gives you the origins of all dried fruits.

8.03 a.m.

> **To Naim:** Oh good, I can use it to hit you over the head. Thanks.

8.04 a.m.

From Naim: If you're looking for an excuse to get physical, we can negotiate something ;)

Haha – he is full, to the brim, of crap.

9.40 a.m.

From Jawad: To be honest, I could tell from your attitude you weren't interested, doesn't take a genius to work out that the meeting was a waste of time. I guess that you only decide to meet me to gather material for your book. It's amusing and 'ironic' how girls always complain about guys not being interested in them due to their age, but when someone does show an interest, they start acting all weird. Anyways, Insh'Allah you will find what you're looking for.

What the hell? That was the most passive-aggressive 'Insh'Allah' I've ever heard. God will not be willing with that tone, young man. Maybe I *should* stop mentioning the book to fake dates. Also, when did I complain about non-interest because of my age, as if I'm a hundred and fifty-two? Although, in Muslim years …

11.28 p.m. Sshhh, I've been told off for coming home late. Mum has this fear of rapists, murderers and hooliganism, exacerbated by the fact that I'm an easy target as a scarfie. Told her she needn't worry – tattooed neighbour seems to be awake all hours. Although, not sure how useful he'd be. He was pacing up and down the street,

97

on his phone, when I came home and completely ignored me and my friendly smile. Anyway, who cares about that after what happened this evening.

Naim and I went to Edgware Road for a spot of people-watching. I ended up having sheesha (throwback to my teens) because I didn't want to just sit there with him smoking cigarettes, while I looked on, longingly. A rather big part of me wanted to say that a person should share things, but I couldn't quite bring myself to it. I shouldn't complain about double standards if I just sit there with my mouth shut.

Anyway, I took his phone and put it in my bag because I think paying attention to a person is important.

'I know what we should do,' I said, 'We should make up fitting Bollywood songs for people walking past us.'

A man with greasy hair tied back in a ponytail strutted by, shouting, 'Bruv. Listen. Listen, bruv,' down the phone.

'OK, so he'd be: "Hero Number One". Obviously,' I said.

Naim moved his chair so we sat facing the same way. A girl with a camel-hump hijab walked past. I noticed her look Naim's way, smile and then I'm sure her hips swayed a little more than necessary.

'She'd be: "My name is Sheila, I am a hijabi …"' he said.

I laughed and took the sheesha from him.

'I didn't say you could ad-lib,' I replied.

'Why can't you be nice and smiley like hijabi Sheila?'

'Camel-hump with the four-inch heels? Doesn't she look at herself and think: *people know my head is not this big*.'

'You're so judgemental.'

'I'd call it *observant*.'

'I'm sure God wouldn't mind if you wore stilettos with skinny jeans. I don't think anyone would.'

Honestly. He turned towards me and I handed him the sheesha. 'Better safe than sorry.'

'Well, your hijab means you're safe. It's like a social condom.'

'Yes, to protect me from socially transmitted diseases. Like you.'

'Is this how you speak to all your fake dates?'

'Just the special cases.'

I took my phone out and saw I had a new message from that bloody Jawad. As I read it, Naim complained about me taking his phone, but he must've seen the look on my face – whatever look it was.

'What is it?' he asked.

I shook my head and re-read the message. He waited before I handed the phone to him, explaining that I'd gone on a fake date the day before.

From Jawad: I am actually disappointed in your behaviour. I would have thought that for someone your age, you would be more mature about this process. It seems you have a lot of time on your hands. Your last message, 'would be good to stay friends', smacks of arrogance. It insinuates that I am desperate, which I find very offensive so you need to work on your people skills. You looked older than me when we met but I still thought that if this is a decent girl, who is intelligent and has a good character, it's worth pursuing, but it seems like you have a chip on your shoulder. I hope that you were putting on a fake act as I wouldn't even want to be friends with someone like you, let alone get married to.

You can put up this whole charade of being an independent person and doing your own thing but, at the end of the day, you're like every other girl; single, lonely and looking for some guy to take care of you and like you for who you are. For your own sake, I hope that you get your priorities sorted out.

'God ... Essay,' he said, looking up at me. I stared at him for a moment and I don't know why, but it seemed so ridiculous. I started laughing. Then he started laughing and we were both laughing so hard people began staring at us (also, I think I caught the waiter rolling his eyes).

I tried to compose myself and took my phone back, reading the message again.

'Oh, God,' I said, wiping my eyes, 'I do find it offensive that he hopes I was putting on an act. Being myself is clearly not a good idea. Also, poor English.'

Naim was still catching his breath. 'I'm sorry, it's not funny, it's fucking rude.'

'It's bloody hilarious. The man's a psycho. Hang on. Maybe he's right: maybe I am arrogant. Only an arrogant person would laugh at a message like that.'

'You must be. An arrogant woman, looking for *some* guy.'

'Any guy will do. I'll ask greasy-haired bruv to come back.'

Naim took another cigarette and lit it up. 'Come on, why bother with him when we have this?'

I could feel the curse of the blush re-appearing.

'*This* being Bollywood songs and psychotic text messages?' I asked.

He leaned forward, flicking some ash into the ashtray. 'The foundation of all great relationships, no?'

I tried to think about anything mundane: stock exchange, house prices, weddings …

'You hungry?' he asked. 'I'm hungry. Let's eat.'

Honestly, conversation shifts are like being in the *Matrix* sometimes. But I went along with it, and pretended he never said anything. And when we said goodbye at the station I pretended the same, all the way home. Now I'm going to carry on pretending while I pray and go to sleep.

Friday 21 October

12.20 p.m. Emailed the girls re last night's incident. Mixed responses. Anyway, must focus. Also, Naim messaged this morning, completely normal. Maybe I misheard what he said? Perhaps a person unintentionally starts making things up in their thirties.

Saturday 22 October

8 a.m. Wedding day! I'm off to Hannah's to help her get ready before we make our way to the Mughal marquee. Mum's been asking if I'm sad that Hannah's getting married because after today, apparently, I won't see her again.

'She's not emigrating, Mum.'

'Haan, but remember Ambreen? You were always together and then she got married and left you.' Wish Mum didn't make me feel like an emotional filler. 'When people have used their time with you, then they say, "who am I, and who are you." Every one forgets everyone.'

Honestly, Mum is so cynical sometimes.

3 p.m.

From Naim: What we should've done was get your friend Hannah to hire us for musical entertainment. Have a good time at the wedding, and careful your mom doesn't get you married off!

Hmmm, what a weird thing to say.

11.30 p.m. Soon as I got to Hannah's house, her dad sat me down. He shook his head. I could hear Suj and Hannah discussing lipstick upstairs.

'My daughter is going to be a second wife. You think I am happy?' He leaned back and rested his hands on his legs, shaking his head again. 'But they say, "The shadow of a man is better than the shadow of a wall."'

I wanted to say: there can't be a shadow if there's a hole in that wall, but Hannah's mum came in and exclaimed, 'Yusuf! Sofia's a clever girl, she doesn't care about shadows,' and walked back out. I'm glad she gets it.

Hannah walked in, swan-like, glittering silver and gold. My heart swelled a little when I saw her. The pressure of it caused a tear to surface.

'Doesn't she look amazing?' said Suj.

Hannah beamed. 'Courtesy of Suj.'

'I *love* this face,' I said. 'Well done, Auntie and Uncle, for making this face.' I kissed it and said a little prayer for her, because thinking about the future makes me nervous. Praying, I've learned, is the only antidote to nerves.

'You kept the hijab on your wedding day?' said Mum to Hannah, when we got to the marquee. She hugged her, examining Hannah's face and all the material wrapped around it. Then she looked at me, and, I'm sorry to say, snarled. Presumably because she assumes I'll also wear my hijab on my fictitious wedding day. Honestly, reasons for not getting married just keep stacking up. Suj and me ushered her away with Dad and Maria to the furthest table in the marquee.

'But I can't see anything from here,' Mum complained. Before I knew it, she'd managed to move herself to the front table.

Fozia turned up late, and came stumbling in asking for a safety pin because her bra strap kept slipping off her shoulder.

'Is Han angry I'm late?' she asked.

'Look at her,' said Suj. 'She wouldn't notice if we were Morris-dancing on the table.'

'Kam just dropped me off,' said Foz. Mum came back and poured mango juice into her glass, eyeing up the centrepiece.

'Is that why you have an unruly bra strap?' I asked.

Suj leaned forward and whispered, 'Until he tells his fucking family that he's marrying you, tell him to keep his paws off your bra.'

'Fozia, look,' Mum interrupted. 'Hannah wore hijab on her wedding day.' She moved the centrepiece towards her and looked at it with as much scrutiny as she generally eyes my scarf.

Maria poked at the flowers. 'I don't really like the wildflowers.'

Dad kept fiddling with his handkerchief, looking around, and patting his suit jacket every few minutes.

'They do look happy, don't they?' said Fozia as I pinned the strap to her kameez. She looked at them wistfully, and was only momentarily brought back to earth when I stabbed her in the shoulder with the pin. It's wistfulness that's got Fozia into this mess in the first place.

'Haan, it is all happy shappy in the beginning,' said Mum, pushing back a daisy and looking inside the centrepiece (what exactly was she looking for?). 'When you live together, then you know what you've married.'

I do wonder why Mum is so obsessed with me getting married when she has such a bleak view of it.

'To be fair,' I said, 'he's only going to cock up half as much, because he'll only be there half the time.'

Maria pushed the centrepiece back. 'Wonder what his wife and kids are thinking. They're all at home, watching TV or whatever, while her husband and their dad is at his own wedding.'

Dad shook his head, frowning. 'Damn fool, this man. He will see what headache it is to have two wives. Damn, damn fool.'

Everyone tucked away their opinion as Hannah and Zulfi came and sat at the table. I now understand the term 'flushed with happiness'. Everything about Hannah sparkled. More to the point, everything about Zulfi sparkled too.

'Should I expect you girls to turn up at our hotel lobby?' he joked as he poured a drink for Hannah and himself.

'Only if we get an emergency call from your wife,' I replied.

'My wife?' he said, looking at Hannah, 'My wife is the *cause* of all emergencies.' He laughed and took her hand.

Dad had his eyes fixed on Zulfi, in an attempt, it seemed, to understand his soul.

'Acha, your children didn't come?' asked Mum.

There was a palpable pause. Dad's eyes shifted. Foz sipped on her drink and Suj pretended to look for something in her purse, while Maria fixed her stare on the centrepiece.

'No.' Zulfi cleared his throat and looked at the table, his sparkle dimming under the scrutiny of reality. 'No, they didn't.'

Hannah straightened up in her seat. 'We all make choices.' Zulfi watched her, queen-like on a throne of white sheet and red organza. She looked around the table, defiant and steadfast. 'Who knows what'll happen?' she added.

Suj and Foz both looked at her, and I'm sure I saw a tear in Suj's eye – perhaps she was thinking of Charles. Disquiet seemed to have replaced the quiet. I'm not fond of either.

'No one knows,' I said. 'Except, you know...' I pointed upwards. 'God. Obviously.'

It was time to leave. Mum shoved a centrepiece into everyone's arms and prompted Foz and Suj to pick up the one on the table nearest the marquee exit. So we all left the wedding with a rather heavier load than when we arrived.

Note for book: If you want to keep the centrepieces from your wedding, attach them to the table with strong adhesive. If you want to keep your sanity, learn how to drown out the voice of your family.

Sunday 23 October

10 p.m.

From Hannah: We're off in twenty minutes! Can you please tell me if there are any dates while I'm away?!

10.05 p.m.

To Hannah: They aren't dates. Remember; get cultured, not killed xx

Tuesday 25 October

9.35 a.m. Hmph. Katie asked about the book, but I told her that every time I sit down to write, some wedding disaster occurs, or the phone rings.

'Your phone is rather a pain. We weren't meant to live life with our head in front of a screen,' she said.

Which was rather rich given that's exactly what most people in offices do. I clutched the phone to my chest.

'No. We weren't meant to meet potential husbands on the Internet either.'

Not that I've met a marriage potential. Obviously. Fine, Suj says that there's no such thing as men and women only being friends, but I disagree. The odd comment Naim throws out doesn't mean anything. Nothing ever does. All it means is that he makes me laugh. A lot.

'I don't know why you don't try going out with a non-Muslim,' said Katie out of, hello, nowhere. I laughed.

'Have you *seen* me? Why the hell would a non-Muslim do that themselves?'

I got a packet of cigarettes out of the drawer and Katie tutted at me.

'Sweetu, I hope you don't pray with the smell of nicotine on you.'

Oh dear. I put the packet back in the drawer.

4.45 p.m.

From: Bramley, Dorothy
To: Khan, Sofia
Subject: Chapters

Thanks for contract. Your remittance has been transferred.
I'd really like to see some draft chapters ready next month?

Note for book: MUST WRITE IT!!!!

NOVEMBER 2011

Never Say Never

Muslim Dating Book

Muslims are big on charity and sacrifice. In fact, we're so big on it that every year we sacrifice a goat to share it with friends and family and (charitably) feed it to the poor. (Or that's what you're meant to do – never trust a Muslim with a whole goat in their freezer.) The universe/God is fond of sacrifice. What nobility!

But not everyone understands sacrifice. A bit like people who say that being Muslim doesn't matter when dating. The pool's miniscule and opportunity doesn't knock, it crawls. On hands and knees. Especially after your thirties. You take what you get (or what's given to you), and you make it work. Why not widen the net, say our non-Muslim (hereinafter NM) friends? We have to smile and try not to shake our heads at their lack of understanding. How can they know that dating a devout Muslim is like dating someone back in the nineteenth century? ~~And to be quite honest – that shit must seem whack.~~ We'd rather not have to put up with the indignity of having to explain this to people with bemused faces, who then throw around furtive glances at the oddness of our practices. Nor worry about having to put the brakes on spiritual development because, actually, you don't really believe in the same (main) thing. Thick skin and a vague nature are a must when explaining to well-meaning NM friends about the true nature of what it means to date as a Muslim.

Wednesday 2 November

8.30 a.m. Bollocks, bollocks, bollocks. Must remain calm. I've made an excellent plan for the month in order to get the chapters written for Brammers. I *can* do this. I just need to maintain focus.

Ooh, Naim calling.

Sunday 6 November

10 a.m. Dad came sneaking into my room, looking over his shoulder, while I was trying to write.

'OK, give me a cigarette.'

'Sorry?'

'O-ho. My cigarette. I need one.'

Poor Dad. On one hand I wanted to be the dealer who gave him the happy drugs, but on the other, I didn't particularly want to be the reason he clogged his arteries. I shook my head.

'Baba, you've managed to cut down so much in the past six weeks. Carry on. Good man. Instead of smoking, why don't you take up golf or something?'

'Sofi...' He gave me one of those looks that, as a child, made me hunt out Maria for protection. Thankfully, I'm now far less prone to being intimidated by dark, narrow eyes and a threatening voice.

'Sorry, Baba-kins. No can do. Mum's right.'

'Fittaymoo. You took my money.'

'Yes, but to be fair, I've only received half of the promised four hundred.'

Before he could respond, Mum came into the room and he froze. He turned around and looked at her. Then he glanced my way and was about to say something but instead stormed out.

'He thinks I don't see. I see everything. Acha,' she continued, 'We need to give out more wedding cards in afternoon.'

Maria walked in and started showing me the wedding menu.

'We can't do the seating plan until we've sent out all the invites and everyone's RSVP'd – and we know that 'Stanis (*Paki*stanis! as Dad would correct us) never RSVP...'

What happened to the good old days when we used to go to weddings in school halls and eat dinner from paper plates? I miss the 80s. Even the shell suits.

'What should we get for the chocolate fountain?'

I was going to say that depends on what ice sculpture you have and lo and behold she pulled out pages ripped from magazines.

'And which ice sculpture do you like?'

Let's have winged angels, unicorns, sodding centaurs and any other mythical creature to go with the theme of fantastical wedding.

10.23 a.m.

From Suj: OMG, I LOVE him. But it's not going anywhere. He is so fit though. And he makes me laugh. But I'm gonna tell him today that I can't see him any more. xxxxxx

10.24 a.m.

To Suj: OK, tell the man you think is gorgeous and who makes you laugh and who you seem to love spending time with that you can't see him any more. Makes perfect sense.

9 p.m. What is the point in people? Mum, Maria and I went to Ambreen's to give the invitation. Ambreen, because she can't help herself said, 'Come on, Sofe! Find a husband.' Honestly, married people live in a bubble – husbands don't just pop out from nowhere, like a jack-in-the box. I ignored her and Ambreen's mother-in-law looked at me and said, 'See, Sofia, this is progress. Ambreen has two children now – what progress have you made?'

I stared at her for a moment and was about to say, 'Well, I'm writing a book!' But then I thought; if it doesn't involve a human the size of a cantaloupe coming out of my vagina it mustn't be very impressive.

Mum straightened up in her seat. 'If Sofia had found her husband in college and dated for so many years like others, then she too would have babies. Lekin education is more important than looking for husbands.'

Cue silence and shuffling around in seats. Ambreen flicked her hair and tittered. I actually could've hugged Mum. (Perhaps I could take up a PhD in order to be prepared for future questions about *why* I'm not married? All of life is about preparation, really.)

10.50 p.m.

From Hannah: Darling! Been having brill time. People didn't know what they were talking about telling me not to marry Zulfi. No one else in the world would've wanted to come to Kazakhstan for a honeymoon! Why do I have to come back again? Oh yes, life. Miss you girls X

2.10 a.m. Rather late call from Naim. I wanted to remind him that, despite his restaurant being quiet, I still have a job, except he didn't sound very chirpy. The conversation was rather one-sided, but when I said I should go he asked why and, well, he sounded so bloody forlorn I stayed on the line. In the end the silence felt ridiculous so I told him I'd read a book aloud in order for him to benefit from literary wisdom.

'Hang on. We're following two people on the same day of each year they know each other?'

'Exactly,' I replied.

'And they're friends?'

'Best friends.'

'Is she ugly?'

'No, Mr Mature, she's not ugly.'

'What's his problem then?'

'Oh, you know, the general narrative of commitment phobia.'

'Well, aren't you positive today.'

Silence.

'You should read it yourself for purposes of emotional evolution.'

'God, no, it takes me like six months to finish a book.'

If it takes him half a year to finish a book, what does that say about his life's momentum?

'And anyway, why do that when I have you, or others, to read it for me?'

Others? Why are my literary habits exchangeable with *others*?

'Co-dependency is an illness, you know.'

He sighed.

'The best kind of illness, Sofe. The best kind.'

He fell asleep, but thanks to him my sleep is shot.

Monday 7 November

10.45 a.m. Hurrah! Hannah's back!

Odd that being awake most hours of the night gives a person a boost of energy; I've sent out copies of *My Life After Dracula*, emailed jacket images to *Glamour*, sent a pitch to *Loose Women*, and have even refrained from rolling my eyes at the new (fagless) workie who printed out a hundred, instead of ten copies of Shain Murphy's interview. But I'm serene and efficient, juggling balls in the shape of work, book, sister's wedding and unprecedented Internet friend. And prayers. Obviously.

11 a.m. Oh dear – I've spotted two typos in my pitch.

11.02 a.m. Arrgghhhh! Three! Three typos!! I missed out the 'o' in count. Shit, shit, shit, shit, shit, shit, shit.

11.03 a.m. OK, calm. Maybe they won't notice.

11.07 a.m. Oh man, I hope Brammers doesn't find out. Bloody hell, *why* is Naim calling at this time of day??

11.09 a.m.

From Naim: Pick up your phone. It's urgent!

11.35 a.m. I rushed out of the office with the phone.

'I'm being stalked,' he said.

'What?'

'I have a stalker.'

'*You* have a stalker?' I said, trying to sound incredulous. What bloody stalker??

'Girl, I can turn on the charm. You just haven't seen it yet.'

Why haven't I seen it yet? What's wrong with me that he doesn't feel the need to turn on any charm? Hmmm? I know we're only friends, but still. I realised I'd stopped listening to him.

'... I had to pretend I wasn't home and then she called my house phone. This is what I mean about girls making leaps from coffee to marriage. What is that?'

'*This* is your great crisis? For future emergencies call 999.'

'You're not being very helpful about my stalker situation. I'm giving you material for your book here. We can talk about my cut later, by the way.'

'If she's stalking you I think *she* needs the help.'

'Are you this irritating to people you date?'

'No, I'm a peach to them.' He'd gone quiet so I added, 'Much as I'd love to chat about harmless stalkers,' (the CEO happened to walk past me at this point) 'I have my own emergency to sort out.'

'You're useless. Go and sort out your problem, but don't ask me for help when you need it.'

'Naim! I just left the "o" out in "count" in an email to the producer at *Loose Women*.' I put the phone down, which was just as well as God knows how long his laughter would've lasted.

To be honest, I was thinking less about typos and more about why I've been shown no charm ... Everyone can do with a bit of that, surely?

12 p.m. Called Foz who was like, 'What? Why would he do that when you're *just friends*.' Fozia and her bloody tone.

So I then called Suj who apparently is now Fozia's tonal doppelganger. I don't know what's so difficult to understand here.

Saturday 12 November

9.20 a.m. There's been an explosion in the living room in the shape of maroon favour boxes and cream ribbon. Mum and Dad have gone to Homebase to get fairy lights. These are, in traditional Pakistani style, to be splayed around, outside and inside the house. Thankfully, Maria's getting married New Year's Eve, so I can pretend to people that we've broken with tradition and decided to celebrate Christmas this year.

'What are these net thingies for?' I asked, as I lunged over the stuff to get to the kitchen.

Maria was on the phone. She's started her beauty regime and Saturdays are cleansing mask day – a stone-coloured thing that cracks every time she opens her mouth to speak.

'Why don't *I* do everything, and *you* just turn up to the wedding,' she mumbled, before throwing her mobile on the sofa.

'Lovers' tiff?' I asked.

'He's so annoying. He's all, *why are we bothering with centrepieces and favours and stuff?* Does he even want to get married?'

'He mentioned centrepieces, not mortgages.'

She looked at me as one would a mad person, then seemed to realise I'm not mad but, in fact, just a child.

'Sofe, if he doesn't care about the wedding, what does that say to you? All I wanted was for him to find a photographer, and did he?'

I know being highly strung is in her nature, but surely she should be glad that after so many years of searching, she found Tahir. Ironic as well, given how many useless men had come to the house, then Tahir walks into Carphone Warehouse; she as the manager gives him a discount, and now they're talking about centrepieces. I think she's missing the point, and was about to tell her this, while I searched the cupboards for chocolate, when she'd already come into the kitchen. She tried to keep mouth opening to a minimum.

'Soooo. Dad came into my room yesterday and started asking me if you're seeing anyone.'

I stopped mid-search. What the hell?

' "She's always on the phone," he said. Tried to get information out of me. Mum and Dad only want to make it easy for you if you are.' Argh! I have such sneaky parents. 'Are you?' she asked.

No I am not! Though I do feel I have a weird nameless relationship with Naim.

'No, no. I mean, Naim and me, we're just friends ...'

She clearly forgot about her face situation because she made the mistake of frowning, then froze when she saw flecks of the mask falling on the kitchen tiles. She squinted at me so hard I had to lean back.

'Are you sure?'

'Yes, I'm *sure*, nosey.'

'Why does he call you all the time? Is he bored? If he's bored, tell him to take it somewhere else. You're too old to deal with a waster.'

Bloody hell. My sister needs to take a pill. A strong one at that.

'Actually he's being very useful. Research-wise.'

She looked at me and then her phone rang. It was Hannah. Mutual wedding experiences bond people.

'Oh my God, I'm so glad you called. Tahir is acting as if the wedding is *my* thing – like he has nothing to do with anything.'

There was muffled grumbling in the background that I couldn't quite make out.

'Was he? Really? Why are men so useless?'

8.30 p.m. The only part of the house that's not decorated with fairy lights is the bathroom, and that's only because of the potential to get electrocuted – otherwise the toilet seat would also be alight with the joy of marriage.

9.35 p.m. I called Tahir, who sounded panicked to within an inch of his life. I told him he just has to *pretend* to be interested in everything she's interested in – wedding-wise.

Did feel sorry for him. Maria has no sense of perspective sometimes. Imagine if they were like my parents and didn't want to speak to each other unless it was a special occasion; like a funeral.

Ooh, Naim calling.

Sunday 13 November

1.35 p.m. 'Toffeeeee! I tried telling Charles that I don't think we should see each other any more and he was like what the fuck?'

I was going through FB as Suj spoke on the other end of the phone. Who is this new friend on Naim's Facebook? She's rather booby.

'And then he said, "Is it cos I'm black?" Toffee! I felt so bad cos how can you give that as a reason?'

I mean he meets about a hundred new people a week, but must they all look the same?

'So I just said, well, I'm seeing other guys so he can do what he wants.'

Not that I care who he's friends with. Obviously.

'He was well pissed off and put the phone down. Oh, God, I have to go now. The old man wants to watch a Bollywood film. Toffee?'

'Hmmm, yes,' I replied. 'Love you, call you later.' I put the phone down and continued to scroll through his FB page. It's just so uninspired. I wonder if these are also people he meets on marriage websites.

2.30 p.m. Typical! I was praying and missed Naim's call. Maybe it's a sign from God.

6 p.m. Tahir and his family are coming over for dinner in half an hour. Apparently I'm not allowed to come downstairs in my pyjamas.

10.25 p.m. Tahir's dad consumed any chance of there being left-overs. Three helpings of rasmalaai, a cup of chai and three satsumas later – because apparently they're good for one's digestion – the subject of my wedding came up. I wonder what the cut-off point is for that question? When does it become uncomfortable because the idea has become hopeless? Late thirties? Forties? Also, it's annoying to have to come up with a new answer each time (to avoid wanting to poke a pen in my eye from sheer boringness of question), but perhaps it'd be far worse when people stop asking. That is when true spinsterhood begins.

'To be aahnest, girls are very fussy nowadays,' said Tahir's dad, suppressing a burp.

The word 'fussy' doesn't even rile me any more. I pity people who think a girl should marry a man who's so overweight beads of sweat drip down his forehead, or a man who, at the age of forty, wants to marry someone no older than thirty, or one who wants his wife to spend her life walking in and out of holes in the wall. I said to Tahir's dad that I'll gladly pass on any of the above's number for his younger sister who's looking to get married. It wiped the smug look off his face.

Dad cleared his throat and Maria widened her eyes at me. Mum was busy placing tea cups on coasters.

When I went into the kitchen Maria said, 'Can you try not to say that kind of stuff to my future in-laws?'

Trust me, I don't like to make a commotion, but I said, 'I'll happily stop saying shit to people as soon as they stop saying shit to me.'

Sigh. We single people are lone warriors.

Friday 18 November

12 p.m.

From: Bramley, Dorothy
To: Khan, Sofia
Subject: Book

Will the opening pages/first chapter be ready soon?

Why, why, why haven't these been written yet? Must bring all my notes into a cohesive chapter. If I'm going to replace the fact that I don't have babies with fact that I *do* have a book, then writing is rather instrumental in that. I've told her she'll have it after the weekend.

Argh! Also, Shain Murphy's launch is in under two weeks and I haven't sent out the invites.

5.23 p.m.

From Maria: We found a photographer! Tahir found him! It's his cousin. Families are the best.

Note for book: People in love suffer from selective amnesia and distorted sense of reality.

8 p.m. Maria came into my room just as I was about to start writing.

'The thing is with Tahir, he does do nice things like sort out a photographer or get me flowers when I'm angry or in a bad mood.'

I wanted to point out that he generally inspires this anger. Then she looked at me and there were tears in her eyes as she smiled. 'I do love him.'

Just for a second I thought, I've never met anyone who's made me smile and brought a tear to my eye simultaneously. I mean, I've met people who have induced both actions independent of each other – but never together.

9.20 p.m.

From: Hopeless Romantic
To: Hello, Publicity

Hi. Thought I'd drop you a line. You seem like a pretty cool person. That and I have a thing for spiritual ladies who happen to look incredible in hijab. Is that corny?

Abid.

Hahahaha. That has to be the funniest message, ever. What a cheeseball email, coupled with a cheeseball name. Then I looked at his picture. Now, I'm not one to be swayed by handsomeness (much), but he did look like he'd stepped off a catwalk. I couldn't stop staring at him. I'll forgive him for cheesiness – for obvious reasons – but won't be waylaid by immense hotness. Obviously.

In the meantime, maybe I'll take a snapshot and send it to the girls.

10.45 p.m.

From: Hello, Publicity
To: Hopeless Romantic

That was totally corny. But a person can get away with it now and again.

Sofia.

11.55 p.m. Naim called and asked why I wasn't being horrible to him (he's such an exaggerator) and I just mentioned the tears, happiness combo.

'Sofe, are you being sentimental?'

'Don't be annoying.'

'It's OK, it's OK. It's what humans call emotion. Let me walk you through it.'

I laughed and told him to shut up.

'One day, Sofe, you're gonna fall in love so hard, and it's gonna make me so, so happy to see *you* lost for words.'

Hmph. Whatever.

Saturday 19 November

8.20 a.m. Today I'm going to switch my phone and wi-fi off so I don't start YouTubing babies dancing salsa, or cats and dogs on skateboards, or – more importantly – check Facebook.

8.45 p.m. Hurrah! I have the opening pages of the book! I hadn't realised how exciting writing is. I can detach myself from my surroundings because I'm involved in a superior form of creativity, which, if you think about it, should run parallel with spirituality. All of this unleashed because a man called me a terrorist. I should go out and celebrate and take a bloody hard-earned break – two thousand words down – only eighty thousand or so more to go. Think I'll call Naim.

8.48 p.m. Ooh – thirteen messages and four missed calls. Funsies!

> **From Suj:** Toffeeeeee! Where are youuuu? I'm having to fly out to LA – with C! I apologised. Can you believe it? Spoke to Han just now. Do you think she's OK? FaceTime you all when I land. Love you! xx
>
> **From Fozia:** I hate my job!!
>
> **From Naim:** Where are you? And why the hell's your phone switched off?
>
> **From Maria:** Er, you wanna come down and have lunch? Mum's been calling you for ages.
>
> **From Hannah:** It's wife's day off! One of the pros of polygamy. Come over tonight and we'll watch back-to-back episodes of *SATC* and scoff our faces with (homemade) brownies. Foz is bringing pizza.

12.40 a.m. Girlie evening of DVDs and brownies indeed. (On a side note, if you're going to be in a polygamous marriage, then definitely make sure he's rich. The house Zulfi's bought Hannah is so lovely, I almost wanted to be his *third* wife.) We'd had pizza and I'd made tea. Hannah put the plate of brownies on the table while Fozia inserted the DVD.

I was about to bite into a brownie when Hannah said, 'Are they having sex right now?' Foz turned around as Hannah looked at us. 'It's fine for him to say that he loves me, but are they basically having a shag as we're watching TV?'

What I wanted to say was 'No! Of course not,' which in the short term would've meant I could eat my brownie but also that I was a liar. I put down my brownie.

'Nooo ... I mean, you can never *know*, know. But they're probably not ...' Probably ARE.

'But there is a possibility? Isn't there?' She started tapping her fingers on her legs. 'Isn't there?'

'Nothing's ever certain, is it?' added Fozia.

Hannah shot up off the sofa, remote control flying through the air, and almost knocking over a plant.

'Let's go to the house.'

'What?' Foz and I said together.

'Sofe, we'll take your car.' She'd already walked into the passage to get her hijab. 'He'll recognise mine.'

Foz stood up and by the time I'd got off the sofa Hannah was wrapping the hijab around her head. I was caught between whether we should be a part of this unhinged behaviour, and whether it made us bad friends if we stopped her. Foz looked a bit out of her depth, so I grabbed Hannah by the shoulders. She looked half mad and half helpless. 'This is crazy. Now sit down and have a bloody brownie.'

We led her to the sofa and made her sit.

'Why is Suj in LA? She'd understand,' said Hannah.

Foz kneeled on the floor and took Hannah's hand. 'Darling, we can use her tracker device and night-vision goggles whenever we need, you know that. But it has to be for the right reasons.'

Hannah stared at her and nodded. Crisis was eventually averted, thanks to God. We went through a detailed account of Zulfi and his first wife's relationship: arranged marriage, close family friends, children: ties that bind and blind etc.

It'd be different if we lived in a place where this kind of thing was acceptable, but talk about a marital fish out of water. When I said this, Hannah looked at me a bit wildly, to be honest.

'I don't give a shit what people think or say. They're not living my life. I don't even care about the fact I'll never legally be his wife.' She pushed her hijab back and sat down. 'Maybe this would be easier if I didn't love him so much.'

Crikey. I opened my mouth to say something, but I hadn't quite the words to comfort her. This love business is a tricky thing. Foz passed a brownie to her and patted her leg. We both looked at each other.

'Once I have a baby,' said Hannah, 'it'll be fine.'

I don't know why dirty nappies seem to be the logical conclusion to happiness, but I put my arm around Han.

'And won't it be a fat and lucky thing, with a mum who makes the best brownies.'

It was probably the only appropriate time to eat said brownie and nod in approval.

Sunday 20 November

3.45 p.m.

From: Hopeless Romantic
To: Hello, Publicity

OK, I'll avoid all corny lines now. Let's talk about some serious spiritual stuff. I'd like to grow a beard. As you're a hijabi, I'd like to know your thoughts on this.

Oh my God. How random, but if he grew a beard I think I'd *die*.

Monday 21 November

9.25 a.m. I've just sent the draft opening chapter to Brammers. God, this kind of pressure and stress can give a person alopecia.

5.25 p.m.

From: Bramley, Dorothy
To: Khan, Sofia
Subject: Opening

This is good. I think you're on track. When can I expect some more pages?

SOFIA KHAN IS NOT OBLIGED

On the one hand, thanks to God! On the other, Brammers is very impatient. I've let her know that she can wait a sodding month. Although it was put in politer words as I do value my job and fifteen thousand pounds.

Tuesday 22 November

9.45 a.m.

> **From: Murphy, Shain**
> **To: Khan, Sofia**
> **Subject: Launch**
>
> All geared up for the big day on Thursday! By the way, I'm going to bring some Bibles, hope you can sell them!

WTH? Bibles? What do Bibles have to do with hippos?

10 a.m. I've asked Brammers. Apparently Shain's been religiously enlightened ...

10 a.m.

> **To: Hopeless Romantic**
> **From: Hello, Publicity**
>
> Salam. Well, I think a person should appreciate a beard. (Although note that I don't think a beard is a true measure

of religious enlightenment, but it's a good start.) There's the added benefit of beards being in fashion – if it's good enough for Clooney etc. But, if you go abroad a lot then you have to consider whether time spent at Immigration is going to be worth that added sense of spirituality. Me? I don't mind the headache.

PS I'm selling Bibles at an author's launch party. Almost feels traitor-like. Do you think I should take copies of the Qur'an to hand out too?

Note for book: Chapter title: Love and Marriage Go Together like . . . Bibles and Hippos?

Thursday 24 November

9.45 a.m. I miss bent-out-of-shape Benji. At least he could laminate show cards properly.

10 a.m.

From Naim: You wanna grab a coffee tonight?
To Naim: It's like I'm talking to myself sometimes – tonight's the hippo launch, remember. Could meet afterwards – 8.45ish?
From Naim: Sofe, you know I hang on to every single word you say – until you give me something else to hang on to ;)
Will see you at 8.45ish.

I looked at the message and laughed. He is such a compulsive flirt.

8 p.m. Well, isn't the world a shrunken place? I got to Daunts in Hampstead and had just begun placing Bibles next to the hippo books when I was interrupted by a camera flash. Who should be with Shain but tattooed next-door neighbour! Turns out he's a photographer and a friend of Shain's from Ireland.

I was obviously a little surprised. 'Oh, hello.'

'Hi.' I'm not being sensitive here, but he *was* curt. Nevertheless, I haven't forgotten about killing people with kindness etc.

'You're my neighbour and I don't think I even know your name.' I held out my hand. 'I'm Sofia.'

He shook my hand – firm – 'Conall.' He looked at the table and moved one of Shain's books before taking a few shots of the display.

'On this side we have facts about hippos, and on the other we have facts about God and the universe,' I said.

He put his camera down and frowned.

'All you need to know on one table.' I smiled as widely as my mouth would let me, which, incidentally, is quite wide. 'Don't tell Shain, but I've left the upgraded version of the Bible at home.' I leaned forward. 'The Qur'an.' Honestly, I don't know why I said that but then that's one of my ongoing problems. I pointed at my scarf.

'Right.'

He took a few more pics and walked away. He returned twenty minutes later, and I tried to get him to buy a Bible or two, but to no avail.

'You two are getting on like a house on fire. Conall – take some feckin' pictures, will you?' Shain slapped Conall on the back and gave him a glass of orange juice. This friendship didn't make much sense to me. Shain's, well, *nice*. 'And don't forget to buy a Bible.'

'Don't need more than one. Why aren't you selling the Qur'an? I've heard it's an upgrade.' Shain looked a little surprised. I couldn't tell if Conall was joking or not.

'Eejit. That's what you're missing from life. Should ask Sofia for that one,' said Shain. He then put his hand on Conall's shoulder and said, 'And while she's at it, she'll get you some Viagra.'

Note for book: Try not to sell religion and sexual enhancement drugs at the same time.

11.30 p.m. While waiting for Naim I'd dropped my lipstick on the floor and bent to pick it up. The bloody thing had rolled under a parked car so I had to get on my hands and knees and reach under to fish it out. I swivelled around on my knees and was about to get up when I saw a pair of legs in front of me. More specifically, was faced with an area of a man's anatomy that really I have no business with at this point in time.

'Well, this is promising.'

I looked up and there was Naim, smirking down at me. I stood up and brushed down my dress.

'That's optimistic,' I said, with what I hoped to be a pronounced raise of one eyebrow. Honestly.

We ended up driving to the usual place on Edgware Road and sat under the warmth of the outside heaters.

'Any more fake dates?' he asked, looking at his phone. Why can't he leave it alone for a minute?

I hesitated.

'Not really. I am emailing someone who seems normal, though. Not sure what he's doing on Shady. He's far too beautiful.'

Naim put the phone down. 'Do you know how many people put fake photos up?'

God, how naïve am I that I didn't consider that? What if they are fake photos? Does that make me superficial?

'I wanna see this guy,' he said.

I put my hand over my phone at first. Then, reluctantly, I went to his profile and showed it to Naim.

'*Those* photos and Hopeless Romantic? A total fake.'

I had to suppress my urge to laugh at his pissed-off face.

'You're just cynical,' I said. If I didn't know better, he almost sounded jealous.

Just then, an email popped up from Abid.

From: Hopeless Romantic
To: Hello, Publicity

Hey, you're meant to be supporting the cause. I wanted to hear, 'Do it! Forget what people think.'

'What does he have to say?' said Naim. 'Assuming he does anything other than pose for photos.'

I pulled the phone away from him.

'Bugger off. Show me the messages you're always getting on your phone.'

'Sure. I've got nothing to hide.'

Now, I'm not one to look into people's private matters, but I wondered if he knew this about me – was this reverse psychology? I put my hand out.

He leaned forward. 'Sofe, all this time we share and you don't trust me?'

'You don't have a trustworthy face.'

He put his hand on my knee and I became very aware of how small the table was. 'Lying to you would be like lying to myself.'

I took his hand and put it on the table.

'Shut up, please.'

He leaned back and took out a cigarette.

'Trust me, I've had enough of lies.'

And then, as if out of nowhere, he began telling me about his ex-girlfriend! Which, apparently, was a two and a half year unfulfilling relationship that fell to pieces. Because she was cold? Or was it him that couldn't commit? Judging by the look on his face it didn't seem as if his commitment was the issue. I asked for another cappuccino.

'God, let me tell you – love? Man,' he exhaled dramatically, 'love can be the most beautiful thing ever. And the most devastatingly heart-breaking thing ever.' He flicked ash on to the floor and smiled at me.

'Guess you wouldn't know, huh?' he said.

Imran sprang to mind. I wonder how he is. When it comes to feelings, I think that's as far as a person really ought to go. What exactly has loving excessively done for Naim, who sat there, looking . . . a bit hollow?

'You don't want to hear this,' he said.

There was some kind of tug going on, because I didn't want to hear, but then I did too. This is what they must call conflict.

'I don't think I slept for about three months after me and Zainab broke up. And then Mom died.' He stubbed out the cigarette and held up the butt. 'Gotta love sleeping pills and cigarettes.'

'Sleeping pills can be handy.' I smiled at him but he was staring at the ashtray. 'Although, not when they're used to send people to bed early.' I told him that Mum sometimes puts a pill in Dad's tea when he's doing her head in.

Naim smiled and took out another cigarette. 'That is awesome,' he said. 'So I guess being aloof runs in the women in your family?'

'Aloof? We are all deeply involved, thank you.'

'I wanted to text you something a few days ago,' he said.

'Oh yeah?'

'Yeah, but then I thought forget about it. Oh, did you sort out the cunt?'

'Hain?'

He laughed, 'The typo in your email?'

'Oh. Yeah. Fine.' I was desperate to ask him, *What? What were you going to say?*

He tapped the pack of cigarettes on the table. 'You know, you are entirely lovely.'

Now, the thing is, if you're going to say such a thing at least have the decency to avoid eye contact.

'Oh.'

When Imran said things like that I used to roll my eyes because he'd say them so often. But this was different; less is more and all that.

'And you're pretty.' There it was again. The curse of the blush. 'You know, I was finding it tough here. Then I met you. Weird how these things happen, right?'

'Totally.' I kind of wanted to lean over and give him a hug, because what can you say to a person about a break-up and parental death? For someone who's apparently a writer now, I am about as articulate as a dog.

'You're still a khothi, though,' he said.

'Well, thanks – nothing quite like being called a donkey,' I said.

'I can't be too nice now can I, Sofe? People will ask what the hell happened to me.'

Isn't it odd how one day you don't know a person and then one day, without realising, you feel, well, *close* to them.

Friday 25 November

10.25 a.m.

From: Hello, Publicity
To: Hopeless Romantic

I thought you'd have inferred my backing a beard due to my chosen form of headgear. Keep up, Abid.

Why don't you sport a beard, I'll carry on wearing a hijab and we can keep a tally of the highs and lows of keeping faith.

6.20 p.m. Shain's just emailed a picture of me holding a Bible and smiling – captioned: 'If Islam doesn't tickle your fancy, how about Christianity?' I should try to be a better publicist for my own religion. It's a sign from God that I'm obviously in the wrong department. In publishing, that is, not religion.

Monday 28 November

1.35 p.m. Bloody hell. My makeshift prayer room has been turned into a medical room with an entry code. I had to call Facilities and explain why I need it. There's always that uncomfortable feeling of someone judging me for being religious. Like when doing publicity for books such as *The Inanity of Religion* – bit weird when you are a walking, talking sign *for* religion. There were a few raised eyebrows at *that* launch, and definitely no mention of me in the author's speech – though probably because throughout the campaign he referred to me as 'that Muslim girl'.

'Facilities,' said quite possibly the most bored voice ever.

'Hi, I'm really sorry but I was wondering if it was OK if I had the code for the medical room. The thing is, I use it to pray and now it has a lock and I just wondered if that was OK? Sorry.'

'Oh, yeah, er do you wanna hold for two seconds ... Dave! What's the code for the medical room? Yeah, someone wants to pray in it – yeah, pray. No, we don't have a prayer room. Well, I dunno, do I? Sorry, two seconds. No, she doesn't want a prayer room, just the code. Is it just you who wants to pray?'

'I think so.'

'Just today or every day?'

'Well, every day.'

'What, all year round?'

'Yes, please.'

'So you pray *every* day?'

'Yes.'

'Blimey – and what, just the once?'

'No. Five times.'

Then he exhaled and I heard him tapping on his computer.

'All right, love, we'll email you the code and you can use it whenever you like.'

2.30 p.m. Well, I have the entry code but for some reason they've changed the door, which now has a huge glass pane so everyone in the post room is also able to see my arse in the air.

8.40 p.m.

From: Hopeless Romantic
To: Hello, Publicity

My beard's grown. (I'm just showing off how manly I am.) How are you? Over the weekend I went to the mosque with my dad – we do that every Saturday, it's our quality time. It's amazing the things you can learn from your parents.

Mum and Dad were downstairs arguing about whether to invite his cousin in Birmingham to Maars' wedding.

He told me when he came to the country he didn't have anything. Just this tie his dad gave him when he knew he was leaving. Never saw his dad again after that. Won't bore you with details, but it makes you realise we don't really have problems. Our parents faced it all. And they did it with a smile.

At which point Dad shouted that Mum never has liked his family and Mum said she certainly liked them more than him.

Note for book: You might, accidentally, end up feeling close to some-one, but sometimes, the closer you are the noisier it is.

DECEMBER 2011

Let it Snow, Let it Snow, Let it Snow

Muslim Dating Book

What a luxury anything organic is: to take your time; to have the lived experience. To hear what a person has to say about love and say, 'Yes! I know that feeling. It shattered my soul and it was beautiful ...'

But you'll probably lose your sanity as well as that money you spent to go online. So it's just as well that Muslim dating works in dog years.

'Don't exaggerate!' I hear you NMs say as you throw back your last sip of red/white ~~(whatever)~~ wine and look at me with incredulity. Well I nod to you solemnly, my ~~un/~~ disbelieving friends. There's a schedule here. Thirty is O-L-D. So we leap, bound, dive, blindly into eternal bliss, and keep faith that it's the right thing. What, after all, are we waiting for?

Friday 2 December

7.40 a.m. Argh! Why do I have to write a book as well as have jeans that are now cutting off my blood circulation? How am I meant to write when life (and weight gain) is literally moving in fast motion?

> **To Fozia:** Darling! Meet after work? Panic re book. Need help. PLEASE.
>
> **From Fozia:** Consider me there xxx

9.55 a.m. OMG, I just switched on my computer and whose bloody picture is plastered over the company intranet but mine! Selling the bloody Bible – I mean not the *bloody* Bible – obviously the Bible is *not* bloody,

Sorry, God, for saying bloody Bible.

10.10 a.m. I've had to undo my jean button as it's puncturing a hole in my intestine. It's too early on in life to ruin my digestive system.

1.20 p.m. Hurrah! When you accept things such as the window in the medical room through which one's arse can be seen, then

God fixes them for you anyway. I went to pray and George from Facilities was putting up blinds.

'Din't wantchya to worry about people seeing ya when you pray.'

I really could've hugged him but it felt a little inappropriate as I remembered my jean button was undone, plus he was wearing a kilt.

7.25 p.m. I've come home to Mum who's in a state of panic in the kitchen. Chachu Zahid is arriving tomorrow and apparently he needs five different dishes for lunch. It's all, 'Clean the floors, Cinderella, grind the garlic and ginger, Cinderella.'

7.55 p.m. Oops. I mixed up the salt and sugar and have been told to get out of the kitchen.

8.15 p.m. Maria and I were upstairs going through things she wanted to throw away. I came down to make us both a cup of tea and caught Mum and Dad whispering in the kitchen. As soon as they saw me, Dad began adding spices to the curry and Mum didn't tell him off. Hmmm. Odd.

Right, now I will transcribe my chat with Foz. Thanks to God for her.

Me: OK, tell me about all these dates you went on. Before you decided to settle for, ungh, Kam.

Fozia: You remember all my running around? (Pause.) Truth is, I just don't know what to do with him. How long is a person meant to wait? Sorry, this isn't about Kam. What was your question?

Me: No one should have to wait this long.

Fozia: I was so happy when I was single.

Me: Or maybe you just think you were happy. Anyway, I think you just answered your own question about what to do with Kam.

Fozia: Forget about that. So, my dates. Do you remember the one who made me walk for two hours and didn't even buy me coffee?

(I laugh.)

Me: Yes. The girls and I met you after because Imran had just told me about the wall.

Fozia: Things are never simple, are they?

(I sigh.)

Me: As simple or as complicated as you make them.

Fozia: Oh, shut up.

(Pause.)

Me: What else?

(Fozia exhales, loudly.)

Fozia: It was a bit of a slog, but they weren't all so bad. And remember Riaz? Lovely Riaz?

Me: I miss him. Generally, though, these dates – how did they make you feel?

(Long pause.)

Fozia: Like there was hope.

Saturday 3 December

8.20 a.m. Dad's outside, de-frosting the windshield and speaking to Conall. Wonder why Dad's looking so earnest. Will go and join them.

8.30 a.m. Hmph, by the time I got my headgear on and made myself look presentable, Conall had gone back inside. Now I've been guilt-tripped into joining Dad to collect Chachu from the airport.

11.30 a.m. Why is it impossible for 'Stanis to go to or come from Pakistan without being at least thirty kilos overweight in luggage? Perhaps they like living up to stereotypes. Thanks to Chachu's suitcases, I've discovered my contortionist skills. There were two cases in the boot, along with three boxes of mangoes, disguised as normal luggage (which Chachu somehow managed to wangle through Customs) and my face was still pressed up against the window.

'I shaved my beard this morning,' said Chachu.

I wanted to say that beard or no beard, it's a bloody wonder Customs didn't stop a fifteen-stone, six-foot-two brown person.

Dad turned around and said, 'Flight from Jamaica had come in.'

That explains *that,* then.

6.20 p.m. Chachu left to go and explore the area over two hours ago. Didn't know he was that curious. Hope he hasn't gone and lost where we live.

Suj called. I was relating the wedding palaver build-up and she asked if I was inviting Naim! Am I meant to invite him? Would it be rude not to? On the other hand, if I do invite him then what am I inviting him as? A friend? Which will prompt questions from everyone as to where this friend has come from. I can't possibly invite him as something *more* than a friend. That would be lying (and prompt questions as to when we're getting married). If by some providential turn of events he ends up coming to the wedding, is that like a date? I mean, let's not all get the wrong idea here. Would he think it's a date? Would *I* think it's a date?

6.35 p.m. Impossible. He cannot come. Dad already has suspicions and Mum will start asking him about his bank balance, invariably comparing it to Imran's, making her question why I didn't marry Imran because he was rich, even though there was a hole-in-the-wall.

All this because of one invite.

6.36 p.m. It would be nice to have him there, though. We could laugh at the ice sculpture.

8.45 p.m. 'Stanis have no courtesy. We slave in the kitchen for hours on end, only for Chachu to come home and go straight to bed without eating a thing. Mum and Dad were fine about it but, honestly, would a simple phone call have gone amiss?

Sunday 4 December

10 a.m. Don't know how I managed to sleep through Chachu's booming voice this morning. When I got up I had a message from Abid.

From: Hopeless Romantic
To: Hello, Publicity

Hi. I was reading a book and thought of you. How are wedding preps going for your sister? Wouldn't it be nice to live on a desert island and just be the person you want to be without questions about marriage and babies?

I was wondering ... I know you must be busy, but do you think we should meet?

I think I gasped. If not on the outside, then most certainly on the inside. *Meet?* It is the logical thing to do but what do you say to someone who's so, well, beautiful? I'd probably trip over myself as well as my words. Maria walked in and said, 'Are you mad? Of course meet him. You just tell me when and where in case he's a criminal.'

I'm seeing Naim today and will give him an invite. I wonder if I can squeeze in a meeting with the hottie. Or perhaps I should rein in my eagerness.

1 p.m. We were sitting in the living room while I decorated a wicker basket for the bangles to be handed out at the mehndi. Doing such mindless stuff is surprisingly cathartic and gives a person a chance to *think* about things, like wedding invites and dates. I got my phone out.

From: Hello, Publicity
To: Hopeless Romantic

Yes, sure, why not? How about Thursday?

Chachu looked rather restless. He stood up and started pacing the room. Mum kept glancing at him.

'Baby and Bobby taw have become like English person since coming here. Don't speak Urdu any more. Have birthday parties for the children and invite only friends as if family is nothing. All this running, running here and going nowhere,' he said. 'And no servants. You know, Gulzaar? The one who came in nineteen ninety-nine to marry that PhD boy. She wants to come home.'

Chachu's son, Bobby, really should consider changing his and his wife's name – linguistic Feng Shui. Dad listened while Mum adjusted the curtains. She turned around and said, 'Everyone comes here and complains, but no one ever goes back.'

They all agreed that reasons to go back were diminishing. It does make one grateful for one's home. Mum talks about how the rich in Pakistan have a luxurious lifestyle of shopping and dining, and dining and shopping, but that sounds like, quite possibly, the most boring thing ever. Not to mention depressing given that you have limbless people begging for money from those coming out of chauffeur-driven cars.

10.50 p.m. Hmph. So much for that. I began talking to Naim about the wedding and without even mentioning the invite, he said, 'Oh damn! I would've gatecrashed only I'm going home for the holidays.'

So I left the invite in my purse because what is the point in giving one to a person who A) can't make it anyway and B) doesn't have the courtesy to inform a person of trips he might or mightn't be taking.

'I'll be gone a couple of weeks – maybe three. I dunno.' And he rubbed his face, taking his phone out to read a text.

While he responded, I felt the need to look over to see exactly who and what he was messaging.

'Well, I expect some sympathy from across the ocean when I'm faced with handing out favour boxes.'

'Why do you hate weddings?' Naim asked.

'I don't hate weddings. I just think ice-related objects should remain either in the sea or, at a stretch, be put in one's drink. Remember the *Titanic*?'

'But Jack found Rose.'

'Yes, and Jack ended up twenty thousand leagues under.'

'But, Sofe, without a wedding there isn't the promise of all those future years of anniversaries – you know, when the husband forgets and the wife complains, and they argue and make up. Where's the fun without that?'

'Oh please, anniversaries! And don't even get me started on birthdays and *especially* Valentines.'

'What are you, the Grinch that stole life?'

'Are you telling me you don't want to gag every fourteenth of February when you see idiots walking around London with heart-shaped balloons and bouquets of clichéd roses?'

'You don't care about any of that stuff?'

'Not at *all*.' I bit into my chocolate cake and was briefly too happy to register what he said.

'You wanna get married?'

'Hmm?' Then the words he'd spoken formed in my head. 'Ha. Yeah, sure.' For some reason it seemed a winged creature went slightly mad in my stomach.

'You know what your problem is?' he said.

'Enlighten me,' I said, trying to get the creature to settle down.

Naim is always making these throwaway comments. It doesn't mean anything.

'You need to get laid.'

Excuse me? The creature was forgotten.

'Fuck off.'

He burst into laughter. Honestly, I don't *need* to have sex. I mean, is my state of perpetual virginity unnatural? Fine, yes. Is it marginally mortifying given that the age of consent is sixteen? Yes, it is. But I don't *need* to get laid. What has getting laid got to do with opinions on weddings and anniversaries anyway?

'Maybe one day I will. I have a date on Thursday.'

'A fake date? With who?'

'Yes. No. Not fake. Well, maybe.'

'Glad you got that figured out.'

'With the hottie. From Shady.'

He poured milk into his coffee.

'Well, good luck to you.' He mixed in some sugar, tapped the spoon on the cup and put it in the plate. 'He's probably going to be less romantic and just hopeless.'

The sullenness was rather endearing, to be honest. Until he said, 'I mean, do you think he's serious about you?'

I felt my face flush.

'What's that supposed to mean?'

'Look at him, Sofe.'

I mean, it's not as if I think he and I would look great together. He is *way* out of my league. But it's different when someone else thinks it. Especially when you realise that person means something to you, though it's not clear what.

'What am I looking at?'

There was an earnestness in his expression that I don't think I've seen before.

'You know what, you're a grown girl. I guess you can look after yourself.'

'No, tell me. What am I looking at?'

He then smiled in that suggestive way that I find both irritating and entertaining in equal measure.

'Oh, come on, Sofe. Arguments are for boring couples. What we have is special – we got it figured out.'

How does a person go from earnest to suggestive? Sometimes I wish I could peel through the layers of his words just to get to the heart of the matter.

Thursday 8 December

9 p.m. Who are these people who seek perfection? I'd like to sit down with them and discuss the date I just had.

I waited for the hottie (whose name I should probably start using) at Waterloo. The conversation with Naim kept playing in my head and it made me keener than usual to prove him wrong. I kept glancing around, waiting for a familiar face to appear. When Hottie called, I realised it was the first time we'd spoken. Weird. I looked around at people on the phone, seeing if I could find him before he found me. Then the crowds parted. The station became a blur. I caught his eye and he broke into a smile which, in turn, almost broke me. When he was in front of me I don't think I actually spoke. Maybe words came out. If they did I'm not sure what they were.

'We finally meet,' he said.

I love you.

For a second I understood how beautiful things might induce people to behave in stupid ways.

'So many people look different, but you look exactly like you do in your picture,' said Hottie.

So do you! Naim – you were wrong.

'Where's your beard?' I asked.

He rubbed his jaw. Who'd have thought such a simple act could make your knees weak.

'That's for the next time we meet.'

Next time!

We sat and had coffee on the riverside. The London Eye's Christmas lights twinkled in the background. He kept asking me questions about me: where did I grow up, who's my favourite author, do I prefer pasta or biryani. I didn't know what to make of all this attention. As I answered his questions, I thought, well, isn't this *linear*. Conversations with Naim jump from Lemon Puffs to Bollywood music.

He got up to use the bathroom, which was a good opportunity for me to recollect myself. There was an elderly couple next to us and the woman leaned over.

'Is that your boyfriend?' she asked.

I laughed and said no. Although the idea was pretty fetching.

'He is absolutely *gorgeous*.' She watched him as he walked away. 'Now let's keep that between you and me.'

Something felt odd, though. Warm, friendly, but *normal*. We walked back to the station and stopped just outside. He said, 'So, Sofia Khan. Until next time?'

Isn't it odd that when something goes well you can feel redundant? As if you know that it could've been you or anyone else and the whole thing would've probably gone the same? It sounds stupid, but I feel like I'd read about this before, or watched it in a film. Whatever else it was, it wasn't new.

'Next time I expect a beard,' I said.

He smiled, the cardboard cutout of a beautiful face.

'I will try my utmost.'

But when I think of him, I have to admit, my heart can't help but flutter.

9.55 p.m.

From Naim: You'd better be home in the next five minutes. Or I'm going to come to that fake date of yours and make a scene.

Ordinarily that would've made me laugh, but I'm finding a residue of annoyance when it comes to Naim and his words. For that reason, I'm going to ignore his call.

10.20 p.m.

From Abid: Salam, Sofia. It was really nice to meet you. Let's do it again soon.

Odd things are happening in the world. *Flutter, flutter, flutter.*

Friday 9 December

7 p.m. As soon as I walked through the door, I was instructed to walk right back out. I had to post leaflets to the neighbours to let them know there'll be noise over the weekend because of the dholki. It seems necessary to us 'Stanis to spend a whole evening beating a drum, singing songs and dancing around the room for entertainment.

When I came back, Chachu's voice was resounding in the living room. He was pacing up and down, on the phone, shouting in Punjabi at Bobby for not picking him up from the airport last week, or in 2001. Sigh. Went into the kitchen and Mum was making roti, looking over at him.

'He's been on the phone for half an hour. And I can't ask him if he is calling a mobile or landline – they don't think about phone bills.'

10.50 p.m. Naim called asking where I've been. I had to tell him it's been manic the past few days.

'Don't give me that bullshit.'

'I don't deal in bullshit,' I said.

'But fake dates aren't bullshit, right?'

Honestly. I knew why I was being an arse but what was his excuse?

'So?' he said. 'How hopeless was he?'

I looked at Maria's mounting boxes in my room.

'He was the opposite of hopeless.' I was damned if I was going to say anything more. 'And, as it happens, he didn't seem to think the idea of seeing me again was completely ridiculous.' Apparently I am damned.

'Why would it be ridiculous?' said Naim.

'You tell me, Naim.'

'Huh?'

The worst thing about people who are oblivious to what they say is when you're really pissed off and then have to explain *why* you're pissed off. So you've been walking around, seething, and they've been pottering about without a trace of excess emotion.

'Oh, *now* you play stupid.'

'OK, I don't know what's going on.'

So I had to remind him – that he found it difficult to believe Hottie would go on a date with me. It wasn't something I particularly wanted Naim to know bothered me, but it was either that or be pissed off without explanation, which can make a person seem a bit like an *ungh*.

'Where the fuck did you get that from?'

I repeated our conversation for him.

'Oh my God,' he said. 'For someone who's doing research I hope you're paying better attention to people's stories. That's not what I meant at *all*. I meant you're a *hijabi* and, so you know, you're a certain way. There's depth and whatever to you – maybe not depth of understanding conversations ... I can't believe you thought that's what I meant.'

I took in what he said. There was an inclination to believe him, but something pinched at any propensity to really trust him.

'Hmmm.'

'Sofe, if *ever* you decided to get married ... that man? He'd be the luckiest guy on earth.'

Oh, his words! Sometimes they're like tiny splinters, catching at the fabric of my focus.

'You have to say that because you're scared I'll shout at you, and then who'll put up with your nonsense?'

'I may say a lot of shit. But I don't *have* to say anything.'

'Right. Fine.'

'Can we move on to discussing important things now?'

I paused.

'Fine.'

He paused. 'Let's have sex.'

I laughed. He really is such an idiot. 'Next time you say something like that, you're going to get punched in the face.' If it were anyone else, they really *would* get punched in the face.

'Just once. Please?'

'You need lessons on how to speak to a hijabi,' I said.

'What are you talking about? Islam is all about manners, and I said please. Plus, my parents taught me equal opportunities.'

'Any opportunity here would be close to a miracle.'

He sighed. 'And that is why I will *always* have faith.'

Argh! Another splinter, but before I could stop myself I said, 'Good. You should keep it.'

'Oh yeah?'

'Absolutely.'

Don't know why I said it. Don't know where it came from, but maybe Katie's right. Maybe I should be keeping an open mind.

Note for book: If you edge towards a cliff slowly enough, you should be able to catch yourself before you topple over.

Saturday 10 December

6 p.m. Dholki day! Woke up super early to write, which means I have circles under my eyes. Does Brammers understand the consequence of her eagerness? Maria's given me a cream that apparently takes ten years off. I'd just dabbed blobs of it around my mouth when Fozia opened the door.

'Ugh,' she said. I looked at her in a royal-blue outfit and bronze sequins scattered everywhere, hair in disarray and no makeup.

'Oh, I love all the decorations in the house,' cried Suj as she waltzed in with Hannah.

'I feel like I'm living in a theme park,' I said.

Suj looked into the mirror and re-touched her lipstick before adjusting the wild curls in her hair.

'The wedding industry has gone mad,' said Hannah.

'Have you heard from the hot guy again?' asked Suj.

'We're texting.' I wish my heart would bloody well stop fluttering at the mention of him. 'I don't know about these sleeves,' I said, inspecting them. 'My arms look like chicken drumsticks. Look.' I shot my arm in front of Hannah.

'Oh, shit. I forgot to defrost the chicken.'

Mum then walked in – my room had turned into a wedding venue.

'Hannah and Maria married. You must all do something now,' she said, looking at Fozia, Suj and me. 'Maybe you two are not as fussy as Sofia.'

'Don't ask me, Auntie,' said Fozia. 'I'm waiting for Kamran's parents to stop being so *backward*.'

Mum scoffed, 'Very clever. He has spent the time with you and *now* his parents care that you're dye-vorced. Tell him, if you don't marry me I leave you. Tell him, *I damn care*.' Mum waved her finger in the air. 'Acha Suj, show me this lipstick.'

Girls and I glanced at each other. Fozia fiddled with the sequins on her outfit, looking intently at her lap as Mum inspected all the lipsticks Suj handed to her.

'I will take this one.' And she walked out of the room, leaving the proverbial elephant behind. Suj offered to do Fozia's hair when my phone rang.

'Oh my God.' I looked up. 'It's Hottie!'

I realised that I'm sure the girls and me have had this very moment, many times, like a decade ago. Some things never change.

'Hi,' he said.

'Hi.'

I put him on speaker. Foz forgot all thoughts of Kam as she kept mouthing, *marry him. Marry him.* Haha.

He asked what I was doing so I told him about dholki day.

'Are you going to cause trouble, Sofia?'

'Only when absolutely necessary.'

It was a perfectly decent conversation that lasted ten minutes, and then he said he'd leave me to it. We said goodbye and he hung up. I sat down on the bed and stared at the girls.

'I don't get it. He's so, so, not of this world.'

'Don't you dare tell him about the book,' said Foz.

What am I doing? What exactly am I doing? To be fair, it doesn't feel like *I'm* doing anything.

Note for book: No matter what you keep telling yourself, you'd better come to terms with the fact that we are all life's marionettes.

Wednesday 14 December

2.45 p.m. I was in the medical/prayer room, sitting on the patient bed, post-prayer, thinking of life and sorts when Suj called.

'Toffee, I can't stop eating, and I can't be arsed to be bulimic.'

'One day I'm going to have my stomach stapled, I think.'

'Your stomach is beautiful.'

'Fudge.' I prodded said stomach, and my finger was in danger of getting lost in its folds. 'I'm very happy to be alone for ever; going out, seeing the world, that kind of thing. But what about when we're sixty?' No one wants to be the Mad Woman in the Attic. 'Am I going to be a cat lady?'

'We'll have each other, Toffee. Anyway, you shouldn't think about that. Overthinking causes stress, which gives you wrinkles. And maybe a heart attack.'

I kicked my legs in the air.

'You're not going to be alone, Toffee.'

I made the valid point to Suj about it being fine because it's a choice and all ... but just because you make a choice, doesn't mean it's the *right* one.

7.50 p.m.

From Abid: Hey there. You should know the beard's coming along nicely. Meet up after Christmas? Would be good to catch up.

Without sounding pernickety, I did want to ask: catch up with what? I hardly know you. Which just made me determined that the next time I see him I'll try to puncture a (tiny) hole in the veneer of his perfection. I will *get* to know you.

Friday 16 December

5.10 a.m. I've woken up in a panic re book. Prayed and now I can't sleep. Maybe I should use my time productively and do some writing. Wonder if Naim's awake. Will just look at his Facebook.

5.20 a.m. Who is this new girl he's friends with? And why can I see her bra through her T-shirt?

6.10 a.m. I've rummaged through kitchen cupboards and Chachu seems to have eaten my stock of chocolates. I also want to know why there are four tubs of butter in the fridge with everything in them but actual butter. Everything is Tupperware for 'Stanis.

6.12 a.m. I need to see that picture again.

6.14 a.m. How can someone *that* thin have such big boobs?

6.17 a.m. Argh! Looked in the mirror. Shouldn't I seem youthful and fresh given abstinence from partying and drinking? Maybe it's that occasional cigarette … might as well join a convent and be done with life altogether – except I'm the wrong religion.

Speaking of which, it's the work Christmas party tonight. I'll decide what to wear, right after I've looked at that picture one last time …

1 a.m. We were at Millbank and it was the usual paper hats, cheesy music, Christmas cracker situation (which I always rather enjoy). People were getting increasingly inebriated as I chugged back glass after glass of Diet Coke. At least two people from Editorial told me they loved me, and someone from Facilities complimented my arse, which isn't the worst thing in the world, though it did make me question my decision to wear this particular green dress.

Katie came and put her arm around me and said, 'Sweetu, I love you *so* much. You are my *best, best* friend at work.' She gasped and then stroked my hijab. 'And look how beautiful you are, sparkling like a brown Christmas tree.'

'Yes. Thank you. Now let's …'

But before I could say let's call a taxi, Katie exclaimed, 'Sweetu! Let's go to Heaven!'

'Errr, yes. Great idea.'

'You'll come to Heaven. With *us*?'

I laughed at how alcohol can make a person think about the deeper questions to do with life and death.

'We'll *all* walk through the pearly gates together,' I said. 'But right now, let me call that taxi.'

'Guys! Sofe's coming to Heaven with us!' Katie exclaimed.

At which everyone cheered and I was swept out of the building by a charge of publicists et al. with Fleur following suit, grabbing people's coats on the way out.

Except I hadn't quite realised that Katie wasn't talking about the afterlife kind of Heaven, but rather the current life, *club*, Heaven.

'Are you mad?' I said to her. 'I can't go in there.'

The music thumped as crowds of people – wearing such little material that I felt cold just looking at them – gathered outside.

'Don't worry,' she said. She leaned forward as if she were letting me in on an exciting secret. 'They're mostly gay! Isn't that great? You can take your scarf off.'

I laughed and held her by the shoulders as the work lot queued outside.

'Sweetu. You know I'm a boring cow and don't do bars or clubs. As wonderful as the prospect of being around gorgeous men sounds.'

She looked so disappointed. I almost went in just to put a smile back on her face. Before she could contest too much, the girls dragged her into the club and Katie waved at me, shouting, 'It won't be the same without you!'

I turned around to call a taxi and bumped into a rather tall man. I looked up to say sorry and started.

'Oh, hello,' I said, smiling in surprise. It was Hottie! I was rather startled to be so pleased to see him.

His face fell.

'What are you doing here?' I asked.

He seemed to be lost for words.

'And where's this beard you're meant to be growing?' I added.

Then he looked over my shoulder. I turned to see what had caught his eye – it was only the club entrance. Why was he looking so *uncomfortable*? He still hadn't answered me and so I waited. Come on, Hottie ... what's happened to your perfect ability to have a conversation? Katie's voice trickled into my head. *They're gay! Isn't that great?*

No way.

'What are you doing *here*?' I repeated.

Surely not ... But his silence ... No, that just *can't* be right. I'm imagining things. He opened his mouth a little, but no words came out. Then he tried again. Something crept up on me one silent second at a time. Another silent second, and another. Then it snowballed until the truth almost bowled me over. What??

I had no idea what to do. What the ... I've not punctured a tiny hole in his veneer – I've exposed everything completely. A rush of sympathy gushed forth. He wasn't going to be able to salvage this. Despite my state of incomprehension, I knew what I had to do. I had to pretend.

'Waiting for some friends?' I said.

'What? Yes. Exactly.'

'Christmas mania.' I rolled my eyes in exaggeration. 'Apparently I look like a Christmas tree. But one tries to fit in.'

The flicker of a smile. But argh! Why did I mention fitting in??

Silence. I smiled, ignoring the flashing lights and Lady Gaga, playing inside. 'I'll leave you to it, I'm sure your friends will be here any minute.'

His sigh of relief perhaps wasn't meant to be so obvious. But it was.

I realised I'd probably never see him again. It felt sad, but for reasons I'd never imagined. *I can't believe it.*

'Look after yourself.' I paused. 'You'll be OK?'

He pretended not to know what I was talking about. I smiled and as I went to walk away he called out, 'Sofia.'

I turned around. He stood isolated in the middle, cast in the shadow of flashing lights.

'I really do love going to the mosque with my dad.'

In that moment he looked so beautiful and so sad, I wanted to take him home and make him a cup of tea. But I couldn't. He won't ever want to see me again. I smiled and nodded. 'Never doubted it.'

Saturday 17 December

3 p.m. Found it hard to concentrate on writing. I called Naim and ended up telling him what happened last night. He burst out laughing as I waited on the other end of the line, quite frankly, annoyed.

'Naim, it's not funny. Can you imagine how he must feel? And what if he got married? Poor girl.'

'Sorry, sorry. You're right. That's tough … But of all the people to bump into it had to be *you*.'

This brought on another bout of laughter. I was going to put the phone down, but he managed to get his breath back.

'OK, no, it's not funny. I shouldn't have laughed, and yeah, I do feel for him. But man … only you, Sofe. Only you.'

Sunday 18 December

10.20 a.m. I walked past Maria's room, minding my own business thank you, when I heard, 'What do you mean they think the ice sculpture's excessive?' A drawer, or similar, was slammed shut. 'But you said it was fine, so now it's not fine because *they* say so?'

Of all the things that happen in the world, my family choose an ice sculpture as the one object of incessant discussion.

'Of course they're gonna pay for it. We're halving it, that's what we agreed.'

Mum, having ears like a hawk, came out of nowhere and nodded towards Maria's room. I briefly wondered whether she had magical powers.

'But it's already been ordered. No, I can't cancel it!'

'What cancelling?' Before I could say anything, Mum pushed past me into Maria's room, demanding to know.

Dad joined me outside as he scratched his head.

'You girls,' he said. 'God has given you everything and you want more, more, more.'

'Baba, if we all lived in contentment you'd never have immigrated. And look at your wonderful life.' I spread my arms out as we heard Mum's raised voice.

Dad looked at me over his glasses. 'Always an answer for everything.'

'Maria,' we heard Mum say, 'don't be ridicklus. What if it becomes all water, water, anyway?'

Dad took off his slippers and threw them down the stairs. 'Mehnaz,' he called out. 'Where are my slippers?'

Mum came out and looked at his bare feet. 'Tst. This is how you'll get cold. I'll find them. You talk to our daughter.' With which Dad rolled up his sleeves and entered Maria's room.

Friday 23 December

10 a.m. Argh! I still only have some flimsy opening pages, which I've not been able to turn into anything substantial ... i.e. a first chapter. I had to pre-empt Brammers' nagging by confessing my complete lack of professionalism.

'Right. Well, meeting a deadline is necessary, Sofia.'

Unfortunately using your sister's wedding as an excuse isn't quite good enough. If Brammers were brown she'd understand. Who said cultural divides don't inhibit understanding?

11.55 p.m. Subsequent to the ice sculpture debacle, Tahir called saying there'd been a problem with his cousin photographer. I was Whatsapping Hannah, who'd had a dream that she fell into a well, but then someone pumped her with air and she floated out, except once she started floating she didn't stop. *Is her marriage to Zulfi a mistake? Will she be adrift for ever because of him? And why isn't she preggers yet?*

What does a person say to that?

Anyway, turns out cousin photographer's been arrested on charges of terrorism!

'You hired a terrorist to photograph our wedding?' exclaimed Maria.

'Maars! He's not a terrorist, the police are being racist.'

'So what, they're not going to let him out until when?'

I put the phone down and said it might be a while – the guy might be wearing an orange onesie soon! Tahir tried to explain about South London's new detainee and his innocence etc. but Maria looked as if he'd just told her there was a tornado coming and she only had three minutes to gather all the favour boxes.

'It's just like Tahir to do something like this,' she said. Apparently he's to blame for anti-terrorist laws. Honestly, where was the perspective? Apparently weddings also trump socio-political issues – which convinces me that if there were less focus on weddings there'd probably be fewer problems in the world. Maria pointed out that he might actually be a terrorist (in which case, excellent work, Scotland Yard), but when she told me which cousin had been arrested, I was like, 'What? Khalid bhai? The one who fundraises for charities in his spare time?' Maria looked a little embarrassed, and my heart sank.

'It's not about him, it's about Tahir,' said Maars.

Well, exactly. That's the problem – skewed focus. Then I heard Mum shouting at Dad for having a cigarette so I had to go into the conservatory and settle that dispute.

By the time I'd come into the living room, Maria had gone, leaving a message saying that she told Tahir he can forget the wedding. Her car keys were gone. I tried calling her but it was going straight to voicemail. *I was only gone five minutes.*

'Did you know Tahir had fundamentalist cousin?' said Mum, ignoring the curls of smoke emanating from Dad's mouth. 'If his cousin is one then what is he?'

Dad looked at Mum. 'Mehnaz – his cousin gets arrested so he is also like that? And we don't know the story.'

'Haan,' replied Mum. 'But look at you. Bad habits run in families.' Of course – perfectly normal for a wedding conversation to move from bickering over an ice sculpture to playing a guessing game of *who's a fundo*.

Dad got his car keys and before Mum could ask where he was going he'd shot out of the house. Five minutes later there was banging at the door and when I opened it Chachu stumbled into the hallway. He looked startled to see me as Mum came rushing out. What was wrong with him and why couldn't he walk straight? And then he opened his mouth and I smelled it.

Since when did my dad's brother drink? He raised his arms and exclaimed, 'Hai my sister. You are so lucky. Look at your daughters … my son doesn't even know he has a father.'

Of course we're all geniuses when collecting pieces of puzzles based on hindsight – the going missing, the coming back late, the secrecy with which my parents would go about as if it was utterly normal for Chachu to come home at two o'clock in the morning. Makes me wonder – anything else I might've missed in life?

'Call your baba and tell him to come home,' said Mum.

Baba, it turns out, is at Tahir's cousin's house where the mum is crying and the dad is saying it is all Allah's will. How awful. Before I could add that his brother was pissed and that he should be careful of the slippery roads, he'd hung up.

I knew Chachu liked to have a cry about his son as often as the fancy took him, but I didn't know he liked that cry to be accompanied by a bottle of vodka. My phone rang and it was Maria. She'd pulled up to speak to Tahir, but now her car wasn't starting.

'Dad's taken his car and gone to T's cousin's house,' I said.

'Why's he gone there?'

'Because no one else was giving a shit that a poor guy has just been arrested for no reason?'

She paused. 'What am I supposed to do?'

I kept calling Dad but he wasn't picking up, so the next best thing was for me to call a taxi.

Before I knew it, Mum had walked out of the house in her shalwar kameez and shawl and was knocking on Conall's door. She proceeded to tell him about my stranded sister, managing to relate the story of my drunken uncle and Tahir's newly arrested cousin. (And yes, she told him under what charges.) What must Conall *think*? I preferred it when he thought we were just a bunch of mad 'Stanis. I wished I had a St George's flag to wear as a hijab

– just so, you know, he knows we're not *that* type of people. But, honestly, the constant need to have to prove oneself is exhausting.

'Colin ...'

'Conall, Mum.' I crossed my hands under my arms.

'Yes, wohi. Very sorry, but very kind of you if Sofia could use your car?'

He looked at me and then at Mum.

'She's not insured.'

'Oh, doesn't matter about that. She only had two minor accidents this year.'

'Conall, really, it's fine – I'm calling a taxi.'

He went back into the house and emerged thirty seconds later with his coat on and keys in hand.

'You won't get a taxi in this weather. Tell me where she is and I'll take you.'

He spent the journey practically silent. I kept trying to think of interesting things to say. What *can* you say to a silent stranger? Ended up talking about the weather and how much I hate snow, then how much I like the smell of cars, which led to my love for the smell of petrol, and isn't it weird that nothing tastes as good as it smells.

'Not that I've tasted petrol. Obviously. Just as well – it'd be as disappointing as what you get at the bakery. Don't you find that bakeries ...'

'Do you always talk this much?' he asked.

'Oh. Sorry.'

He tapped his fingers on the steering wheel.

'But you see that's how you get to know people – by talking,' I added.

He doesn't seem to like me very much. Why? Why doesn't he like me? Am I not friendly enough? Is he like this with everyone? Is it my scarf?

'Which way from here?' he asked.

'Oh. I don't know.' I looked out of the window. What was I looking for, one might ask: a sign that says 'Maria is here'?

He sighed. 'Do you want to phone your sister and ask the exact location?'

'Ah, yes. Good idea.' I glanced at him, his elbow casually resting on the window frame. What a stony expression he has. Can't make out if he's pissed off or bored. According to Naim, a person can tell exactly what I'm thinking by the look on my face. I think that's rather thoughtful of me. I wished Conall would pay the same courtesy. You know, after he'd finished with the current one.

We found Maria, who spent most of the journey home staring out of the window.

'What will people say?' she said.

About the ice sculpture or MI5's newest hostage? She shifted to the middle of the backseat and leaned forward, placing her hands on either headrest.

'Have I been unreasonable?' she asked.

She lowered her head and I looked over at Conall, who'd been silent the entire time. I wished we could've had this convo when we got home.

'Just a bit. A sorry might be useful,' I said.

That head shot up pretty quickly.

'Sorry?'

'Yes. That magic word that shows remorse for having acted like a dickhead.'

'But he …'

'Just sorry, Maars. That's all. That's his poor cousin.'

Conall had pulled into our street. As we got out of the car, he fiddled with the lock and then turned around.

'You know, if you don't find a photographer, I'm free.'

'You're a photographer? You'd really do that?' Maria seemed so relieved I thought she might hug him.

He looked a bit confused. 'Yeah, 'course, it's fine.'

We all walked to our respective doors, and Maria thanked him as she went inside. I gave him the friendliest smile I could muster in the hope that he'd repay the favour. He just nodded and walked into his home. Shame.

Saturday 24 December

11 a.m. I've been in Chachu's room for half an hour. You'd think a grown man could look after himself. But he didn't look so grown-up to me. I just sat with him. Sometimes a person just needs someone to sit with them.

2 p.m. 'Where the hell have you been?'

What was Naim's problem?

'Excuse me. Busy with wedding madness. Obviously.'

I left out the part about the drunk uncle.

'Hey, if you can't talk, fine, but get back to me so I don't think you're lying in a gutter somewhere.'

Yes, I'm sure he was very concerned whilst he was making new friends on FB!

'The only thing in the gutter is your mouth, and mind for that matter.'

'Sofe, how are you ever going to get married if you're too busy being distracted by other people's weddings? Think about it – you'll never get laid.'

Hmph. 'You're such a prick.'

'Now whose mouth's in the gutter?'

'I don't consider "prick" a swear word. For most people it's just a state of being.'

I thought he might suggest meeting. I waited, and retorted and did what we've been doing for really what feels like for ever. But, alas, he was out and so he had to go, and I, as a result, had to stay. Here.

2.04 p.m. I've just looked at his Facebook and OMG, why has he been checked in with new well-endowed FB friend at BFI? He was *just* on the phone to me!

3.45 p.m. Wonder what film they're watching. Or maybe they're having a cosy lunch. I mean, honestly, Southbank at Christmas ...

5 p.m. I went downstairs instead of moping around in my bed-room. All kinds of questions were flitting around in my mind about the meaning of this Southbank episode. Dad was on the phone to Bobby, and I managed to convince Chachu, to be, you know, more open-minded about seeing his son. Before either father or son could change their mind, Dad said he was bringing Chachu over to Bobby's. Thanks to God. Bobby and Baby can't go through life having such ridiculous names *and* ignoring Chachu. Hurrah!

So they all scampered off, with Mum exclaiming that they can't take long because she has Christmas lunch to prepare for tomorrow. (Just because we don't celebrate it doesn't mean we can't partake in national day of stuffing ourselves with turkey.)

It's a Christmas miracle!

Except I don't believe in those. Obviously. Although general miracles are fine.

10.55 p.m. Maria came into my room and looked out of my bedroom window. I was trying to write and missed what was essentially a snowstorm. Tufts of white swirled and blurred in swathes. Already the ground was covered and the sky was this dense greyish brown, which made it look ever so slightly like the world was about to end.

'Mum and Dad just called. They're going to stay at Bobby's,' said Maria.

Typical. You don't speak to a family member for years and then you decide to set up camp in their house.

'I said sorry to Tahir,' said Maria.

'Did you die a little inside?' I know what it takes for Maria to say sorry.

She smiled. 'I wanted to tell him about Chachu's drama, but if he knew we had a drunkard for an uncle the wedding would definitely be off,' she said.

'That's healthy. And Chachu's not a *drunkard*.' I said. 'He has problems.'

'I know that, but you can't tell the person you're marrying everything.'

She looked outside again and the snow was now falling thickly, but without chaos. I always thought that's why people got married – to tell them things. Well, *most* things, at least.

'There are some things you have to be careful about,' she added. 'It's hard to accept a person, warts and all. Think you should put that in your book somewhere.'

Note for book: No one falls in love any more. (Bit sad? Tough. That's life.)

11.57 p.m. Erm ... Naim called so I asked what he'd been up to. He said he'd just been to see a film with a friend. It occurred to me that I must also be one of these friends and wanted to put the phone down, but as soon as I said I had to go he said, 'Where do you have to go on Christmas Eve, close to midnight? You an Elf?'

I told him Mum, Dad and Chachu were at B&B's. Chat, chat, chat, blah blah, blah, and he said, 'I should pop over for a cup of tea then.'

Ha! As if he was going to drive all the way from Slough to South London in this snow in the middle of the night. So I was all, 'I'll just put the kettle on, shall I?'

He's going to be here in forty-five minutes.

Bollocks.

2.54 a.m. I'm not entirely sure that bringing tea and biscuits to a man parked outside my house would impress my dad. It's obviously fine to meet a man of my own accord, but not in the middle of the night, in a car. 'Stani parents are so suspicious – they think the moment you're alone with a member of the opposite sex you'll end up *having* sex. How was I supposed to know he'd actually do as he said? Who drives all that way in the snow for a cup of tea?

'I hope you're not expecting to come inside,' I said as I handed him tea and got into the car.

'I got tea, I got snow; I'm happy,' he replied. 'Don't know how long it'll last. Flying tomorrow and you guys are shit at dealing with shifts in weather. Flight'll probably get cancelled.'

I sat inside and suggested that he should just stay in his land of opportunity if he didn't like it here.

'Sofe, I already have stuff on my mind. Why spoil one moment I'm actually happy?'

'What stuff?'

'Just, you know, stuff.'

'That's specific.'

'I should kick you in the shins.'

'Then I'd have to report you to police and you'd definitely miss your flight. Here …'

I took out a packet of biscuits from my coat pocket.

'Hahaha, are you kidding me?'

'When it comes to Lemon Puffs, I never kid,' I said.

He took a biscuit and dipped it in his tea.

'There's too much milk in this.'

'There is not too much milk. '

'You had forty-five minutes to make me a cup of tea and you didn't even leave the tea bag to brew long enough.'

You're so ungrateful.'

'I drive all the way in the snow to see you and *I'm* ungrateful?'

'Well, instead of appreciating that I brought out *Lemon Puffs* – not just any biscuit, mind, but *Lemon Puffs* – and saying thank you, you criticise my tea-making skills.'

'Yeah, OK, let's call them *skills*.'

He took a bite from the biscuit and the rest fell into the mug.

'Serves you right,' I said.

He reached out for another one and I pulled the packet away.

'You are the worst host.'

'You criticised my skills,' I said.

'Who puts that much milk in tea?'

'Who spends this much time complaining about it?'

He looked at the bit of biscuit floating around in the mug. I saw a light come on and thought Maria had woken up. Looked up and it was only next door.

'OK, can I at least have your biscuit then?'

I couldn't help but smile. 'Fine, you can have my biscuit.'

He took another Lemon Puff as I put the packet on the dashboard.

'Imagine if we had kids,' he said. 'You'd be like, pick up the kids. And I'd be like, no you pick up the kids.'

I'm sure my brain had formed some words, but they seemed to have got lodged somewhere between my throat and mouth. I don't know how the conversation had gone from bad tea to kids, but there we were, in the snow, arguing about who's going to pick up our children. WTH? I felt myself getting ever closer to that cliff's edge. The problem with edging forward is that your steps sometimes quicken without you realising. And everyone knows when it snows there's ice – a person's bound to slip on ice.

'No one would ever invite us for dinner,' I said.

He turned towards me and rested an arm over the headrest. 'Who gives a fuck about anyone else?'

Argh! Words, lodged. Tongue, tied. Before I could dislodge anything he sat back.

'I guess I should say thanks for the tea and biscuits.' He looked at me and smiled. 'Thanks.'

'That's OK,' I said. 'Lemon Puffs for a lemon puff.'

'Sofe?'

'Yes?'

He looked at me and I had to take a deep breath.

'Can I use your bathroom?'

'What?' Honestly. What was I expecting him to say? 'Oh, yes, fine.'

Had to be super quiet so Maria wouldn't wake up. We stopped at the bottom of the stairs and I was suddenly aware of my arse being in his face if I were to lead the way.

'Go ahead,' I said.

'Oh, no. Ladies first,' he whispered, smiling.

Never has the house felt so small, or my arse felt so big.

He came out of the bathroom and looked around.

'So where's your bedroom?'

Putting my hand on his shoulder, I led him towards the stairs as he looked back insisting he was just curious.

I opened the door to let him out and he stopped for a moment.

'Sofe?'

'*Yes*, Naim?'

He put his hand on the outside handle. 'You don't wanna be single for ever, do you?'

I gave a mini shrug. 'Maybe not.'

'Good,' he said. 'Merry Christmas, Puffs.'

I waited for him to say more, and as the moment stretched I could've stepped closer and kissed him. (I didn't. Obviously.) Where the hell did this *affection* spring from?

'Merry Christmas, you lemon.'

Oh dear. Affection, affliction – same thing.

Sunday 25 December

10.25 a.m. So this is how people must get caught having affairs. I opened the door and Mum said,

'Who came to the house?'

For a moment I thought, *shit, are there cameras here? Does Mum have access to local CCTV* (this would not surprise me). *Were Mum, Dad and Chachu hiding in the background, spying on me and my deviant (but innocent by general standards) behaviour?*

'Chalo, chalo,' said Dad and Chachu, who pushed past Mum and me to get into the warmth of the house.

'No one,' I said, searching for the voice of conviction.

'So whose footsteps are in the snow?' she asked. I looked down at the prints. My brain, much like the weather, had frozen.

Then Conall came out of the house with some rubbish.

'Hello, Colin,' said Mum.

Mum started chatting to him about being stuck at Bobby's house yesterday all the while I was thinking argh! Excuse, Sofia, *any* excuse. Then she asked what Conall was doing today. She almost invited him for lunch. Thank God he said his brother was visiting with a few friends. Not that I'm not all in the Christmas spirit of things, but we'd all have to be on best behaviour and that doesn't work very often.

'Taw whose footsteps are in the snow?' asked Mum, looking at me – the woman who never forgets. *Junk mail! Jehovah's Witnesses! Local window cleaner! Naim, Naim, Naim!*

'Carol singers,' said Conall as he put the lid on the dustbin. Of course! *Carol* singers. Stupid, small, brain. Mum seemed content with that as she went inside.

Conall looked over at me. 'Happy Christmas,' he said, before walking into his own home.

Felt bad about being pleased that he wouldn't be joining us: for that moment he was my actual guardian angel.

7.55 p.m. Everyone argued over what to watch for Christmas TV. (I was outnumbered by Bollywood lovers.) It didn't matter, though. I managed to get some writing done. Who cares that there might not be ice sculptures at my sister's wedding, that we have to watch B4U, or that pockets of fat are developing in places I didn't even know were possible. I don't think Naim cares so much either. Just as I had this thought, Maria ambled into the room and threw a Twix at me. I missed it, and looked up at her as I said, 'Something terrible's happened.'

And there I was, explaining to Maria that I was looking over the edge of the cliff.

Monday 26 December

7.55 a.m. Potential of having a relationship with Naim:

Cons: 1) *If* we were to get married, I'd be up at 4 a.m. to pray, while he'd be stumbling back home from a night out with friends. Will this lead me to be a disapproving nag? No one wants to be a nag.

2) What if we didn't end up getting married and there is *another* relationship break-up? Emotional energy crisis? Bad timing?

3) We bicker a lot. What if we end up like my parents??

4) That bloody scarf of his.

5) Also, is he smug or does he just *look* smug? Does it say something about my judgement that I can't distinguish between the two? Does it say something about him that it feels indistinguishable?

6) The above shows this is making me slightly neurotic. A nagging neurotic? Definitely to be avoided.

7) Also, questions to ask oneself: how will he enhance my (Islamic) life? Does he want children? If so, how many? If he expects to have a brood, will I be angry with him for expecting one when *I'll* be the one carrying them?

Pros: 1) I've never laughed with anyone as much as I laugh with him. Oh dear.

Oh dear, oh dear, oh dear.

Suj came over and listened to me repeat the pros and cons.

'Why are you worried?' she asked.

'Fudge! I don't know. Because it wasn't part of the plan? Because he's inappropriate? Because he doesn't even seem like the type of guy who'd go for a hijabi?' I paced up and down the room. 'And what if he doesn't feel the same?'

'Toffee – you guys are practically in a relationship without being in one. I just don't think that's possible. I don't think anyone does.'

I sat on the edge of the bed and thought about Imran. A person can coat it with whatever grains of sugar they can find, but here is fact: there came a fork in the road and Imran went towards the one with the hole-in-the-wall. I don't even think he looked back. Naim and I speak all the time, but words are just words. Imran spoke all kinds – constructed sentences that built something that resembled hope. I can't remember if I even really wanted to be with him, or if it was because that's what was expected.

'Don't worry, Toffee. I know you. You have your shit sorted. When it comes down to it, you'll know exactly what to do and, just like always, it'll be the right thing.'

Note for book: Fear of rejection isn't a sophisticated feeling. You know it thwacks you in the gut. But no matter how hard you try to look for it, you will probably never see it coming.

WEDDING SHEDDING ...
Friday 30 Dec – Sunday 1 Jan

Mehndi Day! *(Note for book: Otherwise called a henna party, involving the ritual of putting henna on the bride and groom's hand, feeding them sweetmeats, followed by drum beating and dancing. Aunties are never so happy as when they're at a mehndi.)*

From Suj: Toffeeeee! Can't wait for tonight and tomorrow. Just a quick q, tho. Can Charles come tomorrow? Love you! Xxxx

To Suj: Of course. Btw, do you have purse to go with my green outfit? Xxxxx

From Fozia: Suj told me you said Charles could come to the wedding. Well done. Sod what people think. Does this mean I can bring Kam? X

Sigh. All I can say is, thanks to God there's no alcohol at Mussie weddings (unless Chachu was carrying a hipflask) – just a DJ, some chicken korma, a few belly-dancing accessories and the aunties are on the dance floor as if their life depends upon it. Aunties who, by the way, were queued outside my room before each function saying, 'Soffoo, Beta, make my eyes like yours ...' Why are sixty-year-olds obsessed with recapturing their youth in the form of liquid eyeliner?

There were (and possibly still are) sixteen people living under the same roof. I've spent most of my life not knowing one relative from the next, and now I even know the colour of their knickers. Any mental capacity I might've had to think about Naim was superseded by their dietary requirements. On top of which I kept having mini convulsions at the idea of everyone's reaction at Suj turning up with a black guy at the barat, and then being horrified at my own sense of inherent racism.

We were preparing brunch and Uncle Scot (as in Scotland – his name obviously isn't Scot) was all, 'London is so rush, rush. Also, there are so many of our people here now.'

'We have a lot of Sri Lankans,' replied Mum, picking up Dad's glasses from the table and cleaning them.

'And Polish,' added Dad.

'Le, here you don't even know your neighbour,' Uncle Scot shook his head. 'Not like Glasgow.'

'Nahin, we are lucky,' said Mum as she went to answer the doorbell.

'Irish,' added Dad.

Uncle Scot nodded thoughtfully. 'Haan. They're different to English.'

As if on cue, Mum ushered in a harassed-looking *Colin*. Everyone stopped talking, which is when he looked like he wanted to get the hell out of there. Dad asked him to take a seat. Yes, please, neighbour, come join us and our casual racism.

'These goray like our things nah,' Mum said to me when I asked why she'd invited him. 'Bechara, he probably has no one to cook for him. You shouldn't be mean, Soffoo,' she added. 'Not everyone is miserable like you.'

Well, wouldn't you be miserable too if you'd just discovered unfortunate feelings, which all evolved from an unfortunate task TO WRITE A BOOK. It didn't help when every time I mentioned 'chai', everyone's ears pricked up like I'd just announced my engagement.

While I was making seventeen cups of tea, Cousin Scot, Ayla, came into the kitchen, saying, 'O em gee who is that hottie with Dad?' She peered into the conservatory, looking at Conall. 'He is *fit*.'

I remember Ayla when she was in nappies. Now she's sixteen, twirling her straightened hair around her fingers. Since when are teenage 'Stani kids allowed to wear sleeveless tops and be dripping with accessories? We were lucky if Mum and Dad let us use Vaseline.

'Oh my God, oh my God, he just smiled at you.'

Which was so surprising I had to look behind me to check there was no one else there. I wanted to impart wisdom and say: maybe you don't have to walk around in skintight clothes to have a hottie smile at you. Though he probably wouldn't want to do much else.

'It's OK, Ayla,' I said. 'The only reason he smiled is because I'm bringing him tea.'

Someone wanted hot milk and someone wanted it cold and some wanted cardamom in their tea and one could only have Canderel, while having no problem with having their hand perpetually in the box of ladoos.

Auntie Reena extended her bejewelled hand and said, 'Beta, this has so much milk in it.' The world now knows I can't make tea. Conall looked slightly perplexed and I realised it was because everyone was speaking in Punjabi.

'Too much milk in the tea,' said Chachu, helpfully demonstrating this by extending his cup for Conall. I had to make sure Chachu wasn't making his tea Irish.

Ayla sat next to Conall and began translating conversations for him. Honestly. I asked a million times for everyone to speak English.

Chachu turned to Conall and said, 'Shakeel told me you photographed in Kashmir?' Conall rested his cup on the floor.

'Yeah – six months.'

Uncle Scot shook his head as his daughter tried to take pictures of Conall on her phone.

'Blady Indians. They will stop at nothing to get revenge on Pakistan.'

'With all due respect, sir, there are two sides to a story.'

(Turns out Conall isn't so uncomfortable voicing his opinions. Choose your audience, love.)

'Oh, so it's Pakistan's fault?' Uncle Scot's eyebrows knit together as if a caterpillar was plastered above his eyes. 'And what is solution then? We give up?' His arm shot in the air, hitting Auntie Reena's elaborate coif.

'Hai hai, don't ruin my hair talking about your politics, sholitics.'

'And where is the justice?' added Uncle Scot.

Conall was about to say something but then seemed to think better of it and went back to sipping his tea. The room had become so tense I had to say something.

'Uncle, you're Scottish – you should know something about wanting independence.'

There I was, helping Conall out, and not even a nod of acknowledgement from him.

'Well,' said Ayla. 'I think Kashmir should be given its independence, right. And so should Scotland.' She looked pointedly at her parents. 'And me.' She turned to Conall and gave him a rather brilliant smile.

'You've a very smart daughter,' said Conall.

Maria and I almost choked on our (milky) tea. Ayla – the girl who'd been called into school for using text language in her exams. She looked at him with such gratefulness though, I had to ruffle her hair.

Thank God Conall doesn't understand Punjabi because Uncle Scot added, 'And what would an Irish man know about how our people suffer.'

'A lot more than you realise, Uncle,' I replied in Punjabi.

Conall was finally allowed to leave the house to get his camera equipment ready and come to the hall later. As evening approached, Auntie Reena came into my room, wanting me to thread a stray chin hair. Sigh. Dad said she looked like she'd been whacked on the chin as he passed her when he came into my room. Don't think she cared much for his comment.

He sat down on my bed, looking at my phone, while I finished re-applying my makeup (which I'd had to take off because I forgot to do my ablutions to pray. NB: Is my forgetfulness a product of wedding household, Naim, book or innate scattiness?).

'Dad, why aren't you downstairs, at the door with the keys, ready to leave?'

He really has no sense of timing. He looked up at me, patting the bed. It was no time to sit down and have a chat, but he looked so serious.

'You spend a lot of time on the phone, haina?'

Where was Maria?? It was beginning ...

'There's a wedding going on,' I tried to explain.

'You know, Soffoo, if you like someone you can tell me.'

It was like I was eighteen, trapped in a thirty-year-old's body. Shame. Why didn't Dad need to leave the room and have a cigarette? Why couldn't I have a cigarette?

'You know what I want, Beta?' he said.

A watch? A daughter who doesn't pray compulsively? A wife who has a verbal filter?

'I want you to be happy and married too. Like Maria.'

He looked at my phone again and I prayed that it wouldn't be the moment Naim decided to message.

'OK.'

'I want to know you'll always be looked after.'

'Dad ... I could do the shocking thing of looking after myself.'

He smiled and took off his glasses, rubbing his eyes.

'Haan, haan, I know you will,' he said, putting the glasses back on. 'You know, it's not fair, but women always have to make the compromise.'

I laughed in a suitably incredulous manner.

'I don't say it's a good thing,' he continued, 'but *everyone* has to compromise, Beta.'

'Next thing you'll be saying marry someone who writes "lol" and uses emoticons.'

The wrinkles around his eyes seem to be etched deeper. Naim crept into my mind and suddenly I wished the stupid bugger were here. Oh, inconvenient truth.

'Baba,' I said, putting my arm around him, 'there are so many more important things in the world to worry about. Famine, for example.' I stood up, giving him my hand. 'And fairy lights.'

He furrowed his brows. 'Nothing is more important than my daughters.'

That's the nice thing about dads; they actually believe this. I kissed him on the cheek and looked him in the eye.

'I'm afraid the world would disagree.'

Actually, half the world was at the mehndi where Auntie Scot managed to get locked in the toilet cubicle. Honestly. Conall in the meantime was capturing all this and the general cultural calamity with his camera. It all must've been quite an education for him. Perhaps an education he could've done without; but no one said you just learn the things you want. Ambreen waltzed in with her mother-in-law, her husband lagging behind with the baby and child who began running around and tipping over chairs.

'I can't wait to have a third baby.' Ambreen rested a hand on her chest. 'Honestly, motherhood is just the most beautiful thing. Finally life has *meaning*. Who are these people who think one or two children are enough? Ugh!' Hannah looked on stony-faced, not that Ambreen noticed. 'And I'm sooooo old,' Ambreen said, touching my shoulder. We are, of course, the same age.

Ayla interjected, 'No way. I hope I look like you when I have two kids.'

My poor, young, stupid, cousin.

Ambreen giggled and patted Ayla's arm, 'Oh, don't, I'm so *ugly*. Look at the size of my nose. Sofe never cared about the size of her nose.'

Conall hovered in the background, snapping away.

'I couldn't worry about the size of my nose *and* my arse,' I said putting a mini kebab in my mouth.

'You're curvy. I'm so skinny, ugh. It's annoying.'

Suj flicked her hair and said, 'Yeah, I couldn't deal with boobs the size of poached eggs.'

Ambreen's face fell for perhaps a millisecond before she recovered her composure and twittered. 'That's what *I* say, but Ibrahim's says, "no one likes a fat person".'

'Who's fat?' Ibrahim came and locked his arm around my neck. 'Sofe,' he said, 'How are you, voluptuous thing? And when are you tying the noose, I mean knot,' he asked, clearing his throat.

'Ibraheeeeeem,' Ambreen exclaimed. 'I hope you plan on getting me the new BMW.'

'Yes, Princess Ambreen,' he said, pointing his fingers to his temple.

Note for book: All that glitters is not a BMW.

189

Auntie Reena, while dancing, had somehow, quite miraculously, bent down so low she was having a hard time getting back up again.

'Tst, look at Reena,' said Mum, shaking her head.

Conall smiled – I noticed it's rather lopsided, as if he can't quite commit to full-on smile. Don't know what it is about him. I thought he was moody, but the more I see him the more I think he just looks sad. He has broad shoulders. Looks like they carry a lot of the world's weight.

'It's all craic, Mrs Khan,' he replied.

She laughed as if he'd said the funniest thing.

'Haan! She is taw completely crack.'

Annoyingly, Ayla decided to scamper up to me, telling me to come and dance with her.

'Can't, dear, have to be careful of my arthritis.'

She looked at me in surprise and then rolled her eyes. 'Oh, come on, you're the best dancer.' Punjabi MC began pounding, which had Ayla forgetting all her zeal to get me on the dance floor as she did a rather good job of occupying it herself.

'Dancing makes God angry?' asked Conall.

I looked at him, mildly surprised that he even noticed I was there. It's so boring having people ask me what might or mightn't anger God with that ironic tone, especially when I know exactly what they're thinking. Also, not being able to shake my hips for a few hours? I am being robbed of life itself.

'Yes, it's going to send me to hell as a matter of fact.'

'No one else seems to care about that,' he said, gesturing towards the dance floor.

It made me think of sheep again. Black, black, black sheep. Wherever I go. Sigh. I leaned over to look at the pictures he'd taken. I'm no photographer, but they really were very good. There was a photo of the mehndi trays lined up in the front with a blurred image of me and Maria in the background. I'm adjusting the flower in her hair.

'Blurry is a good look for me,' I said. 'Well done.'

He nodded. Take a compliment, will you. Everyone was busy dancing so I just stood there with him, lost, surprisingly, for conversation.

'Do you like the Bollywood music then?' I asked.

'It's er, interesting.'

Ha! I've heard that one before. 'My uni tutor once said I have an *interesting* face.' I looked up at him. 'We all know what that's a euphemism for.'

Conall didn't think it necessary to respond. I thought about Naim, wondering what he'd have made of the mehndi. Would he have got on the dance floor? Or would I have been standing next to him instead of speaking to the photographer? Something squeezed in my chest. Like an irresistible, unknown, but so very possible, scenario. He is not here, but he could be here. Argh! I looked at the girls who were sitting with Maria and Tahir, chatting and laughing.

'Did you know the Dalai Lama wakes up at four o'clock every morning to meditate? He was once asked why and he replied, "Because through discipline I achieve freedom."'

'That's very philosophical,' said Conall.

I nodded.

'I'm a very philosophical person; when I'm not selling hippo books.'

'Or Viagra.'

Hmph.

When we'd got home and put things away, given everyone their fiftieth cup of tea, Maria and I settled into bed (along with my sanity I've also lost my room to the Scots so am sharing with Maars).

'Tired?' I asked.

'No, weirdly. More excited.'

I leaned over to check my phone. And at that exact moment I got a message from Naim, asking how the wedding was going. I related the Ambreen exchange.

From Naim: BMW? If that was my wife I'd park a Fiat up her ass. Anyway, forget her – I've decided your nickname's going to be Daisy.

To Naim: Why on earth would my nickname be Daisy?

From Naim: It suits you perfectly.

To Naim: They're an ugly flower.

From Naim: What are you talking about? Daisy Duck was hot. Anyway, a daisy is a single blossom, on a single stem, long and vibrant; like you. Except for the long, and not so vibrant at weddings.

But electric otherwise.

There was that squeeze again. Maria turned around, and was snoring within minutes. I had weird dreams of marquees being blown up and ice sculptures in the shape of Auntie Reena's coif.

Barat Day! *(Note for book: Known as the wedding day, which involves a civilised dinner, where everyone's abandoned the much-loved drum-beating.)*

I thought today was going to be a nightmare, but maybe I need to learn to be more optimistic. Apart from the fact that the display fruit didn't arrive in time, table twenty had run out of 7-Up, Auntie Reena's bumpit was showing, Dad was caught having a cigarette and Mum forgot to wear support pants, the night went quite well. Not least when Fozia arrived alone and announced that she broke up with Kam! Girls and I did a collective cheer. I distinctly remember the camera flashing at us.

Maria and T had their first dance and when the clock struck twelve, everyone was in a foray of congratulations. I looked at the couple, holding hands. The only thing in my hand was my phone. No one noticed that Chachu had accidentally touched Tahir's mum's boob when leaning over for more rasmalai. Dad gave Mum a peck on the cheek, at which point everyone cheered and Mum blushed profusely. And not an eyelid batted at the fact that Suj was there with a black man. Perhaps the family isn't as racist as I thought.

As most guests congregated on the dance floor, I saw Fozia looking on, gloomily. I walked up to her and offered her my hand.

'I'll have to do,' I said, 'until a new and worthy man stumbles along.'

She took my hand and looked over my shoulder, into the distance. 'I did the right thing.'

I spun her around and her dupatta got caught in my heel.

'I make a lousy dance partner. Sorry,' I said.

'You're my dance partner for life, darling.'

'Even when we're old and you have to wipe my bum because of my arthritic hands?'

'This is just in-between stuff. That's when the best part of life will begin,' she replied.

Note for book: There are people who will clean your shit up for you, literally. If a person can't match this – they're not worth the effort.

'Look at Suj with Charles,' Foz said.

I turned around to see them dancing, looking like something out of a magazine shoot. I hoped Conall was taking pictures of them.

'I don't think she should let that one go,' she added.

I agreed wholeheartedly. Hannah and Zulfi were in some kind of deep conversation. That's the thing with those two – every time Hannah's around him she crackles with energy.

'You know you did do the right thing,' I said.

'Remember when I was getting divorced?' she asked.

How could I forget: hours and hours of sitting with her in silence as we both filled the room with cigarette smoke. My parents forgot what I looked like because I didn't go home for weeks.

'And I went back and forth about whether I was doing the right thing or not? You said something.'

'Words of wisdom? From me?'

'You said, "If you're going to make any decision in life, be fearless about it."'

'Ha. Oh yes. Sod the consequences. Being scared is useless.'

I couldn't quite look her in the eye. Yes, it's useless. Doesn't make it any less real, though. We both moved to the sidelines and watched as everyone began bouncing to the more upbeat tempo.

'I think about Riaz sometimes,' she said. Hmmm, second mention so far. 'I'm probably just overthinking things because I'm single again and I *still* can't stand my job. It's all in the past, after all. But I wonder, if only I hadn't met him so soon after my divorce, and we'd been set up by a friend or something, rather than just meeting at a work do ...'

Dreadful place the past can be. Poor post-divorce Riaz. People don't lie – timing is everything. And it doesn't matter how much you tell a friend they're missing out on a good thing, you can't help it if their heart's jammed between an ex-husband and a hard place. I stood by her side, letting her have her silence and re-reading the messages that Naim and I had sent one another. I didn't think about it too much because, like Suj says, overthinking leads to wrinkles.

To Naim: Come home, already. I bloody miss you.
From Naim: Puffs! I was sitting at my aunt's house and had the sudden urge to message you the same. Cross-Atlantic telepathy.

'You're missing everything.'

Conall stood behind us, but Foz was still staring into space. People who are always on their phone are so annoying, and yet there I was – an iPhone extension.

'In my defence I also use it to take notes.' I put the phone away in my purse.

'For?'

'Oh, just this silly project for work. A book type thing.'

'You're writing a book?'

'Not like a masterpiece or anything.' Should really stop saying that every time the book is mentioned. 'But yes, I suppose. A book.'

'Well, this is grand material.' He gestured around the huge chandeliered room.

'Let me show you.' He brought up a photo of when Dad gave Mum a peck on the cheek at midnight.

'Look at that. You captured it.'

I smiled at their expression: two old folks giggling as if they were teenage sweethearts. Don't know why it brought a tear to my eye.

'We could title it: "It wasn't such a bad life, after all",' I said.

For a moment I'd forgotten who I was speaking to. Why does the next door neighbour, of all people, have to know about my disgruntled parents? Really must think before opening my mouth.

'Or something normal,' I added.

Not sure whether it was Naim's messages, or the photo of Mum and Dad, or the fact that as I looked around everyone seemed to be so, well, *content*, but perhaps I was wrong. Perhaps weddings aren't so bad, after all.

JANUARY 2012

Should Old Acquaintance be Forgot

AYISHA MALIK

Muslim Dating Book

If one of your New Year's resolutions happens to be to get married ~~(or whatever), try not to go to any weddings. They'll only make you feel that there's a partner-shaped hole in your life (not wall). And it's all an illusion! A few hours of seeing a happy couple or listening to your best friend talk about the one that got away can shake up your emotions and make you do stupid things, like call your ex, or elope with the next man that offers you a mini kebab. And when you don't end up getting married or finding love (ungh), that partner-shaped hole will only continue to grow (SNOWBALL) in size.~~ For a blind bit of optimism, go to a wedding.

Monday 2 January

9.45 a.m. And if your NY's resolution is to write a book? Then definitely don't develop *feelings* for people. We plan and plan, but God is the greatest of planners. Sigh. I will not panic (re Naim or book). The deadline for the first draft is July, which gives me plenty of time, but I *still* don't have opening chapter for Brammers ... I do wish everyone would stop breathing down my neck about it. Everywhere I go in the office I'm asked, 'How's the book coming along?' I can't even take a piss without the question being thrown at me before I've managed to zip up my jeans – which, incidentally, means sometimes I forget.

3.10 p.m. Brammers called me into the office. Her smile didn't quite reach her eyes as she clasped her hands together.

'Sofia, are you finding this challenging?'

I assume she meant the chapters, but in my head I was thinking of Naim and ended up nodding.

'I mean, no,' I said. 'Yes. Only because of how busy it's been at home, but don't worry. It's all under control.'

How, how, how?

'Just a few more weeks,' I added.

She didn't look entirely convinced, despite my attempt at an utterly convincing tone. *Attempt* being the operative word.

7.35 p.m. I was on my way home, wondering how I'm going to get any writing done. As I got to the house Conall was walking out.

'All right?' He opened up his umbrella.

'When can we see the photos?' I asked. 'Weddings and wars. That's what I'll call the album.'

'Where's your umbrella?'

'Why do you think I wear a hijab? Part religious reasons, part good sense.'

He put his umbrella over my head, not a flicker of a smile. Tough crowd.

'And how's that book coming along?'

Argghhh! If it wasn't so cold and my hands weren't jammed into my pockets, I think I might've jammed them somewhere else.

'I've decided to ban people from asking that question until I get enough peace to actually write it.'

'You need quiet?' He hesitated for a moment and then said, 'You can use my house. If you want. It's empty on weekends most of the time. I'm out on projects and stuff.'

'Really?'

'Sure.' He nestled his face into his scarf. 'Come over Saturday. If you want.'

I'm not sure how much he meant that, given the repeated *if you want*; perhaps he was just being polite. I was about to say thanks, but no thanks, when the looming deadline made me catch my tongue.

Whoever said prayers are futile?

9 p.m. I told Mum and Dad that Conall had offered his house to me on the weekends to write and they both looked at each other as if I'd just announced I was moving in with him.

'It is proper for you to be in another man's house, alone?' asked Mum.

Honestly. I had to reassure my imaginative parents that I'd be in the living room tapping on a keyboard, not in the neighbour's bedroom, tapping on something else.

Sunday 8 January

6.45 p.m. At first I wasn't sure about taking Conall up on his offer, but by ten o'clock in the morning the house phone had rung five times, Chachu and Baba were having a full-blown debate about the Pakistani economy and, for reasons unbeknownst to me, there was a child singing tunelessly. Whose child it was, I don't know. And no Maria in the next room to suffer with me.

I knocked on Conall's door at about half ten. He opened it and, much to my consternation, was still in his boxers! In January? WTF? Mum and Dad's shifty looks came to mind before I realised I was staring, looking even shiftier.

'I'm sorry, I didn't realise it'd be too early.'

He gestured for me to come in as he grabbed his robe and put it on. In the passage there was the distinct smell of paper and

I walked into the living room where the walls were lined with shelves, stacked with books. They were everywhere; on the floor in piles, resting on cabinets and the coffee table. Some were opened on the floor by the sofa.

'I fell asleep going through some stuff,' he explained.

He went about closing them and picking them up from the floor, marking the pages as he did so. It was so quiet I wished the TV or something was on, and since I mention things being on, I wished that clothes on his back were one of them. Why wasn't he tying his robe?? I might be of a holy disposition, but you'd have to be blind to ignore the fact that he looked like he was practically photoshopped. Made me breathe in the entire time I was standing there. Gave me a backache.

'Tea or coffee?'

'Sorry?'

'Tea or coffee?' he asked as he left me alone in the room.

'Oh. No, I'm fine thanks,' I called out after him. 'If I'm interrupting I could always come back later?'

He appeared at the door, 'What?'

'If you're busy I could come back another time?'

'You're here to work.'

He stood in the doorway, and I don't mean to be a prude or anything but it was as if it was perfectly natural to be shirtless, tattoo-armed in your boxers in front of, hello, a hijabi. I mean, it would've been inappropriate with anyone really. I couldn't look directly at him, so kept on searching for interesting places I could focus on.

'I just didn't want to disturb you,' I said clearing my throat and putting my bag on the table.

'It's fine.'

He then walked up the stairs. Thanks to God.

Before he left, he gave me the spare keys to lock up and said I could use them when he's not there to answer the door, which is a little trusting of him. I had a snoop of his bookshelves, obviously. He had most of the classics, books on philosophy, politics (those are books I clearly need to borrow), lots of Karen Armstrong, Dalai Lama, Simone de Beauvoir (hmmm, interesting), Steve McCurry, Sabastio Salgado, Henri Cartier – photography types. Made me feel terribly uncultured that I hadn't heard of any of these names.

Such productivity. I think Naim would be very impressed with my professionalism.

Friday 13 January

11.05 a.m.

From Naim: Honey, I'm home.

Thanks to God we're both in the same country again, but what am I going to doooooooo??

10.30 p.m. NAIM CALLING!

Saturday 14 January

12 p.m. Have come a bit late to Conall's, but at least he's not here. Slept through my alarm for morning prayer. I wish missing fajr didn't form part of Naim's return. I thought it might be a little weird that we've not spoken for weeks. I began wondering whether our conversations were as funny as I remembered them to be or if it was just a figment of my stretched imagination. It *so* wasn't. Apart from when he mentioned partying most nights. Not sure how much time you get to pray when you're partying and then I realised I sounded like a boring old cow. Maybe because I *am* a boring old cow.

2 p.m. I want a fag. Is it unethical to smoke in neighbour's home?

2.10 p.m. I've just tried to unlock the door to the garden and the damn thing won't open. It's just not meant to be.

2.45 p.m. Ha! Huge window in toilet. I had to stand *on* the toilet seat to lean out of the window with my cigarette, but I can't have his house smelling of smoke. That would be rude. I kept thinking about this partying business with Naim. But then what's a relationship without a few hurdles?

3 p.m. Oh my God, my eyes keep closing involuntarily as if a small person is tugging at my eyelids. Maybe I'll have a short nap. To rejuvenate. Conall's sofa does look comfortable. His washing is drying on it, though. Bit weird touching any boxers that might be there. Maybe will just have a peek.

3.02 p.m. Only T-shirts and jumpers mostly. Surely that's fine. Few minutes will have my writerly ideas flowing.

7 p.m. Balls! A few minutes turned into three sodding hours. I was awoken by keys rattling in the door. Leaped off the sofa, whipped on my hijab and ran to sit in front of my laptop as if I'd been writing all day. Conall came in and stared at me.

'Hello,' I said as brightly as I could to disguise the fact that I felt I was having an out-of-body experience. 'I was just finishing this sentence.'

He didn't say anything. Then something felt odd on my head – not inside it, rather more around it. It felt as if my scarf had shrunk. I could see an odd bit dangling from the corner of my eye. I put my hand on my head and then caught a glimpse of my scarf draped over the arm of the sofa: *what the hell is it doing there when it's on my head*? There was a three-second window where I was perplexed at the improbability of such a thing. Then I realised; if my scarf was on the sofa, then it definitely wasn't on my head.

Conall's mouth twitched. 'I've had girls wear my T-shirt before, but never quite like that …'

Argh!! I straightened up and tried to look as dignified as a person can when they have someone's T-shirt on their head. 'It's the only place it would ever fit.'

The two short sleeves flapped at the sides. He walked over, got my scarf and handed it to me. Then he just stood there, looking at me and the stupid T-shirt. I fiddled with the scarf, thinking, *shit, what do I do?* (And also wishing I could glance in a mirror just to see how ridiculous I must look. One gets the idea, though.) Do I act worthy and ask him to turn around so I can make the switch as if I'm about to expose my bra rather than my hair (which hadn't been washed in five days – the hair, that is, not the bra), or leave the room casually, which would of course involve walking past him. The longer I thought about it, the longer the T-shirt remained on my head, which wasn't very good for my sense of self.

I'm not sure how long these thoughts lasted because the moment had drifted into uncomfortable silence when Conall cleared his throat. Just before I was about to stand up and announce that I needed the loo, he helpfully turned around to remove his coat and hang it up in the passage.

He came back into the room and I handed him his item of clothing.

'Thanks for that.' I closed my laptop, wishing he'd go into the kitchen or something. 'There's some biryani in the fridge for you, by the way.'

'Oh. Thanks.'

'Mum made it. Not me. If I made it you would not be thanking me. You'd be making your way to the hospital.'

I got up, packed my stuff away and left as fast as humanly possible.

Thursday 19 January

10 a.m. I've just sent Brammers the first *four* chapters! Not one, but *four*. Ha! I should've made some tweaks, but had to give therapy to my out-of–honeymoon-phase-worryingly-soon sister.

'I come home from work and if I don't step into the kitchen to help right away, his mum's all "Mother-in-law's cooking and daughter-in-law's resting – world has changed." And I want to say, "Yes, you fat cow, the world has changed – you didn't have to work 9–5 when you got married, did you?" '

It did send a shiver down my spine, cementing my conviction that I made the right decision not marrying HITW Imran.

'And Tahir just sits there and increases the volume of the TV, pretending he hasn't heard. He could at least tell her to calm down.'

To me, it didn't sound very different to how Tahir has always seemed. But what's a person to say?

Note for book: After a person's married they will not suddenly do things in the complete opposite way. People might change, like Zzzz Zulfi pulling his finger out and marrying Hannah, but they don't get new personalities.

I always feel so much wiser than my years.

Monday 23 January

9.50 a.m.

From: Bramley, Dorothy
To: Khan, Sofia
Subject: Chapters

I've attached with a few suggestions, can you tweak? Generally looking fine, though. Good work. Carry on, keeping my suggestions in mind, and let's show Lucinda something solid in the next month or so.

Tweak? Any excuse for Brammers to use Track Changes.

Saturday 28 January

8.30 a.m. I'm seeing Naim tomorrow. Not sure how I feel about this. On one hand I might end up jumping on him (obviously I won't, I'll settle for the halal handshake), on the other hand what does it all *mean*?

Suj believes because we're 'brown' there's no shame in bringing up the 'M' word. (Do I need to put money in the jar?) I want to climb under a rock. Times like this, a person appreciates a reliance on alcohol. Don't suppose Chachu left any behind when he went back home. Focus. Hannah (who I can now confirm is definitely a romantic), said it all makes sense – Naim has come along at the very moment I decided to be alone. It's a sign from God. 'Be brave!' she said. 'Fuck it!' said Suj. 'Where is the John Lewis catalogue?' asked Dad.

'What?' I said, being brought out of my reverie. He wanted me to distract Mum with it so he could cook without her interfering about what he should or shouldn't put in the chickpeas. I think Mum's missing Chachu – at least he kept Dad distracted. Sigh.

Sunday 29 January

12.45 p.m. The deal is that I use the key if Conall's not home, but I didn't expect him to answer the doorbell at this time in the afternoon. At least he was fully dressed.

'Top of the mornin' to ya,' I said in, might I add, an admirable Irish accent.

'You know that no one in Ireland speaks like that?'

Hmm, this was news to me. I stared at him for a moment, before he sighed and then sprinted up the stairs.

2.30 p.m. He's been pacing up and down his room for the past hour and a half, speaking to someone on the phone. Can't really hear anything. Not that it's any of my business. Obviously.

2.45 p.m. He just walked in, grabbed his coat and said he was going. Have realised that he's run out of peppermint teabags. Will get him some more, I think.

5.50 p.m. Fozia called asking if she can borrow my black suede shoes for a date she has tonight. I was too busy wondering about how to act in front of Naim. Normal? (Whatever that means.) Jaunty? Ungh – jaunty is a euphemism for bubbly, and everyone knows bubbly people are fat. When I said to Foz that I will just be myself, she said, 'Yes, OK, but maybe a little less "fuck-off" face.'

Hmph.

'But what do I say? Do I say *anything*? The person who invented *just friends* is an annoying bastard.'

'Darling, you can't say anything. Where's your pride?'

'Just behind me. Before I fell.'

'No, no. You want to wait for him to say something.'

'Hmm, yes, you're right. And I'm sure he'll say something. Because so many calls and so much of seeing him – it can't all mean nothing, can it?'

'Exactly,' she replied. 'Exactly.'

Conall,

There are peppermint teabags in the kitchen again. A person should never be without these.

S

PS There's a documentary on tonight about Helmand. BBC2 at 9 p.m.

Helmand, Kashmir. Surely it's all the same war-torn stuff.

10 p.m. When I saw Naim walking towards me, he hadn't noticed me. My nerves seemed to evaporate at the sight of him – I was about to practically *skip* up to him. He looked a bit sombre so I thought one-sided excitement might look desperate. When we sat down it *appeared* the same, but something was odd. A weird kind of heaviness I wasn't sure how to shake off.

'You missing home?' I asked.

'Not really.' He looked at me and seemed to be thinking of something. 'My friend, Haroon, asked about you by the way.'

'Oh?'

Nerves, nerves, nerves! I thought this was it; this is where the conversation begins about what *this* really is. The waiter came and put our coffees down. 'Since we're constantly saying shit on each other's Facebook.'

'What did you say?'

'I said, "That's my Daisypuffs."' *My* Daisypuffs. He was looking at me, but I couldn't for the life of me decide what kind of look it was. Scrutiny? Indifference? Affection/affliction?

'Can I have more milk (*and oxygen?*), please?' I asked the waiter.

'He said you're pretty.'

'Oh, right.' I turned the little vase on the table that had a flower in it: *must remain calm.*

He sighed and leaned back. 'Man, all my friends were like, when are you getting married?'

My heart began pumping significantly faster than usual. He looked at the table as the waiter brought more milk.

'And?'

'Aaand . . .' he said, leaning forward and moving the vase to one side. He put his hand on my knee, and I didn't have the heart or inclination to move it. I waited for more words to fill this weird silence when his phone beeped. It took a second before we both looked at the screen. There was a message from someone called Zainab. Why did that name seem familiar? I only read the first line before he snatched the phone. Something like: *Don't forget to call me early tonight . . .*

And then I remembered. Zainab is his ex-girlfriend from New York . . . And if she's his ex then why the hell was she messaging him to call her . . . early? What did she mean? What did he mean when he leaned forward and put his hand on my leg? What did he mean, driving to my house in the middle of the night in the snow? He read the message and put the phone in his jacket pocket. The moment – that window of time where my heart thumped with such anticipation I thought he might see it beating through my chest – was gone. I moved the vase back to the middle.

'Where were we?' he said.

I broke a petal off the flower.

'Will you leave that damn thing alone?'

'Marriage,' I said.

He tapped his fingers on the table, looking at me, seeming to contemplate something.

'Ever have something that's like, *perfect*. You know, not like boring or anything but pretty much all anyone could ask for?' he asked.

Why was he looking at me like that?? I kept thinking about the message, but then there was that look, and I was in the process of stilling my heart.

'I'm suspicious of perfect things,' I said.

'You're a pain in the ass.'

But I couldn't still my heart. Or my mouth it seemed.

'Yes, but just imagine spending the rest of your life with me,' I said.

For a moment he looked serious before that ever-present suggestive look in his eye emerged.

'Daisypuffs, I imagine it all the time.'

But I needed more than playful words. Something had gathered my nerves, consolidating them into a little ball, which I held in that place where our instincts apparently live.

'Why's Zainab messaging you, Naim?'

He sighed and waved his hand as if he were getting rid of an annoying fly. 'I dunno. We hooked up in New York. Talked about getting back together.'

The little ball burst inside me. I didn't quite understand. I tried to search for any conversation we'd had, which made me think we were *ever* more than friends.

'You know, Haroon asked if you and I were getting married.' He causally put two cubes of sugar in his coffee. 'And I was like, are you kidding me? Me and my Daisypuffs? We belong on a stage together, or on the road, but in a house?'

Thwack. Which strand of offence was I meant to tackle first? The idea of life with me only being imaginable if it involved a road trip or pantomime of some kind, or the fact that just a moment ago he'd leaned forward and I thought he was going to say *something*. When did it shift into *nothing*?

'We'd be a complete disaster,' he continued. 'Can you imagine?'

I shook my head.

'I don't know about Zainab,' he continued. 'I don't know what's right.' He picked up the fallen petal. 'You're the one writing a book, you tell me.'

A book full of silly stories – not a life guide. And all I was thinking about was *this* story. How with each new page was a revelation that I just didn't see coming.

'There's always Poopy Poo,' I said, my mouth dry.

'Oh, God.' He dropped the petal on the floor.

I wanted him to reply, *There's always you*. I lifted my cup in the air – *make sure your hands don't shake. Make sure you don't spill your drink – and certainly any more of your stupid heart.*

'May you both live happily ever after.'

FEBRUARY 2012

Forget You and Forget Her Too

Muslim Dating Book

~~You don't know what you're doing. You've never been here before. You wanted something different to what your parents had, but no one gave you a guide. You are undecided, caught between wanting something and knowing you might never have it. You are Generation have-it-all (that's why your parents immigrated, after all) but you just don't know how to have it all.~~

Come on, Sofe. Keep the catharsis for your diary and leave any heavy(ish) stuff to the real authors. This is a job like any other – get it done, and get on with it.

Yes, we are devout, but don't we have the same struggles as most other girls? (With the additional pressure of keeping God on side for the afterlife.) We smoke behind closed doors, don't always tell our families who we're seeing that evening, but never forget to set the alarm clock to wake up for morning prayers. We fast during Ramadan whilst working full time, we pray on our lunch breaks, go out on dates with men who we meet on the Internet and marry married men. We love our God and our city. We're confused, assertive and romantic, and most of the time don't know how we feel about skinny jeans or beardies. Faithful, flawed, trying to learn the true meaning of jihad as we teach it, we're also girls who wouldn't have it any other way.

Argh. That last line makes me want to VOM.

Thursday 2 February

11 p.m.

From Naim: Why aren't you picking up your damn phone?
To Naim: Sorry, busy. Will call you back.

In another lifetime.

If points were to go to who's the biggest fool, no guesses on who'd win. Fozia got a packet of cigarettes out and handed me one.

'Toffee, that's filth,' said Suj, looking at me as I stuck the cigarette in my mouth and lit a match.

'I'm a prick,' I said. I must be. Me and my *Oh, I'm going to be alone, I'm going to be alone* – blah blah bleugh bleugggghhh.

Hannah brought me a mug of tea and sat down. 'I married a married man. Your prickishness doesn't impress me.'

Suj opened the window, sticking her head outside. 'Han, love, if fancying someone equals prickishness, then I'm the biggest one of them all.'

That's the first thing that made me laugh all week. Fozia held out a cigarette for Suj. 'Go on,' she said. 'Trust me, it helps the pain ...'

'Yeah, until it kills you,' replied Suj.

'Oh my God,' I exclaimed. 'I turned into one of those optimistic people.'

Suj exhaled, shaking her head. 'We all do that when we like someone.'

'Did he ever mention marriage?' asked Han.

I shrugged. There was the mention of kids, but suggestions are not commitments. I looked at Fozia who, bar handing me a cigarette on demand, hadn't said much.

'He's called me eight times in the past three days and I'm running out of excuses for why I can't pick up. Why doesn't he call his bloody girlfriend?'

I showed the girls a picture of her, Zai-knob, lying in a field, hand resting on forehead as if posing for a magazine shoot.

'Oh, Toffee. He's a prick who wears a scarf in Sainsbury's and she's a prick, posing in a field – they're made for each other. This is what you do,' continued Suj, pulling her head back through the window, 'you tell him to fuck off.'

'You know my theory,' said Hannah. 'To get over someone you just have to move on to someone new. Just make sure he doesn't already have a wife.'

'Forget that, Toffee, where does he live? We'll go over there and slash his tyres.' Suj stood up and grabbed her car keys. 'Come on. Let's go. Hannah'll keep watch and, Foz, you can keep handing out those death sticks to Sofe.'

Yes, I'd like Suj to slash his sodding tyres! Why the phone calls, why the meet-ups, why the flirtations? But then every time my anger rises it's quelled by the fact that *I'm* the one who was all about it being platonic – *it's all for the book.* Pfft. Maybe Suj is right about men and women being friends – and especially when you're all Muslim. Scarcity (of Muslim men) breeds potential for emotional dependency.

I finished my cigarette and stood up.

'Fun as that sounds, can you drop me home instead?'

Note for book: On one hand not sleeping with someone saves you from increased emotional drama (which I'm still glad about to be honest – imagine how much worse I'd feel if something had happened), on the other hand, without it – without a kiss, or grabbing someone's hand, holding it as you walk down the street, you can never be sure as to what it really is. Also, if you're going to have male friends, keep it safe and make sure they're not Muslim.

Saturday 4 February

8.10 a.m. Mum came into my room and started vacuuming as if I wasn't comatose in bed.

'You have to write anyway. Waisay you say you're too busy to do housework but every evening you come home and don't get out of bed.'

'Mum, I feel ill.'

She switched the vacuum off and put both her hands on her wobbly hips.

'When I had you and Maria and your baba was at work I had hundred and two temperature. There was no central heating, it was December and your grandfather had just died. I couldn't even go to the funeral in Pakistan. Lekin I got up, washed both your clothes by hand, and started painting the walls. I'm very strong.'

I've obviously heard this story before, but sometimes I forget that beneath her ever-present need to clean and *do* something, there's an immigrant woman – full of stories about death, and washing clothes in a cold climate.

I heaved myself out of bed, kissed her on the cheek, and decided to dress myself.

8.40 a.m. There are several ways in which I could react to this situation. I could succumb to classic Bollywood grief and give way to listening to melancholy songs, re-read all his messages and use his FB profile picture as my phone's screensaver before taking my sister up on her offer to 'beat the shit out of him'. Or I could write this book. But no one did that, sitting in their home, crying over crumbling Lemon Puffs.

8.45 a.m.

> **To Fozia:** Darling, apple of my eye, sanity in my ever-so-slightly ridiculous life – time is ticking for the book and I need new inspiration … do me a favour and come speed-dating with me tonight. PLEASE.
>
> **From Fozia:** Lordy, darling. Can't. The thing is, Kam called me last night …

I didn't bother reading the rest of her message before calling her.

'Don't do it!' I exclaimed. Whatever happened to our poignant conversation on the wedding dance floor? 'Stay away. Remember

The Terminator? Kam's an indestructible knob sent to stamp on your will. *Don't let him.'*

'But what if ...?'

'Ah! Shh. Listen. I have a great plan. We'll go speed-dating, and this'll take your mind off Kam, and my mind off What's-his-face ...'

'Are you OK?'

'I'll be a lot better if you said yes to that speed-dating.'

She paused. 'OK, fine.'

I put the phone down and pushed thoughts of Naim into the less well-lit corners of my mind.

Note for book: Whatever you do, don't play heartbroken damsel to his Casanova complex.

10 a.m. I told Mum I'm going speed-dating with Fozia. Her response? 'She doesn't wear a scarf. She will grab all the men.'

Note for Book: Scarf for spirituality – excellent.
Scarf for speed-dating – apparently bad.

10.30 a.m. Conall was brushing his teeth when he answered the door. He went into the kitchen and switched the kettle on. Then he came into the living room and switched the TV on, all the while brushing away. When he'd finished, he left the toothbrush on the kitchen table top.

He sat on the floor with a drawer resting on his lap, apparently looking for something. I was thinking about Naim and began typing – a sudden bout of inspiration.

'You're stabbing at your keyboard like you're about to murder it,' he said without turning around.

'Let me ask you a question. If you call a girl every day, give her nicknames, that kind of thing, what do you *mean*? You know, from a male perspective.'

'Is this a hypothetical question?'

'Of course.'

I logged onto the Internet to check Naim's Facebook.

'Well, seems I like her company.'

Like her company? Why don't you just tell a person they're ugly and get it over with?

'That's nice,' I said.

'Are you talking about someone in particular here?'

I moved the laptop to one side and looked out of the window. The weather had cleared up and the sky was bright blue.

'Hannah said it all boils down to the fact that he can't be arsed to be woken up for fajr. Morning prayer.'

'I know what fajr is.'

'Oh.'

Conall looked outside the window too, probably wondering what I was staring at.

'Don't suppose this has anything to do with a certain someone who was outside your house Christmas Eve.'

I looked back at him.

'What does it matter, anyway?'

He stood up and put the drawer back in the cupboard. As he put his coat on, he asked what I was doing tonight. I hesitated for a moment. Not exactly the type of thing you want to shout out about, but since I doubt that Conall cares much, I told him.

'Muslim speed-dating? What's that then? Dating without any alcohol, behind a screen or something?'

'Not behind a screen, Mr Offensive. Though there won't be alcohol. For obvious reasons.'

'Why, in the name of Christ, are you going speed-dating?'

'Multi-tasking. This way my mum will think I'm serious about finding a husband, and I will find material for my book, obviously.'

'You *don't* want to find a husband?'

Had to think about this. Husband sounds so impersonal and contrived. Mission marriage. But then there is that partner-shaped hole. Or is that specifically Naim-shaped? I can't quite decide.

'Whatever really.'

'Well, it's always good to see passion.'

'I'm *fine* being alone.' I looked at Naim's FB page. Conall picked up a book and put it in his bag.

'Apathy and conviction aren't the same thing,' he said rather quietly.

Well! Aren't we Mr Philosophical.

'And you don't know what *alone*, alone really is.'

'Right, thanks.'

He said you're welcome (albeit ironically) and left. When he was out of the house I realised that he seems kind of *alone*, alone. Perhaps I should've said something nicer than 'thanks'.

5.45 p.m.

Conall,

*   I put your toothbrush back in the bathroom. Where it generally should be. You don't want to get ants and stuff.*

*   Sofia.*

10.25 p.m. Oh my actual God. Thank God Fozia's a better person than me and hasn't used the hideousness that was this evening to verbally beat me with. Turns out there were precisely two (circumstantially) nice-looking guys there who didn't in the space of three minutes put me to sleep. Although she got both their numbers, so I suppose she couldn't be too mad at me.

I live in a world where Mum is right.

11.35 p.m. Argh! Naim calling again! Do I pick up? Do I ignore it? His name flashing on my screen is giving me a headache. OK, be calm, will pick up and be casual.

Or … just ignore it until one day he gets tired of calling and goes away.

11.37 p.m. He's just left me an angry voice message. A person can (reluctantly) get used to the idea of someone not wanting to be with them. It's when that someone doesn't leave you alone, it gets a little confusing.

Does saving the message make me the type of person I'd roll my eyes at?

I don't need to call anyone to answer that question. Shame.

Sunday 5 February

11 a.m.

> *Sofe,*
> *I didn't know we got ants in the middle of winter ... And don't worry – they don't like mint.*
> *Conall.*
> *PS How was last night? Book material? Husband material? Surfacing of passion/feelings?*

I find it rather judgemental of Conall to assume I have no passion. Also, I've just Googled this and apparently mint is a good ant *deterrent*. Wish brain were its very own Google machine.

7 p.m. I am sat on my bed, crosslegged, staring at my phone with Naim's name flashing on the screen, *again*. Gone. OK, good. I wish he'd get the message.

> **From Naim:** What the hell is wrong with you? You haven't replied to my messages, you're not picking up the phone and I've called you a million times because I need to speak to you.

Oh dear.

7.25 p.m. So this is how the conversation went.

'Hello.'

'Oh, yeah, *hello*. Where the hell have you been?'

'Here.'

'Are you fucking Houdini?'

'Nice language by the way.' I mean, who the hell is *he* to speak to me like that? 'What did you need to talk about?'

Pause.

'Do you realise we haven't spoken properly for over a week?'

'Doesn't time fly when you're left in peace?'

More silence.

'OK, I don't know if you're on the rag or what your problem is but maybe you wanna have a conversation when you're over it.'

'Sounds reasonable to me.' Silence again. 'Well, bye then.'

Pause.

'Yeah. Bye.'

Note for book: The best way to get rid of a person is to act as if you don't give a shit. The person you're trying to get rid of will believe it and, one day, you will too.

Monday 6 February

9 a.m. What is the purpose of Poetry on the Tube? No one wants sentiment when someone's armpit is shoved in your face.

10.30 a.m. Here's the thing: why is it that the minute some-one decides to be alone, a person comes along and scuppers it? I was being sage-like. I *am* sage-like. Actually, I'm more rage-like. I was la-la-la-la-la-la-la, and then *bam!* Someone picks up a packet of my Lemon Puffs. And then Brammers piped up, interrupting my mental rage, at the end of the catch-up meeting.

'Can everyone make sure they put the date in their diary.' She looked at Katie, '9th March, Katie. Why don't you write it down now?'

'What's going on?' I asked as we walked back to our desks.

'School photo, Sweetu – for winning Publisher of the Year Award.'

'Oh.' Katie stopped at my desk as I looked for my chair, which for some reason had gone walkabouts. 'Where the hell is it?' I asked.

Katie looked behind her and stole Tasha's chair from Marketing.

'Don't worry. She won't notice.'

'I want *my* chair. Why can't people leave things where they are?' Katie began rolling the chair back to its original place.

'Shall we get a muffin?' she said.

'I don't want a muffin, I want my chair. Actually, I want to eat a muffin whilst sitting on my chair. Not Lemon Puffs. Muffins.'

Katie walked me out of the office towards the canteen while I explained exactly why it's essential that things remain where you leave them.

Saturday 11 February

11 a.m. I called Fozia to remind her that we have a 'Muslim professional networking event' (which we all know is just code for scouting for single people) to go to tonight. She reminded me about the creep at speed-dating who kept stroking our hands. Ugh. Also, I think he straightened his hair. When she asked if we could get a refund for tonight's event, I told her we most definitely couldn't – even though I hadn't yet paid. She'll be glad when she ends up meeting someone, and can thank me for it later.

Maria had come over for the day and she looked at me as I told Foz this ever-so-slight white lie.

'I know,' I said to Maars. 'Don't judge me. It's for her own good.'

She laughed. 'No. Good. She needs to get over that stupid Kam guy and you … Well I'm just glad you're getting on with things.'

12.10 a.m. OMG, I cannot believe it. The event took place in a church (ha!). The organiser gave a speech so everyone huddled towards the altar. I stood there, eyeing the buffet, which was a lot more attractive than anything else in the church – man-wise that is. My eyes began to wander around the room. Looked to my left and the side profile of someone seemed familiar. He had a slightly hooked nose, a mop of black hair and his arms were folded as he kept on shifting his feet. Then he turned my way and oh my *actual* God, it was hole-in-the-wall Imran!

I turned my back to him and tugged at Fozia's red dress.

'*Imran's* here.'

She looked at me, confused, and then realisation began to dawn.

'No!'

'Over there.'

She peered over my shoulder and grabbed my arm.

'Shall I go ask if he still has a hole-in-the-wall?'

'What is he doing here? Why isn't he married?' I said.

I wondered if I should say hello, but Fozia said I should wait for him. (Why should women always wait for '*him*'?) But I did wait. Then I waited some more. It was when I was speaking to someone who asked when the buffet would be served (because I looked like the waitressing staff?) that he approached us, answered her, looked at me, and then walked away. Looked *right* at me. Then walked away. Unbelievable! As if I wasn't the girl he once wanted to marry. What is wrong with the world? There's the man who apparently wanted to marry me, who ignores me, and there's the other man who doesn't want to marry me, but calls me all the time.

Sunday 12 February

5 p.m. I went out for a walk and it was all red roses and heart-shaped balloons in preparation for the fourteenth. People skipping around, carrying poxy teddy bears.

'Is it me or is anyone who takes Valentine's Day seriously a bit of a knob?' I said, walking through Conall's door. Before he answered, I carried on. 'I mean, last Valentine's Day I was seeing

Imran and I felt the same about it then as I do now, so it's not anything to do with being single.'

'I think you're right.' My respect for Conall has grown as a result of this.

'Same with fireworks really,' I said.

'You don't like fireworks?'

'Oh, they're all nice and pretty when they're being launched into the air, but what about all the mess they make?' Conall looked at the table that I'd strewn with books and papers before looking back at me. OK, so I make a bit of a mess now and again.

'Well, I don't, you know … *blow* smoke.'

'Not much.'

Hmph.

Monday 13 February

7 a.m. I told Suj and Hannah about Imran ignoring me at the event. Hannah seems to think it's because I broke his heart, so I had to remind her that he was the one who wanted to live in his weird communal family system. Suj called him a prick. I don't think him ignoring me warranted calling him a prick, but then Suj is defensive like that. I believe it's called bias.

Love Suj.

Sunday 19 February

8 p.m. I managed to get to Conall's early, so he was at home, making breakfast. He came and sat at the dining table and brought me a mug of coffee. I looked into it.

'What?' he said.

'I kind of feel like tea.'

He sighed and took my mug, giving me his instead.

'Does it have sugar in it?' I asked.

'No, your highness. Would you like me to get some for you?'

'Yes please,' I said, smiling, reaching out with mug in hand.

'Get off your arse and get it yourself.'

'I'll just have the coffee.' I swapped the mugs.

He opened his laptop. Guess he wasn't in the mood for a chat. I stared at my computer screen. Stories, stories, stories.

After a while I looked up and he was focused on editing photos. I think he noticed me staring into space.

'What's up, Sofe?'

I shook my head and he went back to what he was doing.

'I'm just a little stuck, story-wise. I mean, I *have* stories. I'm just not quite sure how it all fits together.'

I swear I could've said I'm not wearing knickers and he wouldn't have looked up. Fair enough.

'I just don't think I have the tone quite right.'

'Have you tried interviewing your parents?'

He said it so quietly I wasn't sure whether he was speaking to me, or mumbling something to himself.

'What would they know about Muslim dating?' I mean, really.

He looked up. 'You're *not* going to interview them?'

Seems I'd missed something here.

'The people that gave birth to you, and probably your ideas?' he added.

'My ideas are all my own, thank you.'

Conall looked a little incredulous. Maybe he had a point. But then that'd require telling them what I'm writing about and, to be honest, I'd rather wait until it's finished before I break it to them.

'Well, I wouldn't mind reading it if you want an opinion,' he said.

'Read it?'

He nodded. 'Sure.'

'About Muslim dating?'

'I'm intrigued. Tell me about it.'

I mean, he doesn't need to know my life story, but there was no harm in telling him about HITW Imran.

'Does he have to be Muslim?' he asked.

'Of course. Unless someone wants to be kicked out of bed before the crack of dawn for morning prayers. And dragged to Mecca at some point in their life for Hajj. Also, who would want to fast at least a month out of the year unless they were Muslim? And . . . it hardly makes sense to marry someone with whom I can't share what's essentially the main part of my life.' I pointed at my scarf.

He took a deep breath and nodded.

'And the last thing I want is to deal with another person in the world that has a problem with my hijab. I mean, I love this thing, but not every one feels the same way, I'm afraid.'

'Well, sure. Makes sense.'

Yes, thanks, Conall. Sometimes fake solidarity is all a person wants.

'Did you love him? This hole-in-the-wall guy?' he asked.

We're too old to talk about *love*. I shrugged. 'All I know is no one in their right mind lives with a hole-in-the-wall.'

'Sure,' he said picking up his mug, his gaze fixed on the keyboard. 'But no one in love's in their right mind.'

I leaned over and moved his laptop to one side.

'Conall. Are you secretly sentimental?' I said, smiling at him. It was kind of funny – the sentimental man with the tattoos.

He moved the laptop back, but I shifted it to the side again.

'You just never struck me as the type, that's all. I'm surprised.'

He stood up, rested his hands on the edge of the table and leaned over. He can be a little scary – his expression gives nothing away sometimes. I wasn't sure if I'd pissed him off.

'Don't worry. Your secret's safe with me,' I added. 'No need to have a face like thunder. It's not very friendly, you know.'

'But it works wonders.' He is an odd one. Just as I opened up a new tab on my computer, he turned around and said, 'I suggest you get typing, Sofe.'

As if I was about to do anything else. Well, OK, fine – I closed the Facebook tab, and I got typing.

Now I must go home and somehow sneakily interview my parents. What a dedicated researcher I am.

MARCH 2012

Love Thy Parents. Sigh.

Me: Baba, how old were you when you and Mum got married?

Baba: Twenty-eight.

Mum: Nahin, you were twenty-seven.

Baba: Oh, nahin, Mehnaz. I was twenty-eight.

Mum: Le. You were twenty—

Me: Doesn't matter. Was it weird not knowing each other and then, you know, suddenly sharing ... life?

Baba: Beta, this is how it happened then. Doing what you people do now would have been strange for us.

Mum: Hai, weird ke weird? (Pause.) Just think. One day I am with my family, and then one day I am with a strange man.

Baba: But, Mehnaz, this is how it happened.

Mum: Haan, I know.

(Silence.)

(Baba sighs.)

Baba: Acha, I'm going to sleep now.

(He leaves the room.)

Mum: (Lowers her voice.) Now he's gone, I tell you. So weird it was that I spent week before the wedding crying to my parents that I don't want to get married.

Me: Mum ...

Mum: Then we get married and there is wedding shoon shaan. Everyone enjoying and I am crying because I am leaving my family and going London. Hai. What is London? My sisters and me used to play on the street and look up at planes when we were children, and I used to think, 'Oh, Allah, I want to go on plane.' But time came and I said, 'Oh, Allah, I want to never get on plane.' (Long pause.) Before barat your grandmother came into my room. She grabbed me, like this, hard. And shook me. I remember her red shalwar kameez, her black hair in *a thick plait, kajol bringing out her big almond eyes. You have her eyes. Lekin, you are darker than her nah.*

Me: *Yes, Mum.*

Mum: *People always said how beautiful she was. She said, 'Mehnaz, sambhlo.' (Pause.) 'You are scared. You will be scared for many months in your marriage. Maybe you will be scared for ever.' (Pause.) 'Lekin, never show him. When people know you are scared, they make it your weakness. Don't be weak.' (Pause.) She had tears in her eyes and then she hugged me very hard and said, 'This is a new life.' (Mum sniffs.) 'And when you get on that plane, make it yours.'*

Thursday 1 March

10.30 p.m. I came home and Mum and Dad were sitting watching Geo News. I plopped myself on the sofa when they told me that one of Auntie Reena's friend's blah blah blah called with a *rishta*. Pfft, I know their idea of a *suitable match*, so I think they were surprised that I didn't roll my eyes, or tell them I'm busy washing my hijab. I was rather surprised myself.

'Tell Auntie to tell him to email me.'

Dad looked at me over his glasses.

'Haan. I said that but she said I should call his mother first,' replied Mum, adjusting the coaster on the coffee table.

'It's one of those,' I said, looking at Mum. I've thought all day about the story she told me about marrying my dad. 'OK. Tell them to call.'

Mum and Dad exchanged a look that only two parents who aren't sure what's got into their daughter can exchange.

Monday 5 March

9.05 a.m.

From: Bramley, Dorothy
To: Khan, Sofia
Subject: Book

It's been a good six weeks since I last saw those chapters. How much more have you completed? Can you give me a date for delivery of those? I want to send something to Lucinda in the next few weeks.

Honestly, thanks to God for Conall, otherwise Brammers would have given me a hernia.

Friday 9 March

11 a.m. Argh! Katie and I both forgot it's school photo day!!

12.20 p.m. Phew. Made it just in time. Have to say, it was a rather proud moment. Not that any of *my* campaigns contributed to the award, but efforts are collective and there's much to be said for teamwork. I just wish Katie wasn't pointing at the sky and that I wasn't adjusting my scarf when the camera flashed. Oops.

7.55 p.m. Kept looking at my phone, wondering if Naim would call. It's just as well he didn't, otherwise I might've caved and answered just to tell him about the school photo faux pas. He loves a faux pas. Perhaps because he *is* one.

Saturday 10 March

6.30 p.m.

> **From Hannah:** I've taken yet another pregnancy test. No luck. Let's meet soon. I could do with some good news if you can muster it.

8.05 p.m. Came home and Maria was there. I asked where her husband was and she snorted.

'Probably sitting at home, watching Zee TV with his *mum*.'

Oh dear. Our own mum was upstairs getting ready to go to the cinema with her friends and Dad was sitting in the conservatory having a cigarette. I sat down and took the bag of crisps she was eating.

'She had the nerve to say I'd already been to my parents' during the week. Why did I have to go again today?' She flicked through the channels until she got to Zee TV. 'Can I give you one piece of advice, Sofe?'

'What?'

'Never live with the in-laws.'

'Well, already dodged that specific bullet.'

She rested her hand on her stomach. 'You did. My brave little sister.'

I nodded as if I'd given up happiness on a principle. *No one in love is in their right mind.* Hating the in-laws must agree with her – she did look incredibly fresh.

'When do you think you'll be up the duff then?' I asked.

She looked at me and smiled, rubbing her stomach.

'Shut your face!'

I flung myself on her. Mum walked through the door, diamanté earrings sparkling in the light, and sniffed.

'Keep smoking! When you die and leave me insurance money I'll be able to get the kitchen re-done.' She looked at Maria. 'Start drinking lots of coconut milk – Auntie Reena tells me that makes baby very fair – I don't want a dark, dark baby.'

10 p.m. Really wanted to tell Hannah about imminence of becoming an auntie, but she sounded so deflated I thought it best to wait. On top of which Zulfi was with his other family.

10.30 p.m.

From Fozia: There's an all-day dating event and I think we should go.

To Fozia: Listen, I know you're all about the dating scene now (you can thank me whenever you want), but I'm going to sit this one out until I hear that Imran's married. There's only so much rejection a person can take in the space of a few weeks.

Sunday 11 March

10.30 a.m. What's with all the censorship? All I said was something about the all-day dating event being full of annoying Pakis and Conall went into one.

'It's a vile word,' he said, slamming books into place.

'All right, PC Police.'

He charged into the kitchen, banging cupboards and dropping cutlery into the sink.

'Next thing, some arse will think, *she says it so it's OK for me to say it*, everyone will laugh and then what? We all start? With that, and ni— Ah! filthy.'

'I would *never* use the "n" word,' I retorted.

He marched back into the passage, saucepan in hand, and stood in the doorway.

'It's everything that's wrong with the world.'

'I'm what's wrong with the world?'

'Whatever happened to moderation, Sofe? You,' he pointed the saucepan at me, 'you, should know fu— . . . know better.'

You can't do a thing right, sometimes.

'It was just a joke. God, lighten up.'

Of course, it struck me as being not a little bit funny that whitie was accusing me, *brown* hijabi, of being a racist. What's a person to do but laugh?

'Very grown up, Sofe,' he said, walking back into the kitchen. 'I'm surprised your parents haven't married you off already. Got rid of you,' he shouted over all the noise he was making. 'Shouldn't you have five children to teach your values to?'

'Now who's being un-PC with their stereotypes, hmm?'

Ha, didn't have much to say to that, did he?

'Anyway, What can I do?' I said. 'No one wants to marry me.'

I looked at Naim's Daisy message for about the hundredth time.

'No one?' he said.

It'd gone quiet.

'Not one person.'

He came into the room wearing bright yellow rubber gloves.

'What do you want, then? Tea or coffee?'

Wednesday 14 March

8.30 p.m. Perhaps parents setting you up isn't a bad idea. Perhaps this time Auntie Reena's friend's cousin got it right. After Mum called Beardie's mum (he's a beardie!), my praying five times a day and hijab-wearing impressed them, and so she said Beardie would call me. And call me he did.

I've learned not to waste my time speaking to men on the phone for more than half an hour, so after thirty minutes I said I had to go. You see; we live, we learn.

Thursday 15 March

10 p.m. Beardie called me today, and it was a bit of a yawn to have to speak *again*. The thing about beardies is that they always make you feel *bad*. Like you're not religious enough because you don't fast or pray enough. This one fasts every Monday and Thursday. I wanted to say that I did too when I was on the 5:2 diet last year, but it's not quite the same thing. Obviously.

'I just love East London ...' he said.

Had a fleeting thought of Imran and how much I do *not* like East London.

'It makes me really angry,' he continued, 'when our people start berating the country we live in. We should remember that we're guests here and so need to abide by their rules.'

Guest? *Guest?* Er, thanks but being a *guest* would leave me without a country. If that's what you think you are, then time to pack your cases, my friend. I mean, obviously I concurred with him about how great London is, but if he wants to give a lecture about it, then that's what Speaker's Corner is for. *You* might be a guest. I am home.

'... Muslims aren't so lucky elsewhere ...' and then I heard a double beep, and who could it be, other than Naim? Bloody, bloody hell. I watched the screen. It flashed, and flashed, until finally he hung up. Am I not being mean enough or is he just relentless? Was our last conversation not the very essence of 'piss off'? Beardie was still speaking, though God knows about what.

'Hello?' he said.

'Hi.'

'I mean, just look at Turkey and Tunisia – women can't even wear a scarf in the workplace.'

I paused, and looked at my screen once more. 'Hmm, yes. Some things just don't make sense.'

Saturday 17 March

9.20 a.m.

> **To Fozia**: May the force be with you today.
> **From Fozia:** Sod that for a laugh. I've got cigarettes.

Apart from the potential for lung cancer, the rest of Fozia's dating rampage is a very healthy state of affairs.

10.45 a.m. Oh my actual God. I've been ambushed! I was about to go to Conall's, and Dad was sitting on the sofa, polishing his shoes.

'They're coming at three o'clock, haina?' he said.

'Who?' I asked.

Mum came scampering from the kitchen, because the polish was going all over her new Persian rug, and looked at me.

'Hai hai, make sure you come back early to change,' she said.

'Change for what?'

I had to wait several seconds while Mum picked up pieces of polish off the floor.

'Change for what?' I repeated.

Dad was pretending to hit her over the head with the shoe.

'People, I have a book to write. Can someone answer my question?'

'O-ho, the rishta boy you're talking to,' said Mum.

WTF.

'What, the beardie?'

'Haan. Who else?'

'Soffoo, no need to make that face,' said Dad.

WTH?? So Beardie called yesterday and he suggested we meet, and I said, *yeah, great, coffee.* But he intervened. 'Oh no, if you're going to do something, you should do it properly. With the families.' Excuse me? That's fine for you, but I'd rather not meet someone for the first time as a potential conglomerate.

'No one believes in the sanctity of families any more.' Blah, blah, bleugh. I thought: *if you think I'm going to sit around and serve chai and samosas to a bunch of muppets, you've got another think coming.* Apparently *I've* got another think coming. Perhaps a clearer 'no' on the phone would've prevented this eventuality, because now the extras have gone ahead and started making all the decisions.

Dad put his hand out as if to tell me to calm down. 'O-ho, Soffoo, what is one cup of chai?'

'Oh my God, my parents are forcing me into marriage.'

At which Mum snorted a little too loudly.

11.30 a.m. 'I'm just saying if, somehow, mysteriously I go missing then I've probably been gagged and shipped off to Pakistan.'

Conall was sitting on the sofa, reading the paper as I put my laptop on the table. He didn't look up.

'It would take an army to gag you.'

'And I wouldn't be surprised if they had one ready,' I replied. Honestly, Conall can be so *rude* sometimes. 'I think I'm going to hide my passport.'

I heard this weird stop/start kind of noise – looked over and Conall was laughing, shaking his head. Well, at least he laughed. I went and sat on the sofa.

'Anything interesting happening in the world?' I asked. 'Or is it all, doom, doom, doom?'

'All doom.'

'Don't bother telling me then.'

'I don't know what you've heard, but ignorance isn't bliss.'

Isn't life depressing enough? It feels like gloom is layered with gloom with a bit of doom for filling. There's a reason the two words rhyme. It will be lifted. It *must* be lifted. I just have to carry on praying.

'Forget that. Tell me, when they come over, should I pretend to have a speech impediment?'

Conall sighed.

'Lazy eye?' I added.

'How can you pretend to do that?'

'Easy. Look.' I demonstrated this rather useless talent. Well, useless until *now*.

'*How* do you do that?' He leaned in closer to inspect this phenomenon. Hadn't noticed that he has flecks of grey in his blue eyes. Began to think I should've kept my useless talent to myself.

'Anyway,' I said, adjusting my eyes, 'I'll think of something.'

He leaned back and opened out his hands. 'Like be an adult and say you're not interested?'

I pat him on the arm. 'Let's just call that Plan B.'

Note for book: Write a list of how to put off potential husbands. Include anything, even if it is to the detriment of your dignity. Better to be undignified for a few moments, than undignified for a lifetime.

7.30 p.m. Suffice to say, I'm never doing that again. No one likes an awkward silence, but then no one likes entertaining *forced* marriages.

The beardie walked in behind his parents, and I was sitting twiddling my thumbs, wanting to throw my phone at someone, namely him when he came into my line of vision. I rather like a beard – a nice neat one, bit of stubble etc. – but there is something about a beardie who walks in, eyes lowered to the floor, that quite frankly makes me feel contrary.

The mother sat down, looking around the room.

'You have a lovely home, Masha'Allah.'

Mum smiled her faux modest smile, then Beardie's mum looked at me and said, 'Beti must help to keep it looking so nice.'

Ha! Mum looked at me and tried not to laugh.

'Oh you know today's girls. Becharis, they work all week – where can they have the time?' said Mum.

'But for the home you must make time, haina?' said the beardie's mum. Beardie was still looking at the floor. I wanted to go and peer up at him and say, *well, this is a fine situation you suggested*.

Then the conversation went on to boring details like what the beardie does – something about business – surprise, surprise.

'Beti, what do you do?' asked the dad, who by the way seemed to be having a mid-life crisis with leather jacket, pointy shoes and more gel in his hair than his son.

'I work in book publicity.'

'Book publicity?'

'Yes.'

'Ah. Book *publicity*,' he repeated.

I nodded. He frowned. 'And what is that?' He looked around the room as if everyone required an explanation. So I explained the daily routine of a publicist.

'Today's children, haina? There are all kinds of jobs people do,' said his dad.

'Haan, I think best job for girl is taw teaching,' his mum added. 'So many holidays, and good when you have your own family. Wouldn't you like to teach, Beta?'

She looked at me expectantly.

My dad threw up his hands and leaned forward. 'Oh this is so common, teaching sheaching.'

Mum followed on from this with, 'Sofia used to help the students in university sometimes.' She laughed. 'She said, "I'm never going to be a teacher!"'

Cue dissatisfied silence. Happily, Mum was able to break this with promises of chai and nibbles. The dad, mum and beardie looked at me as Mum went into the kitchen. Dad had already picked up the remote and said we should all see what's going on in the world, so switched the news on. I looked – pointedly, might I add – at the TV.

When the clatter of the tea arrived, I gratuitously stood up to hand the plates around. I gave one to the beardie and he looked at me for as long as I stood there handing him pakoras. Well! What's wrong with the oh-so-fascinating ground now?

I sat back down when his mum asked, 'Do you like doing housework?'

Was this a trick question?

'I don't think anyone likes housework,' I replied.

She laughed and her husband also chuckled, saying, 'Very good, very good.' I don't remember that being a joke.

'Did you help your mama makes these pakoras?' she asked.

'No.'

Her husband leaned forward, in apparent good humour and asked, 'What did you make? Tell us, don't worry, we will think all is delicious.' He glanced furtively at my dad, who'd furrowed his eyebrows.

I smiled, in the sweetest of manners, and replied, 'Nothing.'

'Too busy, haina? But you do cook?' the mum asked.

'No.' Then I thought of tea and Lemon Puffs. 'I make tea for people sometimes. But it's not very good.'

Mum flashed me a look and then, as if bitten by something, the beardie shot up off his seat. 'I need to pray – where is the kaa'ba?'

Dad stood up to show him to the other room, but the beardie looked at his parents.

'Oh, Beta, you pray. We will pray later,' said the dad, raising his hand in the air, as if to say, God's not going anywhere.

Mum handed tea to the mum, and the dad continued, 'Nowadays children do all this praying.' He laughed, although I'm not quite sure what was so funny.

'This is not a bad thing,' said Dad, looking at beardie's dad's shoes.

'Our son is always telling us what we are doing wrong,' said the mum.

Mum looked at her. 'Acha, he isn't a fundamentalist nah?'

Beardie's mum's teacup halted mid-air. 'No, no!' For a moment I felt sorry for them. After all, I know what it feels like when people make assumptions based on the spectrum of your religiosity. Mum put chutney in her plate, took a pakora and before putting it in her mouth said, 'Because we are not extremists.' Argh!

Note for book: Don't suggest someone's an extremist just because they like praying on time.

'We taw are normal.' She was then distracted by a piece of dirt on the floor, which she picked up and put in the bin.

'No, no,' said Mum after they'd left. 'So much religious is not good.'

'As if I'd let my beti marry someone whose father wears such pointy shoes, anyway,' added Dad.

Seems I am not the only fussy one.

7.45 p.m. 'What a waste of time that all-day event was.' Fozia came over and was lying on my bed. I had the urge to pour the drink I was holding over her.

'I would've traded,' I replied.

'That would've been interesting,' she said with a weird kind of smile. She sat up and took the drink. 'Are your parents arguing downstairs?'

'No.' I sat down and asked whether it was a room full of 'dat' people.

'Mostly.'

'Who started this ugly mutation of the English language?'

Fozia sighed and shook her head. 'Not a lot out there.'

'Who cares? Rather spend a lifetime alone than having to give elocution lessons.'

'Beardie a no-go then?'

'No, I think I sufficiently put them off. This is why people think I'm a snob.' I took her drink and finished the juice. Fozia put her arm around me. 'No, darling. You're just misunderstood.'

Love Fozia.

Sunday 18 March

9.55 a.m. It's been twenty minutes since I've been tapping on my laptop, and not once has Conall asked me about yesterday. Instead he's been running up and down the stairs, looking for something. How does he know I'm not getting shipped off to Pakistan and sold into a family who'll have me shackled to the kitchen, making chicken korma for the rest of my life?

10.20 a.m. He came into the room and was chucking back books, looking under newspapers and grunting.

'What are you looking for?' I asked. He ignored me, and carried on throwing things around. 'Tell me and I'll help you find it.'

'Phone number.'

'The one you were writing down yesterday?'

He looked up. 'Yes.'

'You put it in the first drawer in the kitchen.'

He looked at me as he walked out and emerged a minute later. 'How did you know?'

'You took the number down and then the kettle boiled so you went into the kitchen. I came in after you, because I didn't know if I wanted coffee or tea and you put it in the drawer.'

'Right. Thanks.' He fed the number into his phone.

'Important?'

He nodded.

'Well, now that's out of the way you can hear about my near-miss with the forced marriage yesterday.'

'You know there are people who are *actually* being forced into marriage?'

253

'Yes, I was almost one of them.'

He shook his head and saw the bookmarks I'd left on the table. I told him he should use those instead of creasing the pages of his book.

'Oh, thanks.'

'No worries. Anyway, listen.'

By the time I got to the point where Mum asked whether the beardie was a fundo, Conall was in full-fledged laughter mode.

'She *is* gas.'

'Yes. Lethal.'

4.05 p.m.

To: Khan, Sofia
From: Haque, Imran
Subject: Meeting

Hi Sofe, how are u? It was weird seeing each other at that event. Weird that we didnt speak. I mean, how could we be in the same room and not talk? Don't know if you wanted to ignore me, but I thought I'll be a better person and just email you.

It'd be good to meet for coffee, if you're free? Unless you're already married ... xx

OMG. What does this mean?? Is it a sign from God? If it is, then a sign for what exactly? Annoying thing is, as I looked at the email, I couldn't help thinking of Naim. And also how for a lawyer, Imran's grammar is pretty shoddy.

7 p.m. Meeting Imran in my current state is like proving that he was right, that I'd not find anyone who wouldn't want me to live with the in-laws. Smug bastard. Mind you, Naim doesn't want his wife to live with her in-laws. But then Naim doesn't want me to be his wife.

Told Fozia that Imran emailed me. It took her a moment before she said, 'Oh. Right. What did he say?'

Perhaps yesterday's event has zapped her energy. She thinks I should email him back because apparently it's not as if they're queueing at the door. Yes, thank you for reminding me. I need Hannah's anthropological take, but she is in the midst of having her ovaries tested so has better things to worry about, and Suj's phone isn't working abroad. When I phoned to ask Maria she took a few moments before she slammed a door shut.

'Can't even talk in this bloody house,' she said. 'Oh, Sofe. Stop making all these men your friends and marry one of them already ...'

9.25 p.m.

From: Khan, Sofia
To: Haque, Imran
Subject Re: Meeting

Hello, how are you? Not married quite yet. Would be good to see you. I'm free most of next week – let me know what suits.

There, that's fairly nonchalant and cool.

9.28 p.m.

> **From: Haque, Imran**
> **To: Khan, Sofia**
> **Subject: Monday?**
>
> Great! Hows Monday? We can meet in Charlotte Street. Remember that restaurant we went to last time? Lets go there again. xxx

What restaurant? I'll ignore the lack of apostrophes in email and be thankful that he is not a 'dat' man. Plus, there's no harm in having an amicable catch-up with someone you thought you might marry at one point.

Note for book: Remind yourself of that time where you had hands in prayer, asking for reasons as to why your potential husband was obsessed with living with his family post-marriage, because whatever the failings of your latest (non-)relationship, it's handy to know that you can wash, rinse, repeat – as needed.

Monday 19 March

8.26 a.m.

> **From Hannah:** Give me news that doesn't involve ovaries or babies, please.

8.28 a.m.

To Hannah: Since you ask – I'm seeing Imran on Thursday.

9.04 a.m. 'Do you think he wants to get back together? Is he still single?'

'Of course he doesn't, and I don't know.'

'Interesting.' Hannah paused. 'What if he turns around and says he'll move out?'

'The problem is, of course, that you can take the boy out of the hole-in-the wall ...'

'The only hole-in-the-wall should be a cash machine. Although, you can see how it goes and if one day you decide you don't care any more, you can marry him.'

'I will *always* care about the hole-in-the-wall.'

'Even when you're thirty-five and a virgin?'

Hannah is so grim sometimes. But she really does think ahead.

Note for book: Stop living day to day and think about the future?

10 a.m. We've all been given a copy of the school photo. Katie and I have just spent fifteen minutes laughing. We look like we're pointing to high heaven – as if we've seen God himself.

10.20 a.m. Have just emailed the tweaked chapters and an additional three to Lucinda, copying in Brammers. What if she thinks they're crap? What if they no longer want to publish it because I can't actually write??

2 p.m. Trumpet and Lucinda were admiring the school photo that's been put up on the wall. I was walking out of the kitchen with tea when I heard him say, 'Look at that. A black person, a gay person *and* a Muslim. We really are diverse.' Hahaha. Had to run and tell Katie. Trumpet really does come up trumps sometimes.

10 p.m. The good thing about not fancying someone any more is you don't end up doing things like missing your mouth, or spilling coffee. My brain and body movements were in perfect harmony when I saw Imran. The only time I felt slightly disconcerted was when he got up and looked as if he was about to hug me, but then seemed to think better of it. To be honest, it was nice not to have to talk about the disaster-dating scene, sperm counts and racial conflicts.

'How've you been?' he asked.

'You know, you could've asked me this at the event.'

He looked at the table. 'Sorry, it was just weird seeing you and I...'

'Oh, forget it. I'm joking. It's fine.'

He seemed relieved.

'You still look the same,' he said.

I had a feeling it'd be awkward seeing him again; that we'd both stumble over sentences, have awkward silences, but it was just so *friendly*.

'Well, you only saw me last month,' I said.

'You know what I mean.' He paused. 'It feels longer, doesn't it? Since we were last here?'

I thought of Naim and all that's happened in between.

'It really does.'

We've decided to be friends. He told me about some Parveen girl who he'd been seeing for a while, but that it didn't work out. Couldn't quite bring myself to mention Naim.

I'd told Mum I was seeing Imran, and she was more excited at the prospect of turning my room into some kind of beauty parlour if I married him than anything else. When she asked how the evening went, I didn't tell her it ended in friendship. This way she'll get off my case about meeting someone as she probably thinks I'll end up marrying Imran, and when the time comes to tell her that I'm not marrying him, I'll just say that it turns out his parents are shipping him off to Paksitan to get married. Excellent.

Friday 23 March

9.30 a.m. Argh! Lucinda wants to see me in her office re draft chapters. Bollocks.

10 a.m. A stack of manuscripts blocked the entrance to Lucinda's office door – a literary fence, about two feet high. I had to stand over them, as if poised to do a star-jump. Stupid tight jeans.

'This way only people who have a serious thing to discuss can come in,' she said, looking for something in her drawer. She took out a Toffee Crisp and unwrapped it, gesturing for me to take a seat as she ate a chunk.

'I like that colour scarf on you,' she mumbled through the gooey mix of chocolate and crispies.

'Oh, thanks.' I adjusted the ruching of the scarf. Before I knew it she'd stood up, leaned over, and had my head in her hands.

'How do you pin it all?' she asked, moving my head side to side as I looked at her plump, pink face. 'Would you ... would you mind showing me?'

The thing is, when you're the circus freak, sometimes you have to give the crowd what they want. So I unwrapped my hijab and then she asked if she could see my hair.

'Erm. Sure.'

I took my hair out and she gazed at me.

'Wow! It's so beautiful.' She took a handful of it and looked at it closely. 'It's so thick!'

You're *so close*. It was embarrassing – I felt like a show pony. I explained that Pakistanis generally have good hair.

'Aren't you beautiful?' Which sounded like more of an accusation than compliment.

'Oh, erm, thanks.'

She sat back down and picked her Toffee Crisp up, watching as I put my scarf back on in haphazard manner (no mirror).

'So, this book,' she said, taking a bite that filled out her cheeks. 'Dorothy and I've discussed it. Fascinating subject. Fun. Unusual the way it came about but, on the whole, it's worked out well, hasn't it?' She handed over the chapters with red lines and writing drawn all over the pages. 'Have a look at my notes.'

She rummaged around her drawer and took out another Toffee Crisp.

Does this really happen? How do these people feel? were amongst some of the comments scratched over the paper. Sentences were crossed out and words underlined. Is this what you call something that's 'worked out well'?

'Let me know what you think,' she said, throwing the wrapper in the bin. 'But I think we're OK for you to carry on without showing us any more until the first draft is due.'

'OK' I stared at the pages, realising that this would probably just be a one-book deal. It didn't occur to me I might've wanted more. I lifted myself and my disappointment off the chair and smiled. I was in star-jump position, about to leave, when Lucinda said, 'I like you, Sofia.' She patted around in her drawer. 'This is going to be good.'

Good? I suppose a person should trust a senior editor. I just can't see how.

Saturday 24 March

12.45 p.m. 'Ugh. I just about managed to escape the manicured clutches of Auntie Reena,' I said to Suj on the phone. ' "What are you looking for, Beta? You shouldn't be so fussy nah. No one is perfect." No one's normal, more like. As if they know what it's like.'

'Please. They know jack.'

'They were told who to marry and just got on with it. Now it's all, "You're too religious; you're not religious enough. Why aren't you taller? Thinner? Too educated. Not educated enough. Too loud, too quiet. Too Muslim. Too *westernised.*" That's my favourite, really. Well, where do you live then, mate? Sodding Saudi?'

I wonder which of the above Naim thought was a problem. Too religious, probably. Sigh.

'The next time an auntie asks me, "What are you looking for?" I'm going to say, "I'm looking for a man who I can sit next to and watch a film with, whose pants I can just put my hands down."'

Then the stairs creaked. As did my heart – before it plummeted to my feet. I hung up the phone as I saw Conall walk down the stairs. Of all the things I could've inherited from my parents, why did a Punjabber voice have to be it?

He came into the room, his mouth clamped together as he looked at me. I, on the other hand, began to find the flooring incredibly mesmerising.

'I did ring the doorbell, but no one answered.'

'I was in the shower.'

I prayed please, God, if you are beneficent, please let him not have heard that my criteria for a husband is wanting to put my hands down his pants. It's obviously not the *only* criteria. I mean fine, it's in the top five, but why should he have only heard that one? He went into the kitchen, made his coffee and came in ready with his bag and a full flask. Perhaps he hadn't heard. I breathed an internal sigh of relief.

'Well, I'll be off then.' And then he turned around. 'Oh, and Sofe, next time you're on a date – best way to get a man hooked is leading with, "I want to put my hands down your pants."'

I never want to see Conall ever again.

6.20 p.m. Left Conall's before he got home. Imran called and asked what I was doing at the neighbour's house. He didn't seem to understand the concept of human kindness.

'He probably fancies you.'

Honestly. Because Imran at one point in his life fancied me, he thinks everyone else is so inclined. Which is a nice idea for me, obviously, but I wish he'd get with the programme. He asked if I wanted to catch a film next week, but I told him I'm being productive. I can't dilly-dally around going on non-dates when I have to write about actual dates.

'Don't your parents care you're in some strange man's home?' he asked.

Do my weekends at Conall's go into the 'too westernised' category?

Tuesday 27 March

6 a.m. I woke up in the middle of the night and the downstairs light was on. If someone had broken into the house, I'd have to go charging down with Dad's old cricket bat – or, you know, call the police. I walked down a few steps and saw Dad sitting alone with his head in his hands. He saw me and leaned forward as if to stand up, but then didn't quite manage it. When I asked if he was OK, he said he was fine, except his face was very pale.

'It's just my back hurting, Beta. It's nothing.' But he kept rubbing his chest. So I made him a cup of tea and sat down with him, rubbing his back and telling him about the launch party where an author once said, 'Gosh! You're rather *exotic*. Wasn't like that back in my day.'

Dad should know better than to carry on smoking. Will plan an intervention with Mum and Maria to put a stop to this immediately.

4 p.m.

> **To Imran:** I'm too tired to do any work. Still want to go watch a film?

I'm going to the cinema with Imran and will have stern words with Dad as soon as I get home. I can hardly do it when he already looks miserable. Hopefully today he'll be better and I can shout at him without feeling guilty.

11.35 p.m.

> **From Imran:** I'm going to take you wherever I go! Only you could make that man keep his shop open so we could have those waffles! Haha! Nyt nyt. xxx

NYT NYT? How did I not notice this when we were together??

Note for book: Never marry a man that can't be bothered to spell 'Night' properly. Lazy with words, lazy with life.

Thursday 29 March

2 p.m. I've had to cancel lunch with Lucinda and Brammers to have an urgent meeting with Hannah. I can't let little things like careers get in the way of helping friend in the midst of a marriage crisis. It turns out that tests for Hannah have come back; she won't be able to have babies.

'The worst thing is, Zulfi doesn't care. Why would he? He has a readymade family.'

She got teary and pushed her uneaten lunch to one side. I was going to say it's Allah's will (which it is. Obviously.), but the time and place to say that is not when someone's on the brink of an emotional breakdown. I'll wait to tell her that no one knows what's around the corner. As vision goes, ours is pretty limited.

Seeing Hannah sad has made me want to consume the canteen's entire collection of muffins. Here's a question: if you spend X amount of years wanting something and then realise that you can't have it, and the person who you wanted to share it with doesn't really mind either way, is that time wasted?

Forget years. Even months can feel like years when you meet a person who makes you laugh. It's as if they've been making you laugh all your life. Bloody Naim.

9 p.m. Imran called and said I sounded weird. He asked what was wrong so I told him about Hannah.

'She actually married that guy? She could've done better than that.' Of course Imran loves generic statements. How could I have forgotten? 'So she can't have babies?'

'No.'

'You girls, man. She marries someone with a wife and kids and *you* can't even ...'

'What?'

'It's not as if I was asking you to do anything weird. Everyone knows girls move in with their in-laws.'

'Let's all be clones.'

'I don't get how you let Hannah even do that. Oh my God, how did her parents agree to it?' Then he started laughing out loud. 'Sofe, man. You have some crazy friends.'

Saturday 31 March

8.45 a.m. What a drama, and it's not even nine o'clock. The house phone rang at eight and Mum picked up. After a few minutes came Mum's raised voice, 'No, listen, Bhai Saab, everyone learns as they go along ... Nahin, she only came once this week. She is married but we are her parents. If boys want to look after their parents won't girls want to as well?'

Then Dad took hold of the phone. 'Bhai – these things should be discussed in person, haina?'

'What do they think? Maria is a servant girl who we brought up just to do their dishes?'

I haven't seen Mum angry like this before, but for once we were on the same page. 'And she is so much better at cooking than Sofi.' She turned to look at me. 'This is why I tell you learn something now. You don't know what your in-laws and husband will be like.'

Dad sighed, patting his trousers for his packet of cigarettes. I got up and took the packet from him.

'Calm down, Mehnaz. We have to listen to everyone's side of the story.'

'Dad, what side? This is what I mean by living with the in-laws bol ...'

'Soffoo ...'

'Business. It's so unfair.'

Mum then tried to call Maria, but she didn't pick up.

'Mehnaz, you know these people are traditional. When girls are married, they are another family's.'

I looked at my dad as if he'd gone mad. He rubbed his eyes and sat quiet for a few moments.

'Acha. That is what you think – she is no longer ours. Well done. Very good job we both did all our lives.'

Dad nodded at her. 'I know, Mehnaz. She's ours. But let me rest and when they come we will talk about it.'

He stood and made his way up the stairs as Mum stormed into the kitchen. She started peeling onions and chopping garlic.

'Mum, what are you doing?'

'They'll be here lunchtime. Won't they want food?'

7 p.m. I've just crept into my room after being with Maria for the past hour. She managed to sob herself to sleep. They came at two o'clock and when they were about to leave, she said she wanted to stay here. T kept looking at the floor, clenching and unclenching his fists.

'Maria. Are you sure?' Dad asked her.

She nodded and Mum stepped forward, standing next to her.

'Sister,' said T's dad, 'Mothers should learn to step back once their daughter is married.'

Ha! Coming from the man whose wife tells Maria when to wake up, what to cook and where to go every day.

'Bhai,' Mum replied, 'if you were a mother you would know that she stands in *front* of her daughter so bad things happen to her before her child.'

Mum watching all those Bollywood dramas has come in handy.

8.55 p.m. Imran's called three times but I don't want to speak with him and his live with the in-laws type. T left behind the mother of his unborn child. Must pray as it's the only way to calm down and not want to round up all these men and shoot them one by one.

9.30 p.m. I sat next to Maria and asked how she was feeling.

'Get your Dictaphone.'

'What?'

'That thing you use when you're interviewing people.'

'Oh.' I got it and walked cautiously back into her old room. 'What do you want me to do?' I asked.

'Switch it on then.'

Maria: Living with in-laws is bullshit. Fine, it can work for some, but most of the time we know it's bullshit. (Pause.) You know why? (Pause.) Because you realise your husband's not on your side. (Her voice cracks.)

Me: T is on your side.

(Pause.)

Maria: No. You are.

Me: Obviously, silly moo.

Maria: Don't you dare just settle, Sofe.

(I sigh.)

Me: Is there anyone else you'd have wanted to marry?

(Maria lets out a frustrated noise. She shakes her head.)

Me: Well, then. You didn't just settle.

APRIL 2012

Once More, With Feeling, Please

Muslim Dating Book

Not all in-laws have a hole-in-the-wall (obviously), but many seem to be intent on drilling a hole in your head. It all boils down to forgotten history. The mother-in-law's forgotten what it was like when she was in that very same situation thirty-odd years ago. The tables have turned and instead of changing things, she wants to take a slab of her past and whack it into her daughter-in-law's present.

Oh, bloody hell. They're not all like that. It's just unfortunate that my sister's are.

The issue, of course, is keeping the words you should be saying out loud in the confines of your overwhelmed brain. But you have to be careful: these words can either pierce the tension and release it, or inject and inflame it, until the tension swells so mightily every one is bogged down with the weight of it.

That's the thing with words. Whatever you do with them – in or out – you'll have to live with the consequences.

Sunday 1 April

10 a.m. I came to Conall's for the morning and he was still home, gardening. He walked into the house and took off his gloves.

'Any hands in pants potentials this week?'

I'd completely forgotten about the previous week's debacle.

'Oh, right. Not quite. What are you planting?'

'Seeds.'

I got my notebook and laptop out and plugged it in.

'Obviously seeds.'

'Wildflowers.'

'Hmm.'

'Chamerion angustifolium.'

'What?'

'Rosebay willowherb.'

'Why are you just saying things?'

'That's what they're called.'

'Right.'

'They need a lot of space and light.'

'Space is important.' I sighed.

'And light.'

'And that.'

'Deadline's looming. You'd better get on with it,' he said.

I opened Word and looked up at him. 'You know what really pisses me off?'

He raised his eyebrows.

'Patience,' I said.

Conall pulled up the chair opposite me and sat down.

'I hear it all the time about marriage. You must be patient with your husband. If he asks for five curries for dinner or wants you to live with his parents, then you must comply. If he wants his shoes licked clean, then why do you think you have a tongue? Oh, I don't know – maybe to have an opinion? Worse is when people start using Islam to tell you to be a bloody doormat.'

'Incidentally, how does Islam feel about anger?'

I had to push down what can only be described as non-sage-like feelings.

'I'm not angry.' I shook my head in what I hoped was a calm fashion. 'I'm merely highlighting the injustice of it all. No one ever told men to be patient.' You know what else I can't stand? When people get all judgy.'

'Judg-y?'

'On how things *should* be done. Not everything is black and white, you know.'

'Why don't I make some tea?'

He went into the kitchen and I checked my phone.

From Imran: Pakistan Vs India! Bastards better watch out! Lololol.

He came back with two mugs of tea and chocolate digestives.

'There, that'll cheer you up,' he said, pushing the plate of digestives towards me.

'No, I'm not in the mood.'

Am I so fat that it seems as if biscuits are the only thing that make me happy? I took two and dipped them both in my tea. Then I ranted about Hannah not being able to have babies, Imran and his insensitive comments, Naim and the fact that he's finally decided to leave me alone (I should be glad, shouldn't I?), Dad and him not feeling well – though not sure how that fits into the whole polygamy thing. And poor Conall sat and listened, nodding every now and then.

'The problem with the world, Sofe, is not everyone can be bothered to change it.'

Yes, well, thanks, Mr Optimistic – I am (was?) also a proponent of that theory, but I'm beginning to see that *one* person can't change anything at all.

Then he said, 'Maybe your book'll change things.'

Ha! 'Yes, dating books change things all the time.'

He said he knew that. What was with the irony? 'So maybe you write something different.'

'This is for work.'

'Just odd. Seems to me you have a fair bit to say. Most people do – but not everyone has the same – *you* might say God-given – opportunity.'

I screwed up my face. 'Are you giving me guidance?'

He laughed. Doesn't happen very often, but when it does it really is very kind laughter. 'Well, there's no leading you astray. Next best thing.' And then he tapped the table. 'Something to think about.'

I stared at the heading on my laptop: '*Poke Me Once Shame on You, Poke Me Twice, Shame on Me.*' But there was no deleting it. I had to carry on – resilience and resignation is apparently part and parcel of life, not *just* marriage. Conall stopped at the door and turned around.

'If you think this Naim person is the one who might give you a bit of optimism in life, I wouldn't let it go that easily.'

I looked at him as if he were mad. 'Erm, hello, there's my *pride*.' (As Fozia had correctly pointed out.) What did he take me for? After all this time *I* should be the one to say something to Naim? No, thank you very much.

'I thought truly spiritual people didn't let things like pride get in the way?'

ARGH! Bloody Conall and his *reasonableness*. But he doesn't know that Naim *laughed* at the idea of marrying me. Laughed. In my face! The humiliation!

'I'm not telling you to write the man a feckin' love letter. Sorry. I'm just saying; don't let a person read between the lines.' He smiled his lopsided smile. 'Listen, if a man turns up outside a girl's house he's probably mad about her ...'

'Or?'

'Or he's just passing his time until something else comes along.'

'Great, thanks.'

'All you need to know is if you're tough enough to live with the worst of the two outcomes. It'd be shit, to be sure. But not for long.'

'Hmm.'

'And then there's the possibility of the *best* outcome. Trust me, you don't want to live with regret. I know what I'm talking about.'

When he left the room his words flitted around in my now-strained brain. I felt bad for his regrets. What-ifs' are the worst. People end up popping pills for the rest of their lives because of 'what-ifs.'

1.30 p.m. Have just prayed and I have a *feeling*. I feel that Conall's right. Something about the way he said it; pride and not living with regret. And also, all these unhappy people around me. I could live with being the Mad Woman in the Attic – but I don't think I could add 'regretful' to the title.

9.45 p.m.

To: Sharif, Naim
From: Khan, Sofia
Subject: Hi

Hello,

Sorry I've been ignoring your calls. Contrary to what you think, it's not PMT, thank you. It's another thing. I discovered something a little inconvenient. Apparently I have feelings for you. I know. If it's a shock to you, then imagine what a shock it was to me.

Anyway, this is my way of explanation as to why I don't think we can be friends any more. It's distracting.

Look after yourself, and have a Lemon Puff on me.

Love,
Sofia

Like Conall said, it didn't have to be a bloody love letter. I looked over the email more than a few times. If I were American too, I believe I'd call this closure. Thanks to God I'm not.

I have to say, even at my thinnest I never felt as light as I do now, though something keeps tugging at my thoughts. But this isn't about hope; this is about the opposite of regret.

Tuesday 3 April

8.50 a.m. Maria's still here. T hasn't called or texted her. I've not received anything back from Naim. What was I expecting? Some kind of declaration of – ugh – *love*? Only in films, Sofe. Hollywood has ruined an entire generation of women.

5.45 p.m.

From Imran: You don't seem to be your normal self past few days. Think I should take you out to cheer you up. I'm waiting at your reception. Better not have a date with someone else! Lol.

11.20 p.m. I never quite appreciated the importance of staying friends with Imran. We walked down Southbank and I mentioned how nice it might be to go travelling. Holidays and breaks are all very well, but to really try and see the world would be amazing. Except he just laughed and said I was too old to go travelling and should worry more about where I'm going to find a husband. Honestly! I thought of my empty inbox, and then he added, 'Cos girls like you should get married and have kids. It'd be a waste otherwise.'

Even when I'm a moody cow and don't deserve it, it's just like Imran to see the best in me.

Saturday 7 April

9 a.m. What is it about chocolates in the shape of eggs that are just so delicious? I've bought Conall an Easter egg. I should stop staring at it. Staring leads to eating.

I've had zero emails from Naim. Zero. Is he utterly horrified? Is he glad he now doesn't have to speak to a mad hijabi who goes silent for months and then blurts out feelings via email? Perhaps I made a mistake. Bloody Conall. But then I think about it and feel it was the right advice. Bloody, *right*, Conall.

He's given me a collection of Richard Yates to read. If you are what you read then, judging by some of these short stories, Conall is a bit of a depressive. Speaking of which, I'll lend him *The End of the Affair*. He will appreciate a bit of Graham Greene.

8.20 p.m.

From Naim: Daisypuffs. I think we need to speak. Can you meet on Monday? I've missed you.

ARGH!!

Calm, Sofia. Must remain *CAAAAAALM!*

Easter Sunday 8 April

10 a.m. When I told the girls, their response was a variation of 'Oh', 'Well done!' and 'Good. Fuck it.' At first, I didn't want to mention my email, but then one shouldn't be ashamed of one's actions. Most of the time. They asked how I feel: like I want a fag, that's how. And then they asked whether I was excited. Excited? My insides seem to be stretching and splattering about the place, but I wouldn't quite call that excitement.

Easter Monday 9 April

12 p.m. It's raining so heavily my hijab is soaked just from walking out of my house and into Conall's. He's not here, but there is a Lindt bunny with a note that says '*To help keep your mouth otherwise occupied.*' Cheeky bugger.

7 p.m. When Conall walked into the house, he asked where I was going so I told him. Oh, God, I want to be sick.

He brought a chair round and sat next to me at the table. 'Whatever happens tonight, Sofe,' he said, being so kind I could've hugged him. 'You'll know what this man is made of.'

It wasn't particularly comforting; but it was true. Truth is a good thing.

7.05 p.m.

To Suj; Hannah; Fozia: Battery low, on way to see the American so don't be distressed if I can't respond to all your messages. I know there will be plenty. Xx

7.30 p.m. Stupid battery is dead and I'm fifteen minutes early. I've just looked over at a couple who are fawning over each other. Get a room. I'm nauseous enough, thanks. Not that I'm expecting anything to come of this (I'm sensible like that, after all).

7.33 p.m. Whyyyyy has time decided to stand still?

7.45 p.m. In the meantime I have to look at the fawners. OK, fine, they look happy. Oops, they saw me staring. Will focus on the door.

7.55 p.m. The *one* time I need my phone so I can rant about his lateness to the girls ... Typical. He's going to get a telling off as soon as he's here. Makes me realise: I do want him to be here. Oh dear. Whatever he has to say now, it better be good.

8.05 p.m. Why can't I get the nausea to go? I'm trying to concentrate on reading a book, but keep on jumping every time the door opens. We were meant to meet here, weren't we? Yes, I'm sure. He said it himself – Patisserie Valerie in Leicester Square – our first fake date. I'll get that apple tart and leave the raisins for him. It'll be funny.

8.20 p.m. The waitress keeps looking at me. Maybe because I'm eating the apple tart whilst staring at the door. But I know he's going to walk through it any minute, because he might be ridiculous and a little immature, but he's not the type of person to make me wait.

8.40 p.m. The fawners smiled at me as they left. I made the waitress leave my empty plate with the raisins.

How long are you meant to wait for a person? Minutes, hours? Months? I don't feel the nausea any more. Something's kind of sinking inside me. It's not the apple tart.

8.55 p.m. The problem with waiting is you think if you stick around for just another minute, things will come together. And the problem with that is you realise you were waiting for things to come together.

9.30 p.m. Waitress came to let me know that they close in half an hour. He didn't come. I waited and he didn't turn up. Even more stupidly, of all the scenarios that played out in my head as to how this might go, this wasn't one of them.

I never realised that the weight of disappointment rests mostly on your heart.

10.40 p.m. Got home. Conall was waiting at doorstep. Didn't understand. He stepped forward and just looked at me.

'Sofe. It's your dad. He's had a heart attack.'

Tuesday 10 April

5 a.m. So tired. Must pray and sleep and maybe when I wake up things will be better.

11 a.m. Came downstairs and Mum was getting ready to go to the hospital. She'd vacuumed, cooked, done the laundry and gone to the bank before I'd even woken up.

'When your Chachu calls, tell him to call Auntie Zeenat in Karachi. She will tell everyone there. Auntie Reena said she'll come to hospital.' I nodded and felt a lump in my throat. 'Let Maria rest and you both come together.'

Why didn't I charge my phone before I left on Monday night?

In moments like yesterday's you think everything will be a blur, but I remember every second. Conall stepped forward and I looked at him as if something was meant to follow – that he would take it back and tell me it was a joke. I glanced at the house and no lights were switched on.

'We tried calling, but no one could get through.'

And then I put it all together. Switched off lights, Conall at doorstep, dead battery. Dead. Then I tried to remember if Conall said 'He had a heart attack' or 'He's had a heart attack'. Because one meant I was too late and the other meant there was still hope. I went to go into the house to get my car keys, but Conall took me by the arm and drove me to the hospital.

In that nine-minute journey I could do nothing but pray that I would hear the beeping of machines, because then his heart would still be pumping blood and I would still have a dad.

The sound of my shoes echoed in the hallway, and through the window I saw him lying there, a mask attached to his mouth, wires coming out of his arms, and a line on a machine that went up and down, up and down. He was breathing; and so could I.

9 p.m. Dad is stable for now. Will be in hospital for a while. Perhaps bypass needed. T turned up. Don't think he and Maria spoke, but he didn't leave her side. Naim keeps calling and messaging, but have no energy to speak or care.

Maria held my hand and this memory came to me. I was around six, and Mum and Dad were shouting at each other – I can't recall what the argument was about. I remember darkness and me sitting up in bed, crying. Maria crept into the room, got under the covers and hugged me, telling me to be quiet and that everything would be OK.

Next day, I remember Mum's bags being packed. She's at the door and Maria and I are holding hands, ready to leave with her. Dad takes the bag Mum's holding, looking as sad as I've ever seen him.

'Mehnaz, please, I'm sorry. Not you *and* my daughters.'

Mum hesitated. She looked at us and then at him. In those few moments it was as if some kind of agreement passed between them. She let go of the door handle, put her hands on our shoulders and led us back into the house. The arguments didn't stop, but life's routines punctuated tense silences: Mum having to pick Maria and me up from school, Dad counting the family savings so Mum and he could send money back home to help whichever family member needed it. Apparently Maria and I were not their only responsibility.

Or perhaps I'm misremembering things. I don't know. But I think I'm grateful for that agreement. It means that over twenty years later, we are at least in this hospital together.

Wednesday 11 April

7 a.m. You spend time worrying about the small things and then, when a big thing happens, you wish to be troubled by all those small ones if only the big thing could be better. I know whatever's meant to be *will* be, but there's a whole unlived future he needs to be a part of so I have to pray for him to get better because there is no reason for him to go – not yet.

8 a.m.

> **From Naim:** Sofe, please pick up your phone. I'm so sorry. Just answer my call.

1.40 p.m. Have begun to use waiting room to pray. Couple came in and I had to ask them whether they minded my arse being in the air while they sat and waited for news on their daughter. They've been coming in for four days now. The daughter was in a car crash and she's only nineteen. The dad looked up at me as if he'd seen me for the first time.

'Sorry?'

'You don't mind if I just pray here in the corner, do you?'

'No, that's quite all right. You go ahead.'

4 p.m. Conall came to hospital. Did I once say he either looked bored or pissed off? His was the friendliest face in the place. I didn't even get a chance to thank him for bringing me to the hospital. Uncle and Auntie Scot got the plane down last night and are doing my head in with the cups of tea they demand.

'Sorry, I should've asked before I came.' Conall looked around at the various faces that were staring at him.

'No, of course not.'

He seemed to struggle before he said, 'Sofe, I'm so sorry. I feel it's my fault you weren't home in the first place.'

As if I had the energy to be annoyed at anyone. When he looked down at me I wanted to cry and hug him. But I'm a grown woman and shouldn't need a hug from a person just because my dad's in hospital.

'You let me know if there's anything I can do,' he said.

'Maybe book a plane to get the Scots back up north?'

He smiled.

'I could just arrange their disappearance altogether.'

Ha. Conall is capable of telling a joke.

The girls have been messaging. Times like this you're glad for people on standby, who know you and what you need, even if the thing you need is space. Imran keeps texting to see how I am. I realise I'm perhaps being unreasonable, but I feel I'd be a whole lot better if he'd stop asking me – sympathy conversation is the worst.

11 p.m. I was in my room, trying to get an early night and ignore the voices coming from downstairs, when the phone rang. It was Imran and I was going to ignore it, but then picked it up, ready to cut the conversation short.

'What if I said I'd move out?'

I wish I were the type of person who had their head about them. It's especially necessary when there's chaos in the form of Maria and T having a heated argument downstairs with Mum in the passage, eavesdropping.

'What do you mean?'

'I mean, I'll move out. If that's what you want. Let's do it.'

Random words cluttered around in my head, only they weren't quite stringing together.

'I still want to marry you,' he said.

'Yeah but ...'

'Thing is, I've met girls, but it's just not the same.'

'Oh.'

'Don't you want to get married?'

Not really the sort of convo you want to have over the phone, but his voice went so quiet.

'Yeah, no, I mean, I suppose so, but ...'

'It's you, Sofe. There's no one else.'

Oh dear. You can't just say no to someone without at least pretending you've given it some thought.

'Have you met someone else?'

I paused, remembering the empty chair the evening Naim and I were meant to meet.

'No. No, I haven't.'

Thursday 12 April

10.40 a.m. 'Is this a joke or something?' Suj and I sat in the hospital café, she being a distraction to all hospital staff and patients, and me being distracted by a new life conundrum. 'So he'll move out?'

I nodded as she opened her fourth packet of Canderel and put it in her coffee.

'It's about time,' she said. 'But what will you do?'

I shrugged.

'Has that knob called you any more?'

'Not for a few days,' I replied.

I went through my phone and showed her all the Whatsapp messages he'd sent in the past five days.

'He fucking well should be sorry. If he'd have told you he wouldn't be able to make it you'd have been at home and … Anyway, it doesn't matter. It's all OK now.'

When I wander the halls of the hospital I keep thinking that my dad shouldn't be here. This is the place where lives can fall apart. Every day is like having to look at the possibility of death. Every time I go home I feel like I reek of it – you know, if death smelled like cabbage soup.

2.45 p.m. I was at the vending machine, getting a bag of Maltesers for Maria, and that man whose daughter had an accident was behind me. He gave me a nod and I was just about to walk past him when he said, 'I remember travelling around Turkey and Morocco many years ago.'

It wasn't quite the time to tell him that I'm Pakistani.

I smiled and then he said, 'A lot of beautiful mosques.' He looked beyond me, as if recalling those memories. 'You know the nice thing about Muslims? Even if you don't believe in this notion of God, and I certainly don't …' He gave me a sad smile. 'They'll always offer to pray for you.'

I tried to recall the last time I offered to pray for anyone.

'Could I ask you something? Could you pray for us?' he said.

I'm not sure how I managed to say, 'Of course,' because all I felt were these annoying tears surfacing. I walked away before he could see them stream down my face.

Saturday 14 April

10.10 a.m. The post came today with a card from work. It did make me smile. Heartfelt messages interspersed with jokes about campaigns being at a standstill without me. Katie wrote she's going to bake a cake when I get back. (*Well, buy, Sweetu. I think that's safer.*)

10.40 a.m. Dad's still in and out of consciousness. I didn't even want to think about Imran and his proposal at the moment. Hannah came over to the house and when I told her about him, my pregnant sister overheard. As if she needs more things to worry about.

'I don't know how appropriate it is to offer to move out when someone's dad's in hospital.' Hannah smoothed down the crease in her dress. She looked worried. She really needn't be; I'm reintroducing compartmentalising into my life.

'Emotional capitalisation,' she muttered.

'What?'

'He's *taking* advantage,' Maria interjected. Her thunderous face looked so much like Dad's, it seemed they'd morphed into one person. I told her to stop getting angry, or the baby might pop out early.

Hannah stood up and we all trundled off to the airport to collect Chachu. My thoughts bounced around, wondering about cynicism and cigarettes.

5 p.m. These family members are like hyenas. They sniff you out no matter where you. I sat in the hospital café, having redrafted the pages Lucinda gave me, and emailed them to her when Uncle Scot plopped himself at my table.

'Beta, you must get married now, haan.' He was clearly ignoring the fact that I had my laptop open. He was also ignoring the fact that there was a 'Marriage' jar and that he was now due to put at least ten pounds in it just because of how annoying he was.

'Yep. Insh'Allah.' I gestured towards the hospital ceiling, where, apparently, God was waiting to will my marriage into being.

'No more Insh'Allahs. A parent's biggest dream is to make sure their children are settled and happy. Whether your baba says anything or not, he is always worried about you. Some girls listen more easily.'

I wanted to say that perhaps parents should dream of their children just being content, whatever the circumstance. Bar that, perhaps dream bigger.

Monday 16 April

11.21 a.m. 'O-ho – everyone is acting as if I've already died. Your faces would make a healthy man ill.' Dad winced as he tried to sit up.

Auntie Scot shook her head. 'Bhai, you shouldn't joke about these things.'

'Haan. When you don't have wires and tubes connected to you, then make jokes,' said Mum.

12 p.m.

From Imran: How's your dad? If you can meet tonight, then let's but don't worry if you can't. It's alright. Xxxx

Wish he'd stop being so nice; it makes it very hard to remain focused on telling someone thanks for that offer of marriage, but no thanks.

1.23 p.m.

From Naim: For God's sake, pick up your phone, please. How many more voicemails do I have to leave before I come to your house and start banging at the door?

2.35 p.m. 'I've been calling you every day. Why haven't you picked up?'

'Busy.'

'Listen, Sofe, I'm so sorry. An emergency came up at the res-taurant. I called but it was going straight to voicemail. You got my message, right?'

'Yes.'

'Were you waiting long?'

I paused. 'A half hour or so.'

'There was nothing I could do.'

'Doesn't matter, Naim. It's fine.'

'Where are you?'

'Home.'

Which was not a complete lie as the hospital has become like a second home. Enough of the family is here for it to feel zoo-like.

'Can you meet tonight?'

'No.'

'Tomorrow?'

'Definitely, no.'

'Well, when then?'

'I don't know, Naim. Things are a little mad at home.'

'That's new.'

'I'm busy.'

'Uh-huh.' There was a pause.

'Dad's having an operation tomorrow, so maybe after that.'

The last thing I wanted was for him to feel sorry for me, so I told him that everything would be fine.

And now I must go and see Imran to tell him that I don't think I can marry him, even *sans* hole-in-the-wall.

10.35 p.m. We were in Green Park, sitting in a café opposite the Wolseley and I kept on seeing flashes of Dad in hospital. It was raining so hard I couldn't take my eyes off the slanting downpour. Every time I wanted to say that I just don't feel that way about him, the words wouldn't come out.

'Listen. I know things are hectic. Once the op's over, just talk to your parents and tell me what you want to do.'

'The thing is, Imran ...'

'Just don't think about it for now. Man, I'm hungry, and you need to eat.'

So I never told him. Not yet, anyway. One shouldn't make hasty decisions. Especially when you're trying to get it right. Especially when there's a person opposite you who's there to pick up pieces of life if needed.

Tuesday 17 April

9 a.m. Mum is looking very haggard. When she's not running around doing things, she's sitting and praying. It's as if she doesn't even notice anyone around her. Every time I've asked Auntie Scot to do a task Mum needs completing, she picks up the rosary beads and starts rubbing her knees, saying, 'Hai hai, my arthritis.' Where was your arthritis when you danced at my sister's wedding, hmm?

She was drinking tea (rosary beads in hand) while Mum made breakfast in the kitchen. Auntie looked like she was about to cry.

'Bhai has been so good to everyone. Mehnaz, every night before I sleep I say, "Ya Allah, keep him alive and healthy to see his daughter get married." Don't leave this poor family widowed and orphaned.'

I thought Mum dropped something because there was a bang. When I turned to look in the kitchen she was standing at the sink with her back to everyone.

'I am *not* a widow yet.' She looked over her shoulder at us. 'And if, God forbid, I become one ...' Her voice began to crack. I felt useless. I can't remember the last time I saw Mum like this. Perhaps it was when she had those bags packed, holding on to the door handle, almost changing the course of all our lives. 'My daughters will not be orphans. They will still have me.'

I looked at my hands. Auntie Scot cleared her throat. 'Haan. Of course. Also, thanks to Allah you have Tahir, at least.'

I wanted to point out that you'd get more use out of a used teabag than my brother-in-law, but I didn't trust that my voice would be quite as strong as Mum's. And plus, it was some comfort that from the corner of my eye I saw his hand resting on Maria's.

10.12 a.m.

From Naim: Daisypuffs. Hope it goes OK today. Mother Mehnaz will be getting Uncle-ji to put up the solar lights in no time. Let me know if there's anything I can do.

10.13 a.m.

From Naim: PS I hope you can see how nice I'm being. See, I'm changing for you.
To Naim: Of course you are.
From Naim: I knew you'd respond to that. Most guys would do anything to get a girl to sleep with them; I'll do anything just to get a response from you. This love–shove business

isn't easy. Don't worry about anything for now, though. You just do what you do best – pray, and I'll even do the same. Your dad will be fine.

Typical. Every time I want to ignore him, he thaws my cold resolve. Bastard.

2 p.m. No one's ever been this quiet before. Everyone is on the floor with their Qur'an or rosary beads, praying Dad's operation goes well. Nothing like a bypass to shut everyone up.

9 p.m. It went well! He's out and in intensive care, but it went well. Thanks to God in the hospital ceiling.

Thursday 19 April

3 p.m. Dad woke up while Mum had gone to pray and Maria had gone home to rest. He took my hand, smiled and said, 'You will send your baba to the grave before you get married.'

I smiled, stroking his grey hair. 'It's good you're well enough for emotional blackmail.'

I held his hand in both of mine. He was about to say something, but he just fell back asleep. It's different to when everyone around you is telling you to get married. Very different when your own dad takes your hand and asks you to do the same. Especially when he's attached to wires and tubes.

Very different.

7 p.m. I was on my way out to get some fresh air and Conall was walking into his house. He asked about Dad and if there was any way he could help. Hmmm, I don't know, change the conversation? I know getting married is part and parcel of life, but it's not *life*. Everyone's obsession with it is bordering on the obscene, especially when there are people who are trying to mend their heart.

'Are you all right, Sofe?'

'Yeah, just the …'

'… random thoughts buzzing around your head?'

'Exactly.'

'Everything will be fine.' And before he walked into his house he said, 'Everything will turn out just grand, you'll see.'

8.25 p.m. There are times in one's life when you have to ask yourself, *what am I doing*? This must be that time for me. Not voluntarily obviously – I keep pushing the damn thought into any dust-filled corner in my mind. Imran, Naim, Naim, Imran … Where are those empty, cobwebbed spaces when you need them? But as much as I try, an answer keeps bouncing back; *I don't know*. And then a whole conversation begins which, no matter what direction it takes, keeps coming back to that moment when I held Dad's hand and he said those words.

Friday 20 April

10.30 a.m. What the hell, man. On my way to work I got splashed by two cars, then a bus, the Victoria line was delayed, a man picked his nose and wiped it under his seat (not my seat, but might very well be my seat some other day) and now Brammers wants to see me in her office.

10.50 a.m. 'Sofia, how *are* you?' She leaned forward and clasped her hands together, concern etched in her furrowed brows.

'Fine, thanks.'

She scratched her head and sniffed her finger. Ugh.

'Well, I just wanted to say that I'm really impressed with your professionalism here. Considering.'

'Oh, thanks.' I was rather impressed myself, to be honest. Didn't think I had it in me.

She cleared her throat and glanced at her computer screen, tapping her fingers on the table.

'So we've had a read of the redrafted pages, and I think you could do *more*.'

'Sorry?'

'Have a look at the notes, and see if you can revise it a bit more,' she said.

Ha, the concern etched in her brows wasn't for *me*. I smiled as graciously as possible, and left the office.

I've had a look at the notes: *Do we need this? Could you give some more examples? The tone isn't quite consistent throughout – we begin with something light, though a little formal – please amend – and then it becomes a little serious. Whilst heartfelt, remember what kind of book this is. Keep it light.*

And it went on, and on. But mostly I just stared at that comment – *keep it light*. Sigh.

Why is nothing *ever* good enough?

7 p.m. 'You don't need to write the book,' said Imran, clearly not understanding the situation.

'That's not the point. I want to write it, I just don't think I want to write what they want me to write.'

'So, just do what they're asking. You're already halfway there. No point in starting over. It's like the law, isn't it? It's not what I want to do, but it's what I've done, because well, that's what the plan was.'

'You didn't want to do law?'

How did I never know this? Weird.

'Who gives a shit about it? But it pays the bills and more. Plus, Mum and Dad love telling people I'm a lawyer.'

That didn't particularly fill me with confidence, but I had made a commitment to work. He was right. And anyway, what were the options when I'd already pocketed their money? Must remember that money. I could do something useful with it.

11.05 p.m. It was kind of impossible to think about the book and *not* think about the person who was there from the beginning. After looking at Naim's name on my contacts list for twenty minutes, I thought, sod it, I'll call him. He'll be glad to hear from me.

His phone rang for ages before he picked up. There was all kinds of noise in the background. Namely, loud music.

'Sofe? You OK? What's going on?'

Life! That's what's going on.

'Where are you?' I asked.

'I can't hear you.'

Then I heard some girl shout out his name.

'Hey, can I call you back? Won't be too late, right?'

'Never been too late before,' I said in what was supposed to be a light (I'm practising for the book) tone, but which came out perhaps a little stiff.

'Huh?'

'Nothing. Yes, of course, that's fine.'

Why should it bother me that he's out? That girls are calling out his name? He's making more friends in London. I should be glad. I am glad. Ecstatic.

11.58 p.m. Naim hasn't called.

12.55 a.m. Been a while since I've been up at this time waiting for a call from Naim. Point is, never really had to wait before.

2.12 a.m.

From Naim: What are you wearing?

WTF??

2.13 a.m.

From Naim: Oh, shit, sorry, Sofe. Are you awake? Shall I call you?

Erm, hellooooooo? Who the hell was he messaging? No, don't call me. Don't even *think* of calling me. ARGH!

Saturday 21 April

6.35 a.m. I had to call Suj and rant (though she was half asleep). What was I expecting? I just thought … *maybe,* just maybe, there's something here. Suj listened and obviously cursed him several times and said all the things best friends are meant to say. It's just hard to believe them sometimes. Especially at this time. Most of all at this time.

8 a.m. I've thought about this, and when a man asks you to marry him and basically does everything you want him to do, it'd be unreasonable to say no. Very unreasonable. I'm completely capable of making a decision based on pros, cons and compromise. I'm finally a grown, mature woman.

So I've decided, I'm getting married. I'd better call the man I'm marrying and let him know.

8.20 a.m.

From Imran: Cant wait to spend rest of my life with you. You spoken to your parents yet? Let me know so mine can call and then we can come over. I think May wedding would be good xxxxx

Arghhhh! Come over? Already? Could at least wait until Dad doesn't have to be fed through a drip. May does sound OK, though. Maybe it'll give me some time to think of another book: one that I *actually* want to write.

9.12 a.m.

To Imran: Will have to wait until Dad's out of the hospital, obviously. May is good.
From Imran: We better start planning then. Only a month away! xxxx

WTF??

To Imran: I meant next year! Next month? No way – not with Dad in hospital.
From Imran: Hahahaha, if you think I'm waiting until next year you've got another thing coming xxxxx

Think coming. Not *thing*. Honestly.

Naim calling. No, Naim. Just, no.

10 p.m. I'd rather have spent the evening with the girls discussing at length Hannah's attempt to marinate chicken, Suj's fling with Calvin Klein model (which was fine, apparently, as she and Charles weren't talking that week) and Fozia's latest man who, it turns out, is now a Buddhist, but failed to mention it to her until date three.

Instead we sat in my room and Maria came in, slumping on the corner ottoman. Now was as good a time as any to let them all know I was engaged. It wasn't quite the reaction I'd been expecting. Maria leaned forward, looking confused. I explained about what happened with Naim and Fozia put an arm around me and said, 'He was hardly marriage material.'

AYISHA MALIK

No, but I was willing to overlook that. Turns out he *wasn't* willing to overlook it.

'Oh, he was a prick,' said Suj.

Hannah concurred on both counts.

'Are you sure this is what you want?' Maria asked.

I nodded, but felt something clench in my chest.

'It's an all-rounder, right,' I replied.

They looked at one another. 'What does that mean?' asked Suj.

I wanted to explain about Dad and the wires and his hand on mine, the lack of Naim, the presence of Imran, but I didn't have the energy. Here's the thing about faith: just because you're not a hundred per cent sure about something doesn't make it wrong. In fact, doubt can be good – it stops you from that head in the clouds scenario, which is exactly when people make mistakes. Every time I feel like my insides are being flipped around like pancakes, I just close my eyes and think about Dad and how happy he'll be.

'Don't worry. I know what I'm talking about.'

Hannah cleared her throat. 'OK, I have something to say,' she said, taking a deep breath. 'I'm getting a divorce.'

'What?' said Suj.

'I know they say the first year is the worst but, quite frankly, I'm not having it,' replied Hannah.

'Having what?' asked Foz.

'Joint wifehood, a baby. Any of it. Well, the baby is Allah's will but I can't just sit here crossing out dates on some calendar, waiting for my husband to come home.' She looked around at us. 'Different if I was going to have children, but look at me. If I can't make a baby, the least I could have is a full-time husband.'

'But, love, you knew he was going to be a part-timer before you got married,' said Suj. I nodded. I know I was the one who had at

300

one time mentioned divorce as an option, but what happened to 'til death do us part?

Fozia kneeled on the bed. 'Are you *sure* you want to do this, Han?'

'So now you all think I should be with Zulfi?'

'No,' I said. 'It's just, you spent so many years fighting for this …'

Maria rested her hand on her stomach, looking at all of us.

'So it's my fault?' Han said.

'No …'

'I shouldn't have married a man with a wife?'

'It just …'

'And now I can't have babies I can't just change the rules?'

'I never said that, but.'

'Well, Sofe, let's see what you think when you're married and live in the real world.'

OK, perhaps I should've kept my large mouth shut, but since when did Hannah believe in the marrieds' mantra that single people don't live in the real world? You can't help feelings but people make choices: good or bad, you need to live with them. Does no one fight for anything any more? She stood up and said she was going to make a move.

'Just stay,' said Suj.

'No, I should go.'

I was going to go after her, but felt, well, *annoyed*. I thought of Dad in hospital. Real world? My world feels real enough, thank you. Foz got off the bed and said she'd go and speak to her.

Maria, Suj and I sat in silence. I thought maybe Foz and Han would return, but after half an hour we were still sitting, waiting for who knows what.

'Suj,' I said, clearly on a roll, 'stop messing about and just be with Charles.'

I'd had enough. Everyone needs to deal with their problems and stop pissing about as if we live in a Hollywood film. When Suj didn't respond, I thought maybe she'd storm out too.

'I know, Toffee.' She played with her car keys and looked up at me. 'I'll get my shit together. You're right.'

Suj left and Maria was still sat on the ottoman. 'Bloody hell,' she said. 'Talk about drama.'

10.15 p.m. I heard Maria and T whispering in the next room. Obviously eavesdropping is wrong, in theory, but there are a lot of things that are wrong in theory – skinny jeans with hijab, for instance. But it'd be nice to know that at least someone was happy.

'Sorry, baby,' I heard Tahir say. Then there was silence.

10.25 p.m. I've had a panic at the potential of making a similar mistake as Hannah and marrying the wrong man. Where is that istikhara prayer??

10.40 p.m. Found it! Let's see … normal prayer followed by istikhara, asking for guidance so that which is good for you is made easy, and that which is bad for you is made difficult. I will pray this and the rest will be in the hands of God.

Oh, Lord, please help me. Naim calling.

10.50 p.m. 'Oh, hey. You picked up,' he said.

'Shall I hang up?'

'If you hang up I'm coming to your house and throwing stones at your bedroom window.'

I let him do the hard work of filling in the silence as I thought about my argument with Hannah.

'So listen,' he continued, 'we need to talk. I know things are a little crazy because of your dad.' He paused. 'Here's the thing, Daisy-puffs, I'm being serious, I'm so flattered you'd feel that way ...'

Oh my *actual* God. It's like that nightmare you have, only you realise it's unfolding before you in reality and you can't jolt your-self out of it ...

'... but look at us. We're so different ...'

I sat up in my bed. I couldn't quite believe the words he was pouring into my ears, like lava, heating up more than my brain.

'Oh, Naim, please *stop*. Tell me something I don't know.'

'OK, so you get it?'

Excuse me? The lava spread.

'Save the pep talk.'

'Hey, don't get defensive. I'm just being honest, and I'm telling you how flattered ...'

ARGH!

'OK, fine, whatever. I have to go.'

Silence.

'Come on, Sofe. Who else can I share Lemon Puff jokes with?'

Bloody, bloody, Naim.

'I'm not going to have time for those seeing as I'm getting married.'

Oh I hated the phone in that moment. If only I could've seen his face right then.

'What?'

'Married.'

Silence. Turns out someone doesn't want to join me on stage or on the road, but in actual life, I wanted to say. Moron.

'But, your email …'

'What can I say, Naim? Feelings change.'

'Oh, right.'

I stared at my red paisley bed cover.

'When are you getting married?'

'Imminently.'

'That was fast.'

Ha. My family would disagree. It's been about ten years coming.

'Listen, appreciate the call, but really must go now …'

'That's it?'

'What else is there?'

Silence.

'Well, he's a lucky son of a bitch.'

Before I could think about how he could genuinely feel this and say what he's just said, I told him goodbye and hung up.

You think it'll be like in the films where you either feel you've shifted excess weight from your life (and/or body), or that there'll be some kind of symbolic denouement (see? Hollywood). But there was nothing. Just hollowness. The only catharsis I could find was to delete him from my Facebook. I must say, the ritual of letter burning would've hit the tired and angry spot.

I looked at the istikhara prayer, resting on the bed, picked it up and did what I had to do.

11 p.m. It's no use. I've prayed, but can't get my mind to settle. Have just seen Conall's light on next door. All I want is to see a friendly face. And have a fag. Conall won't judge me if I smoke.

12 a.m. When I knocked on his door I must've looked like crap.

'Are you OK?' he asked.

I said I needed to be out of the house. 'And also,' I added, taking out the emergency cigarettes, 'I kind of needed a cigarette.'

'Thank fuck you've finally told me. I was wondering how long you were going to use the bathroom to smoke while I was out.'

'Oh shit, you could smell it?'

'From a mile, Sofe.'

'Why didn't you say something?' How embarrassing!

He just shrugged as he led the way into the kitchen and opened the door. We both sat on the step as I offered him a cigarette.

'Filthy habit,' he said.

'Yes, thanks. Just so you know, I'm not a smoker – it's just in emergency cases.'

'Of course.'

I inhaled and looked at the stars. I could still feel my heart pumping so fast the heat spread to my face. Then I thought of Hannah. Arguing with her is the worst. She's the one who tilts my head in a different direction when I don't like what I see. And I've told her to keep her heart in a place she no longer found contentment. Whatever she might've said to me was probably said out of sheer frustration. A person doesn't get divorced every day. I am a bad friend.

'Unhappy marriages are a bore, aren't they?' I said.

'Generally unhappiness is,' he said. 'Ah, fuck it,' he added, taking a cigarette and lighting it up.

'This is nice. Shared smoking experiences are better.'

'Not the healthiest.' He looked at the cigarette and then at me. 'Aren't hijabis meant to be a good influence?'

'I'll try again tomorrow.'

'Where were we?'

'Unhappiness.' I was beginning to realise how small the step was – there was barely an inch between us. 'When I was at the hospital, waiting for Dad to get better, I kept thinking about my parents and how much of it was, well, a struggle.' I looked for a place to ash the cigarette. Conall reached behind me and handed me a cup. 'Forget it, I'll shut up,' I said.

Don't know why I was bothering to say all this – ranting is one thing – but lately it feels like it's a lot to keep in. I never used to have this problem. Perhaps as you get older you have less emotional storage space.

'Don't half-finish a thing. It's annoying.'

I took a deep breath.

'I just feel *glad*. Despite the fact that my parents were either shouting or ignoring each other through most of my childhood, I'm glad they stuck at it. Selfish person that I am.' I rubbed in some ash that fell on the grass. 'If I was my mum's friend, I'd have told her to leave, and I'd probably have been right.'

She might've had a better life, but I wouldn't have had my dad in the same way. Mum with her solar lights and sacrifice.

'Maybe she didn't stay just for you,' he said. 'Not great times in the Khan household?'

'Oh well, it's not a particularly original story. Anyway, all's well that ends well etc.'

'And,' he said, 'At least your dad wasn't a raging alcoholic.'

That was another dot to add to the bigger picture of Conall's life. It was his turn to look at the stars. I wonder whether he still speaks to his dad. Whether the dad is even alive? I didn't want to pry, though. No one wants to be reminded of a crap childhood on a reasonably starry night.

'That's not a great time, either,' I said.

He shook his head. 'No.'

'Disgruntled Asian immigrant parents and an alcoholic Irish father?' I sighed. 'Aren't we a pair of second-generation clichés?'

Conall tends to fix his eyes on things; the ground, the sky, the cigarette. *Me*. He looked at me as if I owed him a debt of information. Except I didn't know what that information was, and for a moment I wanted to give it all – whatever I had inside – information-wise. I could've blurted out my entire family history there and then.

'Here,' I said, handing him another cigarette, hoping to distract him. I didn't want to give more than I already had. 'For your troubles.' Then I realised that my stupid scarf had come off. I hadn't pinned it because it was the middle of the night and I wasn't going to stay long. I put it back on as quickly as I could as he looked away. *Awkward*!

'Take a lot more than a cigarette for my troubles, Sofe,' he said after a few minutes. I wish I had something useful to offer – words of wisdom, a profound statement that might help to bundle up his sadness into a manageable size.

'I'm afraid it's all I have right now.'

A siren blared in the background.

'Your dad's going to be all right, you know.'

I nodded. 'But no one lives for ever,' I said. 'And that's not being pessimistic. Unless you want to try and prove me wrong?'

'I'll prove you wrong another time.' He handed me the cigarette after taking a puff. 'A cigarette shared …'

I raised it towards him. '… is the chance of lung cancer halved.'

'To clichés,' he said, smiling.

We sat in silence until I threw the stub in the cup. Never been at Conall's when it's this dark and it had already been a bit awkward, but for that moment I was so grateful that he lived next door, and so grateful that he was next to me that I leaned in and kissed him on the cheek, without even thinking. Despite the cigarette smoke, he did smell very lovely and *clean*. 'Thanks for listening to my crap.'

'Oh, yeah, fine,' he said, not seeming sure where to look. Way to make a person feel uncomfortable, Sofia. I got up, picking up the packet of cigarettes.

'I think it's time for me to give these up,' I said, throwing the packet in the bin.

'Thanks for getting me to smoke after eight years and *then* deciding to give up.'

'You're welcome.' I thought about Naim. 'It should be easy enough to give up the things that are bad for you.'

He smiled as he stood up. 'Ever the philosopher, Sofe.'

Sunday 22 April

7.30 a.m. I didn't think it was possible, but I ended up sleeping well enough last night, and I've woken up with a bit of that hollowness filled. That must be the answer to my prayers.

Tuesday 24 April

8 a.m. Dad's coming out of hospital at the end of the week. Thanks to God. This does mean I have to announce to the family that I'm getting married. Called Hannah to say sorry, and then she said sorry, and we carried on saying sorry to each other for about ten minutes. Must be grateful for friends who forgive and forget. They are the best kind.

Maria and T are still in quiet talks. Every time Mum and I try to eavesdrop, they go quiet. That's the thing with couples – one minute they're telling you everything that's wrong with their marriage and partner, and the next minute they're defending each other with sanctimonious silence.

'What's with all the privacy?' I asked her.

She locked her arm in mine and just smiled. Which was good enough for me.

9.30 a.m. Imran called as I was on my way to work. The least a person can have in the morning is peace. We were speaking and he was telling me about the cricket match from the night before – me wanting to poke myself in the eye to keep awake and, all of a sudden, he said, 'Isn't it weird how me and Fozia were at the same singles' do?' Huh. What? 'Like it was a sign or something?'

Well, I don't know. I'd think something if I knew what the hell he was talking about. What singles' do? Did he mean the one Fozia went to without me? And what did that have to do with emailing me? Of course it's important to maintain a sense of sisterhood, so I pretended as if what he said made perfect sense.

'Yes, totally a sign. They're very useful.'

The only thing this was a sign for was dodgy dealings. And now Fozia isn't picking up her phone!

9.40 a.m. Why isn't Fozia picking up her phone?? Need caffeine. Must go and make coffee.

9.55 a.m. Still no answer and now Brammers wants to see me in her office.

10.30 a.m. Book, oh book! Between hospital-ridden Dad, preggers sister, friend suffering marital breakdown and a man in my life who insists on talking about bunting for the wedding stage, I haven't done nearly as much work as I was supposed to.

'I know with your father it's been very difficult, so we can push the deadline forward a little for you, but you know, it's er, well, still tricky.' Brammers moved her head side to side.

'No, of course. I'll do it. I'm just ploughing through.'

ARGH!!

10.45 a.m. Sign shmign! Cannot believe that one of my best friends would coerce person that is now my fiancé to email me in an attempt to divert my attention away from Naim! It's so underhand, so calculated, so interfering. So *me*.

'You're engaged, aren't you? That's what you wanted,' she said when I started shouting at her down the phone.

I can't actually remember saying that's what I wanted. Is there a template for all expectations and wants?

'You meddled. If you hadn't told him to email he probably wouldn't have and ...'

'And what? You'd still be speaking to that dirty dog and going back and forth. Sofe, listen,' she said. 'I've been thinking so much about Riaz and when I saw Imran at that do, I just thought ... I don't want *both* of us to regret things. One of us should be happy, right?'

How can anyone stay angry with this girl?

'Please just find him on Facebook and message him,' I said to her.

'No, darling. I couldn't. It'd be different if he messaged me.'

'Oh Lord help me. OK, fine, let's wait for that to happen. In the meantime, I hope your pride makes a comforting bedfellow.'

'Let's just focus on you right now.'

'Me? I'm great. And FYI, I didn't need Imran to get over Naim; I'm engaged to him because it's a reasonable thing to do. You know, when someone says they'll move out. I'm being reasonable.'

'But you do love him?'

There should be a ban on the 'L' word too.

7.40 p.m. Auntie and Uncle Scot have made at least three comments about Chachu not being home, raising their eyebrows in judgemental unity.

9.35 p.m. It's bad enough that I have a dad with a failing heart, but now I also have a chachu who probably has a battered liver. Can everyone please act responsibly towards their organs?? I'm going to find this chachu of mine. I don't care if I have to walk into every pub in London.

9.37 p.m. Right after I get some coriander from Bismillah Grocery store because they're selling five bunches for the price of three, according to Mum.

'Oh haan, and also get some garlic and chillies. But fat ones.'

Sure, Mum. I'll just walk around as if I'm poised to cook a curry.

11.45 p.m. Turns out I just had to go to the pub around the corner (not before I stopped off at Bismillah's, obviously). Felt like an idiot hijabi strolling into a pub at ten o'clock at night.

I looked around and Chahcu was sitting at the bar, ordering a drink. I marched over to him and prodded him on the shoulder, so I could tell him off in finger-wagging fashion. He turned around and for a moment I don't think he realised who I was. He looked so sad that any thoughts of wagging my finger went out of my head. Then he clearly added all the factors together in his alcohol-addled mind: niece is here, I'm in pub, therefore niece must be in pub too – cue look of horror.

'Soffoo. What are you doing here?'

He stumbled as he tried to stand up. I got him to sit down as the barman placed his drink on the table.

'Chalo, Soffoo, I have to take you home.' But his second attempt to stand up was no more successful than the first.

'Don't look at your chachu!' He put both his hands on my shoulders and looked at the floor. I wasn't sure whether he was about to say something profound or that he'd just fallen asleep.

'Let's try this again, Chachu.' I held him around the waist and he got up, knocking the barstool over. Then the plastic bag with the stupid shopping got caught in the stool leg, the bag ripped, and all the items fell to the floor. Chachu went to pick them up and was about to fall flat on his hammered face when someone came and grabbed him.

'Time to go home, eh?' I looked up to see Conall drape Chachu's arm around his shoulder. I had to put the garlic and chillies in my inside pocket and bunch up the coriander. Conall looked over at me.

'Christ, *what* are you doing?'

I stood there cradling coriander and was about to explain that there was an offer on, but he was already at the door.

'Love,' called the barman. 'Who's gonna pay for the drink he didn't have?'

Bloody hell. Paying for alcohol is just as bad as drinking it but then not paying for something is also bad. It was quite a moral dilemma. I fumbled around for my purse, trying not to drop anything, paid the man for the whisky and got out of The Hog's Head.

Mum distracted the Scots while Conall took Chachu to his room. Conall managed to get him on the bed and when he turned around I realised I was still cradling the coriander.

'He'll sleep that off. But, Sofe, I really think he needs help. I've seen him in there getting drunk, a lot. Who's Bobby?' Chachu let out a huge snort and his leg fell off the bed. 'Listen, if he wants, he can join me in one of my AA meetings.

'You're in AA?'

He nodded.

'I'll give him the number. Don't worry,' he said.

Conall's in AA? I thought about it and actually I've never seen any alcohol in his kitchen, but I'm so used to not seeing alcohol I didn't think anything of it. And at the launch he did just have orange juice. Then there's the dad. Is that presumptuous of me – just because his father's an alcoholic, he'd be too. But I have a feeling we do inherit our parents' problems.

'If you're in AA, why are you in pubs?'

He sighed.

'Helping a friend.'

'Oh.'

'How's your dad?' he asked.

I went to lift Chachu's (hefty) leg back on the bed and pulled the covers over him.

'Back tomorrow. He'll be just fine when I tell him I'm getting married.'

I turned around but couldn't see Conall properly with only the pale light from the street lamp. Plus I didn't know what to do with the coriander.

'How long have you been in AA?' I asked.

'Who the hell are you marrying?'

'Shhh. Keep your voice down.'

'The American that didn't show up?'

'No. Not the American.'

'Forced marriage, beardie?'

'Er, no. Imran.'

'Who?'

'Imran.'

'Imraein?'

'Imraaaan.'

'*Hole*-in-the-wall?'

I nodded.

'You're getting hitched to the hole-in-the-wall, after *all* your ranting?'

Chachu let out another snort and shifted his bulk towards us, his knuckles scraping the floor.

'What in the name of Christ made you do that?' Conall whispered so loudly he might as well have used a Tannoy.

'I don't have to live with the hole-in-the-wall any more.'

His response was to exhale. 'Oh, well done.'

'It's *progress*.'

I had a horrid recollection of Ambreen's mum-in-law watching me hold Ambreen's newborn baby.

'Have you *even* thought it through?'

'What is wrong with everyone, acting as if I don't have a clue about life?'

'Oh, you have a clue.'

'I live in the real world,' I whispered back, pointing to myself with the coriander.

'Is it that easy to switch feelings for people, Sofe?' He rested his hand on the wall and leaned over, shaking his head.

I don't know. Is it?

'Feckin' hell.' Then he walked past and I followed him down the stairs as he said goodbye and walked out. Why was he angry with *me*?

'I'm just trying to do the right thing,' I said to nobody but the closed door in my face.

Saturday 28 April

8 a.m. You can't say that Dad didn't get a welcome home party given that practically all members of the family were waiting, huddled in the passage. We now have eight functioning hearts that obviously nearly lapsed – mine included – when the news of my pending nuptials spread.

Mum and Maria brought tea for everyone, the Scots were giving Dad pitying glances, Chachu sat there silent, and T was fiddling with his phone. Maria looked around and nudged Tahir.

'He's just going to help me get my stuff together,' she said.

Everyone looked up. 'Now Dad's back, I think it's good for me to go back home.'

Mum and Dad exchanged looks. Dad nodded and Mum said it's just as well they'll have her room back, barely containing her smile.

When everyone had left to let Dad rest, I sat with him for a while. It was on the tip of my tongue but every time I went to tell him it was like the words caught in my throat.

'Chalo now, Beta. No more fussing. Find someone this year.'

Sod it. Sod Conall's angry face. I pushed the words through my mouth and told Dad that I'm engaged.

Of course, Chachu overheard. He leaned in through the doorway, and said, 'You're getting married?' His voice is so characteristically Punjabber, it carried downstairs and I heard Mum say, 'Who's getting married?' This was followed by five sets of footsteps running up the stairs.

'Haw hai – no first telling parents. Bhabi, girls in London are so *advanced*,' said Uncle Scot.

Well, at least now every one knows. Right, off to Conall's. I'm going to act entirely normal when I see him. I'll be the bigger person and ignore his unreasonable anger towards me. I will out-reason him yet.

8.30 a.m. He left the house early this morning. He didn't get to see my reasonableness.

10.30 p.m. I cannot believe that Imran is in a strop because of my continuation of weekends at Conall's. His suggestion? Shut the door to my room. It's unnatural enough for me to be living at home. Shutting the door and having a 'Keep Out' sign wouldn't do much for my sense of self I tried to explain.

'So when's this story going to be finished? We gonna be rich?'

'I'm not writing the next Harry Potter.'

'I never understood how a story about magic got famous.'

Oh dear.

10.55 p.m. Of course it's not important whether someone's read *Harry Potter* or not. Except that they must've been asleep for the better part of this century. Also, one shouldn't off-handedly disparage something they've not read.

11 p.m. Though I reserve the right to do so for self-published erotica. Obviously.

Sunday 29 April

10.45 a.m.

Sofe,

There's semi-skimmed milk in the fridge because I know how important it is to your health when you're having tea and eating Chocolate Hobnobs.

Conall

PS How's your uncle?

Turned the note around to see if there was anything else. Nothing. I wish he could've told me in person.

1 p.m. I told Suj about weird Conall behaviour.

'Oh,' she said. 'He's a good friend to you, Toffee.'

Wasn't what I was expecting her to say. I looked at his note again. 'He is. When he's not shouting at me.'

'Yeah, but white people don't really get us, do they? They all think we're mental, living with our parents until we get married and all sorts.'

Not sure this is about being Asian. But then I'm not sure *what* this is about.

MAY 2012

For Whom the Wedding
Bells Toll

AYISHA MALIK

Muslim Dating Book

There are three things that are certain in life: death, taxes and, if you're Punjabi, a big, fat wedding. Time-honoured tradition in the shape of fried pakoras and henna-painted hands are to be revered, apparently. And in this quagmire of multiplying pakoras and increasingly intricate henna patterns the person for whom – with whom – you're doing all this becomes fuzzier. The elastic boundaries of cultural tradition are stretched and stretched. You just never know how far it can go before it (and you) finally snaps.

Things to do

1. *Venue. YAWN . . .*
2. *Wedding dress. Ibid.*
3. *Caterers. (Apparently people can tell one kebab from another.)*
4. *Take maroon drapes out of shed. (Recycling is environmentally friendly.)*
5. *Makeup person. Suj. Sorted.*
6. *Centrepieces. Seriously, who gives a shit?*
7. *Fruit baskets . . . Seriously, what?*
8. *Mehndi trays. Shed.*
9. *Ice sculptures. Er, VETO.*
10. *Find a photographer . . .*

Thursday 3 May

10 a.m. Bleurgh. It's parent involvement time. I want to keep my eyes shut until someone tells me it's over. Imran's mum is going to call today and I won't be home to monitor what my mum might say. Perhaps I should've taken the phone off the hook before I left.

7.25 p.m. Apparently she called at two o'clock (bloody Imran didn't bother telling me). I was going to ask Mum what she was like but, before I even opened my mouth, she said, 'Did you tell Imran you wouldn't live with his parents?'

'Of course. You know that's why I didn't marry him.'

Then she looked at my dad who was already shaking his head.

'Haw hai. Thinking is one thing but saying is another. What will happen if everyone says what they think?' Which was pretty rich. 'Sometimes you should stay quiet or you'll be back a day after your wedding,' said Mum.

Why am I being told to keep my mouth shut over life's essential matters?

'No matter if you don't like something, Soffoo,' said Dad rubbing his chest. 'Sometimes a person must be quiet.'

Newsflash, parents – this ain't the 1950s and we ain't in Lahore any more, but then who wants to be the daughter that gave her dad a second heart attack?

'Maybe. But I am *not* that woman.' With which I walked out of the room, head held high, in dignified fashion.

Saturday 5 May

8 a.m. Imran and the family are coming over tomorrow evening. Everyone is hyper about getting the wedding organised. I just want to take a nap.

8 p.m. Went to Conall's, and he was still home.

'Hi,' I said.

'Hi.'

'All OK?' I asked.

'Grand,' he said, walking into the kitchen where he was making coffee.

I went into the living room, wracking my brain to think of something funny or interesting to say when he walked in and put a mug in front of me.

'Thanks.'

He sat at the table and pushed a plate of biscuits towards me. There was a muffin in the middle.

'I shouldn't eat any more biscuits,' I said, taking the muffin.

Silence. Conall took a sip from his mug as I searched for words – any words.

'What's the topic today then?' he asked. Thank God! I straightened up in my seat.

'In-laws – as usual, and the injustice of it all,' I said. But this led back to Imran, and it felt weird. I wish I'd just kept my mouth shut. Conall rubbed a scratch on the table.

'Why are you so angry about it? You're not moving in with them,' he said.

'Yes, but it's the *principle*. Anyway, doesn't matter.'

'Maybe he feels his principle trumps your principle?' he said.

'Oh, really?'

'I'm not saying he's right, just looking at the reasoning,' he said, putting his hands in the air. His eyes rested on the clock behind me. 'Well, time for me to go.'

He put his coat on, wrapping a keffiyah around his neck. I willed myself to stop feeling so miserable that he was leaving. All I wanted was for things to go back to normal.

'Where are you going?' I asked.

'Palestine protest.'

Also, why is everything about him just so bloody *good*? And here I was, writing a book about dating.

'You protest about your injustice.' He looked over at my laptop. 'And I'll go and protest about mine.' A few days ago that would've sounded normal, but today there was ice in his voice and I hated it.

'Right. Of course.' I pretended to concentrate on my laptop screen.

He went to leave and then turned around.

'Unless ...'

'Yes?' I looked up.

'Unless you want to come with me?'

We got to the protest, which started at the House of Parliament. Most people were wearing keffiyahs, jackets were plastered with Palestine badges, people carried huge banners and flags, children with Palestinan bandannas tied around their little heads – a foray of black, white, green and red. I've come to the conclusion that London's at its best when protesting. A crowd of white people went past, chanting, 'By the tens, by the millions, we are all Palestinians.' An old man walked with this stick that also doubled up as a chair. Every so often he'd sit down and drink from his flask.

As we walked through Knightsbridge, past the Queen's barracks, there were people sitting out on the balconies, waving Palestinian flags, rainbow-coloured flags, cheering everyone on. Conall had his camera and kept stopping to take photos. It was always remarkable to see what inspired him to pause and capture a moment. One that you might've otherwise missed

When we got to Hyde Park the speeches had started, and everyone was scattered around, sitting quietly or standing up.

Conall put his camera down and folded his arms, looking serious as ever.

'We come together here today because we are a free people. We live in a city and country for which our ancestors fought so that we could exercise that freedom. But with it comes a duty to us all, to use our voice for those who are voiceless ...'

There was scattered applause, and I thought how stupid my problems seemed, how small. I even forgot that Conall was next to me.

'This is the time to unite: to tell the oppressors that we won't be silenced. That we won't shun the gift of previous generations. This is the time to raise your voice and tell them: we will not abandon our duty. We will not forsake the voiceless. Yes, we are free, but in the words of the great Nelson Mandela: "Our freedom is incomplete without the freedom of the Palestinians!"'

At which point the cheers were so loud I couldn't hear my own voice (imagine!). I had to wipe a tear from my eye before Conall saw me. As someone else took to the mic, a group of beardies were walking towards us. They kept looking at Conall and then at me and I thought, what a bloody inappropriate time to be judgemental. I mean, come on, people. Bigger picture, please.

'Bro.' One of the beardies who, incidentally, had the longest beard, beamed as Conall walked up to him and hugged him. I think my hate-dar was generally off all day today.

'Good to see you, man,' said the beardie.

I couldn't hear the conversation. The other beardies nodded from afar – gave me one look and turned away. Conall spoke to him for a while and then Long Beard went on his way.

'Do you think I should've worn a longer top?' I asked when he came back. Mine only just covered my arse.

He gave the length of my top the once-over.

'The length of a hijabi's top or dress should be in direct correlation with the length of a Muslim guy's beard,' I explained.

He looked confused.

'Look, it's not just about *skin*. It's, you know, *shape*.'

Oh, Lord. One does sometimes take for granted how a brown man will just *get* it. Explaining this to Conall just made me super conscious of fact that I was drawing attention to things which I was avoiding in the first place. So that's what people mean when they say, someone's eyes smiled. I guess stretching a smile to his mouth is always a bit of task for Conall.

'I thought you didn't care what people thought?' he said.

'They're not people – they're *beardies*.'

Conall laughed, but I don't know why. It's true!

I think I might have had a few too many coffees, as I was feeling quite jaunty by the end of the day. Up until now I hadn't even thought about Naim. He was slip, slip, slipping away.

'Why don't I go to these protests more often?' I jumped up and down which, granted, caused a few disconcerted glances from onlookers. 'They're just so *fun*. And have a clear moral and ethical purpose. Obviously.'

'Sofe, I'd have thought you'd come to them all the time.'

I say I will but never actually do. Will make more of an effort in the future to shut up and just do a thing.

We got on the Northern line and sat down. Quite a few leftover protestors were looking at pics they'd taken, legs splayed out, sipping coffee. We got off at Tooters and crossed the traffic lights. I asked Conall where he knew Long Beard from. A very different group of boys were walking towards us. Most of them had shaved heads, a few were drinking cans of beer. Conall watched them and he came closer, putting his hand on the small of my back. Bloody hell, we both looked like Palestinian freedom fighters. We had got a bit carried away with the badge buying – Conall had even pinned one on the back of my hijab – he said anyone who saw it would take me seriously as a political activist.

As they walked past I heard 'Fucking traitor', but it seemed to come from another direction because the group of boys had walked on without a second look. Then the rest happened in what seemed like a flash. I felt Conall's hand lift off my back, heard a thud and a grunt and when I turned around he was looking down at the ground with a clenched fist mid-air. There, on the ground, was a man lying on his back, cupping his bleeding nose. He attempted to get up and Conall went to hit him again, but I held him back, and had to drag him away from the scene of this unexpected event!

What the hell! We walked back to the house in silence. He slammed the door and marched into the living room. I followed him but he just stood there, looking around. He turned around and marched into the kitchen. To be fair, I have become quite accustomed to him slamming things. He walked back in and sat on the sofa and kind of stared into space.

'I thought you were a pacifist,' I said.

He shot me a look as if he was about to punch *me*, but then seemed to realise I wasn't the one who'd just called him a traitor.

'I am. Unless provoked.'

'Bloody hell. Can't even support a poor country without being verbally abused.'

He looked up. 'I don't think he was referring to my political views.'

I nodded. 'I know.' I felt like saying sorry to him. If I were white and hijabless, no one would've accused him of such a thing. But what a stupid reason to have to apologise – as if a person can help being brown. 'Maybe you need anger management as well as AA – do you think they have a two-for-one offer or something?' He didn't find that funny.

'What did you want me to do?'

'I don't know. Don't think giving him a nose bleed was the answer.'

'Well, why don't you bake him a cupcake instead.'

'That's not fair, Conall. You know I can't bake.'

I walked to the window and opened the blinds.

'Domestic disaster, aren't you?' he said.

'We all have our version of disasters. Your fist could do with some ice.' I got a bag of peas out of the freezer and threw them on the sofa.

'At least you have another fist that's intact,' I said.

He looked at it and threw the bag of peas on the table.

'I should go back and beat the shit out of him. And then take a photo of it.'

'What is *wrong* with you? Shouldn't you photography types be impartial; assessing the world through Switzerland-tinted glasses?' I asked. Turns out I don't have the monopoly on outrage when faced with prejudice.

'Being impartial's for fence sitters, Sofe. I'm no feckin' fence sitter.'

He doesn't say much that Conall, but when he does, it *stays*. I went and sat next to him.

'You're such an arse.' I handed him the bag of peas again. 'Anyway, no one wants to be a fence sitter. It's very uncomfortable,' I replied.

He turned towards me, clearly still angry, and said, 'Tell me. Why'd you start wearing that scarf?'

Had to wonder whether it offended him in some way – *that scarf*. I looked at his fist and thought about it for a moment.

'George,' I said. 'Michael. Gotta have faith.'

'Do you *ever* give a normal response to a question?'

'Yes, when the question is interesting.'

Though I must say, George did have a point.

'OK.' He turned towards me so we sat face to face. 'I'm asking because I genuinely want to know the answer,' he said.

'OK.'

'Why do you believe in God? I know why some people believe in God, but why do *you* believe in God?'

Crikey. I think I preferred the hijab question. Being asked about believing in God is like having to explain to someone why you're in a relationship with a person who has a bit of a bad reputation.

'Oh, well.' I shrugged. I mean what could I say? 'OK, and don't laugh or snigger or judge, OK?'

He nodded.

'Because I trust you. Do you promise?'

'Promise.'

'I don't know if you've noticed but I'm sometimes of a disgruntled nature.'

'No.'

'Shocking, I know. Anyway, when you're of such a disposition of you know, being pissed off, you tend to like the thing that kind of, well, gives you . . .' I fiddled with the end of my scarf. 'Like, you know. Peace.' He looked at me as if he were trying to catch me out in a lie. 'Also, you can't help what you love.'

'Peace?'

'Mhmm. When I was a child and my parents argued, I prayed. Then, the more I read about it, the more I believed it. Sometimes

I think I'm a lucky cow because how many people can say they have something to lean on. So that even when you have nothing, you always have that. You are never alone.'

He put the bag of peas on his fist.

'Very few.'

'There we have it, my secret un-*veiled*.'

'I can't make you out,' he said, searching my face. I was suddenly very aware of his leg touching mine and also, for some reason, his adam's apple.

'Oh, well,' I said, looking at his fist. 'People are nuanced.'

'Is Imran nuanced?'

I stared at Conall's bruised fist and thought how Imran is the precise opposite of nuanced. Without thinking I touched the bruise – dipping my fingers into the grooves of his knuckles. It was too close, but the bruise meant something, if you think about it. He kept looking, waiting for my answer. Why the hell was I touching his hand? I stood up, perhaps a little quicker than I intended, and he got up and stepped towards me. Was he going to say something? *Do* something. Before I could find out I made my way towards the door. As I opened it I turned around and looked up.

'The thing with Imran,' I said, 'is he gave enough of a shit to compromise. I didn't think people did that any more.'

'He didn't fly to the moon, Sofe.' It came out almost in a whisper.

'That'd be useless anyway. No gravity.'

Which is a bit what that moment felt like.

10 p.m. I'm a liar! But when Imran asked where I was today I couldn't bring myself to tell him that A) I spent the day with another man – however much for a good cause it was and B) that all this time I've spent crying about not having time to write was spent walking around London, dripping in I Heart Palestine badges. So I said that I had the phone on silent in my bag.

'Is everything all right?' he asked.

'Yes, of course.'

'You still want to marry me?'

I paused.

'Do *you* still want to marry *me*?'

'I don't want to marry anyone else.'

Sunday 6 May

8.30 a.m. The two banes of my life – meeting the in-laws and fried onions. How does one prepare the brain for underhanded verbal assaults (I feel Pakistani parents are particularly good at these, though I might be being racist) when my senses are being assaulted by fried onions at the break of dawn? My hair and the rest of me stank before I even got out of bed.

I woke up thinking about the conversation with Conall yesterday. I wish I hadn't touched his fist. What an invasion of someone's space. Or told him about God and peace and blah, blah, blah – you say you believe in God and people look at you as if you've said 'I believe in fairies'. Not that Conall looked like that, but whoever knows *what* he's thinking?

8.50 a.m. Tried to launch a candle offensive but Mum's told me to worry less about the smelly house and more about helping in the kitchen. Having a fiancé is so time consuming – an entire day wasted on preparing food. I'll help, but I'm not going to lie and tell his parents that I cooked any of it. I am just not the sort of daughter-in-law who will pretend to enjoy things like vacuuming and curry powder.

9.45 a.m. I was in the kitchen taking out the big dish for biryani and is it my fault that I dropped it and it fell on my poor foot? I mean, the last thing someone needs after almost losing a toe is their mother losing their temper. I've consequently been banished from the kitchen. Since I'm no use in the kitchen I'm going to go to Conall's and write.

10.55 a.m. Hmph – glad someone finds my limping funny. Last time I ask him how his knuckles are – though I don't think there'd ever be a reason to ask that again anyway.

He looked at my feet. 'Let's hope it's not a dealbreaker.'

'If anything's going to be a dealbreaker it's the fact that everything, including the linen, stinks of fried onions.'

'Nervous?' he said.

'What's there to be nervous about?'

'Meeting the future in-laws for the first time?'

I gestured towards my foot. 'Imran is about to introduce his parents to the girl with the limp for whom he is leaving the nest – I don't think I'm the one who should be nervous.'

Conall tapped his fingers on the table, looking at his fist. 'The only thing he should be nervous about is making sure he's good enough for you.' And then, without looking my way, he got up and left the room.

I think that's the nicest thing anyone's ever said to me.

7.15 p.m. Bloody, bloody hell. I've had to change five times. Apparently any simple outfit is unacceptable. Surely the only unacceptable thing is my attire being dictated by my mum. Dad made a feeble attempt to tell Mum to leave me alone but she said that she has his prescriptions and, if necessary, she will hold on to them. He leaned forward as I adjusted the unruly scarf that refused to pin up properly and said, 'Thirty-three years ago she couldn't speak English. Now she's holding my medication ransom.'

I thought how funny Conall would find that. How funny Naim would've found it. All the world's a stage. And my unwieldy hijab is its curtain.

11.45 p.m.

From Imran: I hope you cook like your mum.

When people have their love goggles on, they don't believe a bad word you say. Sometimes it'd be nice for Imran to say I'm being an annoying cow, which would be completely acceptable as I can be an annoying cow a lot of the time.

Imran's mum, who, by the way, I'm meant to call Ammi (and, please, that is not happening), started digging into the biryani.

'Did Beti make this?'

No, love, *Beti* was dreaming about cigarettes while Beti's mum picked out the nuts in the chevra mix because your husband is allergic to them.

Self-appointed Ammi (SAA) looked at me and smiled. I thought she might take the chiffon scarf off when she came in but she kept it on. Not a scrap of makeup. This is what my mum describes as *simple* people, but it seems I didn't have to worry about any under-handed verbal assault.

She put food on her husband's plate before filling her own.

'Haider always says to me when I go to Pakistan, "Khalda, who will know how much rice to put in my plate?"'

Err, I dunno – you? But Imran was beaming at them. Mum, Dad, Maria and me looked at each other, a little uncomfortable with all this niceness, to be honest.

'I think June is perfect time for wedding,' said Imran's dad, looking over at his wife and nodding.

'Haan, we think the weather is nice and before Ramadan they can also go for honeymoon.'

I felt like my throat was closing up. June? June?? That's next month! First of all, I have to get thin, second of all, that's next month. Mum and Dad sat there, nodding in agreement. I tried to catch Imran's eye but he was too absorbed in setting dates to consult (hello?) the woman he's meant to be marrying. Maria intervened.

'That's quite early, isn't it?'

'Nahin, nahin, Beta,' said Imran's mum. 'All good things should be done quickly. Also,' she continued, 'now they are living away from home ...' His mum looked at her husband who urged her to carry on, 'Haider's nephew is estate agent and he can find them cheap place to rent.'

'Why waste money on house that isn't yours? Hmm?' piped up old Haider.

'And then we think we should help them buy house together, haina?' said SAA.

It was all *first-time buyers! House prices! When two families become one* ... Mum and Dad didn't take two seconds to say that they were glad this was brought up because they felt the same. Don't know when they had that conversation. Or maybe I wasn't listening?

So the collective has decided to help Imran and me with a deposit for a home, and in the meantime faceless and nameless nephew will be providing a flat for habitation. Where? Leyton! Yes. Exactly. And when I suggested something a little more equidistant to my beloved South London, my concerns were pushed aside because, apparently, we'll worry about that when we start looking to buy. I'm not sure whether 'we' constitutes me and Imran, or the people at the table and, possibly, the nameless nephew.

'Are you OK, Bhai?' asked Imran's mum, looking at my dad.

'Haan haan. I'm Alhamdolilah OK. Doctor says I should make very good recovery, and my wife is, ahem, such a good carer.' Dad winked at me and Maria. 'But what I really want is for my daughter to get married, so June is very good for us.'

How can you argue with a dad who looks so happy you have to ask him to keep his heart in check?

Note for book: When keeping an eye on a person's heart, perhaps give yours the once over too.

And so it is. I'm getting married. June 30th.

Monday 7 May

7.30 a.m. I had a nightmare that it's the day before my wedding and I'm spitting out teeth into the sink. Dad comes in and says we're at war with America and have to migrate. Then Mum comes into the bathroom and asks where her Sainsbury's shopping list is because she needs to give it to Maria, who's gone to Moscow (??) for the baby's birth.

7.40 a.m. Had to check teeth were all intact.

8.10 a.m.

> **From Imran:** Have you got your guest list ready? We need numbers so can book the hotel.

Imran's mum insists on buying me a wedding dress. Proviso being that it's her choice. Sigh. Putting that to one side, I asked why we can't just go to the mosque, say, 'I do' three times and get the day over with? Mum is horrified at the idea of a mosque shindig and Imran won't hear of it. Something about his parents' youngest son getting a good send-off.

'We're not going to be living with them, so this is like their way of saying goodbye,' he said. I wanted to say, for God's sake – you're getting married – not going to war. I refrained. I can be disciplined like that. 'Don't you want that?' he added.

'I don't mind, as long as it doesn't involve me being stuck behind a table for four hours, head hurting from all the pins keeping the three-tonne scarf on my head.' But clearly not that disciplined.

He didn't respond.

'It's OK,' I said. 'It's fine. You know, just make sure the scarf doesn't weigh three tonnes. That's all.'

I wanted to add that it'd be nice if he made sure the outfit isn't some horrific shade of red, but perhaps will precede that with a polite conversation.

2 p.m. Why does everyone in the office keep asking me if I'm OK? Of course I'm OK. I'm getting married next month. Which reminds me that perhaps I should tell them. At least I should tell Katie as she will have to save the date.

5.30 p.m. OK, I didn't have time to send a save the date email, but I really did have to chase up those long-lead magazines. And, to be quite honest, it's just good form to help Fleur out with the work experience person and show them where the post room is. I used to be an assistant once too, after all.

7 p.m. Bumped into Conall coming out of the station and he asked how the dinner on Sunday went.

'Fine. Not so much as a misplaced sigh.'

He put his hands in his pockets and nodded. 'Good. Good. Glad to hear it.' He looked at the ground as we walked towards home.

'How's the fist?' I asked.

'Grand, really. I like having a few bruises to show for moral victories.'

'Conall, there is nothing moral about violence.'

'I'm going to teach you how to throw a punch. Then you can tell me that when you're able to box the shit out of the next man that calls you a terrorist.'

Would've been nice, certainly, to knock out that moron on the Tube. It's not a very Muslim way, though, and unfortunately I can't really be innovative with the ways of our peeps; especially if my own ideas of innovation include breaking someone's face.

'Shall I bring my boxing gloves on the weekend then?' I asked.

'You want to box?'

I nodded.

'No worries then, Sofe. I've got everything we need.'

Saturday 12 May

11 a.m. Oh my actual God. Conall wasn't joking. I walked into the house and there were a pair of boxing gloves on the table. He brought in two mugs of coffee and handed me one.

'You're going to need this.'

2.10 p.m. It's official. I can kick ass (ass/arse?). Who knew I could kick that high? More to the point, who knew my jeans had such give? I've been trained in the art of right and left jabs too. I did almost knock Conall out but he should've been paying attention to where I was punching as opposed to something behind me, whatever it was.

'I could be like a hijabi Buffy the Vampire Slayer,' I said, bounding out of the front room. 'A scarfie superhero.'

'Just save yourself, Sofe. That'd be enough.'

Hmph.

8.45 p.m. Perhaps there is a correlation between boxing and productivity. Got an inordinate amount of writing done, have managed to tidy unruly bedroom, wax legs, pluck eyebrows (cannot believe I subjected Conall to the monobrow, *with* sunlight streaming through the front window) and shopped online for jeggings. Controversial, I know, but perfect and necessary for my new lifestyle as Scarf Face.

Ah, Imran calling.

10.05 p.m. Really, I don't know what he means by me being in an especially good mood.

Sunday 13 May

8.50 a.m. I'm being bombarded with congratulations text messages. Have I accidentally announced my engagement on Facebook? Was there a memo sent out to the community of which I'm not aware? Ambreen wants to go shopping for costume jewellery. Who gives a shit about costume jewellery? I have a boxing lesson!

9 a.m. Except I just tried to get out of bed and my legs almost gave way. Perhaps I should've warmed up before high kicks and left–right jabs. Ouch.

9.50 a.m. Hobbled downstairs, and Mum and Maria were in the TV room with a guest list. Mum's been calling everyone to announce the wedding date. I never knew this could make you feel like you have a stomach ulcer.

Maria ran her finger down the list until she stopped, looked up and said, 'We're not inviting Conall are we? Cos we want him to do the photography. Have you asked yet?'

'Oh, I hadn't thought about it.'

'You've only got six weeks. Ask him today. Maybe he'll do it for free, cos you're mates now.'

Mum's eyes lit up at the word 'free'.

'He has better things to photograph than yet another bride and groom.'

And also, I can't ask him. I know we're friends, but it feels weird to ask him this perfectly normal question. Not sure why.

'Tell me friends you're going to invite,' said Mum, picking up the phone and dialling a number. Before I could answer she was talking to someone called Bilal about tandoori chicken.

Monday 14 May

3.20 p.m. I've just told Katie I'm getting married.

'Oh my God. The American came to his senses.'

'Er, no.'

'Oh.' She put her hand on my arm. 'Then who, Sweetu?'

Told her the hole-in-the-wall retraction story.

'Oh. OK. That's … that's *good*. So this is the one?'

'The one I'm marrying, yes.'

'No, I mean the *one*.'

Honestly. The 'one' is obviously the person you marry because that's whose mug you'll see every morning for the rest of your life. That's a person's *one*.

Saturday 19 May

10.30 a.m. I am Rocky in a scarf! Perhaps next I should take lessons in being graceful. But having a plant right next to the punch bag isn't very good positioning. I tried to clean up the mess, but ended up just hovering over Conall, who began sweeping and telling me I should be careful where I kick my legs. He's left now so I'm going to write, but I should do something nice for him – to make up for occupying his house and destroying it, fern by fern.

10.35 a.m. I know, I'll bake him some cupcakes! Everyone likes cupcakes now. So much of life is centred on cupcakes. How hard can it be? Also, it'd be a nice 'in your face' moment when I hand them over to him, perfectly made. Domestic disaster indeed. Sometimes I'm surprised at how capable I am of doing kind things for people. I'll be an utter genius and make red velvets! According to Googs, it'll take forty minutes. Sorted. I'll go out, get ingredients, bake, and be done by midday and have the rest of the day to write.

11.10 a.m. Balls. Forgot cream cheese.

11.35 a.m. Hmmm, how does this bloody oven work …

11.55 a.m. Oops. I didn't realise I'd turned the oven on and have consequently almost singed my eyebrows. Also, according to my personal deadline, the cupcakes should be done in five minutes and I haven't even mixed the batter yet. Thanks to God for online instructions.

12.15 p.m. Crap. He doesn't have an electric mixer. I'm sure boxing has given me sturdy enough arms to whisk ingredients manually.

Ooh, Fozia calling.

12.55 p.m. Oh my God! Fozia just told me that she emailed Riaz! Hurrah! I had to be sure that this meant Kam was well and truly over. She paused before saying, 'It was over a long time before it was over, darling.'

Quite, Fozia. Quite.

It's not easy keeping the phone pressed to one's ear, concentrating on mixing flour and eggs *and* friend's old love interest coming back on the scene, but I seem to be the queen of multi-tasking.

1.05 p.m. Why aren't 'sifted' ingredients and 'wet' ingredients smooth yet? Arm is hurting. The man has cake tins but not an electric mixer. Honestly.

Argh! Time to pray!

2.35 p.m. Oh dear. I think the oven was a little overheated and now the cupcakes are burnt on the outside but squidgy on the inside.

Just called Maria, who helpfully told me that I shouldn't have left oven pre-heating for so long, and then asked me whether I'm there to write or bake cupcakes. It's as if kind gestures are frowned upon.

Oh balls! Just heard gate close! How can he be home so early??

8.25 p.m. I've always maintained that it's the intention that counts when doing good deeds. Even if said good deed ends in neighbour's kitchen looking like there's been a cupcake massacre. Obviously when Conall walked into the house and smelled something burning, he rushed into the kitchen. I was caught between getting rid of the burned cupcakes and airing out smoke.

'Jesus, what the hell is going on?'

I held out the tray of charred red velvets and tried to give a winning smile.

'Cupcake?'

Spent the subsequent hour scrubbing batter that had splattered in oven, cleaning counter tops and washing dishes.

'To be fair, Conall, it'd have worked out perfectly well if you had an electric mixer.'

He then opened the top kitchen cupboard, took out some pans, and then brought out, lo and behold, the mixer.

'Oops.'

I took the towel from him and gave him the mixer to put back in the cupboard. While I was busy defending my eyesight and justifying my baking skills, I just asked, casually, if he could do the photography at my wedding.

'You don't have to, of course.' I looked at him and rolled my eyes in an, *isn't the whole wedding thing a huge bore,* kind of way. 'It's up to you, and I mean you're obviously going to be a guest at the wedding so it's a bit weird, but if there's going to be anyone who's taking photographs then it should be you. Obviously.'

The words felt all wrong. It was like I'd said something not quite right, but I'm not sure what.

He rolled up the sleeves of his jumper and started wiping down the counter tops. Again. Nice arms and hands are underrated.

'Entirely up to you,' I said.

He carried on wiping, but the surface looked pretty clean to me, even with my apparently crappy vision.

'I'll get back to you on that one.'

'Of course, sure. Whatever, you know.'

Then he turned around and said, 'There's a commission going. If I take it then I won't be around on those dates.'

'Oh.' He won't be there? I kind of need him to be, for the moral support. 'When will you decide?'

He put the cloth over his shoulder and folded his arms.

'Soon.'

Conall took a few paces towards me and leaned in and I was like, WTF is going on here. He reached out an arm – *arghhhh, what is he doing*?? – and indicated to something behind me.

'The door, Sofe.'

'What?'

'I need something from the shed.'

'Oh.' I looked behind and, of course, I was standing in front of the door leading to the garden. 'Oh, right.'

So I turned around because, well, I could feel my cheeks burning, and I unlocked the door but the knob wouldn't budge.

'Here, let me do it,' he said.

'No, no, I've got it.'

The stupid thing was stuck.

'You just have to turn it.'

'I am turning it.'

'The other way.'

'What other way?'

'The *opposite* way ... here, let me.'

'No, I've got it.'

I tried to turn it the other way and that didn't work so I turned it the way I was trying to turn it in the first place.

'The *other* way, Sofe.'

'It's not working the other way.'

'It's not working *that* way either.'

So I gave the thing a little yank – and by little I mean really, it was just the slightest yank, and the knob came out in my hand. I stood there for a few seconds before turning around, not quite looking at Conall.

'Oops.' I put my hand out to give him the now-broken item. 'I'm not very good with knobs.'

Conall took it and stepped forward, holding it up to me.

'Sofe, why don't you go inside, sit at your laptop and do some work that doesn't involve being in the kitchen, or near anything that you could possibly destroy.'

I decided not to argue and did as he suggested. I think it was the correct thing to do.

Thursday 24 May

11 a.m. I'm meant to be seeing Imran today to shop for his wedding suit. Why can't he go with his mates or mum or whoever it is you're meant to go with? I tried to explain that I have a book to write, and he was all, 'All right fine' in that passive aggressive way that I thought only I was capable of.

'OK, no, let's go, it's just one evening,' I said.

'What are you going to do when it's the wedding? Or when we go on honeymoon, or when we're moving into the flat?'

We're going on a honeymoon? Rang Suj and she was like, 'Well, that is what normal people do, Sofe. Where are you guys going?'

Had to put the phone down and run into the toilet. Thought I was going to be sick. Why? Why am I not excited about a honeymoon? The problem, of course, is that I must be ungrateful. There are plenty of women who'd be more than happy to find a doting fiancé, blah blah blah. I think there must be a tic with the hardwiring in my head. It's just a temporary glitch. It'll be fine.

11.30 a.m. OMG. Imran is to me what I must've been to Naim. And I'm late for digital meeting.

Sod it, I need a fag.

10.20 p.m. Right, I've read and re-read translation of istikhara:

If this is better for me in this world and the hereafter, then make it destined for me and make it easy and a blessing,

*and if it's bad for me, my religion and faith, for my life and
end, in this world and the hereafter then turn it away from
me and turn me away from it and whatever is better for me,
destine that for me and make me satisfied with it.*

Hmmm, which is perfectly fine really, but I've made my decision.
And there's not been any divine intervention to tell me *not* to
marry him. I'm being stupid. Obviously.

11 p.m. Dad wasn't feeling very well so I rubbed his back for a bit,
while distracting him with tales of my boxing. He laughed saying,
'Good, good. That's my beti.'

I nodded, rather smugly, at Dad's pride in my boxing abilities.
I was about to tell him about the cupcakes but he said he was tired
and was going to try and sleep.

Saturday 26 May

8.45 a.m. I can't write today because Imran's mum is coming over
with her sisters to bring my wedding dress. Don't most normal
people get to choose their own wedding dress even if the outfit
is a present from the in-laws? Surely a kindly groom's side would
hand over the money for the cost of the dress or – in our case,
because we're only having one big ceremony as opposed to two
separate ones – go halves maybe? But no, no. No, no. Dear Imran's
side *insist* on doing things in the way of our ancestors. Most of our

ancestors didn't have to worry about cameras and DVDs lasting for generations though. Because I've insisted on doing things that are *not* the way of our ancestors by not living with the in-laws, this must be my punishment. Sigh. Imran isn't coming because, according to his family, there should be some distance between bride and groom before the wedding. Ungh. Bit ironic given I'd only seen Imran a few days ago and I had to tell him to stop putting his hand on my leg.

8.20 p.m. Oh dear. Girls came over after in-laws had left. We all sat around what can only be described as a lilac mass. Mum picked the wedding dress up and scrutinised it. She threw it back down and raised her eyebrows. Fozia patted the dress and looked like she was about to say something, but then didn't.

'You chose to marry him,' said Mum.

I looked at the girls and Maria. Suj nodded, by way, I guess, of encouragement.

'Is it that bad?' asked Hannah.

'It'll look nice when you wear it,' Maria added.

My sister is such a big, fat liar.

Sunday 27 May

9.45 a.m. Hmmm, Conall's not home. Maybe I should text him and see where he is. Bit nosy, though. It's like, er, who the hell are you and why are you asking me where I am? It's just that I could've done with punching something today.

10 p.m. I'm now home. Saw Conall walk through his gate. I was going to go out and say hello but Suj called. She suggested I accidentally-on-purpose burn the dress.

Tuesday 29 May

9 p.m. While Mum doesn't take much interest in my life unless it involves wedding arrangements, at least it means there are certain things she's not privy to. Dad, on the other hand, is all inquisitiveness. He asked about the book, so I told him the first draft is nearly done, and what did he say? Well, he said he wants to read it. I'm just wondering how well disguised my friends' dating stories are. More importantly, how well disguised *my* dating stories are. Of course, I was terribly composed, slotting in the fact that it's a competitive market and so a certain amount of embellishment is needed. To which he responded with, 'Acha,' and went back to his reading. It's not getting shortlisted for the Man Booker. Fine, re-reading it last night did make us Muslims look like idiots sometimes (am I unintentionally collaborating with the mass media??) but it has to be funny and I have to take out the 'deeper' things, because as Lucinda and Brammers said, it's not *that* type of book. Isn't compromise a part of life? Isn't that what everyone keeps telling me? Think of *others*. Think of your dad.

What is the line between compromising, and compromising oneself?

Note for book: Search for the line, then be sensible and don't cross it.

Thursday 31 May

11.45 p.m. Dad and I decided to watch Maria's wedding DVD last night. Conall cropped up every now and again, taking photos of bride and groom.

'He's a nice man for letting you use his house,' said Dad. 'Very quiet person, haina?'

Dad looked at me from the corner of his eye.

'Unless he has something to say,' I replied, eyes fixed on the screen.

'What were you two saying there?'

Conall was stood behind me and I was looking at the stage and gesticulating – which, honestly, I should do less of now that I can see that I look like a puppet on strings. He's laughing and taking the photos. Then he says something – can't remember what it was – and I look at my phone – to check if Naim's messaged, no doubt. Hmm, that was the night Naim texted saying something about daisies. Pig. Never noticed this part of the DVD before. (NB: Pay more attention to detail.)

'Can't remember.'

I went to make a cup of tea and peered through the window to see if the lights were on next door. Nothing. When I sat back down I saw Dad holding a wad of paper, and I thought, hmm, what is that? Then I saw the title page with my name on the front and realised it was my bloody manuscript. Clearly I need to have a padlock on my bedroom door. Thanks to God Mum doesn't know how to use my laptop or she'd be reading through my diary, asking questions like, 'What is a shag?'

'Baba, it's not ready yet.' I put his tea on the coffee table and rested mine on the arm of the sofa, looking at the word-studded paper.

He nodded and put his glasses on, then began turning the pages. The pages of *my* book. I was going to add that I'll be publishing the book under a pseudonym so no one will know it's me, but then realised that would beg the question as to why that matters.

'How much is left to do?'

'How much have you read?'

'All.'

I had to reiterate it's not finished.

'Acha? It's funny.'

I paused the DVD, crossed my legs, and faced my dad.

'Really? You think so?'

'Soffoo, I have learned one thing in life, so listen to your baba – nahin, don't roll your eyes. Listen. Only do what you are happy to do. To hell with everyone, and everything else.'

Sometimes parents just don't know what they're saying. One minute they're begging you to stop fussing about and get married and the next they're telling you to be autonomy activists. He handed me the manuscript.

'Recent lesson?' I asked.

'Ooold lesson, Beta. Very old,' he said before sipping his tea. 'But sometimes we need to remind ourselves.'

JUNE 2012

The Halfway House Seems
a Heartless Place

AYISHA MALIK

Muslim Dating Book

Compromise is the name of the game, apparently. ~~And we all do it. Every day. Muslim or not. Don't pin it all on us.~~ If you want babies and the man who's committing to you is already married, well, you know, them's the breaks. If the man who you're with is having a few issues letting his parents know about the small fact that you're a divorcee, well, wait it out. (The clock ticks louder for those without anyone at all.) And what about that perfect boyfriend (who just happens to be black)? Keep him until a nice Indian one comes along and leaves no boxes unticked? (Because doesn't it make perfect sense to sacrifice a thing to please the people who won't actually be living your life?)

But what are our options? Where is this mythical inheritance of choice? Harder to find than a bloody husband.

Saturday 2 June

9 p.m. When I knocked on Conall's door, he didn't answer so I used my spare key. I opened the window, switched on the fan and went into the kitchen where there was the customary note, telling me that the Hobnobs were in the fridge in case they got eaten by ants. I put the kettle on and went upstairs to the bathroom. When I came out I noticed a stack of boxes in the passage labelled 'storage'. I looked inside and there were clothes, books and other bits and pieces. I wondered what it was for, but the kettle had boiled so I went back downstairs to make my tea and eat a Hobnob or ten.

As I settled down to read my manuscript, my thoughts wandered to Conall photographing at the wedding and whether he'd be at mine. Did he mention where this commission was? And for how long? Then I thought of the boxes. What was with the boxes? I went back upstairs and looked inside them again. It couldn't be, could it? I instinctively opened his bedroom door and went straight to his wardrobe. There were hardly any clothes there.

I couldn't concentrate. I wanted to message him and ask where the hell he was so he could come home and explain

355

himself. I waited through lunchtime; two, three, four, past five o'clock. I kept looking out of the window and ignored Imran's call. The little hand on the clock moved to seven.

Around eight-thirty, keys rattled in the door.

'Oh. Hi,' he said.

'Going somewhere, are we?' I asked.

He put his keys on the table.

'I brought you some muffins,' he said, lifting up a bag. 'For tomorrow.' He looked at the untouched packet of Hobnobs on the table. 'Are you OK?'

'Where are you going?' I asked.

He put the bag down and placed his hands on the chair in front of him.

'Afghanistan.'

Yes, Afghanistan. As in the country. As in the country that's in political turmoil. I mean, is it your actual intent to get killed? He pulled up a chair and sat down.

'It's for three months. Stupid to say no.'

'*Afghanistan*?' I might have sounded a little hysterical.

Beads of sweat formed on my forehead, on top of which Conall really should rethink wearing a white T-shirt when clearly you're going to get sweaty in the heat and, you know, T-shirts are very clingy. A person's trying to correct a book. I wanted to leave. The problem was, my limbs felt fairly paralysed.

'Do you want some lemonade? I made it yesterday.' He walked to the kitchen. What is the point in having a Sainsbury's around the corner if a person *makes* their own lemonade? He came back with two tall glasses and put them on the table, taking the muffins out of the bag.

'Blueberry, of course.'

'Is it hot in here?' I said, gulping down the lemonade, which, incidentally tasted bloody nice. He put the fan on the highest level.

'Better?'

Every time the fan faced his way his T-shirt fluttered against his skin, which made me remember the day I knocked on his door and he was T-shirt free.

'When exactly are you leaving?' I asked.

'Three weeks.'

Three weeks!

'Right.' I finished the lemonade and put the glass down.

'My brother's going to come and stay while I'm away. You'll get on.'

I looked at the empty glass. 'So you won't be at the wedding?'

He shook his head. 'Don't worry. I've spoken to a photographer friend and they'll be able to do your wedding if you want them to.'

I couldn't give a fuck about the photographer! Why, why, why does nothing stay the same for more than five minutes? Why does everything have to change all the time?? And just for a minute when you think, here's someone solid, someone who, you know, will just be there; they go and tell you they're going to freaking Afghanistan.

'Oh.'

'Don't you want the muffin?' he asked.

'But I'll miss you.'

I'm afraid my head-to-mouth filter wasn't on; it's an illness.

'You won't have time for that when you're married.' He took his glass and kept turning it around in his hands. 'You'll be happy enough once the wedding's over.'

'Happiness,' I said, watching him. 'It's just an illusion anyway.'

He leaned forward.

'Discuss.'

'I'm not being cynical.' The conversation might've taken a turn, but all I was thinking was, *Afghanistan. Three weeks!*

'Of course. You're an optimist.'

'That's just stupid,' I said, looking at the muffins, that *he* had bought – the lemonade *he* had made, this house, in which *he* lived. 'I'm a realist.'

'So, you're saying you're something between common and stupid?'

I thought about this and then shrugged. 'I must be.' To have not realised that nothing lasts for ever. It's the mistake of humanity itself. Common, stupid, humanity.

He looked at the table.

'Sofe, you're odd, to be sure. But I think we can safely say, there is nothing common about you.'

There is a person who thinks this, and he is leaving.

'Especially when I bring roses and a string quartet to play melancholy music before you leave,' I said.

'Will you be melancholy?'

'I will pop a lot of pills.'

'Sofe,' he replied. 'We're better than surface jokes.'

His mobile rang, but he ignored it. I drew circles on the table with my finger, remembering our cigarette on the garden step, and looked up at him. No words would come out.

'Can't stay in one place for ever, Sofe.'

More's the pity, I wanted to say. But, like an agreeable person, I nodded and tried to focus on my laptop – on a blank page I didn't know how to fill.

Sunday 3 June

9.45 a.m. 'What is wrong with you?' asked Mum. 'You're dragging your feet like your arse is too heavy for your legs.'

'My arse *is* too heavy for my legs.'

'It is because of wedding outfit, haina? So lilac it is.'

I walked into the kitchen, opening and closing cupboards, not knowing what I wanted for breakfast. Mum came in and said she'd make me paratha.

'Soffoo,' she said, taking out the rolling pin and ghee, 'no one will help you in this life.' Oh, God, here comes more cynicism. It's a wonder Maria and I haven't slashed our wrists, 'But when you are married, you will be surprised how strong you are.' She rolled out the dough. 'Lilac lengha is nothing to worry about. You will see.'

From Imran: I can't wait to wake up every morning to you.

Oh, Lord, I think I'm not hungry.

8.30 p.m. Maria and T came over and we'd just finished lunch when, out of nowhere, Mum said, 'Chalo, let's play Monopoly.' It's been twenty years since we last got that out of the storage cupboard. What I wanted to do was crawl into bed and sleep for ever, but then I'd be called anti-social.

Halfway through, T got a phone call from his parents. He went into the other room and we all – yes, even Dad – strained our ears to listen to the conversation.

'No, Mum. I don't know. Well, whenever.' Maria walked over to the door, and Mum started slapping Dad's hand when he went to scratch his stubble. 'We're playing Monopoly. Mum, no, we're not coming home. We're staying here. Cos Maria wants to. And so do I.'

Maria, hand on belly, tiptoed back to her seat as all of us pretended to argue about who had how much money, which is when Maria realised that I'd stolen two hundred pounds from her.

The doorbell rang and Mum went to answer it. It's been so long since we've played Monopoly that I'd forgotten my personal obsession with owning Park Lane and Mayfair. I was snatching the Community card from Tahir as Dad tried to take a fifty-pound note from my pile of money.

'Sorry, I didn't meant to disturb you.'

I looked up and Conall was standing there, next to Mum, with a bundle of books in his arms.

'I told you, I'm not lying, Sofe!' Tahir put the card back in the card pile and looked behind him. 'All right, mate?'

Conall nodded.

'I was just clearing out some books, and thought, well, there are some great ones on the Indo–Pak war, and thought you'd like them, Mr Khan.'

Dad eased to his feet and took a look at one.

'Ah, haan, I've read this one before.' He leafed through the rather well-thumbed copy of *Kutch to* something or another. He looked up and smiled at Conall. 'Come. Sit.'

Conall hesitated for a moment, looking at the now utterly imbalanced Monopoly board.

'No, no – thanks a mill. I have packing.'

'Colin, you're going then?' Mum followed this with a 'Hawww'.

'Conall, Mum,' I said.

'Haan, that's what I said.' She took the rest of the books and put them on the coffee table, knocking off a few of Maria's hotels.

'Come have a look at my potatoes.' He followed her out into the garden where I could see her nodding as he bent down and took a handful of soil. She laughed (at something she'd undoubtedly said) and he looked up, smiling at her. That lovely, kind smile that his face breaks into every now and again.

I turned back, reached into my dad's breast pocket and took out the fifty-pound note. 'Shame on you, Baba.'

'Colin, there will be lots of people coming next weekend so sorry for noise,' said Mum. I'm apparently having a dholki. I've lost the will to argue.

'That's, er, that's grand, Mrs Khan.'

'O-ho, you call me Mehnaz.'

I looked at him and smiled as he was about to walk out. 'Sofe,' he said, 'you don't seem to be winning there.'

Maria laughed saying, 'That's because she wants everything or nothing.'

He looked at me for a moment. 'That's no bad thing.'

What the hell is going on when every word and sentence all of a sudden feels like it means more than it actually says?

Friday 8 June

5.10 a.m. I cannot believe that next month I have a first draft to hand in. I'd like to know how mothers cope without sleep and carry on the daily routine of being human. I can barely keep my hand going when I'm brushing my teeth.

Tuesday 12 June

7.35 p.m. The doctor paid a home visit today. I spoke to her in the passage after she'd examined Dad. Apparently he's doing much better. She stepped out of the house and I glanced towards Conall's as the doctor turned around and said, 'Your dad seems very excited about the wedding – I'm sure it helps that he has that to look forward to.'

Thursday 14 June

10 a.m. Katie and I were having breakfast in the canteen and I told her about the Godforsaken dholki Mum is *making* me have this weekend. Maria and Mum are putting up the fairy lights. I really wish I didn't have to see them again. The fairy lights, that is.

'So exciting,' she said. 'Can I wear a sari?'

'You can wear a bin bag if you want. Just come, clap at the beating drum, smile and ignore any auntie who asks if you're married.'

She cleared her throat and leaned forward. 'Right, so don't make a song and dance about it, I don't want to tell anyone yet, but …' And she gave me this look – a twinkle in her eye. 'I'm engaged.'

'Tom proposed?'

'Last weekend, Sweetu. It's a done deal.'

Gosh – talk about remaining calm in the face of the prospect of getting married – Katie is a kindred spirit, I've decided.

'Are you happy?'

And there it was, the look of a person who has their excitement under control, but who can't hide the ripples that will invariably surface.

'Yes. Very.'

Then for whatever reason, I ended up having to run to the toilet and threw up a perfectly good muffin. I'd think I was pregnant, only there was only one immaculate conception – and if there is ever going to be another one, it won't be from the girl who writes press releases for a living.

Saturday 16 June

8.55 a.m. 'HAVE YOU TOLD THE NEIGHBOURS THERE'LL BE NOISE?'

I'd barely opened my eyes and Mum's voice was blaring in the house. 'Soffoooooo. Soffoooooo. Uff, Shakeel, Soffoo uthi ke nahin?'

'Haan haan, she'll be awake soon,' replied Dad.

The doorbell rang.

'Haw hai. Bilal, what is this? This is taw shocking pink. I said *green.*'

'Baji, this is all fashion. Last week Mrs Naila's daughter had same colour for her mehndi.'

'But how is this going to go with the floor cushions. Sofiiiiiiii. Wake up!'

'Oh my daaays. What is *that*? We wanted green,' said Maria. When did she get here?

Someone came bounding up the stairs and flung my door open.

'Sofe, do you have coral nail polish?'

I squinted and pulled the cover over myself.

'Get up. I need my eyebrows threaded.'

'Why is everyone so loud?'

I sat up and rubbed my eyes. Maria stood, face masked in mud, hair bundled up in some weird substance that was kind of white.

'Oh, it's egg and yogurt. Makes your hair soft.'

I can't believe I'm reliving the nightmare. The house has turned into a melting pot of fairy lights and ladoos.

Argh! Doorbell!

9.03 a.m. Who the hell ordered eight baskets of bananas??

9.15 a.m. Mum, Dad, Maria and I stood around the baskets that were wrapped in cellophane and swirly baby-blue ribbon.

'Very strange thing to do,' said Dad.

'Soffoo – what in-laws you have.' Mum ran into the kitchen to switch the hob off. 'Chalo, we will make banana milkshake tonight.'

Dad walked out into the conservatory to help Tahir unpack boxes of material and Maria and I just stood there.

'Well weird,' she said.

10 a.m.

From Fozia: Darling, I'll be there on time, but in case I'm late don't tell me off. I'm seeing Riaz! Love you xxxx

Hurrah! Hurrah, hurrah, hurrah, hurrah!

5 p.m. 'Why are there eight baskets of bananas in your kitchen?' asked Suj. She dabbed my nose with some blotting powder and held up two different blushers. 'Orgasm or Desire?'

I assessed the two options.

'Both?' I said.

She put one down and started attacking my cheeks with a blusher brush. I sighed and moved my head back as Suj stood with brush mid-air.

'Am I doing the right thing?' I asked.

'Do you want Desire instead?'

'Imran's *nice*, isn't he?'

'Yeah. Yeah. He's, you know ... He'll look after you.'

'I'm not a dog.'

Mum walked into the room and put my outfit on the bed. She looked at my face.

'Make sure you put on thick eyeliner.'

'Mehnaz, is it time for my pills?' Dad hovered at the door, buttoning up his shirt. 'Where did I put my glasses?'

'O-ho, they're on your empty head.'

He felt his head and pulled them off. 'Ah. Acha, Surjeet, Beta, don't put too much makeup on my daughter. She is already beautiful enough.'

Mum chortled. 'Don't listen to him. He doesn't realise even when glasses are on his head.' She made Dad follow her out; something about making sure the solar lights are working.

'Well, there's at least *one* good thing that'll come out of getting hitched,' I said. 'I won't have to live here any more.' But this just made me feel sad. I never realised how much I love this home.

7.45 p.m. People have started arriving and everyone's all *congrat-ulations, congratulations.* I've decided that most people are very annoying.

Monday 18 June

9.45 a.m. I gave Katie one of the smoothies I was holding when I got to work.

'Saturday was epic,' she said, opening the bottle and taking a sip.

'Did you have a banana?'

'At least three.' She perched on my desk. 'I met your neighbour, Sweetu.'

I rested my bag on the desk and looked at her.

'Conall?'

'I apologised about the noise on your behalf.'

'What did he say?'

'He said, "That's nothing. You should hear 'em when they're making Christmas dinner."'

'Your Irish accent is crap,' I said.

'I said you're not nearly that loud at work. According to him you don't shut up. I told him, "Well, you have to love it." I have your back.'

'What did he say?'

She closed the lid on her smoothie. 'Erm, then Tom called and asked if I was on my way home.' She rolled her eyes. 'He keeps telling me I have to get used to someone caring where I am in the middle of the night.'

'Hmmm, right. So, what did he say?'

'Just whether I was getting a taxi.'

'No, I mean Conall.'

'Oh, I don't know. Something like, "That's the truth." Which it is. Obvs.'

'Something like, or definitely?'

'Oh God, it's Brammers.'

With which Katie slipped away and managed to look as if she was in the middle of organising a G8 summit by tapping furiously on her BlackBerry. Why do people not pay attention to the details in life?

Friday 22 June

7.30 a.m. I have seventy-six emails in my inbox, eight mailouts to send, authors who can't travel Economy on the train for a fifty-minute journey to Cheltenham, and a fiancé whom I'm meeting for dinner because *his* mum wants to give something to *my* mum. However, I also have the first draft of a manuscript. I don't feel quite ready to let it go just yet.

8.55 a.m. 'Mum, what's Imran's mum sending you?' I had to whisper into the phone as weird, over-productive people in Marketing were already in the office.

'Oh haan! She wants you to wear the choker she wore on her mehndi.'

Why does no one tell me anything??

'But, Mum! What if it's ugly?'

'You are also ugly.' Laughter from her side of the phone.

Does Imran know about this choker? No. Was I given the slightest bit of notification about this symbolic piece of jewellery that is becoming a noose around my neck and life? Clearly not.

'I told her girls like to wear their own things, but it doesn't looks nice, nah. She will think you are snob. Which you are, but better she knows after the wedding.'

'Bye, Mum.'

'Oh haan, bring some milk on your way home.'

9.20 a.m. I was photocopying when Tasha, the drawler from Marketing came over and asked what I was doing on the weekend. No one *actually* cares about this. What if I decided to lie around in my pyjamas, eating chocolate and watching MTV? I'd be forced to make something up otherwise I'd sound like a lazy cow. This constant need for people to be *doing* stuff is exhausting.

'Oh, nothing much, just … wedding preps.'

Tasha's eyes widened as slowly as her sentences take to come out.

'Oh wooow. How exciting. I had no idea. What's the dress like?'

And on and on the conversation had to go.

'I bet it's beautiful. Your weddings are just so colourful. Our weddings are so *plain.*'

I thought about telling her about the lilac mass, and the as-yet-unseen choker. But instead I smiled, indicated the photocopier was free and dragged my feet back to my desk.

1 p.m. What I need to do is pray and be Zen-like. I can be Zen-like. I've been Zen-like before, I can be that way again.

I reminded myself: *the choker is an expression of a mother-in-law's affection. It is not a form of control. Whilst wearing the choker is an unreasonable expectation, it is just a result of a long line of expectations dictated by tradition. But one should try to respect these traditions. Remember, it is not a noose; sometimes a choker is just a choker. Exhale.*

I am serene. Even this manky excuse for a prayer room, with its dingy grey walls, a bed that looks like it's been carted out of a hospital, and noticeboard with how to perform the Heimlich manoeuvre is beautiful in its own way.

Prayer time over. Emotional order has been restored.

10.45 p.m. I was geared up to be agreeable. I really was. If anybody decided to pay my intentions a visit, I swear, they would've seen a 'Sofia's being agreeable now' sign hung smack-bang in the centre.

'You're acting weird.'

'What?'

I looked at Imran as we sat at our designated table and gave him a lovely smile. All affability.

'Why are you smiling like that?'

'Like what?'

'Like – sarcastic.'

'Can we get a basket of bread, please?' I asked, smiling pointedly at the waiter. 'Was that sarcastic too?'

He handed me a little bag and I looked inside. 'That's to give to your mum, or you, or both. I dunno.' And then, as if on cue, my phone rang and it was his mum.

'Beta,' said the ever-sunny voice on the other end of the line, 'I told Imran to tell you not to look at choker until you get home.'

I desperately wanted to ask the reasoning behind this. And while I was at it, I should've asked about the eight baskets of bananas too, but there was his mother on the other end of the phone, and my mother in my head, saying *It doesn't looks nice, nah.*

'OK, Auntie. I'll look when I get home.'

'Good, Beta. Acha, tell Imran I've made his hair appointment for the weekend.'

I shot a look at him, but he was too busy viewing the menu.

'Erm OK, Auntie.'

'O-ho, I'm your ammi now.'

The serene part of me was unravelling fast. I don't care how mad my mother is, I only have one, and there will have to be an ice-skating show in hell before I start calling anyone else that.

'Oh, I think I prefer Auntie. Auntie.'

Silence, and then a clearing of the throat. This lasted a good five seconds, which might not sound long, but felt rather close to an age.

'Oh. Haan, haan, of course, Beta.' She sounded so aggrieved! And I, of course, felt awful.

'I'm going to have arrabiata.' Imran put the menu down and looked at the bag. 'Have a look.'

'Your mum thinks I should wait until I get home.'

He shrugged. 'She just thinks girls should do everything with their mums.' I'm assuming the look of horror showed on my face because he laughed and said, 'Don't worry, Sofe. She's not going to be like that with you.'

I took it out, and well, it was just so *gold*. A thick strip of gold, with little balls hanging from it.

'Oh, that's ... lovely.' I dangled it in the air, wishing a rabid dog would pounce out of nowhere, grab the choker and run off with it. Preferably somewhere far, far away.

Imran smiled. 'If you don't like it, you don't have to wear it.'

Oh! If only!

'No. I'd love to wear it. Just as long as your mum doesn't ask me to call her ammi again.'

I browsed the menu, reasoning to myself that being annoyed about trivial matters is un-Islamic. Unkind. One can try to make others happy by doing small things. So I'll wear an ugly choker for the day? Who cares? Imran looked so relieved and glad and, gosh, well, I'm learning to bite my enormous tongue.

'You might as well. It's all the same when you become a Haque.' He took a piece of bread and dabbed it in the plate of olive oil and balsamic vinegar.

'Become a Haque?'

He munched on the bread. 'Yeah, you know, when you change your name.'

'I'm not changing my name.'

The munching slowed down.

'But everyone changes their name when they get married,' he said.

'Erm, no they don't. And I don't care what everyone does.'

'What's got into you lately, why are you so, I don't know, short?'

'I'm not *short*. I'm just saying that I'm not changing my name.'

'Sofia Haque. It's got a ring to it.'

'But I already *have* a name. I've had it all my life, why should I change it for anyone just because I'm getting married?'

He leaned back and blew out a puff of air. 'Anyone?'

A figure came and loomed over us.

'Are you ready to order?' Mr Chirpy Waiter beamed at us, but Imran's stare was fixed on me. The waiter turned around and walked away.

'You know what I mean,' I said. '*You're* the one who's always saying things like, that's so *westernised*, that's such a *westernised* thing to say and do. Changing my name isn't?'

'We'll chat about it later.' He took the napkin and laid it on his lap. 'What you going to get?'

'We'll talk about it now.'

He sighed.

'What's got into you?'

'Imran,' I said, putting down the menu, desperate for him to understand. 'If it's not the wedding date, it's the outfit. If it's not the outfit, it's the choker, and if it's not the choker, it's my *name*. You're telling me to change my name.'

'Everyone changes their name.' He ran his fingers through his hair, which just made me remember his hairdressing appointment that his mum made. 'Fuck's sake, Sofe. What more do you want? I'm *moving out* for you. Can't you do this?'

I put my napkin down and realised: I'd miscalculated the measure of his sacrifice. To me, it is so small. To him, it is everything. He stared at me and my unreasonable self. I felt a rush of affection for him, but I knew it wouldn't last. I'd go back to being short and frustrated because reason has nothing to do with it, after all.

'I don't think we should do this,' I said.

It took a few moments before he seemed to realise what I'd said – his face contorted as if I'd sucker punched him.

Oh, God! I had to tell him. I had to say that I just *can't* marry him. Now I know what a person who's been thwacked looks like. Awful, awful, awful!

Saturday 23 June

5.40 a.m God, if today's the day you want the world to end then I can't say I'd mind. Although, if I could get in a little more prayer time that would be helpful – you know, to make up for bad deeds etc. Which now include telling the man I promised to marry that I no longer want to marry him.

5.46 a.m. On the other hand, surely it's much worse to marry someone half-heartedly because you were too spineless to tell them the truth. Now, would I rather be a spineless liar or a person who's too selfish to keep a promise?

Could I just be someone else altogether?

5.50 a.m. How long should a person wait before they text the fiancé they just broke up with to check if they're all right? OK, if I'm making a mistake, send me a sign, God. Any sign. Like, make it rain or something.

I looked out of the window and, of course, it's as bright as bloody anything. Although not wanting to get married is kind of a sign. I must compose myself. I am a mature adult with the ability to make life-changing decisions all by myself. I must not, at the crucial hour, lose my senses.

8.05 a.m. I just have to clear my mind, that's all. I have to see Conall. He'll make it better – he'll understand and tell me I did the right thing.

7.55 p.m. OH MY GOD! I am mortified! Conall opened the door and I was ready to blurt it all out, but something in me hit the brakes on my declaration of guilt. I went into the kitchen to put the kettle on, but couldn't find any mugs.

'Where have they all gone?' I said, looking around as if I'd lost my very sanity. He came in, got one from the mug tree and put it in front of me. I had to walk past him to get to the fridge but he didn't move. 'I need milk.' He turned around and got the milk out. I don't know why but the empty cupboards made me sadder and I wished he would leave the kitchen so I could cry in peace.

'Tea or coffee?' he asked.

'Anything.'

He sighed and mumbled something about me not wanting it, or wanting something else? I was too busy looking at him putting a teabag in the mug, and the more I looked at him the sadder I felt. The empty cupboards, the boxes stacked in the passage.

'Actually, I want coffee.'

He shook his head. 'Of course you do.'

The living room was covered with books, photo albums and papers. I sat and crossed my legs.

'Tell me how I can help.'

I put my phone behind me on the sofa to show how serious I was. He taped a box and moved it to the side. I picked up an album and flicked through a picture of him and his brother at school.

'You had braces. No wonder your teeth are so straight. Unreasonable really for a man to have such good teeth, I think.'

He kneeled and reached over to get a book that was on the sofa behind me and looked at me.

'You prefer them broken?'

He rested his hand on the edge of the sofa and I looked up at him and you know what I thought? I thought isn't that the loveliest face anyone's ever seen. There was that clean smell again – it makes you want to close your eyes and go to sleep. For ever, in my case.

'Go eeeeh.' I bared my teeth to demonstrate.

He frowned. 'Eeeeeh.'

His arm was touching my shoulder and I was caught between wanting to laugh at him and wanting to wrap my arms around him.

'A little chip might've done you some good.'

He held my gaze for a moment before he pushed himself back and put the book on the pile on the floor.

'I suppose the man you're marrying has a chip?'

Yes, and it's probably on his shoulder – quite rightly. What was I thinking? How could I tell Conall, of all people, that the man I was meant to marry next week – I've decided I won't. He patted his hand on the top of the pile. 'These'll be for you.'

'You'll come back at some point, I'll take them then.'

'I think I've stayed here long enough,' he replied.

'You're not coming back?'

'No, Sofe. I'm not.'

'Oh.'

I closed the album, trying to process this.

'What about the American?' he asked.

'What?'

'His teeth.'

'Oh. The American.' I looked at him. 'They were sort of like yours, I suppose.'

He raised his eyebrows and said, 'Is that your way of telling me you had a crush on me?' I'm sure I went bright red. I looked at him, thinking, what kind of a question is that? And then I thought, *Crush? Conall? WTF. What would be the point in that? He's not even Muslim.* But as soon as these thoughts went through my mind they were succeeded by an *oh my actual God* moment. Of course I have a crush on you. I have more than a crush on you. Then one could say I was saved by the bell. But I was saved from one evil only to be plunged into another.

'Jesus Christ, will you hang on,' Conall shouted as someone banged at the door. It didn't occur to me to worry about who it was given the utter inconvenience of aforementioned discovery. 'Oh,' Conall said, and then Mum came storming into the living room.

'Have you gone off the track?' She stood towering over me as I held onto Conall's album and looked up at her furious face. 'Imran's ammi just called.'

Shit.

'No telling me, or your baba! Without anything, you just cancel wedding?'

The thing is, having a disgruntled mother is one thing, but an angry one like the one I met today was a little different. Conall came in behind her and said, 'You're not getting married?'

'Why isn't she getting married? Of course she's getting married.'

I managed to get up, after a faulty start with all the bloody stuff around me.

'No, Mum. I'm really not.'

'What about all the guests? The money? Tell her,' she said, looking at Conall. 'Tell her how stupid she's being. Let's go home. Your baba will talk sense into you.'

Conall stepped over the mess and faced me. 'You're not getting married?' He looked at me and … Oh! I love his face. 'You don't have to go home.'

'Le. Of course she does. She is mad.'

I shook my head and followed Mum out of the door, like a delinquent fifteen-year-old who'd just been caught stealing underwear from M&S. I glanced backwards to see Conall staring at the ground as he ran his hand through his hair.

We got inside the house and Dad was pacing the room. He stopped as soon as he saw us. 'Soffoo, what is this I'm hearing?'

And so it began …

'What is wrong with him?' exclaimed Mum.

'If you didn't want to marry him, why did you say you'd marry him?' said Dad.

'I didn't know.'

'Le, what didn't you know?' For the succeeding hour Mum felt that repeating everything I said would make me see how ridiculous I sounded. Yes, I'm sure I did sound ridiculous. I'm sure that I *am* ridiculous. Then I thought, it's all well and good standing here and shouting at me, but perhaps if you hadn't all been banging on about me getting married so that Dad could 'live to see me happy', this whole thing probably wouldn't be happening. But of course that's not taking responsibility for my own actions.

The phone rang and Mum shot me a look after she picked up.

'Baji, what can I say? I am talking to Sofia …'

Oh, God above and around me, it was Imran's mum.

'Haan, we understand. Of course.'

More looks.

377

'Please, we are talking to her and she will listen. Don't worry, there *will* be a wedding ...'

Dad was shaking his head at the floor.

'Nahin, baji, don't say like this. I'm not saying Imran can't find a girl ...' Mum's tone began to change. 'Taw so what? Men marry girls much older than them.' She glanced at me. 'I understand you're angry, we are also. We speak to her and ... hmm ... nahin, so ...' Mum stood up and started shaking her head. 'Why are you bringing up her age again and again? They are same age ... Listen, she is a child ...'

(Erm, seriously ...)

'They make mistakes ... Well, acha, if this is how it is then we don't want this rishta either!' With which Mum hung up and threw the phone on the sofa.

'Who the hell they think they are?' she exclaimed. 'Same age, same age. So what?'

'Mehnaz. Calm.'

'Hain? What calm?' continued Mum as she got out her diary and looked up a number. 'I told them get lost. We don't want rishta either.

'Haan, Sikandar? Haan, I spoke to you yesterday about the swing for the mehndi? Nahin, it's cancelled.'

'Where was Imran?' I asked. 'Is he OK?'

'I heard him in background telling his mum to be quiet. But that woman? Uff.'

Dad looked at me. If ever there was a look of utter disappointment, there it was.

'We will have to pay them for the wedding,' he said.

Mum put her hand to her forehead. 'Hai hai, all that money. Just think. And the talk that will happen? You should've heard that woman. Waisay, she walks around pretending she is simple, and the tongue on her.'

I hadn't even thought about the money. *Think things through!*

'Sofia, this is not a good thing you've done,' said Dad.

No, I wanted to say, it's the worst thing I could've done. Mum flicked through more pages of her blue book.

'I'll give the money from the book,' I said. 'I'll do something.'

'You have put fire to everything,' said Mum. 'And for what?' she asked. 'Think, Soffoo, for what?'

8.10 p.m. I've realised I've left my phone at Conall's and I can't pop over to collect it with Mum and Dad in not-so-quiet fury downstairs. Disaster, disaster, disaster!

Sunday 24 June

9.10 a.m. I'm a prisoner in my own home. It's all murmuring and stomping downstairs, with intermittent exclamations at how someone must've given me the evil eye. What must Conall think of me? I wish I had my phone. I need my girls! Life is so much more depressing without my phone. If only I could get out of the house to see him and explain that I'm not an *intentionally* horrible person.

9.40 a.m. I can't stand this. I'm going to creep out and hope my parents don't notice.

10.45 a.m. I walked into the living room but wasn't quite sure how to start the conversation. Was I meant to say sorry for bringing zoo-like behaviour into his home? The shouting? The abrupt exit? Before I could decide, Conall piped up, 'Am I going to have to ask what happened?'

I put the phone in my pocket.

'I know. I know I did a shit thing, but I've done him a favour.'

'Feckin' hell, Sofe. Take a thing seriously now and then.'

I could handle my parents being angry with me, but not Conall. I wanted him to tell me it was going to be OK – you know, offer those false words of comfort.

'But my dad,' I tried to explain. 'There were wires and everything.'

'Ah. So it was the pressure.' He was leaning against the door. 'Let's hope for everyone's sake that anyone else you love doesn't get connected to wires then.'

Which instantly made me think of Conall attached to wires.

'I mean that poor bloke.'

One can imagine what being stabbed might feel like; this was like the knife twisting in my guts.

'Yes, I know. It's awful. *I'm* awful.'

I went to walk out of the room but he was in my way.

'You go and blame your family and your dad.'

'I *said* I'm awful, didn't I?' And then I mumbled, 'What would you know about being brown anyway?'

'What?'

'I said, *what would you know about being brown*?'

'Oh, *that* card.'

'I *am* brown.' I pointed to my face to make this absolutely clear. 'It's different, Conall. It's so, so different.' He had nothing to say, it seemed. 'I need to go home. I'll put your keys through the letter-box before you go.'

He looked down at me: I was the sound and he was the fury. I'd have left but he wouldn't move. Then he put both his hands in his pockets, moved to the side and said, 'Fine, drop them through the letterbox.'

As if it didn't matter whether I stayed or left.

11.30 a.m.

From Imran: I'm sorry abt mum calling. She was just upset. Anyway, your dad spoke to my parents and I've emailed my account details. I've also emailed you a list of all the numbers and things that need cancelling too. Let me know when it's done. Transfer the money as soon as you can. Imran.

At first I thought, don't apologise! Then anxiety wrapped itself around me once more. How could I have done that to him? And that money for which I said yes to the book in the first place, is now going to pay for the wedding that never was.

3 p.m. Maria has come over. She came straight up to my room, her belly ever expanding, and closed the door behind her.

'What the hell happened?'

Not sure if it was her maternal look, with her hand resting on belly, or whether it was the concern on her face, but I went up to her and hugged her so tight I think she was scared I wouldn't let go until labour kicked in. I told her everything, from how I think

I said I'd marry Imran because I was scared of Dad dying, to how each time Imran would mention anything about the wedding I'd feel sick and that he thought Hannah was stupid for being a second wife, and Suj shouldn't marry a black guy and that it all amounted to he and I having nothing in common. She sat there, nodding.

'Don't worry, Sofe. You send me that bloody email and I'll call all the people needed.' She put her arm around me. 'Listen ... it's better to do something *now*. Later sometimes gets too late.'

'Mum is furious.'

'Don't worry about Mum. I'll deal with her too.'

God, having an older sister is a relief. She stared at the floor, contemplating something. She then raised her head and looked at me, 'And hey, at least you won't have to wear that lilac lehnga.'

Monday 25 June

7.20 a.m. Haven't slept all night. Ended up just reading the manuscript. Every few pages, I'd stare into space and think of Conall's angry face. But I want this damn manuscript that's ended up being a waste out of the way. Then I can live under my duvet for the rest of my life.

9.25 a.m. There. Sent.

10.25 a.m. Katie came over to my desk and put a Kit-Kat on it.

'Well done, Sweetu. Let's celebrate with fish and chips for lunch.'

Yes, and I can also tell you that my wedding is cancelled. Happy Monday!

1.30 p.m. The canteen shouldn't allow you to help yourself to chips. How is one to know when to stop? Katie sat and listened to me and my awfulness. When she put her hand on mine and said, 'Of *course* you did the right thing,' I almost sobbed into her kale and spinach smoothie.

9.35 p.m. The lights were off in Conall's house when I got home. I had the awful feeling that he'd left early, but then why would he do that? Where is he?

Mum's constantly on the phone telling people what's happened. She flares up with anger, laments with despair, cries with sadness: every other minute a new emotion surfaces. We have nothing, if we don't have variety.

The girls have obviously taken the called-off wedding very well. Incomprehension was speedily replaced with, 'I knew it was the right thing to do', 'There was something not quite right about it, really' and 'He wasn't good enough for you, anyway'. Suj put her glass down on the table to draw a line of finality over the last statement. Love my girls.

Note for when revising book: Always be around the people that see the best in you. Gives you a fighting chance of maybe one day being that person.

10 p.m. Mum and Dad haven't spoken to me. We are all exchanging nods and grunts. I'm not really in the mood to speak to them either, to be honest. I blame myself entirely – for not knowing my own mind sooner and for the sheer weakness of giving in. I just wish they'd understood *me* enough to have known it too.

Tuesday 26 June

3 p.m. I'm praying so hard that Conall's convoy gets cancelled. I know that's against the rules – you're meant to pray for whatever's the best, but I can't help it. Please, please, please convoy be cancelled! *Pleeeeeeease.*

I just don't understand how he can leave home for such a long time. Maybe he's not the settling-down type – maybe he'll always be on some convoy or another: destination documentation, capturing people and moments and truths while I sit by my computer pitching books about hippos.

7 p.m. I walked through his gate. His keys were in my bag, and I was about to put them through the letterbox. I opened the flap but, just as I was about to push them through, I knocked on the door instead.

'Hey.' I felt sheepish. He looked it. After a moment he looked over my shoulder. 'Where are the roses? The melancholy music?'

'Just can't get the help nowadays.'

I glimpsed at the empty passage. My heart felt displaced, as did my life.

'I wanted to give you these.' I held out the keys for him to take.

'Ah, thanks.'

I thought he might ask me to come in and have a cup of tea, coffee, fresh lemonade. Nothing. Goodbyes are the worst. I looked again at the empty passage – just wooden floors and hollow walls. When he closed the door behind him, before I'd even shut the gate, something swelled inside me, pushing tears to the surface. Must be PMT. Though don't know why they call it Pre-Menstrual Tension – more like Constant Menstrual Tension.

Thursday 28 June

7.45 a.m. I woke up early to read some Qur'an so was walking around the house in my burqa and black hijab, as one does when they're praying. The doorbell rang, which was odd. I went to open it and Conall was standing there.

'Oh.' He stared at me and the length of my burqa. 'Oh. Hi.'

'Hi.' I didn't even think of what I was or wasn't wearing; I was all, *Conall's here!*

'I, er, thought I'd catch you before you went to work,' he said. 'Have I disturbed you?' Then he looked at the black shroud once more and I realised I must've looked like I was about to go to Hogwarts.

'Oh, no. I'm in mourning,' I said, picking up the sides of my burqa and doing a curtsey. What the hell? Why couldn't he stop staring at the burqa and why was I curtseying?

'I just wanted to drop by before I left. Sofe, I ...' Before he finished he stepped back and shook his head. 'Nothing.'

'What? Half-finished things are annoying, remember?'

'I wanted to say goodbye and ...' He laughed awkwardly. 'And think twice before you leave the house with that on. You could cause a riot.'

Was that meant to be funny? It felt like someone was wringing my insides. Why did he have to see me in my burqa and then I thought why *shouldn't* he see me in my burqa? Why can't I just wear what I want to bloody well wear?

'As long as it's for the right reasons,' I said.

'Of course.'

'Sometimes it's worth it.'

'Maybe.'

'Maybes are for fence sitters,' I said.

'Is that why you've taken to wearing a burqa?'

I almost laughed and was going to say, *don't be ridiculous! I'm wearing shorts and a T-shirt under this.* But then something stopped me.

'Now I'll be able to eat as many Hobnobs as I like.'

But he didn't laugh. Nor did I. Funny was lost.

'Behave yourself,' he said.

He was really leaving, and I thought something had cracked in my heart and expanded in my throat. There he stood with his tattoos and me in my burqa, and all this space between us. He might as well already be in Afghanistan.

But I thought, sod this space, and I went and put my arms around him. 'Try to stay alive,' I said in his ear. He tightened his grip and nodded. Then he stepped back, turned around, and walked away.

Friday 29 June

8.30 a.m. Dad is looking better than usual. He hovered at the door while I sat on the edge of my bed, brain willing my body to get up and body refusing to comply.

'Have they said anything about the book?' he asked, or barked, rather.

'No.'

'Good.'

I stood up and put my hair up in a clip.

'Why's that good?'

'Time away from something helps you to see more clearly.' He frowned. I wonder how much longer he'll frown at me.

Mum came in and opened my wardrobe. I was going to ignore her, but living in a silent household was getting really depressing.

'What are you looking for?' I asked.

'I can't find the safe key.'

'Why would it be in my wardrobe?'

'O-ho – I change the hiding place every month – but I can't remember where.'

Mum continued to paw around my clothes.

'What's this?' Mum groped into the back for something. My eyes widened in realisation and I threw my hair band at Dad. He looked at me as I put two fingers near my lips, pretending to smoke. Dad's head shot back to the wardrobe, but it was too late. Mum already had the box of cigarettes in hand. She looked at both of us. Dad pretended to look authoritative until the look on Mum's face cracked him. He pointed at me.

'See my daughter? She looks after me. You just give me head-ache.'

I smiled, comforted by Dad's words. Maybe not too much longer until he forgives me. Mum laughed even though she pretended to look annoyed. What an idiot I was, deciding to marry someone just to keep my parents happy (or whatever word you want to use). They've made it through much worse.

The parents will be OK. I will be too. But everything is leaden right now; my feet, my head, that beating organ that pumps blood through the body.

10 a.m. I went into Brammers' office and took a seat.

'So, Lucinda read the draft you sent.'

'Oh, OK. Right.'

'After I spoke to her I thought it'd be good to have a few of the other editors read it too – that's one of the good things about the book – it's an easy read.'

'OK.' My mouth was dry and I tried to detect what she might say next based on her facial expressions. 'And?'

'And ... We all loved it.'

'Really?'

'Absolutely. This, Sofia, is going to be a real gem.'

The door opened and Lucinda walked in, plopping herself on the seat next to me.

'Gem! To be honest with you, I was a little bit pissed when I read the manuscript and I wanted to make sure the reason I liked it wasn't just because I'd had a few chardonnays, you know what I mean?' she said.

I nodded.

'Of course you don't know what I mean. It's amazing. You've never touched a drop of alcohol. You must have the most healthy liver.'

Yes, it's just my heart's that's the problem. She peered at me as if I was some wild animal at a zoo.

'Isn't that amazing?' she asked Brammers. 'Have you seen how beautiful Sofia's hair is?'

Brammers replied that she had not. 'Anyway, so this is great but let's have lunch to discuss some niggly editorial changes.' They both looked at me.

'OK,' I said. I did everything they asked and they loved it. I should be relieved, happy, proud – but I wasn't. I just wasn't.

Note for life: when you write a book, don't do it for money ...

'This is *gold dust*,' said Lucinda. 'And it doesn't hurt when you're marketable.'

Which I thought was kind of ironic given that I'm pretty unmarketable in the marriage world.

I went back to my desk and stared at my computer screen.

'Sweetu, you should be so proud of yourself,' said Katie.

I nodded, but there's a fair bit of a distance between what you should be and what you are.

Ah. Mum calling ...

JULY AND AUGUST 2012

What We Talk About When We Talk About Goodbye

Tuesday 3 July

My dearest Sweetu,

I've wanted to call you all weekend, but I wasn't sure you'd be in the frame of mind to speak, so I'm writing instead.

Oh, Sofe, I'm so, so, sorry. That's not enough, but I am. I won't go on because you don't like that, but if there is anything at all I can do, or if there's anything you need, even if it's just to speak, I am on the other end of the phone, or will come wherever you are to see you.

Your friend Fozia texted me to let me know that the funeral is tomorrow. Of course I'll be there. Everyone at work is thinking of you and sending you big love.

Your dad loved you.

As do I,
Katie xxxx

Saturday 4 August

10.45 p.m. Death turns people into philosophers. Tonight Auntie Reena leaned over and said, 'You must pray for your baba, Beta.' She thrust the rosary beads in my hands. 'Death shows us we are not here for ever,' she whispered, her breath stale from fasting.

'Uff,' said Auntie Scot, shaking her head solemnly, 'you never know when your time is up.'

Mum looked up from reading the Qur'an as Auntie Reena replied, 'Everything stays here. Nobody takes anything with them.' Then there was collective tutting in the room.

Just as I was putting the rosary beads on the coffee table, Auntie Reena added, 'You know, more important than wearing hijab is praying your five prayers.'

Mum turned the page of the Qur'an, glancing at the clock, and Maria shifted in her seat.

'Chalo, it's almost iftari time,' said Mum, getting up with the requisite groan caused by arthritic knees, and going into the kitchen. I followed her.

It's been over a month and Chachu has come and gone again, Ramadan is here again, but at least random people aren't turning up at our doorstep with tear-strewn faces, sitting in the house for hours, waiting for fast to open – now and again picking up a copy of the Qur'an – but mostly whispering about whatever the latest social scandal is. Oh, and the poor dead dad who didn't get to see his youngest daughter get married. All these tragedies.

'Everything is from Allah,' said Auntie Scot. 'Just think, if Soffoo hadn't said no to Imran there would've been a funeral on the wedding day.'

Mum passed me the fruit salad and touched my cheek with her hand.

I should never have called off the wedding. It never would've happened anyway.

11.50 p.m. I keep thinking about that moment when I got to the hospital and Mum looked at me, shaking her head, tears down her cheeks. Maria was sat with her hand resting on her belly as she stared into space, Tahir next to her, gripping her hand.

'Soffoo, your baba is gone,' said Mum.

Gone? Gone how? Gone where? What do you mean – *gone*? She blew her nose into a tissue and wiped her eyes. 'Chalay gaye, Soffoo,' she repeated. I stared and just kept shaking my head. Can someone explain to me where *gone* means?

A doctor came in and whispered to Maria, who listened intently before we were led out of the waiting room. As we followed the doctor I looked at the familiar setting – I'd been here before, and it had been OK – everything would be OK. The door opened. I walked towards a bed where Baba lay as if he were asleep. He's going to wake up and he's going to be fine, I thought. But then some people came and covered his body with a white sheet, and I thought, what the hell are you doing? Are you mad? And then they began wheeling him out and all I could think was: Baba doesn't have his glasses. He needs them. He can't see anything without them. I think I might've begged. I begged for them to wait a minute. That's all I wanted. *One* more minute. But Maria pulled me into her arms, shushing me, and I no longer had the energy to plead. The swinging doors shut and he was now on the other side. Gone.

Now I'm sitting here, alone, and I'm thinking about what I might have done with one more minute. How can you fit a lifetime of 'I love yous' into a minute?

Monday 6 August

9.35 a.m. Death has also made me more efficient. Well, death and fasting. I don't have the energy to explain to Mum or whichever member of the family has decided to stay over that night why I'm not getting up at dawn for suhur. Seeing as I can't be bothered to eat for most of the day, I might as well fast with everyone else. This year it just means I get more work done and even though sometimes I nod off on the toilet, generally I'm more productive – no one needs to be awake while they pee anyway.

12.15 p.m. 'Sofia.' Brammers shut the door as I walked in and she took her seat behind the desk. She smiled. I smiled back. She clasped her hands and rested them on the table. I settled mine under my legs. She smiled again.

'Sofia,' she said, letting out a sigh. 'I have to say you've done incredibly well, working on the book.' Smile. 'Under the circumstances.' Her voice rose a few decibels there.

'Good.'

I glanced over at the manuscript on her table.

'There was just something that we were wondering. It's not that the material is in any way *lacking* ... we just feel that there isn't enough, well,' she leaned forward, 'we feel there isn't enough ... *sex*.'

'Excuse me?'

'Sex.'

'Right.'

'Fascinating stories.' She scratched her head and sniffed her fingers. 'Gosh, do all Pakistani boys really just sleep around and then end up marrying a girl from *back home,* as you call it?'

'Erm ...' I put my hands on my lap, '... as much as *all* English boys get drunk in the middle of the day on the Tube, I suppose.'

Brammers looked at the manuscript.

'Ah, yes, well – of course. Anyway, we do feel that, though entertaining, there needs to be more sex.' I folded my arms. 'Just so that it's appealing to a wider readership.'

Wider readership? What? Like bored housewives and people who need something to read before the next Mills & Boon comes out?

'Can I be candid, Sofia?' Smile. 'It's an admirable way of life, really. No drinking, no sex before marriage, up at the break of dawn to pray. It's really very committed ...' Sounded more like she thought I should *be* committed. 'But it's also a little tricky for people to relate to. And what readers really want is something they can understand.' She twisted in her chair. 'Of course they want something new and unknown, but really it should also be *relatable*, you see?'

'Right.'

'We're not talking about an exposé or anything. Just maybe one chapter involving something sex-like.'

'Sex-*like*.'

I stood up to leave as Brammers began typing an email. Just as I was about to walk out of the door, she said, 'People always get side-tracked by sex. It'll save you from explaining why you decide to live the way you live.'

I didn't know I had to explain my life to people as well as go through the process of actually living it.

3.30 p.m. The new work experience girl came scampering to my desk because Fleur was nowhere to be seen and she was all, 'I'm so terribly, terribly sorry, but those show cards … Everything's got stuck … could you have a look?'

I unstuck the papers from the board and ended up doing the laminating myself while she watched. Her dedication to the job was admirable – she was the only one in the office who didn't have a separate screen open to watch the Olympics.

'Oh, so that's how you keep the air bubbles out.'

She graduated with a First from Oxford and she's learning how to keep air bubbles out.

'I don't know how much you'll need it in life, but it might get you a job around here.'

She beamed at me. And I thought all Oxford Uni students were stuck up. I've thought a lot of things, though, haven't I? Not quite sure what I've been right or wrong about.

'Aren't you the one who's written a book?' she asked.

I nodded.

'That's very exciting. I won't ask what it's about. I bet every writer hates that question.'

I looked over my shoulder.

'One accidental book does not a writer make.'

She picked up a box of jiffy bags.

'It's very lucky. Just think of how many people would die to be in your position and, look, just like that you've managed to get a publishing deal.'

And then Fleur, who was walking down the corridor, caught sight of us and came into the stationary room.

'Margaret, I told you, if there's anything you need, tell *me*.' She gave me an apologetic smile.

'Fleur, it's fine. There'll be plenty more chances to be nice to me – my dad will always be dead.'

Poor Fleur. She went bright red and walked away. But I've never been very good at filtering – so that's another thing death does; fucks up an already fucked up brain filter.

'I'm really sorry to hear about your father,' added my new friend, Margaret.

I began stacking the envelopes in size order. I thought she'd left, but as I turned around to check, she said, 'Not everyone has a daughter who manages to write a book.'

She smiled and stepped forward, taking the show card from me, but I wanted to say I don't want you to take the show card. I want you to tell me what his last words to me were. Every night I stay awake trying to remember our last conversation and absolutely anything he might've said that could at least mean something.

Anything other than, 'Ask your mama where my glasses are.'
Philosophise that.

8 p.m. I still haven't quite got used to seeing someone other than
Conall coming out or going into his house. The day his brother,
Sean, moved in I had to do a double-take, they look so alike. He
smiles a lot more than Conall. I've just not particularly been in the
mood to smile back. But when I went into the garden to get some
pots from the shed and looked over into Conall's garden, I saw that
the flowers he planted are blooming. I had to stop for a moment
and look at them.

Truth is, he's wedged in my thoughts. I'm trying to dislodge
him, but somehow I can't think of Conall without thinking of
Baba and I can't think of Baba without thinking of Conall. And
I can't think of either without wanting them back. Apparently
you can't just wish things into existence; conjure them up like a
magician. Even miracles have their limits. You can't resurrect the
dead. The only thing I should be resurrecting are stories about
sex, apparently. Although 'resurrect' would be the wrong choice
of verb there.

9.20 p.m. The girls have come over. Hannah's asked me for about
the hundredth time (and that isn't an exaggeration) whether I'm
praying or not. No, I'm not. *And I'd appreciate it if you'd stop
asking.* I think she got the message because she started speaking
to Maria about organic baby food. In the past month Maria has
been marching around the house and city with Mum, preparing
funerals, calling mortgage companies, writing to solicitors – the
pregnant and impregnable. Hannah's voice wasn't even strained

when she spoke about Maria's baby – in fact, I almost forgot she can't have a baby. She too has lost something. I suppose we are both in mourning.

11.45 p.m. I went upstairs to sit on Dad's side of the bed. This is a spot that feels far from the madding crowd, so to speak. Which feels closer to him. I came here to think – maybe about God. But all I could think of was flowers that bloom and how withered I feel. I didn't even hear the footsteps enter the room.

'Fast opens soon.'

I looked and Hannah was sat next to me.

'Oh.'

'I brought you some dates.'

She placed the plate between us and we both sat in silence for a while.

'Shit happens, doesn't it?' I said.

'It does.'

'What do I do?'

'I don't know, Sofe.' We both looked out of the window. 'But I wouldn't stop praying. That's counterproductive,' she said.

Then the call to prayer broke out, and she handed me a date.

'I know I shouldn't even think it – but I just can't bring myself to pray,' I replied.

She uttered the supplication to open fast.

'Well, sometimes it takes a while. Eat your date.'

She moved the plate away and sat closer to me.

'I bloody love you,' she said, putting her arm around me. I'm fine when people are neutral towards me; it's when they're nice that something comes undone. I sobbed. I sobbed as if the droplets of tears would cleanse the pain or something. She shushed me, and hugged me, and said it would be OK. But I sobbed until she made me lie down and put a blanket over me.

When I woke up it was dark, and Suj was sitting up, next to me.

'Toffee, you need to eat something.'

'The world doesn't stop,' I said. 'Nothing does.'

She lay down and faced me, taking my hand.

'I know, Toffee. I know.'

I closed my eyes and let the tears fall onto my dad's pillow until I fell asleep again.

Thursday 9 August

2 p.m. 'Brammers wants you to add something about sex?' said Katie, picking out the sweetcorn from the salad with her fork and dropping it back into the large bowl. 'People really shouldn't make such a big deal about it. It's only sex.'

'That's what I thought.' Although, granted, I have no reference point. 'It's all so ... frivolous,' I said.

Katie emptied the salad back into its bowl and picked up a slice of pizza.

'Frivolity,' she said, bringing the plate to eye level and inspecting the pizza at all angles, 'is the nature of the time we live in.'

'Hmm.'

'And the time we live in asks for sex. I know. Very unoriginal.' She paused. 'Don't think I haven't noticed you not praying, by the way. I see everything.'

'Everything but the queue behind you.'

'Oh yes,' she said, walking to the paying counter.

'God won't mind if you don't pray for a while. Why don't you try something less strict?' She put a piece of pizza in her mouth. 'Like Christianity?'

'Not really a *turn the other cheek* type person. Nor the whole Trinity thing.'

She looked at me and nodded. 'No, but imagine if you decided to take your scarf off? Now that would be a story.' I looked at her as she ate her lunch. 'Sorry, Sweetu,' she said, covering her mouth as she munched on her food and I sat foodless. Not that I cared.

'Not a particularly original story,' I replied.

'No.' She put her pizza down. 'I know you don't like speaking about it, but you know I'm here, don't you?' I didn't trust myself to speak so nodded, looking at the table. 'OK, good. Because you should know.'

8.20 p.m.

From: Haque, Imran
To: Khan, Sofia
Subject: Sorry

Hi Sofe,

Sorry it's taken so long. I heard abt your dad last month, but couldn't bring myself to write. I was angry man. I didn't want to be but I was. Doesn't matter how angry I was though. I should've written sooner.

I'm really sorry. I know what he meant to you. He was a good guy. Even my parents thought so. How r u keeping?

I guess it's easier to write now because I kind of have some news. Parveen got back in contact when she heard the wedding was called off. Thing is Sofe you're probably right. These things all work out for the best. She wants to live with the in-laws. She's not like you but you know, I think she really loves me. Sometimes that's enough.

Anyway, like I said sorry it took so long to write. Look after yourself. And well if u need anything, let me know.

Imran. X

I wrote back to him, obviously – as if he should be worried about saying sorry. Have to say, I'm kind of relieved that Parvy-pants swooped in there. It makes me feel marginally better knowing that he's got someone by his side. Life, eh. Bloody life.

Sunday 12 August

11.20 a.m. The time it's taking to start this new chapter, you'd think Brammers had asked me to pen the new *Kama Sutra*. I've spent two days staring at a blank screen. My tabula rasa – waiting for sex to impregnate the page so that words will be born.

I think I will go for a walk, even though Mum has warned me against getting a tan. But maybe my moving legs will have a knock-on effect on my brain.

1 p.m. I walked, and I walked, and carried on walking until I realised I was following the road to the graveyard where Dad is buried. I made my way up the sun-dappled path leading to his grave. Profound thoughts on life and death should've occurred to me. Isn't this the place that's meant to open up your mind to questions about the nature of how we live? *Who* we are? But it got too hot and I couldn't stand there any longer. I walked away and for a moment looked back, as if I was meant to say bye or something. But the time for byes is over.

And now there's nothing to do but write the damn chapter on sex, and get it over with. Not really the appropriate sentiment for a first time.

Monday 13 August

9 a.m. Well, it's done. I've just emailed the new chapter to Lucinda and Brammers. I don't think a huge chunk of my soul died, just a sliver. I can cope without a sliver.

8 p.m. OMG. I was at Waterloo, on the escalators going down, thinking about graves, books and Afghanistan when, on the other side, there was a man running down, pushing people out of the way. He looked so familiar. He carried a brown suitcase, and being a person that never forgets a face (though I might accidentally wear two pairs of underwear on any given day), I realised it was him! The man that called me a terrorist! I looked around, trying to find someone who I could tell, 'Look! There he is!' An impulse compelled me to follow him. I ran down the escalators, but some annoying person had blocked everyone's way – why don't people follow rules! There was a group of people in front of me, all of whom looked some variation of perturbed, bored and resigned when I shouted at them to get on the right side. I had to follow that bloody man. Major rage came bubbling to the surface and something was about to burst.

I reached the bottom of the escalators and a group of Spanish kids, jabbering and sauntering, blocked my view. Then I saw the brown briefcase and I followed it, hopscotching around people; eyes fixed on that briefcase. He cut his eye at a girl with hot-pink spiky hair and three nose piercings. This was for me, for her, for all the people he thought it was OK to be obnoxious to – the brown briefcased, prejudiced bastard! I caught a glimpse of my flushed face and lopsided hijab in a huge poster for a new John Grisham novel. Pushing past people, I knew this was it: this was the moment where I would get my revenge. Then, out of nowhere, an old lady got in my way.

'Terribly hot in these tubes, isn't it, dear?' A lady in a camel-coloured cardigan and carrying a walking stick smiled graciously. 'You must be very hot in that scarf,' she said, chuckling.

I smiled, looking over her old little tightly curled head to make sure he was still there. Next train would be in two minutes. I was on a deadline.

'You get used to it.' *Time to move on now.* I tried to walk past her, but apparently Old Lady wanted a chinwag.

'Ah.' She rested both hands on her stick. 'My daughter-in-law wears one of those. Lebanese. Lovely girl. Always calling to ask how I am.'

Ooh, did this mean her son converted?

'Christmas is a bit of a bore – neither of them drink – but I always get a nice bottle of Shloer. I can't say if my Frank were alive he'd be very happy.'

One more minute. Old Lady was preventing me from reaping my revenge. By the time she had stopped talking, the electricity had somewhat dissipated. I watched The Racist, gloomily. The train came and we got onto the same carriage.

There it was: the holy grail of a long and tiring journey home. And, after the to-ing and fro-ing of people getting off, or getting up for Old Lady, there in the middle of the carriage was a lone, unoccupied seat. I saw The Racist go for it. He was closer than me, but apparently I can be swift when needed. I strode towards it and there we were, for just a moment, face to face before I slid into the chair that by any onlooker's view was rightly his. I tilted my head to the side and smiled at him. He glared at me, nostrils flaring.

'Paki bitch,' he said, audibly enough, as he walked away, looking back as if he'd rather like to punch my lights out. (To be honest, if he wanted to be offensive then he should've just called me a 'fat bitch'. No one likes being a chub.) People cast sideward glances, cleared their throats and went back to reading their Kindle or looking at their iPad. As he walked past her, Old Lady banged her stick on the floor.

'Well, shame on you, young man.'

He looked taken aback at that, but imagine his further consternation when a black guy, built like a house, blocked his way.

'What did you say, blud?'

The Racist cleared his throat. There's no way I'd have elicited the same look of utter fear that my saviour seemed to.

'Nothing.'

'I think we all heard you.' He looked down at Old Lady and smiled, softening his tone, 'Didn't we, love?'

'We most certainly did,' she said.

'She took my seat.'

'I don't fucking ...' At which Old Lady cleared her throat. 'I don't care if she took your pink-laced knickers, bruv. You say sorry or *you're* gonna be sorry.' The Racist stood still. Saviour leaned into his face. '*Real* sorry.'

Most people continued to pretend nothing was happening, but one person shouted, 'Tell him, mate.'

I wanted to add that apparently I'm also a terrorist, but didn't think I needed to add more ammunition to the situation. The Racist then turned around to me and said, 'Sorry.'

The Tube stopped and my saviour strutted off without a second look at the people glancing his way or me, smiling gratefully. The Racist made his way into the next carriage and for some reason the anger came back. Was that it? That completely disingenuous, half-hearted, pathetic, *I'm clearly not having an epiphany about my narrow-minded, prejudiced views* sorry? I got up and people looked at me as The Racist carried on walking.

'Actually, one last thing,' I shouted out. (Sometimes having a Punjabber voice comes in handy.) He turned around and looked as if he was bored by the entire incident. I strode towards him, with what I hoped to be my most 'no-shitting-around' face, and stopped so close to him that he had to lean back.

'You're a cunt.'

That's right. I had no idea *that* word would come out, but it seemed to trump all the rest. He looked unimpressed while a group of people with Team GB shirts on tried to shift their gaze.

Pfft, I'll give you something to be impressed with. I took one step back, jutted back my arm and rammed my fist into his face.

'You crazy fucking bitch,' he shouted, blood streaming down his face.

'Fuck! Argh!'

I'm not going to lie, I got a clean swipe and I think there was definitely some breakage there – unfortunately I hadn't taken into account how much my own fist would hurt. He was bent over cupping his nose and I was bent over holding on to my fist. Conall had made it look so easy.

The next stop came and The Racist's nose was still bleeding, so he got off and a random passenger grabbed me by the arm, leading me onto the platform. People crowded around as The Racist pointed at me, calling me a crazy bitch.

All thoughts about my throbbing fist were forgotten and I lunged forward to take another swipe at him. 'And you're a racist wanker.'

He stumbled backwards but someone held me back as I kicked my legs in the air.

'Come on now, let's stop that,' came the voice of the man holding me back. Then there was more shouting and more expletives exchanged.

'Right, what's going on here?' A policeman and woman parted the crowds – no one was holding me back any more, but I was staring at The Racist, willing him to give me a reason to pummel him.

'That fucking crazy bitch punched me,' he exclaimed.

The policeman looked at me, raised his eyebrows and then looked at The Racist.

'This young lady here?' asked the policeman.

The Racist nodded vehemently.

'*She's* the one who punched you?' he continued.

'I'm bleeding, aren't I?'

'All right, sir, calm down,' said the policewoman.

'I'm pressing fucking charges.'

'Oh yeah? Good,' I said. 'It'll give me an excuse to find out where you live.'

The policewoman raised her hand.

'You're pressing charges, are you?' I shouted over the policeman's shoulder, 'Guess what? So am I.'

'What for?'

'Er, for inciting religious and racial hatred, *waster.*'

'And what were you doing?' asked the policeman, sighing as he took his notepad out.

Then a man, probably in his fifties, walked over to The Racist and spoke to him. He put his hand on his shoulder as The Racist glared at me.

'Can you tell me exactly what he said to you?' asked the policeman.

I was distracted by the conversation in which The Racist was now shuffling on his feet. The policeman repeated the question, but by that time the man was walking towards us.

'Officer, I believe the gentleman is no longer pressing charges.'

The policeman looked over at his colleague who nodded, putting her pen and paper back in her belt.

'Young lady,' said the old man with grey hair – I noticed his glasses; his thin, gold-rimmed glasses – just like Baba's. 'I suggest you stay out of any further trouble.'

I recognised the voice – it was the same man who'd been holding me back. I nodded – words had escaped me.

He peered at me over his glasses and his eyes glimmered as if amused by something, 'No matter how tempting it might be.'

Before I could thank him, he made his way into the crowd and I lost sight of him amongst the throng.

As I walked home, rubbing my fist now and again, I kept thinking about the man. What an unsuccessful day of fasting it was – neither tongue, nor limbs were in my control – The Racist had taken a hit, but so had any remainder of my spirituality. Before I went into the house I stopped outside Conall's gate – just for a few seconds – when Sean came out with a rubbish bag.

'Oh, hello,' he said. Must stop staring at him just because he looks like Conall. He might think I'm a psychopath.

'Hi.'

He nodded and was about to go back in when he noticed me rubbing my fist.

'How'd that happen?'

'Oh, this?' I asked, inspecting the bruising that was getting more purple by the minute. 'I punched someone.'

He laughed and then stopped, looking at my straight face.

'How's the house?' I asked.

'Grand. The garden door's an arse to open, though. Conall can't fix a lock to save his life.'

He tucked in his shirt and rested his elbow on the pillar.

'What you have to do is pull it towards you, twist the knob a quarter of an inch, anti-clockwise, and then push out. I kind of broke it.'

'You wouldn't mind opening it now? It's roastin' in there.'

Unfortunately, it turns out that I'm a bit out of practice. I fiddled with the stupid thing and the door wouldn't move. It didn't help that my hand wasn't in complete working order.

'Try pushing instead of pulling,' he said.

'No, it's definitely pull and then push. Maybe it's clockwise.'

His phone rang and when he picked up he kept saying, 'Hello, hello?' I was rather dedicated to getting the door to open when I heard, 'Conall, I can't hear you. What? Oh, right – you're using your girlfriend Hamida's phone, are ya?' He chuckled.

My throat was dry as I kept shaking the knob. *Hamida? Who the FUCK is Hamida?*

'Ah, well, whatever. What? No, your garden door won't open. No, Sofia's trying right now. Sofia. Yes. She'll make it what? Speak up. Yeah, she's grand – punched someone in the face.' Sean laughed. 'She did, I swear to you – bruised fist and everything. Tell her what? He says: isn't Ramadan meant to be a month of peace?'

My heart seemed to have moved from its usual place – I had organ displacement. *He has a girlfriend.* Worse still – *he has a Hamida* – a *Muslim* Hamida!

'He's asking about your family,' said Sean.

I gave the knob another push and pull and with one last effort the door flew open. Before Sean could ask anything else, I sprinted out of the house.

He has a Hamida. A *Hamida*. Probably some annoying, philanthropic do-gooder in khakis and no makeup who goes around building schools or whatever. But *of course* he's going to find a girlfriend. He's everything that's good.

411

There's still over an hour until iftari. I'm going to curl up in my bed.

No bloody way. Naim calling …

9 p.m. I picked up. If for no other reason than sheer curiosity.

'Happy Ramadan, Daisypuffs.'

For a moment it was so comforting to hear that familiar name. As if everything that's happened between the last time he called me Daisypuffs and now didn't exist.

'You too.'

I thought maybe he'd found out about Baba, but he began making small talk, asking how Rammers had been so far. Blah blah blah.

'What can I do for you, Naim?'

'I miss you.'

It cushioned the jagged edges of my heart a little, those words.

'How's married life?' he asked.

Of course. He didn't know I'm no longer with Imran.

'Do you miss me?' he added.

I paused.

'Why are you calling, Naim?'

He sighed.

'Because I miss you and love you.'

That's right. The 'L' word: throwing it out there as if he'd said it a million times before. You never think you'll be taken in by a person – even for a second. Everyone has such a high opinion of their judgement.

Everyone is an idiot.

'You are amazing, Naim. And I don't mean that in a good way.'

'So you're still uptight?'

'Yes. I'm still uptight and you're still a prick.' I couldn't quite believe it. Right now, he thinks I'm married and this is what comes tumbling out of his mouth.

'Hey, I call to tell you I miss and love you and you call me a prick? I'm being fucking honest.'

'Bullshit.' I paused. 'If you'd *just* left things the way they were I'd probably have looked back and thought, *even though it didn't work out, he was a good guy. At least he cared about me.* So thanks for clearing that up for me, because there's obviously nothing you could be other than a self-serving waste.

'Don't call me again,' I added. 'Ever.'

And I put the phone down.

11.45 p.m.

From: O'Flynn, Conall
To: Khan, Sofia
Subject: Violence

Sofe,

Would you believe I was here, sat in Afghanistan, randomly considering this pacifism of yours, and just when I thought, she might have a point, my brother tells me you punched someone.

It's beautiful here. But I'll tell you something for nothing: this place'd change a person. It's awful. If I had words like you, I'd describe it. I met two girls today, sold by their dad for money to fund his drug addiction. Children no older than six and nine. I've seen things before, but this is something else. I tell you, it'd be a good time to have someone who makes you laugh.

I won't be here for much longer. I'm going to Pakistan. Hamida (she's a documentary filmmaker I met) is making a film on shanty towns. The biggest one in Asia is in Orangi in Karachi. You'd love her. She never stops and she's gone and convinced me to join her. She's a bit like you – hammers on at you until you give in – couldn't say no. Plan is to raise funds through the documentary to help educate kids who don't have money for school. I've done all I can in Afghanistan, and I've run into a fair few problems, so think it's time to leave. We'll be making our way to India from Karachi. Remember the protest we went to and how you loved it so much? I can't imagine what you'd be like if you knew Hamida's plans.

How's the book? I didn't think I'd email you, you being busy with your work, but when you hit someone, well – couldn't quite help it.

Try to keep things peaceful in London.

Love,
Conall

2 a.m. I read and re-read the grammatically perfect email. I now know it by heart. Weird thing is, it wasn't the fact that he wasn't here, but the fact that he was sad, and the reasons that he was sad, which made me feel depressed. *Children being sold*. I looked outside, at the street lamps lighting up the road and, all of a sudden, the comfort of my pillow annoyed me. I switched on the bedroom light and paced up and down the room, thinking of this beautiful, forsaken place he was in.

I've just seen a printout of the new chapter I handed to Brammers, and it's given me that sinking feeling, as if something's out of place. This stupid book – it's not even as if I can give the advance back. And whose fault is that?

Tuesday 14 August

10 a.m. I know feelings can be useless – like when you want something that you will obviously never have – but they can be useful too: like when you know you're making a mistake marrying someone, or you've written a book that is *not* the book you want to write. I couldn't sleep all night. I was willing someone or something to inject an answer into my brain about what to do. And then it came to me. Because the last thing a person wants to do is look back and think, 'Hmm, if only I'd followed my instinct.'

So I went into Brammers' office and I told her. I said, 'This is not the book I want to write.'

She glanced at her computer screen and then smiled at me.

'Oh dear. Well, you're almost there, and the new chapter is just the addition that was needed.'

'No. No, it isn't – the whole thing isn't what's needed.' I sat in the chair opposite as a matter of urgency and leaned forward, 'Is this what it's come to, Bram ... Dorothy?'

I wish I had a hard copy of the manuscript to wave in the air as a matter of example.

'I can do more. Much, much more. We all can. We can publish something better than just a book about Muslim dating.'

'Umm, hmmm, thing is, it's going to be great. No need to fix something that's not broken.'

Actually, quite a lot of things are broken. She clasped her hands together.

'Do you have another book planned?' she asked as I stared at her. 'How would you be able to write something in three months?'

I looked at her as if I was about to tell her I'm putting her dog to sleep, because this wasn't an argument she was going to win.

'I'm sorry. It's not happening,' I said.

'Sorry?'

'I'm taking it back.'

'The problem is, Sofia, that you have a contract and there's no way of changing that. You have to deliver a book in October.'

'Yes, and I will.'

'What?'

'Dorothy,' I leaned forward – for effect, you see – 'I know the deadline's October and I know it sounds incredibly, well, impulsive, but that manuscript you have isn't getting published. But there will be another book.'

'Well, what would this book be?'

Shame I hadn't *quite* thought that through.

'Trust me, Dorothy. It's going to be great.'

Brammers picked up her pen and started tapping it on the table, shaking her head. 'Impossible. This just isn't what we agreed.'

'Dorothy, please. If it doesn't work,' I continued, 'if somehow I don't pull it off then it's not as if you don't already have a book to fall back on.'

She put her pen down and looked at me as that sympathetic smile that I've become so used to surfaced. I had to put all my energy into making sure my gathering tears didn't fall. Wrong time, wrong place.

'Please, I know I can deliver something better.'

Brammers took a deep breath and sighed.

'OK, Sofia.' She reached out and patted my hand. 'OK. But you know you have something good enough already.'

I sighed with relief.

'Thank you.'

She picked up some papers and went to stand up.

'Before you get up, Dorothy, there's just one more thing.' I put an envelope on her desk. 'I'd like to hand in my notice.'

12.20 p.m.

From: Khan, Sofia
To: O'Flynn, Conall
Subject: Violence

Conall,

I'm back to being a pacifist. Every time I look at the bruise on my fist I think, this really should only be used to make obscene gestures at people who take my parking space. People who take other people's spaces are dickheads. If I'm going to make one effort in life, it's going to be trying not to be one of those.

417

I'm not quite sure what to say about your email. At least you're doing something – not just sitting around, sipping tea and eating samosas or whatever. Everything is OK. Complaining about anything when you've seen the things you've seen would be a dickheaded thing to do and I've already established I want to avoid that. I miss not being able to speak with you on weekends, or see you walk in and out of your house, sit next to you on the garden step and have a cigarette. But I suppose there's the greater good at stake.

In other news it turns out I'm not made for publicity. I quit my job. I am totally jobless. I hope to have more profound thoughts on life now I'm not busy writing press releases. I also have a book to rewrite. I don't think the world's going to be a better place for having a Muslim dating book on their e-reader. You were right. Turns out you often are.

Karachi will be amazing, I'm sure. I am jealous. Since you've spent some time with my family and me at least it won't be too much of a culture shock. I'll make an effort to do more for the world after I finish the book, just not sure what that more is yet.

Any thoughts you might have on what book I should write will be greatly received.

Sofia. Xx

It took me an hour to compose those paragraphs. There was no need to mention anything about Dad. I don't need sympathy. Anyway, what's the point in relating information when the only thing a person can reply with is, 'I'm sorry.'

7 p.m. Maria and Tahir are over for iftari. Maria keeps complaining about pains in her stomach, to which Mum replied that if you're not going to be in pain with another human growing inside you, then when are you going to be in pain.

I keep checking my phone for emails. Nothing. But then there's not much to reply to.

10 p.m. Tahir's gone to the mosque so I came downstairs to see what Mum and Maria were up to.

'I gave Sean iftari today. It's rude, haina, all Ramadan we've given nothing to neighbours,' said Mum. I put the kettle on and looked in the cupboards for potential muffins. 'So much like Colin he looks.'

'Conall, Mum!' Maria and I said in unison.

'O-ho, haan, Conall. Muffins are in bread bin – look with your eyes. And then he asked about your baba.' The muffin was almost in my mouth. I put it down. Great. 'Nice hai, Sean. You know how these goray like our food. Also, the kitchen light is not working properly. I'll ask him to fix and give him biryani.'

Maria said that Tahir is more than able to fix things in the house and Mum scoffed and said that it'll be a wonder if he'll manage to hold their baby without dropping it on its head.

Friday 17 August

7 p.m. Everyone's waiting for Eid to be announced. I'm waiting for a reply. I suppose I should give up. But he is in Afghanistan.

Anything can happen in Afghanistan. What if there's been an accident? Or bombing? Maybe I should ask Sean, just in case. I'd like not to come across as unhinged, though. But what if Conall's lying in a ditch somewhere and all that stands between life and death for him is me finding out whether he received my email?

Or maybe he's with that Hamida. Whyyyyyyyyy??

7.45 p.m. Oh my God! Maria just called and said she thinks she's having contractions. The baby's not due for another five weeks!

9 p.m. Bloody hell, I'm in hospital. Mum, being the faint-hearted sort, told me to call her when it's done. God, please let Maria and baby be OK. *Please.* Tahir has just come out of the labour room and Maria wants me inside.

'She says she needs you. To talk her through it.'

'What about the midwife?' I asked. I gag just at the mention of mucus plugs.

'She needs her sister, Sofe.'

I looked at his serious face, and then thought of my poor sister, pushing a *human* out of her vagina.

'OK. OK, let's go in.'

Saturday 18 August

6 a.m. You see a woman give birth, you're going to respect her. Fact. What an Eid present. Yes, today is Eid. I'm officially an aunt – to an as-of-yet-unnamed baby boy. I can't believe a person can be that tiny. Maria's asleep and Tahir's passed out on the chair. There was this moment, when I saw the baby's head, this weird upside down, alien thing – covered in blood and mucus and God knows what other crap – that I felt my eyes well up and actual happiness pop to the surface. It doesn't hit you, really – how you've never seen anything until you've seen one human come out of another.

He hasn't opened his eyes yet and we can't go into the Neonatal Ward, but the doctors say he's going to be all right.

When I checked my phone I thought I'd have an email waiting for me. I'd better go and collect Mum. She wants to see whether the baby's fair or not. The circle of life.

Sunday 19 August

7.05 a.m. Mum told me to get out of bed to help her make samosas for people who'll be coming to visit Maria and baby. I saw my life flash before my eyes. All of a sudden I was in my sixties, living in the same house, making samosas for this same nephew's wedding.

11 a.m. Oh my God. I have lost the will to live. My arms are aching from filling in samosa pockets and I also have the weird paste all over my clothes. I have to now help Mum clear out Maria's old room. As per tradition, she and baby will be living here for at least a month.

I check my phone all the time. Every time it beeps I think it might be him, and it isn't. Perhaps it never will be.

Friday 24 August

1 p.m. Maria and baby are coming home at last. I will be glad to be able to bundle up joy in my arms.

Saturday 25 August

10.30 a.m. 'Sofia! Also bring back Maria's white sandals. People come to see the baby and she's walking around in horrible slippers.'

If it's not kebabs and chocolate fountains, it's formula and breast pumps. When I left to pick stuff up from Maria's home, I sat behind the wheel for five minutes. I started the engine and I took a left towards the cemetery. I still haven't got used to seeing his name engraved on a tombstone. Date of death: 29th June 2012. On the 28th I had a father, and the next day he was gone: from flesh to eventual dust.

I raised my hands in prayer – there's nothing much I can do for bones, but if there's a soul floating around somewhere, unaided and in need of a place to rest, then I'm going to pray for it. It's different when you're crying alone out in the open – in fact, if anyone's ever going to cry anywhere, I'd recommend it be alone, in the open – under some blossom tree or a ridiculously picturesque place like that. There's nothing quite as sad as grief displayed beneath a blossom tree.

12.15 p.m. I was sat, phone in hand – waiting, as ever – and Mum asked me to get her gold bangles from upstairs.

'Gold bangles?' I asked. I mean, on one hand there's someone like Conall (and bloody brilliant Hamida) doing things that mean something, and on the other hand there was my mum, asking me about gold bangles.

'Haan. The ones your baba gave me last year for our anniversary. O-ho, the ones with the rubies in them.'

T attempted to swaddle the baby as Auntie Reena looked over and said the swaddle wasn't tight enough. Auntie Scot said it was too tight. I could see beads of sweat running down T's face.

'Rubies?' I asked.

Mum tutted at T. 'O-ho, *this* is how you do it.' As Maria watched the three of them, fussing over the baby, she burst into tears.

'Tst, Beta,' said Auntie Reena, 'chalo, chalo, you don't cry. Men don't know these things. They don't have wombs, nah.' She walked over and sat next to Maria, hugging her.

Tahir took the baby to Maria. 'Babe, look at him.' He sat on the arm of the sofa. 'He looks just like your dad.'

Maria nodded and smiled through her tears. Mum's eyes filled and I headed up the stairs to get the gold bangles so I could cry alone in my room.

2 p.m. 'Sofia! Door!'

Honestly, can't the world even give a girl five minutes to cry alone? When I opened the door I ... Well, I ... I was like what the *actual* fuck? When you've spent most nights taking turns to soothe a baby, are covered in dubious-looking samosa paste, and have four women collectively telling one man how to swaddle

423

aforementioned baby, then a person sometimes needs to do a double-take. I thought I was hallucinating.

'Conall?'

'Hi.'

I stared at him. I had to look closer because I mean, it certainly looked like him, but he was sporting a beard and looked like he'd wandered out of a prisoner-of-war camp.

'You going to invite me in?'

I opened the door. He walked in and I followed, bewildered, as he entered the living room. Five faces turned to look at him.

'Colin!' exclaimed Mum. 'You're back.'

There was a general kerfuffle as the group dispersed and Maria was left holding the perfectly swaddled baby. She looked up at Conall, blowing her nose with a tissue. I went into the kitchen as I heard everyone asking questions, him saying congratulations etc and all I could keep thinking was, *what the hell*? An aeroplane flew overhead. I watched it make its way over the line of red-bricked houses until it was gone. Gone, gone, gone.

This is a new life. And when you get on that plane, make it yours.

When I turned around, Mum was laughing. Conall sat down, answering questions and looking at the baby. Every now and again he'd stare into space and then be recalled to reality by someone. He looked positively knackered, to be honest. In the meantime, my insides had decided to start hopping around, thumping against my chest, tying themselves up into knots. I walked back into the living room and looked at him. My nephew was equally entranced by this new arrival.

'Let me get the samosas,' said Mum as she got up and was followed into the kitchen by Auntie Reena. Auntie Scot and Maria looked at me and then at him.

'You're meant to be going to Pakistan,' I said.

'I am going.' He leaned forward, clasping his hands together.

'Oh. Doesn't make much sense for you to have come back when you could've just, you know, crossed over.'

'No. It doesn't.' He opened up his hands. 'Not *one* bit of sense.'

I wanted to cry. Actually cry. Only I'm not sure *why*. Because he got on a plane and was here? Because he was going to get back on a plane and leave? Or because he'd apparently done something senseless? Whatever it was, something sprang back into a life that wasn't all about other people's babies and gold bangles.

Mum and Auntie Reena put the tray of samosas on the coffee table.

'Hain, you're going to Pakistan?' Mum asked.

He was still looking at me and it might not have been the light at the end of the tunnel, but sometimes you think *maybe if I make a change I'll find a tiny bloody ray*.

'Yes,' I said.

Mum stopped pouring tea into a cup and looked at me.

'I'm going to Pakistan,' I added.

There was a moment of silent confusion until I started explaining about Orangi and the shanty town there and this documentary film. He didn't have to say anything, and it didn't matter what he said anyway, because I knew I wanted to go to Karachi. I wanted to go to India. I had to leave and *do* something with my life.

'Haan, haan,' said Mum. 'Lekin what will *you* do there?'

Auntie Scot had eyebrows raised to high heaven.

'I don't know,' I said. 'I'll find a story.' Conall nodded at me, as if reassuring me to go on.

Then Auntie Reena said, 'O-ho, she can stay with Nasir's cousin. You know, the fat one who thinks she is always wearing the best clothes. Every year she comes to London, showing me her fat face.'

'I'm not staying with anyone's cousin,' I said.

'Le, taw, who will you stay with?' asked Auntie Scot, taking a bite out of her samosa. I looked at Conall.

'With him,' I said, pointing in his direction.

'There's a group of us,' explained Conall to the bewildered faces.

'Grrup? What grrup?' said Auntie Scot.

Conall stood up. 'I think I'll leave you to discuss the logistics between yourselves.'

Just like that, he left: a ghost who'd come into the house, made a commotion and disappeared.

'Sofe,' said T. 'It's not right.' He was swaying my nephew side to side. 'All I'm saying is, go to Karachi, but stay with some family, not in a random place where there's a bunch of people you don't know.'

'Just hold your son, Tahir,' said Maria.

'You know what things are like in Karachi,' said Auntie Scot.

I wanted to stuff all the samosas in her mouth to keep any more words from coming out of it. Tahir nodded in agreement and then the baby threw up all over him. The doorbell rang again and it was Uncle Scot who walked in and looked at everyone. Auntie Scot relayed what had just happened and he scoffed. 'Le, as if we will send our beti with a strange man. And in Karachi too. So unsafe it is.'

He sat down and rubbed his hands together, reaching over for some tea. I was just about to say, 'I'm going whether anyone likes it or not,' when Mum interjected.

'Those days are gone now, Bhai,' she said.

Maria and I looked at her as she picked the tray up before Uncle Scot had a chance to take a samosa. She walked into the kitchen and placed the tray on the counter. When she walked back in, Uncle Scot was looking around the room, his eyes resting on Tahir.

Mum turned towards me. 'Soffoo, you are sure this is what you want? You get bored of everything, this will bore you too, nahin?'

I shook my head.

'Bhabi, girls in our family don't do this,' said Uncle Scot.

'Bas,' said Mum. 'I'll say it only once more – those days are gone.'

2.50 p.m. Extraordinary! Did Conall actually walk through the door two hours ago?

OMG! I'll be in Karachi while Hamida and Conall fawn over each other! Must go over there instantly. *What* am I thinking??

5 p.m. Very weird things can happen within the space of a few hours. I was half-expecting Sean to open the door and be like, what are you talking about? My brother's in Afghanistan. But it was Conall. Flesh, blood and beard. He rested both hands against the doorframe, and this might not be the most PC thing to say, but with the beard and all he kind of looked like Jesus. It actually *was* like a resurrection, except we don't believe in that, because, you know, he's still alive. Just saying.

I walked into the living room. What was I thinking? Why the hell did I say I'd hop on a plane with this man? This wonderful, lovely, painstakingly grumpy man? It was so unreasonable. He was, after all, just a friend. I couldn't do it. Except the alternative was going back to making samosas for the foreseeable future. This wasn't just about him.

'Why didn't you tell me about your dad, Sofe?'

Suddenly the polka dots on my dress became very interesting to me.

'Oh, you know,' I waved my hand. 'What was the point?' I couldn't quite bring myself to look up. 'Have you seen your flowers?' I went into the kitchen to show him that they'd bloomed.

'Just as well it rains all the time. Broken doorknob,' I said, indicating to the door.

'Hmmm.'

I folded my arms. 'What'll be next then? After Pakistan and India?'

He shrugged and put his hands in his pockets.

'I guess planning is for the unadventurous,' I added.

'Or the short-sighted,' he replied.

'Yes, well, sorry for not being all *visionary*.'

'Pakistan's a good place to start. Now, tell me,' he said, his voice softening, 'why didn't you say something about your dad? No one likes a martyr.'

I had to compose myself. My integrity was at stake, after all. *Get your shit together*.

'What's that, anyway?' I said, gesturing towards his thick, dark, beard, while I swallowed the lump that had formed in my throat.

'This? Yes.' He nodded, looking at the floor. 'Something new I'm trying.' He rubbed the back of his neck. 'Sofe ...'

I looked at the ground because there was no holding the tears back. It's the kindness; it gets me every time. The tears dropped, one by one. I tried to speak. I opened my mouth, but no words came out and then the tears had steadied into a stream. I tried to wipe them away, but before I knew it his arms were around me and I was crying into his filthy T-shirt. His lovely, filthy, T-shirt.

'It's just hay fever,' I mumbled.

'Of course it is. You won't get that in Karachi.'

I shook my head. I can't stay! I have to go. I *need* to go. I released myself from, quite frankly, a rather embarrassing collapse of emotion, and I didn't want to get used to his arms around me.

'Why did you come back?'

He sighed and glanced at the floor.

'I had some things to sort out.'

'Oh.' I focused on the polka dots again. But I couldn't be too disappointed. What did I think he was really going to say? And what did it matter? He wasn't Muslim. I know that I want it all. The sensible person in me knows that even if not immediately, some years down the line I'd miss things like us praying together, going for pilgrimage, learning about our faith and growing with it. With each other. And when you feel *this* way for someone, the way I do right now for Conall, I can't quite bear the idea of him not being a part of everything. That's the thing about that ray of light – you never find it where you want it.

10 p.m. Surely I'm making a mistake? OK, time to get the istikhara out again.

11.20 p.m. I do think, I'd rather be near him than not.

Lord, I've become pathetic! Maybe I've always been pathetic??

Monday 27 August

8.30 a.m. Ticket booked! Leaving Friday. Yes, this Friday. So much to do. Haven't run into any hiccups yet – am waiting for istikhara to show its force and put hurdle after hurdle ... Although I do have to take my nephew (still unnamed) to hospital. Maria has mastitis and has been admitted. This worries me. I said I'd delay flight because I have a newborn nephew, and all these people who need me.

'No!' She leaned over and whispered, 'Trust me.' She gripped the sleeve of my blouse. 'If you don't leave this Friday, you'll never leave.'

The girls were in obvious shock. Also slightly concerned about how I'll get to India, given my Pakistani status. I told them I'll take Conall to Islamabad when I go to get my visa. In brown countries a white person is like a master key (which I'm obviously annoyed about in principle). I don't think the girls' feeling of moroseness lasted very long as Hannah had to go because she's started online dating and had to fill in her profile, Suj was mid-argument with Charles about him being upset that he's a secret and Fozia had decided to write a letter of resignation.

'I'm done. I've said bye to Kam, now it's bye to old job. I've always wanted to go to South America and if you can up and leave, why can't I?'

I smiled to myself at obviously being a source of inspiration before Fozia added, 'Though who decides to leave the country only to go to Pak?'

'And India,' I added.

'Oh yeah. That's better.' She paused in thought for a moment. 'I'll meet you there.' When I asked her about Riaz, she became that wistful person again, but imagine my surprise when she said, 'He's waited this long, he can wait a little more.'

I went to Conall's and he was stuffing the clothes Mum had given him to hand out into his bag. I told him what Fozia said about the boringness of going to Pakistan. He just shook his head and sighed. I've realised our relationship largely consists of him shaking his head and sighing at me. What does this mean? He also seems constantly occupied with staring into space unless a person actively engages him in conversation.

'So, are we going to save the world or something?' I asked.

'You'd be a fool to think you could do that.' He took out some clothes and refolded them. 'Tell me that's the last of it, Sofe.' He zipped the bag.

'Sorry.' I handed him another black bin bag. He sighed (obviously) and said, 'And you'd be an even bigger fool if you never tried.'

Tuesday 28 August

7 p.m. Katie just came to give me a belated Eid present – a new workout DVD, which will apparently change our lives. Tom waved at me from the car.

'I can't believe you're leaving,' she said. 'I have India books. I'll bring them on Thursday. Also, linen trousers. Lots of linen trousers. You're going to come back so thin.'

Tom beeped at her.

'But please not too thin. It's so passé. Call me if you need anything. See you Thursday.'

She was about to leave when she turned around and hugged me. 'I'll miss you so much.' She held me by the shoulders. 'But it's going to be *epic*.'

Love Katie.

Thursday 30 August

9 a.m.

From Fozia: Darling, have you got Hannah's headphones? Also, I'll need to borrow Conall's sleeping bag after all. He won't need it out there, will he? See you tonight! xxx

12.20 p.m.

From Suj: Toffeeeeee! I'll be a bit late. I've just told the old man about Charles! I thought, fuck it. What's the worst that can happen? Shit. I have to go. Promise won't be too late. Love youuuuuuu xxxxx

1.45 p.m.

From Hannah: This guy with the long beard – have you told him I can't have babies? I don't want to be set up with a person only to have to explain I'm barren. It's boring. Actually, I'll ask Conall myself because you always miss out the details. BTW, if Fozia asks you for my headphones, tell her you lost them. She broke my old ones and there's no way I'll get them back in one piece after her gallivanting around South America. Why is everyone leaving the country? Xx

OK, fine, I know I'm going away, but that doesn't mean I have to forsake the responsibility of helping friends with relationship issues. All I did was ask Conall about Long Beard – the thought just occurred to me, quite randomly. Well, actually, I was thinking about the protest day and obviously recollected Long Beard, and I thought, hmmm, Hannah's single, I wonder if Long Beard is too. When I asked Conall about LB he looked down at me, oh so sceptically (after telling me off for calling his friend Long Beard).

'All I'm saying is, he's a single beardie and she's a single hijabi and you like him, right? One should never ignore possibilities.'

And you know what Conall did? He sighed (standard) and texted LB!

'He's not going to be some weird fundo, though, is he?' I asked. I mean, a person never can tell.

'Sofe, he's one of the best men I've ever met.'

It sounded as if Conall should marry him. If only. I wouldn't feel so bad if that's the way he was inclined. That made me think of Hottie Abid. I do hope he's OK.

'Exactly how many miles away will you have to be to stop inter-fering in your friends' lives?' Conall asked.

'Interfering and caring are two very different things. It says more about you that you don't know the difference.'

He put the phone on the table and laughed. I think that's the first time he's laughed since he's been back.

'You talk utter shit sometimes.' What does a person have to do to be taken seriously? Bet Hamida doesn't talk shit. I'll try to be a more impressive person. It might be a losing game, but I will try and try and try.

5.30 p.m. I decided to finish off my packing while Maria sat and nattered away, feeding the baby. Mum came in and looked at the hijabs I put in the suitcase.

'Reena!' Auntie Reena came sauntering in. 'Tell Soffoo what Karachi is like. No one wears hijab shijab there.'

'Haan, Beta. Better to take it off.'

'There taw girls wear little, little sleeves and capri trousers to their knees only. Very modern they are now,' shouted Auntie Scot from the toilet – all these voices that carry ...

'They'll say how girls from London are so village.'

I'm sure they will. Hamida will probably think the same – but there are some things that can't be changed. You can't help what you love, and I think I've at least learned what is and isn't worth compromising.

11.30 p.m. What an evening! House overrun by people. Sean and Conall came over. Tom delighted Mum with ongoing compliments about the food, but he didn't look quite so comfortable when Uncle Scot kept going on about the British Raj dividing the Hindus and

Muslims. Poor Tom. Suj kept on looking at me shiftily and when I asked her what was wrong she said, 'What's going on with you and that Conall?' I feigned ignorance, though I don't know why I bother with Suj. She probably already knows. I've just come to realise that speaking about matters of the heart can be counterproductive. Conall sat staring at his glass before I caught his eye and he smiled. I love his smile.

After dinner, Sean helped Mum wash the dishes. Auntie Scot was looking at him.

'Look there,' she said to Auntie Reena as I picked up rogue napkins from the floor, 'Can you imagine Pakistani man doing that?'

Auntie Reena scoffed. 'Le, our men taw are shit.'

Uncle Scot looked up from watching the news whilst Tahir tried to stop the baby from crying.

I looked at both aunties. 'Come on, now,' I said, 'there's no need to be racist.'

I had to take a moment and look at everyone. Everyone but Baba. There will always be something missing. There's nothing you can do about loss, except fill the hole as much as you can with memories of the people that have been left behind.

Friday 31 August

4.30 a.m. I sat on Baba's side of the bed, thinking of what he might've said if he were here. I can only guess – I'll only ever be able to guess – but I hope that his feelings would be something along the lines of pride.

Fozia stayed over last night.

'Darling,' she said. I turned around and she was standing at the door. 'It's time to go.'

I stood up and got the prayer mat out and wrapped my hijab over my head.

When I sat down afterwards on the mat, I prayed for everyone that was in the room last night. And the person that wasn't. I remembered the couple from the hospital whose daughter had been in an accident, and prayed she was OK as well. Also, seeing as I was feeling generous, I threw in a prayer for the rest of the world too.

'Will you miss me, Mum?' I asked.

She yawned as she put the kettle on and said, 'I'll be too busy to miss you. And waisay bhi, you know how much mess your Scotland Auntie and Uncle make in the kitchen. I'll say thanks to God when they go back.'

When all my cases were in the trunk I went to hug Mum and Maria.

'Acha, make sure you come back thin,' said Mum. She held my face in her hands and tears were gathering in her eyes. 'Chal, my bachi.' *Bachi*. Yes, I will always be a child in her eyes. 'Be careful in India. You know they don't like Muslims.'

'Yes, Mum,' I said, smiling as I hugged her.

Maria started crying. I told her I'd be back in no time and she said, 'Not that, stupid. I'm just happy you're doing this.'

I worried, having to leave them both, but Fozia was there (which reminds me to email the girls separately and assign who's to look after who while I'm away). She put her arm around Mum and told her she'd help her paint the conservatory before she left for South America.

'Make sure Suj doesn't go breaking up with Charles,' I said, hugging Foz, and (I'm sorry) feeling envious of her slight frame. 'I'll see you in India.'

'I'll bring fags!' she whispered in my ear.

8.45 a.m. Thanks to God – we're on the plane and I've sent emails to girls. Really wish we hadn't flown Pakistan International Airlines, but God forbid I say a thing out loud. Conall told me to stop being rude. Let's see how he feels a few hours in when it's too hot, the entertainment system doesn't work and passengers start complaining about the cutlery.

'There are worse things in the world, Sofe.'

Must stop looking at him in puppy-dog fashion. I do have *some* sense of self left.

8.50 a.m. Mum just called and I spoke to everyone on speaker-phone. Luckily no one in the plane really noticed or cared.

'Beta, acha, there is a boutique in Clifton, if you call …'

Maria cut Auntie Reena off with, 'Quick! Put the phone down before everyone starts giving you orders for what clothes they want made.'

The Scots told me that times might've changed but I'm still a girl and still the daughter of Shakeel Khan. I told them it wasn't likely I'd forget my gender (honestly), or whose daughter I was. But when they started saying bye in unison I felt like giving them a collective hug. As I switched the phone off, Conall handed me a packet of Hobnobs. It almost made me cry. I tried not to think of how many nice things he must do for Hamida and focused on being grateful for the fact that I was sitting beside him for the next seven hours.

Because we know now that I am pathetic.

Time at current location: 2.55 p.m. I have to record this right now in case I forget any detail. I can't risk losing a single moment to memory loss.

Some fat man tried to close the overhead compartment and I thought, see, it's beginning – being on this flight *is* one of the worst things in the world.

'Jesus, how heavy is that person's hand luggage?' said Conall, under his breath.

'How heavy is that person?' I replied, not so quietly.

'So when we get there, Hamida'll meet us with her partner.'

I fiddled with the seatbelt and fastened it, attempting to block out any mention of her.

'Hmm, fine.'

'They're a great team,' he said, smiling at the fifth person who'd walked past staring at him. 'Met two years ago on a charity tour. Just got married.'

I looked at him, but he started casually flicking through the pages of a magazine. What was this? Met? Each other? What?

'Oh.' I took the magazine from him and pretended to flick through it in case my heart leaped out of my mouth. 'You mean her *husband?*'

He nodded, saying, 'Sofe, are you always going to just take things from me?' I couldn't speak; I just looked at him. 'OK, when we land we're going straight to Tooba mosque. Put some discipline in you. Plus,' he continued, 'It's Friday. We'll miss afternoon prayers, but you want to go to the mosque on a Friday.'

We? I couldn't speak. I just nodded.

'We'll enrol in some cookery classes, too. Sort this domestic shit of yours out once and for all.'

Ladies and gentlemen, please take your seats and fasten your seatbelts …

'We?' I said, accidentally dropping the magazine.

He buckled his seatbelt and gave a brief nod. The plane began to move and people were still standing, getting things out of the overhead compartments. A baby cried in the back and a man stood, chatting to his friend sitting behind him.

'Sir, aap *please* beth jayein,' said the air hostess to him.

When he ignored her request to sit down, she sighed and stomped off to the cockpit. My heart wasn't just displaced – it had found itself practically in my mouth. But I had to act normal. *It doesn't make a difference. He's not Muslim.*

'You know, you really should trim that beard. You look like a homeless person,' I said.

He sighed.

'Although, I guess where we're going you'll kind of fit in.'

'Jesus Christ.'

'I don't think you should take Jesus's name in vain. Also, I have a point. On both counts.'

He scratched the beard and turned towards me.

'Don't you like it?'

Ladies and gentlemen, can you please *take your seats and fasten your seatbelt. The plane is taking off.*

I don't think I could help smiling when I looked at him, and his lovely face with this unruly beard.

Of course I like it. I love it. I love youuuuuu.

'It's, you know, whatever.'

Conall leaned in, his face not two inches away from mine. 'Whatever? I go and get a beard for you and all I get is a whatever?'

I must've looked confused. Hain? A beard? For me? Also, why was he so close (and yet so far!)? There was the quickening of the heart again . . .

'You'd be surprised what you think about when you're away from everyone. Everything.'

The confusion about his train of thought must've appeared on my face.

'Like the length of your dress being in correlation with the length of a Muslim's beard . . .' he said.

Muslim's beard?

'Some things don't make sense until you have the time to think about them. And then you just have to adjust a few things. You don't mind having to adjust the length of your dresses?'

'Conall . . .' I began. What was he saying? Did he actually mean what I think he meant?

'You better not. Seeing as I've feckin' adjusted my religion.'

Oh my actual, *actual* God.

'There was only one thing I needed to sort out, Sofe. And that was knowing if you were willing to take a risk too.'

Then it all came out. How Afghanistan made him realise that he missed me. (*Me?* If I weren't buckled in, I'd have buckled over. Seriously.) And that my email made him restless, and then the phone call when Sean told him about Baba – it all meant one thing, and that was apparently to come back and see if I felt the way he thought I felt. (Erm, hello? As if I had a choice in the matter. As if I could feel *any* other way.) He held my hand and I threw my arm around him. I'm afraid I cried. A lot. Bloody tears. Blubbered things about feelings that, really, I'd rather not repeat or get into. He seemed to find it all quite amusing.

Imagine, I don't have to worry about tearing myself away from him. Ever. I keep wondering how this could've happened. Does he know what he's doing? I've heard of people converting for their partner, I *know* people who have done it, but that shit always happens to others. Not like this. Not to *you*.

He's queueing for the bathroom (good luck to him). I keep looking back at him to make sure he's still there, and that this isn't just a figment of my imagination. The entertainment system *isn't* working, it *is* too hot, and someone's just asked whether this plane is going to Islamabad (there have already been complaints about the cutlery), so it all feels real enough ...

What do you do for a person who's going to change their life for you? I must think of doing something equally brilliant for him. Don't think cupcakes will work – well, not *my* cupcakes anyway.

Oh my God! I just flicked through my diary and read the Anaïs Nin line: 'We write to taste life twice.' That's it! The book! The book can be about all of this! Nin-ster is a bloody genius!

I will write a whole book about Conall, and *we* will be even.

3 p.m. (Still on plane. Obviously.) Hmph. Conall just came and sat back down. Nosy bugger read the last line of my entry, laughed out loud and said, 'Like fuck we'll be!'

I looked at him – he is so familiar and new. I won't think too much about what all this means. Not yet. There are months spanning out ahead, clearing the space for so many more words, so much more life. What's the rush?

If there's one thing I've learned, it's that these things do take time, after all.

Acknowledgements

Thank you to my first readers: Clara Nelson, for that all-important weekend in Bosham, and without whom there'd be no pigeon sex in the book; Helen Bryant and Kathryn Price, my Cornerstones family, who kept me employed despite my never actually doing those digital campaigns. Thank you also to Ruth Warburton and Fiona Murphy for their encouragement.

I am so grateful for Nelle Andrew's enthusiasm and belief in Sofia. Joel Richardson, thank you for your remarkable calmness and commitment (especially when it came to the font for the author name on the cover).

To the people who suffered the hazards of having a writer friend: Jas Kundi for being on hotline all these years and those coffees in Costa with Sandra Romero, to whom I am also very thankful; Sadaf Sethi for teaching me how to peel an onion and that step on Albion Road; Amber Ahmed, for being my kutiya and international budday blues partner; Shaista Chishty, because you stood on the equator with me and are the spiritual pea in my pod; Kristel Pous, for buying me biscuits and loving me despite the hand that has often been in your face; Sarah Khawaja, for our weekly work sessions and for never saying a common-place thing; Farah Jamaluddin, for Elba (it's nice, inni), dates and *Juan!* Thanks are also due to Nafeesa Yousuf for post-MS-reading giddiness, and Alex Hammond for PoshWatch and debates about things like social justice and porridge.

I am beyond lucky for my sister/surrogate mother, Nadia Malik, who is the only person I'd call if I were stuck in a jungle (reception permitting), and because she gave me Zayyan and Saffah Adam – the best hindrance to writing anyone could ask for. Thanks also to my Pakistan family; Bibi, Naz, Nani Khala and Khaloo Asad, who pray for me always.

And of course *thank you* to my mum and dad who unwittingly taught me the different ways in which love can spring; this life would not have been possible without them.

Lastly, but obviously not least, thanks to God for all of the above and everything in between.

Enjoyed Sofia Khan is Not Obliged?

Read on for an exclusive Q&A with Ayisha Malik, reading group questions and a first look at what Sofia does next . . .

Reading Group Questions

- Have you ever read a novel with a Muslim protagonist before? Do you think it changed the way you read the book?

- Was Sofia what you expected of a Muslim heroine? In what ways was she different?

- What did you think of the title? In what ways is Sofia not obliged? Do you think the author meant to use the term ironically? If so, how?

- Would you want to read Sofia's Muslim dating book? Do you think she was right not to follow through with it?

- How important do you think it is to share religious beliefs with your partner?

- How do you imagine Sofia and Conall's relationship will be? Did she make the right choice?

Want to join the conversation? Let us know what you thought of the book on Twitter using the hashtag #SofiaKhan

An interview with Ayisha Malik

This is your first novel. Where did you get the idea for the story?
There was something about dating in London as a practicing Muslim that struck me as a little ridiculous (and therefore, funny). I've been writing for years, but have struggled to find a story that I've managed to finish – in the end I decided to write what I know.

You've worked in publishing – are the scenes at Sofia's work based on any real life experiences?
Some material was lifted from my time working as a publicist – certainly the aspect of probably being the only hijabi in publishing, and the unique experience that comes with trying to find a place to pray in the middle of an author's book launch. And then trying to explain it to people. At least all those awkward silences and looks finally came in handy.

Sofia's friends and family are such an important part of this book – are they possibly more important than the love story?
I loved writing about them and I think they are. The love story is the happy ending, but without her family and friends Sofia would be just another girl who's to-ing and fro-ing between men and it would've been, quite frankly, a bit boring. The point of her family and friends is to show that there is more than one kind of love, and more than one way of learning about it.

Would you like to see Sofia Khan adapted for film or television? Do you know who you'd like to play Sofia?

Which author wouldn't? I have absolutely no idea who I'd want to play Sofia. Jake Gyllenhaal for Conall though, please. I just Googled him again and my enthusiasm for this casting is still very strong.

Do you like the label of 'Muslim author'?

I think the label is inevitable. For now, I believe it's a good thing and in keeping with the kind of book I've written. I'm not sure how I'll feel about it years down the line – it'll depend on what I'm writing, I suppose.

Sofia's faith is obviously a very important part of her life. Did you find it easy to write about religion?

Mostly, I did. To begin with I thought the harder part would be trying to show the importance of faith without it being difficult to relate to. Religion is so often frowned upon that I knew Sofia had to be a strong enough character to help the reader overcome any aversion to the idea of it. As I continued to write I found that because religion is just a part of the make-up of Sofia – another facet of who she is – then it became, if not relatable, something the reader could understand. Ultimately it ended up being quite fun.

Have you encountered any good Muslim characters in other books?

In a word: no. I don't think I have. Perhaps I did once and I've forgotten.

Do you know what you're writing next?

The sequel to Sofia Khan, and I have to say, I'm rather enjoying it.

Can't get enough of Sofia?
Read on for an exclusive first
peek at what she does next
– publishing in early 2017 . . .

Tuesday 1 January

8.30 a.m. Oh my actual God. I can't believe it. There's a man in my bed! A proper, real-life man. I keep prodding Conall – because who knows when one might have become prone to hallucinating? This might not sound like sophisticated behaviour, but I'd rather be non-hallucinatory than sophisticated. I decided to message the girls. Text message, of course, because we wouldn't have anything as advanced as Wi-Fi in this place.

> **To Suj, Foz, Hannah:** I wonder what I should do with him?

> **From Hannah:** If he's asleep then I wouldn't do anything unless you want to be charged with assault.

Hannah always makes very good points.

> **From Suj:** Jump him!

> **From Foz:** For God's sake. Wake him up. Does he know how long you've waited to have sex??

As do Suj and Foz.

'Sofe, would you please let me get some sleep?'

Conall turned over towards me, raised his head to look at my phone and then flopped back down again. OK, will stop prodding him in case he regrets converting to my Muslim way of life. These are precarious times, after all. I've heard the first year of marriage is the making or breaking of the foundation upon which the marital future is built, blah blah blah.

'You're worse than the doodwalla,' he added.

Having one's level of disturbance being compared to the milkman can be a bit of a passion killer. I looked around the room with its flaking paint and grimy curtains – the lonely desk in the corner, which is meant to be a work area of sorts. Work for what, though? What exactly am I meant to be doing? Conall suggests I write another book, but I don't think I have more than one in me. Even if I did, how would I be able to complete it when we only get electricity six hours of the day?

'Be grateful for that thing called pen and paper,' said Conall.

I'd really rather be grateful for electricity.

From Suj: BTW I'll be a little late tonight. We miss you, Toffeeeee. Come back!!! xxxxxx

I felt a sudden pang. It's been five months since I've seen the girls and each respective life is being lived with undramatic regularity, despite my not being there to, well, regulate it. Plus, there's only so much information you can glean about each friend's life via intermittent messaging and emails. Not knowing things makes me uncomfortable. Almost as uncomfortable as this room.

Billy popped her head out of the bathroom door and meandered over. I took a biscuit out of the drawer and placed it on the floor before glancing over at Conall. He'd stuck his head under the pillow.

'The thing is . . .' I ventured.

Quiet.

'It's not as if we have to stay here.'

More quiet. Billy was nibbling at the biscuit and looked up at me momentarily, tilting her head and meowing before returning to her day's favourite activity. The beeping of car horns, as usual, didn't stop all night, which was punctuated only by the bleating of sheep – all lined up, naturally, outside our block of flats. I can hear the children playing out in the streets already.

'At least at Chachi Nino's we wouldn't be living in *Dante's Inferno* meets *Animal Farm*,' I said. 'And just think – no doodwalla.'

He is exceptionally loud (the milkman that is). A cockroach skirmished in the corner. Vom. It says something about my personal growth that I didn't actually vom. I picked up my slipper to go and kill the damn thing when Conall grabbed my arm and pulled me back under the covers.

'There's another 'roach. It's gross.'

'Shh. Just be useful for once and keep me warm,' he said. 'It's freezing.'

'What do you mean, "for once"?' I said, wrapping my arm around his. 'I've opened your eyes to a new way of life. Before me you were sullen and alone and now look . . .' I sighed. 'Before Sofia. You can call it BS. As in, that's what life used to be.'

To be quite honest, every time I open my eyes in the morning I'm not sure I haven't converted to his way of life. His breath tickled the back of my neck as he laughed. 'Shut the fuck up.'

I enveloped the blanket around us to block out awful Karachi cold – God, I miss central heating – when the door creaked open and Jawad stepped into the room. I slipped my un-hijabbed head under the covers. Honestly, would knocking on the door go amiss?

'Bhai Sahib. Chai?' he asked.

'Please,' replied Conall.

I shot my arm out of the covers. 'Me too, please, Jeeves. But no cardamom. Or boiled milk. And not the leaves. The teabags. Please.'

There was silence before I heard the door creak shut.

'Anything else you wanted to add?' said Conall. 'And call the man by his name, will you?'

I peeked out of the covers to make sure Jeeves had gone.

'I'm trying to get a bit of banter going. Break him down a bit. Get him to open up, you know? He's very . . . severe.'

'I don't think using British cultural references with the serv—' He stopped himself. '. . . with the *workers* is the way to go.'

'It's Pakistan, PC police. Lighten up. Having PG Tips in the morning is the only thing I look forward to. I miss regular milk.'

I looked up at the cracked walls. Sigh. Billy had disappeared. Even she was having none of it.

'At Chachi's there's a generator so we'd have a heater and I'm not saying we couldn't come back here during the day.' I faced him and pulled on his beard. There are more flecks of grey than there were some months ago. Is this life's doing or mine, I wonder?

'I'm not sleeping in comfort while everyone roughs it, Sofe. The whole team's dealing with the same shit.'

Of course he's right. Do wish he appreciated from time to time that I haven't been to Afghanistan or Sudan and God knows where else. Granted, this isn't war-torn awfulness, but wish he wouldn't make me feel as if wanting hot water and electricity was unreasonable.

'Yes. Obviously,' I said. The cockroach scurried under the bathroom door. Eugh. 'Sleeping in twelve items of clothing is so boring though.'

'Is it now?' He slipped his hand around my waist when there was a knock on the door.

Jawad's wife, Meera, walked in with our tea in a tray. Conall got out of bed and took it from her as she drew her scarf over her face, looking up at him and then promptly away.

'Thanks, Meera.' He put the tray on the floor and went to the bathroom. Meera waited until he shut the door.

'Baji, are all men in England like him?' she asked.

Ha! I was going to sit her down and tell her about life before Conall. Why bore the poor woman though? More to the point, why bore myself? I slid my hand into a self-made pocket inside my pillow and took out some money. I handed it to Meera because a) it's part of New Year charitable giving and b) because I could give away all the money in the world – it still wouldn't show enough of my gratitude for the fact that I get to sleep with my next-door neighbour turned Muslim husband.

'No,' I replied. 'Not quite.'

Just then, Billy sprang up on the work desk and deposited a freshly dead mouse on the table.

God, I'm a Londoner, get me out of here.